CHARACTERS
CYKOPATH: BIRTH

CYKO

The protagonist of our story, he lost his parents in a fatal accident and went on to live in an orphanage, where he quickly bonded with the other children. Hot-blooded and determined, he is willing to do anything for his friends and family.

MAGY

An affectionate girl who seems to always be smiling serenely. She strangely enjoys the pain from the experiments done on her, but nevertheless is very protective of those she likes.

MYO

A small, sickly boy who is terrified of nearly everything. He wishes nothing more than to be free again.

SNOW

A cute, snow white cat that Cyko came across one day. How she got in the facility was unknown, but her affections are a great help to the children in relieving stress.

Tela

A girl who is much wiser than her age reflects, sweet and friendly, she is ready to do whatever it takes to save all the other children.

Ellyn

Always in a good mood despite her situation, she loves the feeling of the wind on her body, and being able to communicate with it.

Reddox

Mysterious and quiet, his passiveness hides a powerful aura, although he has trouble being motivated.

Mr. Whale

A rich and influential businessman, he is the founder of Project R.N.G. Paranoid about potential threats from the Creator, he spared no expenses to make sure his project will become a success.

Dr. Gacha

A brilliant individual and the lead scientist behind Project R.N.G. No one knows his true background, but his intellect and devotion to research are without equal.

CYKOPATH: BIRTH

CONTENTS

Prologue
Project R.N.G.
1

Chapter 1
The Children of Tomorrow
9

Chapter 2
Catalyst
75

Chapter 3
The Death Games
131

Chapter 4
Awakening
197

Chapter 5
Aftermath
245

Chapter 6
Rebellion
275

Chapter 7
Retribution
329

Epilogue
The Children of the Future
371

VOLUME 1

LUCA BRAÑA
ARTWORK BY: AVALOKI

⊖Lunime

Cykopath: Birth
LUCA BRAÑA
© Lunime Inc. 2019

Artwork by Avaloki
Edited by Alexa Beck

This book is a work of fiction. Names, characters, places, and incidents are the product of the author's imagination or are used fictitiously. Any resemblance to actual events, locales, or person, living or dead, is coincidental.

Lunime Inc. supports the right to free expression and the value of copyright. The purpose of copyright is to encourage writers and artists to produce the creative works that enrich our culture.

The scanning, uploading, and distribution of this book without permission is a theft of the author's intellectual property. If you would like permission to use material from the book (other than for review purposes), please contact the publisher. Thank you for your support of the author's rights.

Lunime Inc.
550 Fullerton Ave. #87361
Carol Stream, IL 60188

Visit us at Lunime.com
Facebook.com/Lunime
Twitter.com/LunimeGames
Instagram.com/LunimeGames
Discord.gg/Lunime

The Lunime name is a trademark of Lunime Inc.

The publisher is not responsible for websites (or their content) that are not owned by the publisher.

KDP ISBN: 9781099370601

10 9 8 7 6 5 4 3 2 1

Dedicated to the
best fans in the world.

PROJECT R.N.G.

1

Children were being brought in, exiting the black bus one-by-one and looking around in wonder. It was some sort of underground garage, spacious and filled with different vehicles. If the *garage* was this big, then how humongous would this new place be? Would this be their new home?

They had been told that their orphanage would be moved somewhere larger and more comfortable, but was this going to be the place where they would live? Where they would wait until their parents came to take them home?

It was then they noticed the big, mean-looking men everywhere, and one was walking towards the children. He paused, gave them a smirk, and said "Welcome to Hell, kids."

2

The year was 4049 A.C.—the "A.C." indicated that this was "after the Creators" made their presence known to the world. Although the universe was mostly at peace, there was a looming fear amongst its citizens, stemming from the unpredictable nature of these Creators, and the destructive power they were capable of.

Near the top of a towering skyscraper in Neon City, one of the most populous cities in all the cosmos, a gathering of individuals was about to take place to address this concern. As the board meeting was about to begin, a few latecomers stumbled into the conference room and took their seats at the table. Standing before them all was Mr. Whale, the CEO of multiple high-ranking companies and a very intelligent and respected member of the upper-class of society.

"Ladies and gentlemen, thank you all for coming out today. What I am about to present to you will revolutionize the universe as you know it. No longer will we have to live with the distress and anxiety of not knowing what the Creators are conspiring, with no protection against their powers. No longer will you go to sleep at night wondering if you might not wake up the next day, just because a Creator erased your city on a whim."

The ears of most individuals perked up as Mr. Whale's booming voice echoed throughout the room. Standing up against the Creators? This was an idea unheard of for its time as these supreme beings created their very existence. Was it even possible for an entity to challenge them? This prospect intrigued the board members, who now paid close attention to every word spoken out of Mr. Whale's mouth.

"I would like to introduce you all to Project R.N.G. With enough funding, we can make this preliminary concept a true reality, and with enough weapons, we can silence the Creators for good and take back what is rightfully ours!"

As his voice rang out, a complex chart with a wide array of images and statistics was displayed upon the screen next to him. In large, bold letters at the top was the title "Project R.N.G.," the latter initials described below as "Reversing Natural Genes." The pictures showed what appeared to be various children, each displaying an obvious type of emotion or behavior, though it was not easily identifiable by the eyes of the viewers.

"What you see before you results from years of scientific analysis, done in a secret underground laboratory and carefully hidden from the Creators. I am sure that all the images and calculations you are examining right now don't have much value to you, so let me give you a brief overview of what this project entails."

Mr. Whale took a deep breath and exhaled, as if to prepare for a very long, detailed explanation. "I want you all to close your eyes and imagine a world where these Creators do not exist. Now open your eyes.

Unfortunately, a world such as this is logically impossible, and I'm not here to advocate the elimination of the Creators, but rather to promote a viable countermeasure."

The crowd of wealthy executives continued to listen with great intrigue.

"Project R.N.G. will accomplish just this: an effective measure against the unknown threats that these Creators pose. Allow me to further explain the details of this project. Through decades of research, my team of highly trained scientists have discovered hidden natural genes in the human DNA that only appear during the early childhood stages of one's life. Normally, these genes are abandoned by the body as one ages, but through our elaborate experiments, we were able to reverse this process and actually recover these lost natural genes."

The display on the screen changed to a new slide, highlighting extensive details of what Mr. Whale had just discussed. Along with the comprehensive DNA diagrams, more images of children were shown. One such photo depicted a young boy with cyan blue hair, sitting alone on a testing facility's exam table prompted an abrupt question from one of the board members.

"Mr. Whale, are you suggesting that we conduct life-altering experiments on innocent children?"

With a sly grin on his face, Mr. Whale held up his hand to stop the individual from further inquiring about the subject, as if he was expecting such a question would be asked.

"Sir, I understand your concerns, but I can assure you these experiments are harmless. We have conducted tens of thousands of trials to ensure that they would not be detrimental to the current lives of these children, or have any side effects in the future. I wish we could use an older age group for this project, as I'm sure many of you would have volunteered, but unfortunately the concealed genes have already disappeared entirely from our DNA, and we would not be able to reverse the process as we can with the children."

The individual seemed somewhat accepting of the response he was given, but still had a displeased look on his face. Many other members appeared bewildered, provoking Mr. Whale to continue with his speech.

"Now it appears that many of you are wondering how reversing these natural genes in the children will help prevent the Creators from destroying us at any given second. These heredity units are not just common genes that determine your hair or eye color. They are something much more special. Each group of genes carries a unique and powerful ability that when recovered, brings out the true potential of a human being."

The confusion in the room dissipated, and it seemed that the meeting's participants were finally grasping the true nature of Project R.N.G.

"Just how powerful are we talking?" probed an executive.

"With enough luck, these powers could equal that of a Creator, perhaps even surpass one. Why luck, you ask? We have discovered several different natural genes hidden amongst children, yet there is currently no test available to predetermine exactly the type of powers that will awaken. Only after we conduct our experiments will we be able to witness this awakening, which is where the elements of luck and randomness are involved."

"What type of abilities will we see from these children, and will they be able to control themselves without harming others?" shouted one member from the back of the conference room.

"Ah, yes, let me continue. Our team has discovered copious results that occur upon reversing these natural genes. First, I should point out that for many of the children it might be too late for their genes to be recovered. In such an instance, they would be free to leave our facility after the experiments have concluded. For others, new characteristics such as unparalleled accuracy, increased muscle fiber, or unimaginable intelligence will emerge. By harnessing these new traits, along with being trained by our expert technicians, these children will have supreme control over their abilities. While one alone may not be enough to stop a Creator, a whole team of them with the right awakened genes could match the presence of one."

Smiles formed on the faces of those sitting in the expensive leather chairs as they envisioned a universe filled with these powerful super children. A few were still pondering what Mr. Whale had just disclosed, as one questioned, "Are we going to leave our future up to luck?"

"Ah, thank you, that brings me to my closing point. Yes, there are risks involved in this project, as there are in most ventures. Yes, there is a certain level of randomness involved, and we may not succeed with our goals. Yet a world with children—able to stand against the ambiguous intentions of the Creators—isn't this worth the risk? With your funding, we can make this dream a reality. So I ask you today, ladies and gentlemen, do you feel lucky?"

As Mr. Whale concluded his presentation and took a seat in the lone empty chair at the front of the table, not a sound could be heard as each member processed the information that was divulged before them. After a few moments passed, the head administrator of the meeting stood up and cleared his throat.

"We will now take a vote to determine the funding of Project R.N.G. If you believe our firm should supply Mr. Whale with the requested amount of capital, please raise your hand at this time."

A single drop of sweat rolled down Mr. Whale's cheek as he waited in suspense for the movement of limbs around the table. Would the project he had devoted his life's research to finally be brought to life? He lowered his head and peered down at a single section of the conference table he was seated at, afraid to look up and see how many people had voted in favor of his proposal. As he was considering the possibility of failure, he glanced up, witnessing a forest of extended arms all across the room. Every single member's hand was raised.

Project R.N.G. had been approved.

3

A blue-haired child stared at the ceiling of his room, thinking about everything that had led up to this moment. He was an orphan. He had lost both of his parents in a car accident where he was the only survivor. That had been three years ago, and yet he could barely remember it.

He had been taken in by the government of the Blue Faction, who introduced him to his new home at the time, a rather run-down but friendly looking orphanage, run by a kind, grey-haired old lady they all had called their grandmother. She tried her best to make all the children feel at home, despite the circumstances that might have brought them there.

It had been a hard time: grieving the death of his parents, healing from the accident, and adapting to being alone. But eventually, the little old lady and the other children got through to him, and he regained his hopes of a good life and of having a family. He had become a child once again.

But then that all changed. One day, without warning, the old lady disappeared and a huge man came in her place, saying he had bought the orphanage and they would move into a better and bigger house. They were sad leaving their grandma behind, but the fat man assured them she was okay and had just retired.

What a big lie that was. They had been impressed at first, with how big the garage was, but they were introduced to their 'wards,' the place where they slept, and they realized something was deeply wrong. Their rooms were much worse than the ones at the old orphanage. It was a bunk bed in an uncomfortably small room, attached to an even smaller bathroom with a very cold shower and, to make matters worse, they couldn't leave their rooms unless they were told to do so.

The boy grimaced, holding back tears at the sound of screaming and crying. This was the worst part. They all were being taken away, one by one, and from what he could hear, the ones that came back were begging to leave or whimpering. He had no roommates, so he had no way of knowing what happened to the others.

Suddenly, his door slammed open. "Subject Number 444, come," the ice cold voice of a big guard made his fists tighten. Was he not even going to call him by his name? Even though he was just a nine-year-old boy, he knew something for certain.

This was wrong.

THE CHILDREN OF TOMORROW

1

Three months had passed since the approval of Project R.N.G. Far away from the city's center, hidden underground in a remote forest, was Mr. Whale's secret laboratory. With the help of a custom-engineered barrier, the above-ground entrance to the facility was completely hidden from the all-seeing eyes of the Creators. As the moon reflected the bright lights of Neon City, Mr. Whale was seated in the back of his limousine, en route to his life's work to give his final seal of approval before the real testing began.

As his vehicle made its way to the outskirts of the city, a brief moment of doubt entered Mr. Whale's consciousness. *What if this experiment proves to be a failure? Would I go bankrupt and be forced out of this life of luxury?* So many people depended on the success of this project, many of whom believed that this was already a guarantee, and that the possibility of a catastrophe did not exist. Mr. Whale shook his head in denial. Thousands of trial tests had already been conducted and there was no way that such a disaster could occur. Then he started to dream about the newfound fame his results would bring. He would become the wealthiest man in Neon City without a doubt, perhaps even in the entire world. Although he was relatively well known as the architect behind Project R.N.G., his status would soon propel into that of a celebrity idol. As Mr. Whale's thoughts ran wild with these delusions of grandeur, he was brought back to reality by the voice of his chauffeur.

"Sir, we've arrived."

Mr. Whale slowly stepped out of the limousine, grabbed his briefcase, and headed to the entrance of the facility. Stopping briefly in front of a giant pine tree, he pressed his finger against a small button on his watch, unveiling a control panel that was previously concealed beneath the bark of the tree. He stooped down and aligned his eyeball to the device, standing still while its sensors scanned his retina. After validating his identity, a loud rumbling could be heard from below. A short distance away, a portion of the top of the ground could be seen retracting into itself, uncovering the stairs that descended into the laboratory.

Mr. Whale made his way down the steps and was greeted by two security guards, who again verified his status and then allowed him to proceed to the main corridor of the building. As he gazed across the facility, he took special note of all the new technology and machines that were scattered around; newly purchased additions that were made possible by the funding he had received.

The laboratory was a massive underground complex with seven levels of depth, each one serving a purpose, and protected by thick walls of a nearly indestructible material—the best money could buy—and reinforced with rituals and sigils by the best mages available for hire in Neon City.

Indeed, the laboratory had to both be well-hidden and well-protected against a possible raid from potential rivals, berserker experiments running loose, or even the Creators themselves attacking. Highly sheltered and highly efficient (that is one of the key aspects of this project) and so far, results seem to be showing.

A very well-organized installation indeed. It was a good idea to leave the logistics to the science team, Mr. Whale thought, while reminding himself of the current infrastructure.

The very first level, the administration level, was the perceived 'front' of the project, where most of the paperwork was done, and where his personal office was located. Should any footage of the lab be required, the administration was often the very first one to be shown, and often at length. Those who work on the first level, while privy to the location of the facility and the legalities behind it, were often in the dark about the rawer aspects of this project. Well-furnished and visually pleasing, the administration level was the perfect face for Project R.N.G.

The second level was called the dormitory. All of the staff present in the facility was required to live in the plant, even those who just worked in administration. This was to minimize any and all possible information leaks that could make its way to the Creators or any possible adversaries. The Dormitory was designed to be an optimal residential place, with many comfortable dorm rooms, a mess hall, and recreational rooms that had access to television shows. Mr. Whale would be a fool to dismiss the effects that good morale had on workers. But just like its purpose to avoid information leaks, the Dormitory lacked Internet access.

The third level was the security room. On the outside, it was a place where security guards would get outfitted for work, and where those in charge of the security cameras were stationed. In reality, it was a massive fortress outfitted with heavy weaponry and well-trained guards, to prevent people from coming in, or out, without express permission from either Mr. Whale or the head scientist. The remaining four levels can only be accessed through this level and down a large elevator.

The fourth level was a storage room. A large area filled with hardened crates full of supplies strictly for the lower levels, materials that are either of sensitive or volatile nature. Supplies for the upper levels are stored on their respective floors. The floor had two other purposes as well. One as an obstacle for any out-of-control test subjects, employing guards with plenty of cover; and as a buffer between the upper and lower levels, to make sure nothing compromising could be heard or sensed by the staff on the upper floors.

The fifth level was the *actual* laboratory of the facility. A very large floor with dozens of rooms filled with cutting-edge equipment, both magical and scientific. This floor served as a research facility where samples and results from the experiments discovered on the lower floors would go to be thoroughly checked by experts. The lab was a place that a businessman, like Mr. Whale, would surely never be able to fully understand, as it wasn't his area of expertise, but he trusted the man he put in charge enough to take care of all the details. He himself just needed to study it sufficiently to understand the basic concepts so that he could show them in board meetings.

Politely greeting every staff member he came across, Mr. Whale checked the condition of the administrative floor. Everyone seemed to be working as they should, which was a good sign. Workers that slacked off are useless to him, especially in a project as important and sensitive as this one. Even if the administrative floor was the most relaxed section, it was still important work to make sure that all finances, supplies, and logistics were taken care of, and everyone knew that.

His office was located just behind a wall on the far end of this particular sector; a futuristic, sturdy-looking steel door labeled "Mr. Whale." He would have preferred the beautiful craftsmanship of a wooden door, but even he had to follow security protocols; you never know when a catastrophe may happen, especially against the beings he is working against.

"Useless thoughts, this is not like me," he murmured under his breath, figuring the pressure for being the figurehead of this project was getting to him. The magicians and engineers responsible for the security measures assured him that the Creators would be unable to even detect this place, so he *should* feel at ease.

Shaking his head, Mr. Whale stepped up to his office door, letting the scanners read both his fingerprint and retina. Watching as the machine acknowledged his identity, Mr. Whale stepped inside his office: a large, beautifully furnished room with a wooden desk. If he was to work here for an extended period of time, he needed comfort as well. Morale was a benefit both for the workers and for the boss after all.

Walking up to his desk and sitting down, he pressed a button to boot up his digital workstation and began to look at the reports that were in front of him—reports with a large, red mark of CLASSIFIED. The businessman chuckled, this almost looked like a document the government would give to an official, but considering the contents, the label was certainly very accurate.

Normally, one would consider having such documents placed atop their desk to be a very dangerous move. What if the cleaning staff were to come across it and, say, indulge in curiosity? Enter here: the wonders of magic. The document was magically sealed, only those with the cipher could open it. His own cipher was a ring he was wearing on his middle finger. A curious thing, red with a strange symbol in its center. Magicians always had a flair for the dramatic.

Opening the document, he scanned its contents, revealing details about the newest test subjects. Inside was a list of names and ages accompanied with small photographs of the children brought inside the lab for testing purposes, along with a note that a more detailed report will be forwarded to him, once initial testing and diagnostics could be done.

Mr. Whale nodded. This was an expected report since he had sent representatives earlier this week to find and acquire the needed assets. Orphans, juvenile delinquents, and even some teenagers—the tests would determine if either they could or could not be useful. To decide that, the sixth and seventh levels were of extreme importance.

The sixth level of this facility was a second laboratory, however, it differed from the fifth floor in that it was much larger, and both the staff and equipment were specialized in such ways that morals wouldn't stop them. The Experiment Lab was the great focus of all of his efforts. It was where the magic happened, where the test subjects would go to have their genes unlocked through a battery of treatments... or to be deemed as failures and be freed. That particular level, along with the seventh, were the ones built with the most durability and highest security in mind, displayed by a much larger quantity of guards than all the other levels aside from the third; heavily armed and authorized to use lethal force if necessary.

Now finally, the seventh level, the depths of Project R.N.G. as well as its main resource. Named the Coliseum, it was the largest and most secure of the levels where the test subjects were housed. Large rooms with bunkers and the very base necessities for human beings. They were designed to be as uncomfortable as possible while still maintaining just enough relief to allow for sleep. The floor got the name 'Coliseum' because of a future project that the head scientist had in mind, and as such, there was a very large open area in the center.

Looking at the next page of the document, Mr. Whale took at a glance at the proposed methods of the 'Hidden Gene Awakening Treatments' for the subjects that were brought in. *Starvation, electric shock, drowning, suffocation, burning, harsh environment, near-death experience, etcetera.* These looked more like torture methods than any true treatment, but one thing was a fact: those years of experiments made prior to his presentation of the project showed that the best way

TOP SECRET
PROJECT R.N.G. FACILITY MAP

Level 1
Administration

Level 2
Staff Dormitory

Level 3
Security Room

CLASSIFIED

Level 4
Storage Room

Level 5
Research Lab

Level 6
Experiment Lab

Level 7
Coliseum

to unlock the hidden genes was through a stressful situation—through trauma and through adrenaline. Things that would evoke such a strong reaction from the human body, alongside the right chemicals, would trigger a response from the body to try to preserve itself, thus, awakening the hidden abilities of a human being.

Research on the most powerful humans on the planet seemed to indicate that all of them had gone through some form of trauma in their early childhood, allowing for them to unlock their hidden powers. However, this only happened to a precious few, certainly not enough people to put up a fight against the Creators. If this project succeeded, then they would have a whole army of incredibly powerful children that they could shape into loyal, brave soldiers that would fight for the greater good of all humanity. Additionally, should the scientists find a way to make all the humans in the world be as powerful as them, they would need not fear the Creators any longer!

Mr. Whale could already see the massive boost in both his economic power and fame. He would go down in history as a hero for all of humanity, the one who dared to stand up against the threat everyone thought was impossible to overcome.

"Everything seems in order," he murmured to himself while looking again at the profiles of the newest batch of children, his stare resting on a blue-haired boy. Truly, he would have preferred to conduct these kinds of experiments on adults who could understand the necessity of this all, but for the greater good, sacrifices had to be made. For a moment, he wondered what sort of power he would have if his hidden gene was unlocked in his childhood. He shook his head. The last page of the document had a request for a meeting with the head scientist at his earliest convenience, so he should get to that.

Pressing a button near his desk, he spoke, "Please inform Dr. Gacha that I would like to speak with him in my office." Mr. Whale relaxed in his chair to wait for the man, and soon enough, a request for entrance appeared in his terminal. Touching the screen to accept the request, he was greeted by a serious looking individual.

Project R.N.G.'s head scientist was a man of few emotions, a youthful visage despite bolstering a healthy sixty years on his shoulders. His hair and beard were whitened by age—the only tell of his seniority. One would be mistaken to assume him to be a harmless old man, however.

The steel of his red gaze told you to not take neither him nor his intelligence lightly, and indeed, the man walked up to him with only the slightest of nods as a polite greeting.

"Mr. Whale," the man's nearly emotionless voice spoke as he sat down in one of the comfortable chairs in front of his desk, looking straight in his eyes. Mr. Whale had to stop himself from shivering. There was something about him that made Mr. Whale feel uneasy, nevertheless, they had business to deal with, so he spoke up.

"Dr. Gacha, I saw your report about the latest batch, what is it you wish to talk to me about?"

"Yes, it's about the next phase of Project R.N.G." He took a tablet from inside his coat and began swiping his finger across it, his eyes briefly scanning the data it contained, before placing the device on top of the desk. With a glow, a three-dimensional projection of the seventh level appeared. It was different from the current schematics, in that it had a large arena in the center where the open area had been. "As I told you before, the next phase's focus would largely be on the seventh level, and with the new test subjects brought in, I believe we finally have the numbers to start it."

"Oh, I see, that's certainly good news! But, wouldn't you need time for the new batch?" Mr. Whale decided that this was definitely positive news. The next phase, according to Dr. Gacha, would help test the hidden gene's power potential, as well as develop them for the future indoctrination needed to turn these hosts into perfect soldiers.

"Of course, the new subjects will be experimented on and treated during the period of time it will take to prepare for the next phase. It will be a tight schedule, but we can accommodate for it with more intense versions of the current treatments."

"Very well then, but is that wise? The last batch produced many failures," Mr. Whale said with a nod, causing the scientist to frown at the mention of the last batch.

"It was unfortunate, but our project does rely heavily on luck after all, just like a… gacha game. Sometimes you get good rolls, sometimes you get rejects that should be disposed of, to try to salvage something. Fortunately, the other batches before this proved to be useful. Only time and experiments will tell if this one will be viable or not." The doctor took the tablet from the table and pocketed it back in his coat.

"However, that was not the only reason I came here. We finally found a way to catalog all the different kind of powers unlocked through the R.N.G. treatment. As you know, when the treatment succeeds, the subjects show a variety of different abilities, neither being quite the same as the other. If you'd accompany me to the lower levels, I can show you what I mean," Dr. Gacha spoke in a neutral tone, looking the businessman in the eye. Mr. Whale frowned; he wasn't particularly fond of going to the lower levels, but if it was necessary, he would do it.

"Very well, let us make haste."

2

The fifth level of the Project R.N.G. facility, the laboratory, was a very clean and sterile place, yet it contained a scientific beauty that even a businessman like Mr. Whale could appreciate. The staff, both scientists and guards, gave them nods of acknowledgement and immediately returned to their work, a show of how disciplined and dedicated they were.

"As you know, Mr. Whale, in this lab we analyze any samples and results acquired from the lower levels, to better understand what caused them and if we can replicate them." The head scientist gestured towards one of the many rooms, whose insides could be seen through the large glass windows.

"Those people were hand-picked by me, the best in their respective field, and ambitious enough to turn a blind eye to the darker aspects of our research. If this works out, the entire team will receive much prestige, but I digress. We have arrived at my office," he said, moving in to allow the digital scanner to identify him, giving them both access to the room.

Dr. Gacha's office looked like any other lab. A little more conservative on the number of devices present, but each was clearly handpicked for his personal use in case he ever needed to do an in-depth analysis by himself to either contest or clarify a result given by the scientists that worked under him. True enough, his dedication to the work provided many great insights to the project.

"I thought you wanted me to take a look at the subjects themselves?" Mr. Whale asked while looking around his head scientist's office, giving in to curiosity despite having been here many times before. The scientist nodded his head and gestured for him to come closer to his desk, which was located in one of the corners of the room.

"The seventh level is currently being prepared to receive the newest test subjects. Going there would just give both of us needless distractions. As such, I decided to make some use of the failures," Dr. Gacha replied blandly, his left hand reaching for a button that appeared from inside his desk. "Thanks to this, my team now has an easier time cataloging the different kinds of hidden powers that all humans have inside of them."

The moment Dr. Gacha pressed the red button, the room seemed to change. The center space of equipment disappeared in a wave of arcane symbols and in their place appeared seven giant tubes, mechanical in nature, each filled with fluid of a different color…

And the dead bodies of children.

"I assume there's a good reason for this?" Mr. Whale asked calmly, even as he paled in shock. He already knew the price of his project, and had already accepted what had to be done, but the suddenness of it caught him off guard. Not to mention, the bodies inside the capsules were in terrible condition.

"Of course. Each of these subjects had powers that worked in different ways and were deemed failures because their powers were either unable to be controlled, or because of a bodily condition prior to the treatment, such as cancer or insanity…" Dr. Gacha said as he walked over to the leftmost capsule, one whose fluids were a cyan blue color. He took a moment to look at the body, before turning back towards Mr. Whale, who was trying his best to focus on the capsule itself rather than the body inside.

"This subject's experimentation gave him the ability to become stronger, faster and more durable than a normal person, with reflexes and increased thought processes to match. He was able to put a dent in solid metal with his bare hands, seemingly without effort. Not even our physically strongest guard can do that. His speed and reflexes allowed him to dodge bullets fired from regular pistols, something hard to achieve with conventional training." The scientist sighed. "Imagine what level he would have gotten to with proper training, with the indoctrination to be a loyal soldier! Alas, he was deemed a failure because the experimental treatment also triggered a fatal retrovirus. We made calibrations to avoid this in future test subjects, of course."

"So, I assume there are more children whose powers are similar to his?" Mr. Whale asked, fascinated at the tale of such an incredible amount of power. A child! Even the strongest of the factions of Neon City had to train for *decades* to get to such levels.

"Indeed. Many of the present subjects, those who are currently receiving the treatment, displayed the ability to become stronger through a form of energy that they are able to activate or deactivate at will, while others permanently gain the increased attributes without the need to expend energy on them. We call this category, the 'Enhancers,' subjects whose powers allows them to surpass the limit of normal human physical prowess." Dr. Gacha made his way to the next capsule, once again stopping to look at it as the body floated inside the orange-colored fluid.

"Our world is one where both magic and science exist in equal amounts and can thrive together. Indeed, this project is as scientific as it is magical in nature, and as such, some power can't be properly explained with just science, such as the case of this subject." The scientist turned to Mr. Whale, who was looking at the capsule with curiosity. "This subject showed the ability to use telekinesis, being able to lift and control objects several times heavier than himself with ease and also showed some limited form of mind reading. His powers came completely from the mind, and thus, we decided to call this category of subjects, the 'Mental.' Unfortunately, the subject was already suffering from terminal brain cancer by the time he was admitted to this facility, and thus, deemed a failure."

"I see, but what use could someone with mental powers have against the Creators?" Mr. Whale questioned, as while he thought telekinesis in itself was powerful, mind reading would not be so useful against beings who could easily destroy their world with a snap of their fingers. The scientist just shook his head while his face, for a moment, slipped into a smirk.

"You wouldn't know how useful it would be, to always know exactly what your enemy is going to do. Creators still have minds, so theoretically, they could also fall prey to mind readers like any other living being. They would make excellent spies, as well," the scientist said as he moved towards the next capsule, one with a red fluid. Curiously, the capsule was completely empty.

"Why is this one vacant, doctor?" Mr. Whale asked wondrously. He hadn't noticed it before, thanks to the shock of the capsules and their contents, but this one, indeed, does not have a body inside it. The doctor turned to face his boss, a smirk still present on his face.

"That's because the subject who would be stored here for study is still alive. You see, Mr. Whale, this subject so far is our biggest stroke of luck, an ultra-rare pull if you will. The individual is currently the most powerful and successful experiment we have done in this project yet. From inside his body, books came into being. Red books full of arcane secrets and knowledge even our magic researchers found highly complex to learn quickly. But for the subject himself, they were as easy to read and understand as a grocery list," the scientist explained with calm excitement, obviously pleased with this particular result.

"A high stroke of luck indeed! If we could get more like him, then…" Mr. Whale trailed off with optimism. Magic users are not uncommon in their world, but the discipline it took to be a high-level mage was enormous. If they could make soldiers who could learn powerful arcane arts with ease, his project would undoubtedly be a success.

"Indeed. But there is one thing that concerns me, however," the scientist said, losing his smirk and once again turning to gaze at the empty capsule. "This was made because the subject was thought to be dying at the time, his body was filled with malignant tumors, well beyond any hope for a cure. It would be a great waste, but we were prepared to make a thorough autopsy and research in hopes of duplicating his hidden gene, but…"

"But…?" Mr. Whale asked in apprehension, looking at the empty capsule, whose red liquid seemed to shine slightly against the lights of Dr. Gacha's office.

"When we told the subject as to what was causing his body to fall apart… something happened. It seemed as if reality itself flipped, and the next thing we knew, he was perfectly fine. Somehow, this particular subject found a way to completely erase all the tumors in his body, with pure force of will." The scientist turned back towards Mr. Whale, who had a conflicted but thoughtful look on his face.

"Erasing, but isn't that part of a Creator's power?" the businessman asked in contemplation. Perhaps it would be possible to—

"Yes, but the subject showed no other characteristics of a Creator so far," said the scientist, interrupting Mr. Whale's wishful thinking. "As it stands however, his power of erasing things, coupled with his prodigy level of magical ability, will undoubtedly be the most powerful asset in our project, so far in any case. He is both our greatest asset, and our greatest danger. Currently he is kept in the maximum-security ward."

"I see. It is a shame that we cannot make artificial Creators then," Mr. Whale said with a resigned tone. Alas, this was still great news for the project in general. "I guess this particular subject got his own label?"

"Indeed." The scientist nodded. "The category is called 'Magical,' for those subjects who are shown to either have gained prodigy levels of magical ability or are naturally able to use magic. So far, we only have one subject with that label." Dr. Gacha walked towards the next capsule, one that had a vivid green color, with a young girl taking her eternal rest inside.

"This one is an interesting case. She was amongst the first test subjects to be experimented on and receive the initial version of the treatment. However, unlike the Enhancer subject, this one didn't die because of a retrovirus, no. She ascended." He frowned as he spoke before turning to look at Mr. Whale. "Our magical specialists discovered she was in contact with a spirit before she passed. This subject's apparent power used to be elemental channeling of the earth element, but instead, what she got was the ability to talk with natural spirits—beings from the world that are normally invisible to regular and sometimes even magical humans."

"Wouldn't that classify her as a Magical then?" Mr. Whale questioned.

"They are similar, but different. 'Spiritual' are subjects who are able to directly talk and work with spirits, spirits of nature and sometimes of beyond, although we still lack the latter. Through working with a spirit, someone can channel their powers into their body to achieve great feats and in fact, it's not rare for a spiritualist to also be a magician, but not exclusive. In this particular subject, communicating with Earth Spirits allowed her to become stronger, and it's theorized it also allowed her to gain extra senses, such as perceiving steps through the ground.

Although rare, we still have several subjects who fit into this category," Dr. Gacha explained with a contemplative look on his face.

"I see. I can understand how useful they can be, if they can control those spirits, they might even match the power of deities, which would help greatly in stopping a Creator from attacking us," Mr. Whale said while stroking his chin. Already, all of the categories had advantages that could be used to make humanity's greatest defense, but he halted any further thought on this. There was still more to see.

"Absolutely... As for this subject, she greatly disliked our... methods, so she made an agreement with her spirit of choice, and when we found her, she was already dead. Our magical specialists discovered confirmation that a pact had been made, and we feared a possible information leak would occur, but it seemed our worries were unfounded, as our mages managed to track down the spirit the subject made the promise with. She wished for a reincarnation." He sighed, a frown forming on his face.

"Obviously, we now take care to avoid such things from happening. The maximum-security ward is now equipped with special barriers that keeps spirits out, and whenever we need to conduct research on them, we make sure to have a team of highly specialized magicians to oversee the experiment. The number of subjects lost via pacts and deals has dropped down to zero, and thanks to this, we gained precious information regarding spirits and how they work. But, let us move on, we still have three categories of subjects to discuss," the doctor said, dismissing the subject and moving on to the next capsule. It was larger than the others and it was filled with a dark brown liquid, however, the figure could easily be seen and...

"Wait... What? What is that?" Mr. Whale asked in shock as he got a better look at the body inside. It seemed like a man, a fully-grown man, with the head of a lion and a muscled body covered in fur, his nails enlarged to sharp-looking claws. It seemed like it would break free of the capsule and slaughter them both at any moment.

"Those, Mr. Whale, are the 'Mutants.' They are one of the most troublesome subjects we have, and not due to lack of cooperation, but because many times, the awakening of their genes also cause an animalistic side to emerge, turning them into hulking berserkers that had on one occasion required a whole team of ten heavily armed guards to take down. Four of those guards died, by the way," the scientist explained with a casual air, not bothered at all by what he was saying.

"Oh, yes, I remember that particular report, but I didn't think the subject that caused that incident looked like this! Frankly, he looks horrifying, how useful do you think those subjects would be?" Mr. Whale could already see it in his mind, an army of powerful and fearsome beasts, backed by all the powerful soldiers they could make with Project R.N.G. It would be the greatest defense against the Creators!

"Certainly, the mutations tend to turn the subjects into powerful beasts, but more often than not, they must be heavily restrained due to transformation making them much more violent. Yes, there are some that retain their humanity, but most need to be trained like animals. With proper preparation, we believe they would make excellent heavy-hitters. As it is however, we have a better variation of the mutants currently," Dr. Gacha said as he moved to the penultimate capsule, one filled with glowing white liquid. He seemed to look at it almost fondly, pressing his hand against the glass. Inside, the body of a girl rested peacefully.

"This subject, upon receiving her treatment, gained the ability to transform into a falcon. An unnaturally white falcon of great speed and power, easily surpassing the speed of the sound barrier. As a human, she also received improved visibility of faraway objects. Unlike mutants, these subjects fully retain their original personality, sometimes gaining quirks related to the creature that they transform into. We call them 'Shapeshifters,' subjects who are able to transform into one or more creatures without losing their sanity, like mutants do. Some turn into birds, others into insects and a precious few into great creatures of myth." The scientist mumbled something under his breath.

"What was that, doctor?" Mr. Whale asked in confusion, unable to hear whatever it was that he had said. He turned towards his boss, his face expressionless.

"The subjects that are of this category are implanted with special chips that allow us to track their location, because a number of them can turn into small insects or animals. The ones that can turn into stronger creatures are placed in wards with increased security."

"Hmm, they do seem like a better variation of the Mutant ones. I can see the ones that can turn into small creatures being great at spying or acquiring information from others," the businessman contemplated out loud, earning a nod from the scientist.

"Indeed, depending on the transformations, the subjects could have many great uses as soldiers or spies… with the proper training." The doctor turned back towards the capsule. "As for this particular subject, she unfortunately got too careless in one of the experiments and hit a wall at full speed in her falcon form. It was interesting to note that upon her death, she returned to her human form, seemingly with no injuries, but completely lifeless. After a few experiments, we managed to confirm that the injuries acquired in the transformed state vanished when the subject returned to their original form and wouldn't come back should they once again transform," the doctor explained, nodding at the look of wonder and optimism in the businessman's face, who had taken a greater interest in the capsule.

"Completely? A full healing from simply transforming back into their original forms?" Mr. Whale asked in bewilderment. If that was true, those children would be a priceless addition to his army. He looked away from the capsule and back towards his head scientist, who nodded at him.

"Correct, those of this particular category have access to a quick form of healing, making them much more durable than any normal human, soldier, or mage." He shook his head.

"However," he continued, "if they have multiple forms, the injuries will persist should they then transform into something that is not their original form. This gives the Shapeshifters great advantage in combat as they just need to undo their transformation to heal themselves. However, their stamina is not recovered and, as you can see, death is permanent."

After finishing his explanation about the Shapeshifters, Dr. Gacha made his way to the last capsule—one filled with a glowing, golden liquid, and inside, the body of a young boy. Like before, he took a moment to look at the child inside before turning back towards Mr. Whale.

"During the experiments, this subject awakened the ability to control electricity at will as well as sense any electronic equipment in the vicinity. Tests have shown that he could absorb and discharge electrons from machinery, as well as mold electricity to fit his needs, such as creating spheres of lightning that could be thrown like a bullet. Something interesting to note, is that he seemed immune to electricity himself, as any and all electrical attacks were simply absorbed with what the subject described as a 'tickling' sensation." The doctor turned back towards the capsule.

"Wouldn't that make him a Magical then? Many mages in this world can use lightning, such as most of the ones in the Yellow Faction," Mr. Whale questioned, taking his eyes off the capsule to look at the scientist who shook his head at the question.

"We thought the same, too, but our magical researchers confirmed that no magical energy was being produced by his body, nothing beyond what a non-mage was. This means that the awakening of his hidden gene led to him gaining the power to control a facet of nature itself. Later, as more test subjects were brought in, we managed to acquire additional individuals with such powers, often limited to the magical elements of light, darkness, nature, fire, and water. However, it's not rare for subjects who can manipulate something more unique, like a subcategory or a combination of elements." The doctor then took his tablet out of his coat.

"I see, they seem less effective than the Spirituals, but still useful nonetheless," Mr. Whale observed.

"Truly so—the ease at which they can control their elements is something that could be immensely useful as Spirituals need to make contact with spirits to make use of theirs. This category, the 'Elementals,' are those who have the power to directly control one or more elements without the use of magic or control of a spirit. Their control tends to be very instinctual, as if the element was a part of themselves, so, like Spirituals, they sometimes gain one or more senses related to the use of their powers." He nodded to himself in thought. "As for this subject, he died due to a fatal heart condition that could not be cured in time. Ironic that one with power to control electricity would die of a heart attack." He blinked slowly before turning back to Mr. Whale.

"As you can see, Mr. Whale, those are the categories of subjects we have managed to acquire with this project. As of now, we have several hundred subjects in the wards on the last level, and if this project pays off well, many more will be brought in to receive the treatment," Dr. Gacha spoke callously, although a smirk could be seen on his face, a sneer that Mr. Whale mirrored as well.

"So far, I've left all the technical details up to you, so to know we have made this much progress... Before we move on to the next topic, tell me, can a subject show more than one attribute? Belong to multiple categories?" the businessman asked in curiosity, certain that such could be the case, considering the sheer possibility of powers the treatment could unlock across multiple subjects.

"I'm glad you asked. For you see, it's entirely possible for a subject to belong to multiple categories." He started swiping his finger across his tablet, looking amongst the data, before holding it in his palm so the screen was facing upwards. From the device, the holographic projection of a little girl appeared.

She was wearing an outfit that could only be described as a pair of rags; dirty and full of small slashes. The girl had colorful pinkish-purple hair, common to those born in the Purple Faction, and dull, unhappy red eyes. She was staring forward with a blank look on her face. On both of her arms, two purple colored bracelets could be seen, and on the parts of her skin that were visible, some small scratches and bruises were evident.

Mr. Whale stared at the holographic image with stony eyes. This was one of the reasons he disliked going to the last levels. While he was not the most moral person in the world, even he knew that should this operation be for anything else, it would be wrong. However, for the sake of the future of his world, sacrifices had to be made, as many have been for the greatest advancements in medicine. That he would become famous and loved by all was, of course, a welcome bonus.

"*Subject Number:* 47
Name: Magy
Age: 8
Sex: Female
Categories: Spiritual, Enhancer, Elemental
Time in the facility: 1 year
Phase of treatment: Experimentation, already awakened

Description of powers: Can summon forth spiritual scythes from her body. The scythes themselves are the spirit she formed a pact with. Scythes can pass through physical matter to either strike at the soul or pass defenses to cut at the flesh. The weapon seems to be adaptable to her weight as a small increase in size and mass was noted in the previous year. The spirit she contacts is of a dark element, however, she is able to channel dark elemental energy independently from her spirit to enhance herself to be faster, stronger, and tougher. She is able to cloak herself in the shadows for stealth.

Psychological Profile: As with many other children in the facility, she developed an unhappy disposition, which is part of the treatment to empower her hidden genes, however, when going through experiments, seems to enjoy pain. Was observed causing painful attacks on subjects she dislikes, seems to also enjoy giving out pain. Possibly a sadomasochist, but too young to determine.

Value: High, her powers are unique and beneficial to the future phases." The scientist read from her file in the hologram, looking towards Mr. Whale upon finishing.

"This was a short summary of her profile in our database. As you can see, Mr. Whale, this is an incredibly valuable subject with unique powers. Due to the way her powers work, she was classified as Spiritual, Elemental, and Enhancer. She is an example of a subject that fits multiple categories, and we have many more. It's rare for a subject to not be qualified for more than one category in fact, as some Spirituals can enhance their senses or physical power, while some Shapeshifter's transformations can give them powers that can fit in the other categories as well," the scientist explained, watching as Mr. Whale's face shifted from curious to subtly excited.

"This is most excellent; I can already see this project will be fruitful. I am going to make a detailed presentation of everything you told me to the board, they'll love it. We may even get a budget raise! But I am curious about something. What are those bracelets on her arms?" the rotund businessman asked, his eyebrows raised, looking at the girl's wrists in the hologram.

"Ah." The scientist smirked slightly. "Those are one of our best safety and monitoring implements. The wards already have their own form of security and monitoring, such as the maximum security one, but the bracelets are an extra form of safety. A failsafe, if you will. They are created using both science and magic, then sealed on their wrists using the latter. It becomes part of their bodies and cannot be removed without intensive surgery."

"The proverbial handcuff then," the businessman noted, earning a nod of approval from the scientist.

"Exactly," he answered, "many test subjects, such as the Mutants, are dangerous, so we need to have ways to keep them on a leash. As for the bracelets themselves, they provide real time monitoring of both their current location inside the facility and their vitals, such as heartbeats and levels of stamina. For security, the bracelets are able to form a magical chain that can lock into itself and then around the subject. If that doesn't work, they are equipped with numerous magical wards, such as paralysis, poison, or gravity that will greatly aid in subduing the dangerous element," Dr. Gacha explained, turning the hologram off as he finished.

"I knew I was right to put you in charge, Doctor, you truly think of everything. With such security features, we should be able to proceed in peace," Mr. Whale said with a pleased grin. The scientist smirked.

"Yes, and on that note, let us move on to the ensuing topic of this meeting. The next phase of Project R.N.G. I already introduced it to you, but now it's time we discuss the details. Let us take a seat, this might be a lengthy discussion," the scientist said, moving back towards his desk, Mr. Whale following behind him.

"Very well, I would like to know as much about it as I can. We need all the precision we can get to make sure everything goes well."

3

He was spasming, his muscles painfully twitching every three seconds or so as he turned and thrashed in his bed. It hurts, it still hurts, even after the pain he had gone through, it still hurts so much!

"Aargh... Why... Why is this..." he muttered pitifully to no one as he spasmed once again, bringing out another painful groan as a muffled sob escaped from his throat, tears falling from his eyes. This was wrong, this was so wrong! Even if the boy considered himself mature for his age, in no small part due to the accident that killed his parents, this was still too much for his nine-year-old brain to endure.

It had been three months since he had been taken here, three months of constant suffering, of pure torture! He barely got any food, and when he did eat, it was some form of disgusting porridge. "It is good for the body," they said. What a lie! That he could still bathe was a miracle in itself, considering how terribly he was treated in here.

Just a few hours earlier, he had been taken in for another 'experiment.'

"More like torture," he grumbled to himself. According to the guys in white, or 'scientists' as they were called, it's all a part of a procedure to awaken some form of ultimate power inside him or something. He didn't care. They still had the gall to try to convince him that this was for the greater good of humanity and that he should endure it silently. They should do this to themselves, not to children!

"Urgh... Stupid shocks..." he grumbled once again, grimacing as another spasm ran through his muscles. They usually change up what they do to him, but they always take care to not cause any permanent damage. The idiots told him to be optimistic after the torture, saying that he should awaken his powers 'soon.' As if he cared about that. He just wanted to leave this place...

"Goodness... It hurts..." He guessed he should count himself lucky that at least it wasn't as bad as his first week there, where it was harder to shrug the pain off, and when he shed more tears than he does now. All the children seemed to have grown used to the experiments, even if the whispers of "granny" or "I want to leave" could still be heard in the corridors.

"Goddess, uh? Urgh..." He clutched his stomach and bent over. The Creator, the Goddess, she was the very reason those people are doing this, the babbling scientists said. They were to be humanity's shield if any of the Creators ever were to go berserk. What a bunch of garbage, no one can go against the Goddess, and why would they? The lady always seemed nice enough whenever she decided to appear. Even in his young mind, he thought it ridiculous that she would try something after 4,000 years of leaving them be. It wouldn't make any sense.

At last, the spasms were ceasing and the blue-haired boy could now breathe normally again. He would be sore in the morning, but the painful part had passed, for now at least. He raised one of his arms and looked at his palm. He started to focus on it, as if trying to will something, any sort of power that could aid in his escape, before sighing and letting it fall back down.

Maybe he could try praying? Praying to the Creator? No, that wouldn't work, she made it quite clear that people who prayed to her were wasting their faith, as she was not a religious deity. But maybe, just maybe...

He shook his head, there was nothing he could do at this point. The Neon countries had several deities that he could pray to, at least, some he knew from what little time he had at school, but the damned scientist, once again, told them that prayers would be useless. Their mages had created barriers that would block and trap any faith trying to leave this underground prison. It didn't stop the other children from trying though, and most of them, just to spite their captors, were sending their faith to the Creator.

Dang it, if he does get any power from those experiments, he would make sure to find a way to escape—and take everyone with him that he possibly can. This was a shared sentiment, no one wanted to stay here their wholes lives, or worse. He knew some kids did not make it, and that just made their situation increasingly tragic. A child like him should not have such mature thoughts, he knew that, but any chances of a normal life were lost the moment that fat lard first appeared.

The door in his room was suddenly banged on loudly, snapping him from his thoughts with a startle. He hates it when the damned guards do that, and to make matters worse, he noticed that they always seem to do that at set points during the day, and occasionally at night. The boy had no way of telling time, but their harassments seemed to follow a pattern. So, yes it appeared they were doing it on purpose, and not even from being cruel jerks, but likely because someone ordered them to.

He still hated the guards the same anyways.

Then he heard a sliding sound and once again his door was banged on, meaning the awful guards had decided to feed him. He was feeling hungry anyway, so he might as well see what trash was on the menu today. He slowly made his way out of bed, wincing as his muscles still hurt from the spasms.

"Jeez, did they look through the sewers from home to make this?" he whined in annoyance, noticing that the cooks decided once again that he should eat with his hands, as no cutlery was included. Thankfully, he stole some from the meals that did come with them. Even if they were frail, plastic things, it was better than to eat with his hands.

Grimacing at the taste of wet paper and a cardboard-like texture, he ate the meal in silence. All the kids had quickly learned that if they did not eat their meals, they would likely die from starvation, as they got literally nothing else. Water was supposed to be drank from the shower, and these porridges were the only meal they ever received. They would vary in colors or texture sometimes, but other than that, very little changed.

Sometimes though, the idiots would 'forget' to feed them for days on end, making their existence even more miserable. The only good side was that when they did that, they also 'forgot' to call them in for experiments, allowing them some days of peace. If having your stomach gnaw at you is considered peace after all. It was obvious that the starvation was only another part of their sick experiments, but they could do nothing to stop it.

"Ah, at least I can eat it without feeling nauseous now," he mumbled to himself. And there was another part that was driving him mad about this whole thing. Even after three months, the boy still had no roommates, essentially having the whole 'room' to himself. That also meant he had no one to connect to, no one to talk with beyond occasionally seeing other kids when they were allowed to go out. He had no way to communicate with anyone else, unless he decided to shout from his room. It would quickly get the guards mad, though, so it was not very useful.

Essentially, he had to rely on the whispers he could hear from those walking the corridors, from other kids who talked too loudly, or from the scientists themselves, who seemed to love explaining the reason behind every single thing they did to him. Most of the time it was surprisingly informative, but only about each other rather than any information on an escape method, so it wasn't really that useful, although he still kept on listening occasionally, if at least to know how the other kids were doing. They are all together in this.

As he finished his horrible excuse for a meal, the boy looked back up at the ceiling. Sometimes, he just wanted to cry, to beg his parents to come back to him, to save him from this horrible place, but he knew he couldn't. He lost much of that childish impulse in the first months after they died, and had nearly lost it completely those past months here, but he was still a child after all.

Still, crying and begging for help wouldn't benefit him in any way. He learned this, all of them learned this, but the only thing they could do was endure, and hope to find a way to escape this forsaken place.

"Maybe a bath will help me relax... Yeah, right," he moaned as he got up and made his way to the terribly small bathroom, opening the rusty steel door to enter. The space inside was barely enough to fit both the shower and the toilet. That they had even this much was a miracle in itself, but he was sure they would one day find a way to create more experiments even in their safe spaces.

Whatever, he should try to at least take it easy, or he might go mad from all of this.

4

"Gah!" Suddenly waking up due to a heavy bang on his door, the blue-haired boy looked around in shock, before realizing once again that it must've been the mean guard that had woken him up. He groaned. Now, he would have to try to sleep again.

"Get up, rat. It's socialization time," the gruff, robotic voice of the guard loudly called out, making the boy blink in confusion. *Socialization time? What?*

"What?" he asked out loud, making the guard once again grunt at him.

"That means, get up and get out there. All of you rats are going to the big area, those are my orders. Now get up before I get my shock rod," the guard barked, banging the door loudly one more time before stepping back, leaving the boy confused as he made his way to the door. This had never happened before. They were never allowed out of their prison for no reason. The only time they had the opportunity to get out, was when their turn to be experimented on came. What could they have planned this time?

The thick metal door opened, revealing a large guard waiting for him, suited up in power armor that glowed a menacing red, covering his entire body from head to foot. In his hands was a large gun which the boy knew had been used at least once. The guards didn't play around at all.

"The bullets in this gun are rubber, but they can leave nasty bruises on your body, and they can be switched to live ones really quickly. This is the first time you will be allowed out to do whatever, don't get any funny ideas," the guard said gruffly, the red glowing eyes of the powered soldier glared at him. The boy looked back at the ground, silently following him as he tried to glance at other kids also being roused up by the guards.

If they wanted an army so bad why not use those guys? he thought. They are already big, and looked pretty strong, why would small children need so many armed soldiers to look after them? The boy knew, he knew he would have no chance of beating the guard in front of him, or the hundreds that they seemed to have in this prison. Fat chance, even with whatever powers they unlocked. He rolled his eyes at the thought.

"We've arrived. Go inside and don't try anything funny. If a fight breaks out, we will make you hurt," the guard said, snapping the boy from his thoughts and bringing to his attention a very large metal door in front of them. One of the guards walked towards it and pressed a switch, causing it to start sliding upwards, revealing…

"Is that… a gym?" one of the many kids asked incredulously. The door indeed revealed what appeared to be a gymnasium, it was large and had some sports equipment scattered around, alongside a few chairs and tables. The gym was large; much larger than the garage they had been first brought in.

"All right, rats, get inside! Now!" another guard shouted, prompting the security that was escorting them to push them in, forcefully, earning several pained yelps in the process, though no one tried to resist. They had all learned what happens when they do. If they were to escape, they had to be intelligent about it, to think of a plan, like a grown up.

The boy looked around as he stepped inside with many other children, glancing suspiciously across the gym-like room. The door then closed with a loud bang, startling them and making them turn around, confused. *What were they supposed to do now? Talk? Were those guys really allowing them to do this?* Then they noticed that the gym had other giant metal doors all around, some of which were opening, revealing crowds of more children, looking just as confused as they were. *What was going on?*

As the doors closed, everyone looked uncertain, staring blankly at each other, before hearing a loud static sound coming from the ceiling. There were speakers in there, and after a second, a cold voice began talking to them.

"As of now, all of you will be allowed to mingle with each other for two hours at this set time on certain days in the near future," the robotic voice advised them. "The gymnasium can also be used as a training ground for those of you who have awakened your powers, but be advised that use of lethal force against your fellow subjects will result in harsh punishment. Fights are discouraged. Make connections with each other as those of you who survive will become the army that shields the world." After the speech, there was a loud crack followed by silence, making the children even more confused than before.

They spent a few minutes rooted on the spot, looking around in fear and suspicion, unsure about what to do. Was this another experiment that would result in terrible pain, be it on the body or on the heart? Was this a trap of some sort, to identify the rebellious ones? Should they even trust each other? The trauma each of them had gone through in here was making them hesitant to step away from their respective entrance doors. Even the boy was unsure about what to do, he knew he wanted to be able to talk to others again, but…

Then, a person walked forward. She had emerged from the door directly in front of them. The girl had deep red hair and orange-ish eyes, and like everyone here, she was wearing rags that barely fit her. The thing that set her apart was the determination in her stare; the gentleness in her aura. Then the children noticed that they could actually feel a soothing, calm sensation being emanated from her.

The girl looked at all the doors, taking in the vision of all the children in the gym, their weak forms, their desperation, their longing for a better life, their sadness, their anger, but not figuratively. It seemed like she was taking all of their negative emotions in, like she could tell what every single one of them was feeling at this moment. The girl smiled sadly, her own feelings being transmitted to each child's heart.

"*You do not have to be afraid, not of each other.*" The boy heard a voice, making him jump and look around for the source, but the only thing he was met with was the confused look of another kid. Then he noticed that everyone was looking around, bewildered, causing the redhead to giggle slightly, transmitting her feelings of funny amusement to them all, making some kids actually giggle at each other's silliness.

"*I'm the one who is speaking to you all, in the center. The power those... people... unlocked in me was the power of telepathy. My name is Tela, by the way, and I really hope I didn't get named that as a baby on purpose!*" The girl giggled again, making the children reunited here once again feel a funny sensation in their hearts, making them want to laugh, something they haven't felt for months, and for some, years.

"All of us... We are in a terrible situation right now, but we can't lose hope! If there is anyone we should trust, it's each other. We are all in this together, we've all suffered from their horrible 'experiments,'" she made air quotes, "but if we all work together... I'm sure we can escape, I'm sure we can get out of this place!" the girl declared through their minds, sending feelings of understanding and determination through them all.

This girl... She was something else, the boy thought. Amazed that she indeed did have powers, but more than that, that she had such great charisma. He could already see everyone's spirits rising from the bottom. With such few words, she had given the children hope; hope that if they worked together, they might escape this place. The boy himself felt like he could trust her words and that they could trust each other.

"This 'socialization,'" she air quoted again, "*that they call it may seem suspicious, but now, it gives us a chance. My powers... they should allow us to talk through our minds, secretly, without them knowing. We can plan something. We can do anything, I'm sure of it!*" She transmitted her thoughts through their minds, the message laced with bravery and optimism.

Her words, like magic, broke through the ice created by trauma and fear. Slowly, the kids from the different gates began to walk towards each other, and, though awkwardly, began talking to each other. At first with small *hellos* and *how are yous*, but after a while, they began to talk in earnest, with many kids circling around Tela, impressed by her words. Everyone slowly got used to being around other kids, even after so long. Some even tentatively started to play, using the sports equipment that was around.

The boy was taking all of this in with a strange expression on his face, for someone had managed to so easily rally them up, to make them leave their fears behind, at least when they were with each other, a sense of camaraderie between fellow prisoners. He knew he could trust her and that he should trust everyone around him, for the simple reason that they were all going through the same thing. But... he was alone, all by himself for months, just going up to someone and talking to them was...

"Hey, Cyko, is that you?!" A familiar voice sounded from somewhere near him, making the boy turn around to see a small crowd of children, looking at him with surprised faces.

"Y-you guys!" The blue-haired boy, named Cyko, widened his eyes in surprise and shock even as the small crowd began to move closer to him. Those children, they were his brothers and sisters from the orphanage! They are still alive, they are okay! *They're okay!*

"Cyko! You're here! W-we thought you had disappeared, no one heard from you for months, I thought all of us had been placed near each other!" a short blonde girl exclaimed, smiling in relief at seeing one of her brothers okay, relatively speaking. Her name was Anna, a very sisterly and protective girl. Back in the orphanage she used to help the old lady around, and keep an eye on the younger ones, such as himself.

"I-I was placed alone, I had no idea where everyone was, and those guards didn't let us out... Until now at least..." Cyko said with a nervous, but happy voice. If anything, the fact that they were dragged out here was good, if at least for allowing him to see his brothers and sisters again, to finally be able to talk with them after so long.

"Those monsters..." a brown-haired boy said. Matthew always was a fierce child who took bullies head-on when he could, especially those from outside who would come to harass the orphans. He earned many earfuls from the old lady but had the respect of the other kids.

"We're glad you're all right, Cyko, we had feared the worst," a blond-haired boy said next. His name was Geon, a very friendly youth that always tried his best to help the newcomers feel at home, and sometimes, even going out of his way to make prospective parents give more attention to the other children.

"Thanks, Geon, but... Where... Where are the rest, of us? Didn't... Didn't they take all of us to this place?" Cyko stuttered, suddenly feeling a weight in his chest at the possible answer to his question.

"Cyko... We are sorry... We... We never saw them again after the first month... We are the only ones that are still here. Please, don't let it get to you..." the gentle, but sad voice of a blue-haired girl spoke next. Sara, another kind soul amongst his group. She lost her family to crime, but even as she dealt with her sadness, she always tried to help everyone near her. Sara was best friends with Anna; the two were very similar.

"Oh." He clenched his fist, feeling the stab of loss strike at him. The orphanage that the old lady ran was small but had twenty children living there in total. Counting him, there were only eight left... Those monsters—his family was taken from him again.

"Big brother, p-please, don't cry..." a soft, melancholic voice spoke next as Cyko met the tearful eyes of a small, purple-haired girl. Starry was the youngest of the orphans, being a mere three-year-old toddler when Cyko arrived at the place. She should be five now, but was still too young, too young to suffer like this...

Cyko bit back the tears that were accumulating in his eyes and tried his best to give the little girl a reassuring smile. He wasn't sure if he succeeded. "I'm sorry, Starry... W-we need to be strong, don't we?" She nodded sadly, trying her best to smile at him, even though he could see the tears forming in her eyes, too.

"Yes, we do, those brutes, they need to pay for everything!" the fiery voice of a red-haired, short boy yelled, flames coming from his clenched fist. Ironically named Torch, he used to spend most of his time near Starry, being very protective of their collective youngest sister. He always tried to either encourage her or cheer her up whenever she was sad. Regardless, he must feel terrible that he can't help her when those fools decided to experiment on her.

"Torch, you have powers, too?" Cyko asked in shock at seeing the little boy's hand become engulfed in a fire at his rage. In answer, the boy gave him a bitter smile, something no boy his age should ever be capable of.

"Yes, those idiot's experiments did this to me. Look." With a short yell, the boy's red hair turned into fire, his eyes an orange glow and his skin seemed to shine. He looked up for a moment, and with a grunt, he jumped. Faster than Cyko could see, the boy made it to the ceiling and jumped back, falling to the ground with a thud.

"Whoa!" was all Cyko could manage to say. Torch had managed to do something that he thought possible only by powerful soldiers of the Neon factions!

"Yeah, it's cool. And it feels awesome," the boy said with a grin, hair still on fire. But then he frowned. "The first time I 'awakened,' as they call it, I made a big fuss, tried to fight my way out, managed to knock down five of those guards before they put me to sleep," the boy gritted his teeth in anger, "I tried to fight again when the brutes came to do another experiment on Starry. It took ten guards this time and I would've kept going if they didn't threaten to separate the two of us. Cowards," he said, the fire that empowered him was dying out in his shame.

"I think big brother Torch is cool," Starry said with an angry pout. She always gave him praise when she felt he was being too negative, which made the boy smile and pat her head.

He laughed. "Thanks, Starry."

"If we try to fight alone, it will be useless, we need to do like that girl said and join together. This socialization is an excellent opportunity to try to plan for something. The guards, individually, aren't as tough as they look and if we work together, we can take them on," a boy with green hair said, his glasses shining against the light. Henry was always a very smart kid and currently was the oldest of them at twelve years. Affectionately called "nerd" by the other kids from the orphanage, he often spent his time helping others study, or taking care of the old lady's garden.

"Wait, do you guys have powers, too?" Cyko asked in curiosity. Torch was younger than him, but he already had powers. Would that mean that the others also had theirs?

"Some of us yes, others no, although the scientist did say we should feel optimistic as we are near," Henry said with a frown, earning a nod from Cyko.

"They said the same thing to me, and all it did was make me mad. Not like I can be happy while being electrocuted." Some of his friends winced in sympathy.

"Shock-shocky is bad," the small girl, Starry, said with a tremble of her body. If possible, this just made Cyko angrier than before. That they would dare subject this little girl to such cruel tortures for no good reason… It made him want to…

"Cyko, calm down, it's okay…" He felt the gentle hand of one of his older sisters, Anna, on his shoulder, making him turn to look at her. She had a sad smile on her face. "We all know how terrible it is, and we all get angry too, but… We need to keep resisting, and we need to do it smartly. All of us may be just kids, but once we get experienced enough, we can… we can escape."

"Yes… Yes, you are right… It's just, it's hard, you know? Of course, you do, but…" Being around family finally made him notice how stressed he really was, how sad the situation really made him felt, how much he wished everything could just be better, and that he could be back with his parents or back to being a happy family in the rundown orphanage of the old lady.

Then he suddenly felt warmth all around him and was surprised to notice that his family had gathered themselves for a group hug. Warmth and comfort like he hadn't felt in months. This is nice, very nice, the boy thought. He smiled and relaxed for he knew that as long as he had them, everything would turn out okay.

"Let's go, everyone, we should find a good place to sit down and talk before time runs out," the second oldest, Sara, said encouragingly. The small, makeshift family of eight separated from the comforting hug and made their way towards one of the more secluded areas. Despite the inspiring speech from the telepathic girl, they all were still shy and wanted to talk amongst themselves first.

As the place was rather huge compared to the number of children present, they soon were able to find an actual school table that was unoccupied. They barely all managed to fit in, but for the small family, it was enough.

"We should have around an hour left to talk, if I'm not mistaken," the smartest child, Henry, said as he glanced at the ceiling, making the others turn to him. He looked back. "I've been counting the seconds ever since we got in, but I lost count several times already, it's a fair guess." He shrugged.

"It should be enough time, if not to plan an escape, then to at least catch up a little!" the blonde boy, Geon, said with a friendly smile, although he ended it with a grimace. "Even if we don't really have much to share with each other."

"No, you are right," Cyko said, smiling at the older boy. "If at least to make sure where we stand. Now, how are you guys doing?" he asked with a smile, eager to hear from his foster family, even if most of what he will hear is likely bad things.

"Well, the rest of us were placed near each other. We are all in the same corridor I think," Sara said softly. "I am sharing a room with Anna, Mat, and Geon. It's tight, but at least we can have each other for comfort when we get back from the... experiments," she said with a sad smile at the end.

"I am in the same room as Torch, Starry, and one other kid. I thought they had put all of us together because we came from the same place, but with Cyko, it seems I was wrong," Henry said with his hand on his chin. "Unfortunately, I wasn't around when that thing with Torch happened, or I would've told him to not do it."

"Wait, why?" Torch exclaimed incredulously, making Henry turn to him with a deadpan look.

"Because of exactly what happened to you. You may hurt a few of them, but there are a lot of guards, we can't do everything ourselves," he explained while the redhead pouted at him.

"Well, he had good intentions at least," Cyko said, giving a thumbs up to his little brother.

Anna nodded in agreement. "At least we know that once all of us have powers, we should be stronger than them," she said with a smile, before turning it into a grimace, "but we will have to endure more of that torture, at least for a while longer."

They stopped talking at the mention of once again having to go through those horrible experiences. They knew that whatever it was those scientists did would make them stronger, but none of them wanted to continue doing this anymore, they just wanted to go home, to go away and be normal kids. Cyko sighed, it was hard to be cheerful with everything that was happening, but they at least had to try to be optimistic, right?

"Hey, if you guys don't mind me asking, which of you already have powers? Besides Torch, I mean," he asked eagerly, making the other kids perk their heads up. They looked at each other and Matthew, Starry, and Geon raised their hands. So, with Torch, that was only half of them, huh?

"What can you do, Mat?" Cyko asked curiously. The boy gave him a grin, one that made embers exit his mouth.

"It's cool. Apparently, I can breathe fire like a dragon! It's very hot too. When I 'awakened,'" he said with air quotes, something the kids did often, it seemed, "I melted the ceiling and their equipment into a hot puddle. I was so tempted to try to escape then… but…" He began to fidget nervously.

"I-I didn't want to melt anyone… I should've done it anyway, or at least tried!" he continued with an angry hiss, the embers coming from his mouth dripping down to nothing.

Anna reached over to put a hand on his, making him turn to her.

"Don't blame yourself! Like Henry said, we can't do anything just by ourselves, and besides… It's normal to not want to hurt people, even those horrible bullies," she said with a comforting smile, making Mat sigh and return her grin. He was okay now. She let go of his hand and looked down. "We may be forced to anyway," she added under her breath.

"What about you, Geon?" Cyko asked, seeing the somber mood that was beginning to settle on his older sister, Anna. She snapped out of it and also looked at Geon, even if she possibly already knew about it, she was still curious to see his powers.

The blonde boy smiled before putting a hand on the table. Soon enough, it began to shake violently, making them jump in surprise. "I can cause earthquakes, localized ones, and I can control the intensity. It's a little weird, like I can feel the vibrations," he explained as he made the table slowly stop vibrating. A small frown then appeared on his face. "The room that they're experimenting on me in almost collapsed when I awakened, and I seriously considered bringing the whole place down, but… it would only squash us all rather than help us get out, and I don't know if I'd be able to do that, anyway."

"Well!" Cyko exclaimed, surprised. "That is very cool! Earthquakes! We are underground so that means our lives are pretty much in your hands," he joked. Geon gave an awkward laugh at the praise, but seemed to perk up, regardless.

"Thanks, Cyko! But like I said, I can make localized and controlled earthquakes. The scientists called it 'vibrations' instead, but I prefer earthquake. I also noticed that I can feel when the ground shakes, mostly from people's steps. It's a little weird, like a small light appears in my mind whenever someone takes a step. It nearly drove me mad, but I got used to it. I think I can make a map of the place if I concentrate hard enough," the blonde explained, earning a few whistles from his friends.

"Geon, that's excellent news!" Anna said, receiving a nod from Henry. "If you can make a map of this strange prison, then that would give us a big advantage," she said with a smile, making Geon rub the back of his head in embarrassment.

He laughed. "I'll try my best. But I'll need someplace to draw it," he said, getting a nod from his friends.

"We'll think of something later, then. It's a topic to keep in mind after all," Henry said with a smile. Even if it was a small thing, it could still give them hope.

"What about you, Starry?" Cyko asked gently to the little girl who was looking at the others with stars in her eyes. She turned back towards him before smiling and holding up a hand. From her palm, a small, five-point star appeared. The children could feel a sort of energy being radiated from the small star. It felt comforting, calming, and inviting, just like Starry herself was.

"Stars!" she exclaimed after a while, raising both of her arms upwards with a big smile on her face. They all watched as dozens of stars suddenly formed from her hands, flying towards the ceiling in beautiful patterns, some going slow, others going fast. They all stopped before they could strike the ceiling, however, and instead, seemed to float there, giving that particular area of the large gym a pretty purple glow. After a while, the stars disappeared as if they had never been there. Starry was beaming triumphantly at her older brothers and sisters.

"Whoa," Cyko said in amazement, "that was incredible, Starry! You created so many stars, and they were so pretty too!" the blue-haired boy exclaimed. Even more than that, he could feel a dark energy coming

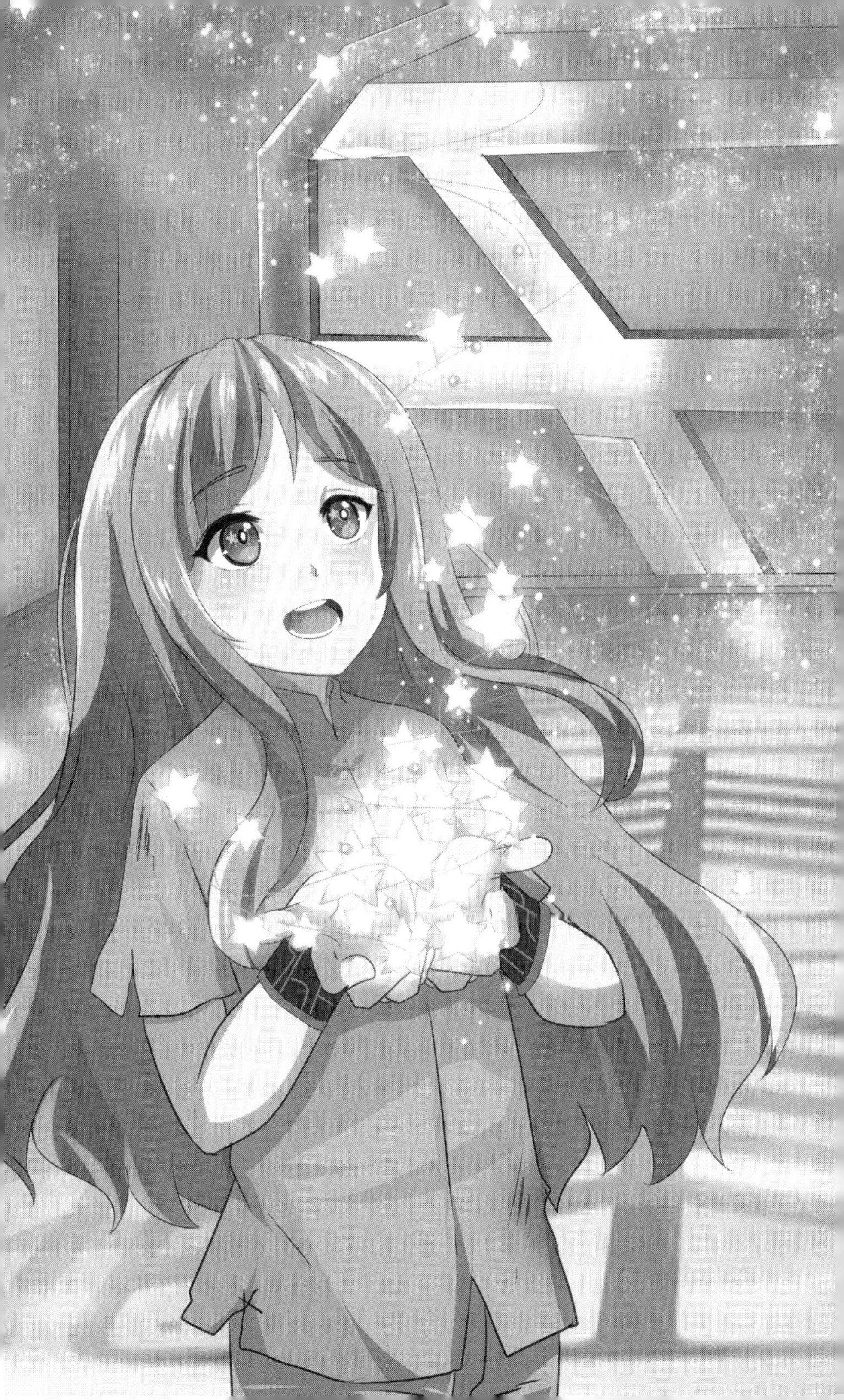

from those stars, and the strength in them was making his body shiver in excitement for some reason; he could already tell that she would be very strong someday.

"Yeah, that was amazing!" Sara declared with a big smile, earning several nods and claps from the surrounding others. They all loved it. The little girl looked bashful for a few seconds before giving them a large, thankful grin.

"Thank you, everyone!" she exclaimed, looking up at them proudly.

Torch gave a laugh and put a hand on her head. "She is something else, you know. Starry is the one who cheers everyone in my room up after the… things that they do to us. She puts on shows every night and they give us the motivation to resist." He smiled sadly, making the little girl blush.

"You are embarrassing me, big brother!" she exclaimed in discomfort, still looking down with a red face. The others at the table laughed at her reaction. Torch tousled her hair gently and their roommate, Henry, smiled at the scene before looking back at the others.

"Her power is to create dark elemental stars, like the ones you saw her shoot from her hands," the green head said, earning looks of curiosity from his friends, "we don't know how strong they are at the moment, we never tried finding out her true strength so far, but she can create tons of them. There is also this thing, that they can somehow make you relax, like being near them is good for you. As of now, she's only used them to cheer us up, so I don't know what would happen if it was used to attack someone, but it's something to think about." He finished his analysis, earning a thankful nod from each of them.

"Well, what can I say? You guys have great powers! I didn't believe those foolish scientists at first, but… Now I can't wait until mine are unlocked, even if it means resisting that torture. I want to help everyone get away from this place," Cyko said, determination and hope filling his voice. Finding his family again managed to motivate him to see if he can get useful powers… his thoughts wandered.

"I know how you feel," Anna said with a frown, "even if we can't do much, if we all work together, we should be able to get out of this cursed place. We will need to endure more, but… It's a sacrifice worth making." She looked sadly towards Torch and Starry—who was gazing at the ground while Torch's brow furrowed in anger.

"I just wish they didn't have to go through it, that none of us had to," she finished, her lips turning down at the thought of Starry or Torch going through what they did. She then felt a hand on her shoulder and looked towards Matthew.

"Don't beat yourself over it, Anna, we will give them what they deserve, you can count on it!" he said, smiling encouragingly towards her as she nodded at him.

Starry perked up then, and loudly said, "I am strong! I won't give up!" Earning a grin from Torch, whose hair turned to fire again.

Cyko, seeing that everyone was motivated, gave a smile. The orphans that he got to meet were always close-knit, and they had accepted him without problems, welcoming him amongst their family. He was grateful for the tight bond that they all had.

"All right everyone," Sara said with a smile, "maybe we should talk about something el—Ahh!" A loud siren interrupted her, making her and her friends jump in fright. They looked around for the source of the loud noise before they noticed that it was coming from the sound boxes in the ceiling.

"Attention all subjects, socialization time is over. Proceed to the gates you entered from to be escorted back to your quarters." The uncaring, robotic male voice sounded all over the gymnasium, earning a few disappointed sighs from the children there.

"Darn it, seems we ran out of time," Cyko said in displeasure. He wanted to spend more time with his family, it had been so long!

Anna shook her head; she was clearly just as sad as he was. "They did say it was for just two hours. Th there is always next time, right?" she asked nervously, forgetting if this was a one-time thing or if it will be a regular occurrence from now on.

"I don't know," Sara answered her and shook her head, "but at least, we could see each other, right? And we are making some progress, I could see a few kids practicing their powers, and I could see that telepathic girl talking with lots of other kids." She was trying to be optimistic.

"Tela, right? Maybe we should try talking to her next time?" Cyko suggested. He did find her interesting, and he would be lying if her words didn't affect him positively. Talking to her is the next step of their plan.

"Then it's decided, next time, we will chat with the telepathic girl. Maybe she will have come up with something by then," Anna said, earning nods from the others. They all got back up as the sound boxes repeated the message, this time with a reminder that the guards were expecting them. They did not want a free beating, so they would comply.

"Well, guess this is goodbye for now," Cyko said, trying not to let his smile drop. His family gave him smiles just as sad as his own, but they all waved to him.

"Don't be sad, Cyko, we'll see each other soon, count on it!" Matthew said enthusiastically.

"Yes! Be safe, and don't do anything stupid until then, remember we will wait for you!" Anna said with a reassuring smile.

"Stay safe, brother, we'll see each other again soon," Geon said, smiling.

"Think positive, Cyko, we'll be waiting to see you again," Sara said gently.

"Take care, big brother Cyko!"

"Yeah, don't let those fools win!" Starry and Torch said simultaneously. The blue-haired boy smiled at them, waving his hands as he made his way to the gate he came through.

"Thanks guys! I'll be seeing you soon, so stay safe!" he yelled to them before turning back towards the way he was going. He frowned. Even if he was happy with meeting his family again, it didn't change the fact that the rest of them were gone now, and he wasn't naïve to think they might be alive. He clenched his fists. This wasn't fair. It wasn't.

"Oh?" Cyko blinked, stopping his walk as he felt something between his legs. He looked down and nearly yelped in surprise. It was a cat! A cat of all things! The feline was white as snow and had golden yellow eyes, and it was rubbing itself on his legs. *Where did that cat come from? How did it even get there?* he wondered, trying to stay calm and undetected.

"What the, where did you come from, little guy?" Cyko crouched down to look at it better. It was a very pretty and surprisingly clean cat. The feline looked up at him and meowed. He started to pet it and the cat seemed to love it, rubbing itself against his arms and legs, earning a chuckle from the boy.

"Attention all test subjects, socialization time is over..." the sound boxes shouted again, louder this time. Dang it, if he took any longer, the guards would get annoyed at him and he would be unable to do anything about it. He should hurry and leave, but what will he do about the cat?

It meowed again. Somehow, no one saw or heard it, preoccupied as they were, either with last minute talking or hurrying over to the gate. Maybe he could try to bring it back to his room? It would be hard, he would be forced to eat less in order to give some to the cat, and he will have to clean up after it, but at least, he would have someone to talk to...

"Hey, little guy, if I put you in my shirt, will you keep quiet?" he asked in concern. The cat just looked up at him and meowed again. Uh, maybe he could give it a try? The good thing about the rag he was wearing was that it was larger than him, so he could fit the cat in there without problems, as long as it behaved.

"Well, I'll give it a try. Come here, little guy," he said aloud. He picked the small cat up. It offered no resistance and immediately snuck in under his shirt and didn't make a fuss, so hopefully it would stay that way.

Making his way towards the gate, while holding his arms over his belly where the cat was, he nodded to a few kids and blended in with them. Hopefully the guards wouldn't ask why he was holding his stomach like that.

Soon enough, the gate opened, and a full platoon of security was already waiting for them. The largest of them, the same guy who 'gently' woke Cyko up, moved to the front. "All right, rats, listen up! We'll be calling for you as we pass through your dorms, don't try anything funny! Those things in our arms aren't just for show! Now move out, quickly!" he barked loudly, the metallic tone of his voice sent shivers down their spines. The children were quick to comply and hastily moved along.

One by one, they entered their wards, waiting for their turn to be called. When Cyko's turn came, he breathed a sigh of relief, none of them had noticed it seemed, so he should just move— "Hey, blue rat." The large guard suddenly appeared behind him, making Cyko stiffen up in surprise. *Oh no, this was bad, this was bad, this was bad—*

"Why are you acting like that? Are you trying to sneak something from the gym into your room, hm?" he whispered in his ear, making the boy sweat bullets. If he gave the wrong answers, he knew he would receive a terrible beating.

"A-a-a, I-I j-just have a… stomachache!" he yelled nervously, desperately trying to keep the struggling cat still. It was so quiet until now, why was it trying to get out so suddenly?!

"A stomachache, eh? You think I'm *dumb*, rat?" the guard spat out, making Cyko shiver even more. He wouldn't ask him to strip down, would he? He just wanted the cat! He wouldn't dare to imagine what those people would do to it, so he had to maintain the lie better!

"Y-yes! A s-stomachache-OUCH!" He held his stomach in genuine pain now, as the cat was clawing him! The boy was desperately trying to stop the cat from moving, but now it started scratching him, and it hurt. Thankfully, he had experienced much worse than that, so he could resist it somewhat, but it was still painful.

"Humph, as if I cared about what you bring with you or not!" the guard shouted in annoyance. "You can't escape, you hear me? No matter how hard you try! This facility is made to keep people *IN* and *OUT*, no one will come for you, and you will stay here forever, so go ahead, bring yourself some rocks, it will help a lot! Not!" He shoved Cyko towards his dorm room.

"Go inside before you pee your pants and make a mess of the corridors! Remember, any mess you make, you clean it, rat!" And with that, he slammed the door closed, the loud bang echoing in the small room. Still shaking, the boy let the cat fall out of his shirt to land gracefully on the ground. He still couldn't believe he survived that. It was way too close for comfort, that guard is so scary—

"Meow." The white cat, now sitting in one of the beds, stared at him. The little thing was back to being calm, must've been nice, clawing his poor belly like that!

"Ahhh," Cyko let out, falling down in the adjacent bed, "at least you're safe now, little guy, but how did you get there, anyway?" he questioned the cat who completely ignored him and started to lick its paws. Cyko sighed in frustration before getting up and moving towards it.

Meow!" the cat exclaimed as it was picked up by the blue-haired boy, who had a look of both curiosity and annoyance on his face.

"So, you are 'she' then. You are a girl, not a boy. Still, how come no one noticed you before?" The cat just stared at his face with an expression that was almost smug, making his eyebrow twitch.

"Yeah, I didn't think you'd be able to tell me how in the world you got there, little girl. Ahhh." He sighed before sitting down in the bed and placing the white cat on his lap. The kitty then started to rub herself against him affectionately, making the boy give a small smile. Well, at least he had company now, didn't he?

"Hmm, I guess I can't keep calling you little girl, huh? I know! How about a name?" he asked out loud as the cat rubbed her head against his hand, purring occasionally. Now, what would be a good name for a cute, white kitten? Ah, of course! "Snow! What do you think of Snow, little one?" he asked the cat who stopped her rubbing to meow at him again before going back to her previous activity. The boy chuckled, did that mean she liked it?

"Snow it is then! Hah!" He started to play with the small cat on his lap, patting her and sometimes making her try to catch his fingers, which she would try and swipe at, thankfully, without pulling her claws out. This was fun, he thought. He would be back to loneliness once the socialization time was over, but now he had a pet! Snow!

He quickly realized that the small cat loved to play around and also loved to be petted. She was a nice cat and Cyko quickly grew to like her. For the first time, he had fun in the small room he was in. Maybe he should sneak her back the next time they let them out? Cyko would love to introduce Snow to his friends, especially the girls as he knew they would fuss over her.

A sudden bang on the door made him yelp, and the cat jumped from his lap to the floor, running to hide under the bed. *Curse that guard! Why do they always have to do that?!* Grumbling in annoyance, he got up and resolved to go back to playing with Snow, before the small compartment on the steel door opened and a plate of food slid in before it closed again.

Realizing only now that he was hungry, the boy went over to get the plate. This time, the porridge was green and had several solid looking… things… mixed in. Sighing in defeat, he steeled his resolve. It would taste horrible, he knew, but at least it would fill him up.

Sitting down in the bed he was at previously, Cyko began to work through the disgusting food, noting that the solid parts tasted and seemed like cardboard pieces. It wasn't that hard to chew, but it was definitely bad tasting. Thankfully it didn't nearly make him puke with each mouthful, *what was that stuff made out of, anyway?* he thought.

Snow meowed, making the blue-haired boy blink. He looked down and saw that the white cat was staring intently at him while licking her lips, then she meowed again. She eyed the plate of food he was eating.

"Meow!" the feline exclaimed again, this time raising her foremost paws and making a clawing motion at the air. She was hungry, it was obvious. But the question was... Would she even want to eat this disgusting stuff? He knew that cats were predators and could eat small critters, but... He sighed, it would be best to make sure his new companion didn't suffer from an empty stomach at least.

"Here, I know it tastes horrible, but you need to eat too, Snow." Separating a small part of his meal with the thankfully provided spoon, he quickly finished his portion of the disgusting porridge, before setting the plate on the ground. The cat started to sniff at the food before turning away with a seemingly disgusted face while meowing. Cyko gave a short laugh at the poor cat.

"I know it smells horrible, and it will taste just as bad, but it's all we have Snow, it's all those mean guards will give us." He told the feline who meowed once again, before reluctantly eating the green paste. She hissed every few seconds—it was apparent the poor thing detested the food, but it wasn't like he could do anything about it.

As he watched the feline eat, he began to wonder about today's events, particularly, about the 'socialization time' as the guards called it. He got to meet his family again and got to see a lot of other children too, including the mysterious telepath who had broken the ice and motivated them all. It was suspicious. Not the girl, but the suddenness of it. Why would they, after months of keeping them confined in those small rooms, allow for the children to go and have fun with each other?

He had a bad feeling about it, but he knew that these meetings would be their only chance of making possible plans for their escape, their only chance of having any happiness at all in this hellhole. He sighed, he just *knew* they were planning to do something, but the question was, what? Exhaling again, he decided to take a shower, one of the very few commodities they were allowed to have. Which was strange, all things considered.

Snow had finished eating the paste and was making a weird face. He really hoped it wouldn't upset her stomach because he literally had nothing else to give her to eat. He picked the feline up and put her in the bed he was previously sitting in, petting her until she closed her eyes. At least she could take it easy, since she was a cat and wouldn't have to worry about being tortured.

As he cleaned himself, Cyko thought about Snow. He had thought about it several times already, but how the heck did she manage to sneak all the way into this place? Maybe… Maybe she was a pet of one of the guards, or possibly of one of the scientists? It seemed unlikely, they were all terrible people, and Snow herself was a very nice cat. He discarded that possibility.

Maybe there was some sort of secret passage? A way to sneak in… And possibly out of this place?! "I mean, what *other* way could she have gotten in? There are guards and giant steel doors everywhere," he mumbled to himself in annoyance. He knew that there were at least two floors in this place, and that it was massive, but he never went beyond where the guards allowed him to go, so it was possible that there was a secret passage somewhere.

Yes, that was another topic worthy of discussing with the others when they were allowed to come out again. If they all were on the lookout for something then they would be bound to find it, maybe another animal would make their way down there, who knows?

Finishing his bath, he went about the next part of his routine. Cleaning his rags. They were the only clothes he had, so he would be damned if he let them stink. Terrible situation or not, he was determined to not let it get to him in such a way that would make him slip in his hygiene. He simply would not.

Still, all he had to work with was cold water, some generic white soap, and detergent that the guards provided every few days, but he did what he could. This was a curious thing as well; the guards would also give them some cleaning supplies. He had a mop that he would use to clean the floor of his room and even had a generic toothpaste and brush set. As he was conservative with what he had, there were quite a few supplies accumulated in the corner of his room. He had even used an old plastic bottle of detergent to fashion himself a small cup to drink water from.

It was as if they went out of their way to make the rooms as uncomfortable as possible, all the while being comfortable enough so that they could sleep without problems. If he was older, he would probably assume that it was because the scientists wanted the subjects to be as rested as possible for the next time they would be experimented on, but as it was, Cyko didn't think much about it, although he still treated everything with suspicion.

Finished cleaning his clothes, he wrapped a towel around himself and left the cramped bathroom, breathing a sigh of relief. Now, all he had to do was hang them off the side of the upper bed in his bunker, and they hopefully would be dry tomorrow. He would have to sleep in the nude, but being a kid, he didn't think much of it.

"Hello, can everyone hear me?" Jumping in surprise, Cyko looked around, before realizing that the voice was from the telepathic girl, Tela. He blinked. How did she get in his head from wherever she was? He heard a few yelps across the corridor, so the others probably heard her as well.

"How did she...?" Cyko asked out loud. She did say they could make use of her powers to talk secretly with her using their minds, but he thought it would only work in the gymnasium where there was nothing between them! The fact that she could do this was amazing; a huge advantage if they were to plan for anything!

He then heard a hum as if she could hear either his or other people's questions. *"I didn't mention it before, but at the time I managed to memorize all of your soul signatures. What are they? It's a name I gave to the feeling I get from individual people. Everyone has a different signature, and that allows me to tell the difference between you and the guards. Anyone whose signature I can't recognize, I don't communicate with. Previously, I could only talk with my roommates and a few children I had seen in the corridors. I don't dare try to talk to guards, they know of my powers."* Cyko heard a buzzing sound, what was that?

"Yes, all of you are located in different wards. There are many in this place, and I can tell you that not all the wards were allowed to go to the socialization time. I don't know what or who are in them, even if I reach out with my mind, I don't have a connection with them yet," she

explained, earning a thoughtful frown from the blue-haired boy. He did see all those different doors, and he had noted that only a few had brought children in, but he didn't think that all the doors led to where they were being kept... Just how many kids were there?!

He heard the buzzing sound again. *"Where am I? It's a place that the guards said has additional security features. All of you know about magic, yes? The walls of this entire building are magically strengthened and sealed, my telepathy can't breach through those walls."* Another buzzing sound, what did these noises mean? They always sound after she starts making some explanation, does that mean people were trying to talk to her, and he heard the buzzing instead?

"How am I talking to you all, then? The ventilation shafts! I heard one of the guards talking about how all the shafts in this floor and the one above us were connected with each other, that's why it's never hot in here. If you look at your ceiling, you may see a very small metal shaft. It isn't big enough for us to crawl through, but it's large enough to allow fresh air to freely circulate through. I am using those to send my telepathy through all the openings," she explained, and this time, the buzzing that he could hear intensified. Blinking, Cyko decided to try to send in a question of his own.

"How does it work?" he thought, trying to make his question focused at her rather than himself, and suddenly, he could feel as if a pair of eyes was directed at him. He turned to look at Snow, but she was happily snoring away, that could only mean that the telepathic girl was focusing on him now, maybe?

"That's a good question, and a hard one to explain," she said amidst the buzzing of likely several questions directed at her, *"I imagine my telepathy as tendrils, and I send them inside the ventilation shaft. Then I make the tendrils poke around everywhere, and whenever they find a person, they ask me if I want to make contact or not. If I recognize the person, I start to talk to them, if I don't, I avoid them. It feels a little weird, and it took me some time to get used to it, but with that, I can talk with all of you at once!"* she exclaimed, and after a pause, the buzzing started again and Tela giggled.

"No, silly! I am not an octopus! Well, you can imagine my telepathy links being like tentacles, but they don't coil around you!" she said in good humor, making Cyko himself chuckle at the strange proposition, for he

could suddenly imagine an octopus vaguely shaped like her putting its tendrils inside the shaft, it was a weird scene.

He felt the focus on him shift away, likely concentrating on someone else to answer them. *"That's a nice question, but unfortunately, I can't map this building using my telepath—I can tell how far you are in relation to me, but I can't tell the way it took to get there, sorry,"* she said, giving out an apologetic-like feeling at the end. So, she couldn't make a map of the place with her abilities, huh? Then it would be a good idea to seek Geon's powers for this purpose.

"Everyone, as you may have already guessed, we will need our powers in order to escape. Everybody here is likely to get powers eventually, we need to make as big an army as we can... That means, we will need to keep enduring the experiments for a while," she said with a resigned voice, and the boy could swear he could feel her sadness and fear at the prospect. The buzzing increased in volume.

"It's terrible, I know, but... Currently, it's our only chance of escaping this prison. It will take time for us to come up with a feasible plan, but... We need to endure, we need to act like grown-ups and be strong! I-I hate the things they do to me, too, but for the sake of you all, for the sake of our freedom, we need to keep resisting!" she exclaimed with both fear and determination, and Cyko noticed he could feel her emotions, which in turn made himself resolved to survive this ordeal. She was a strong ally, he knew, and he felt like he could trust her in this.

"Everyone, we don't have much we can do individually, but... until the next day they allow for another socialization time, be it tomorrow or in a month from now, I would like those of you that have powers to think of ways you can help. If you can map this facility, if you can pass through walls, if you can teleport, anything! Even if your powers are only useful for taking out guards—that is still valuable too. We need all the power we can get. This is war, a war for our freedom." Tela declared through their minds, more assurance being felt by him, and likely by everyone who heard her speak—or think.

He suddenly thought about his twelve brothers and sisters that disappeared, and he clenched his fists. Yes, this was war. And once he had his powers, and they had an escape plan, he would make sure to hurt as many of those torturous scientists as he could! A small grin formed on his face, as if he was excited for the prospect of the bloodshed, but he didn't notice it, focused as he was on Tela's transmission.

"This will be all for today. I just really wanted to let everyone know that we can talk and discuss our plans this way. If you want to talk to me, just think about me really hard and I should feel your intention, hopefully, otherwise, I'll try to send messages every day. Please, stay in touch if you can, we all need each other in this moment." And with that, Cyko felt like a television shut down in his mind, making him blink. It was a weird experience, having someone talk to him directly through his mind, but it wasn't an unpleasant one, as hearing Tela's plans and motivational talk did work for making him, and likely everyone else, more prepared for their future escape.

The blue-haired boy became lost in thought as he looked at the sleeping cat in the bed next to his.

"A rest would be nice, hopefully I can sleep through their banging tonight," he mumbled to himself before laying down, still wrapped in his towel. The bed wasn't the most comfortable thing ever, nor was the pillow or the blanket, but at least he could sleep on them without problems.

He turned to take a glance at the sleeping Snow, the little kitty was now sleeping belly up with her paws in the air. He chuckled softly at the cat's silliness. Having her there with him is definitely going to have a positive impact, he just knew it. But for now, he also needed to sleep and recover from everything that had happened.

Today had been a long day, and tomorrow would be yet another one in this prison where he would wait for his turn to be experimented on. He had hope, however, that he could still get out of this place. But for that, he needed to be as rested as he could.

5

Two scientists sat in the control room of the gravity test area, observing as a particular test subject struggled to move against the increased gravity and pressure of the enclosure. The boy was crying and gasping painfully as he crawled across the ground, trying to move towards the goal where it was agreed that they would stop the experiments for today if he made it in the designated time.

"What do you think?" one of the scientists, a brown-haired man with glasses asked his partner, who was rubbing his beard as he watched the experiment. The older scientist had a frown on his face as he looked at the boy inside the gravity room.

"The subject is using his newly awakened powers to make holes in the ground in order to get a better grip, but... What is the current setting at, again?" the bearded scientist asked his colleague, who looked down towards the digital console he was working on.

"... Only 2.5x the planet's gravity," the younger scientist replied as he pushed up his glasses, also scowling. The bearded one shook his head in disappointment, taking a tablet out from under his coat.

"This particular test subject was always described as being unfathomably weak, even against the non-awakened ones. Even the youngest of the subjects would only struggle this badly when the gravity was set to four, and that is the non-awakened ones. He is already awakened, yet, he can barely even move," the bearded scientist said, his brow furrowed.

"Indeed, the subject also demonstrated incredibly low pain and stress tolerance. Most of the other experiments caused him to faint in just a few minutes, something expected only of newly brought in subjects. Sure, the awakening of his powers resulted in rapid equipment deterioration, but other than that, he wasn't shown to have many useful traits," the bespectacled scientist said as he continued to analyze the data coming from the terminal.

"Not a very good result, I agree. We did have a few useless subjects in the past, but for now, we should continue to observe for a longer moment. The next phase is near. That will decide whether this subject is worthy of anything," the bearded scientist said as he watched the boy faint and stop moving. He had been so close to the designated time, but alas, had failed.

"For now, we shall continue the experiments when this one wakes up, he did fail to arrive at the target after all," he said as he went back to look towards the data on his tablet, which contained the detailed information on the subject they were currently experimenting on.

Subject Number: 443
Name: Myo
Age: 7

Sex: Male
Category: Elemental (Earth)
Time in facility: 5 months
Phase of treatment: Experimentation, already awakened.
Description of powers: Earth Elemental who can weaken structures, such as walls or machinery. However, ironically suffers from myopathy, which worsens whenever the subject makes use of his powers, medical treatment would be costly and unlikely to provide any benefits beyond the health of the subject.
Psychological profile: Meek, shy, and depressed, completely lacks a backbone, shows many signs of trauma from the experiments.
Value: Very low, subject is unlikely to be useful in future phases.

Not good results at all.

6

Cyko gasped as he sat down in his bed, the door closing harshly behind him. Snow made her way towards him and started to rub against his leg, she was trying to comfort him, he mused. He was drenched.

Today's experiment had been gravity. Essentially, they made everything much heavier and told him to try to move towards a goal, and if he failed, he would have to suffer through more experiments until he succeeded. They told him that they had increased gravity to eight times that of the planets, and after that, told him to get to the goal in thirty minutes at most. It was terrible, but at least they didn't shock him this time.

Somehow, the scientists seemed to be in a positive mood as he reached the goal without much trouble, although he still sweat and struggled immensely. They expressed that "it is pretty much confirmed that you will awaken soon, be happy."

Happy? He wanted to smash the smug scientist's face in, but he was too tired to even attempt anything.

"Ahhh, ahhh... Hello there, Snow, how was your cat-nap?" he asked the small creature who continued to rub his legs while purring, earning a chuckle from him. Even if the experiment itself was stressful, just the company of his little pet cat already lifted his spirits back up—he made the right decision in bringing her back here.

"Well, I guess I'll go take a bath, wait here for me, okay? And please don't eat all the food if they slide some in before I get out," he said as he made his way to freshen up. At last there would be no more experiments for the rest of the day, hopefully.

It had probably been a few days since he met Snow, but so far nothing too different from the usual routine had been happening—the only difference was that now he had a little companion with him. The telepathic girl would send messages to everyone daily, most of the time it was encouraging speeches, although she also reminded them to try to come up with a plan for their next meeting.

Still, it had been nice, he felt like it was easier to partake in the experiments now. He couldn't wait until his powers were unlocked and he could be useful in aiding their escape. But for now, all he could do was wait and hope that they would be revealed soon.

"Ahhh." He sighed as he stepped out from the shower, a towel wrapped around him. Since he did sweat quite a bit, he had to wash his clothes again, but hopefully they would dry up fast. He looked towards the bed where Snow lay and smiled, the cat was taking her own cat-bath, licking her paws and limbs.

"You like staying clean too, don't you, Snow?" he asked as he made his way towards the white feline who meowed at him and continued cleaning herself. He chuckled and decided to just watch her, smiling as she finished up and rubbed herself against his arm.

"Hah, who is the cute little kitty?" he cooed as he petted her head, beaming at the purring feline. She really knew how to cheer him up after a hard day and he liked her for that. He should bring her with him when they escaped this place.

A sudden bang on his door snapped him out of his trance and the startled cat dove for the floor and hid herself under the bed. Sighing, he wondered what it was this time. Were they bringing in food, or were they just here to harass him some more?

The door suddenly opened, revealing the same large guard who was looking straight at him. "Listen up, rat, your days as a loner are over. From now on, you'll have another rat to keep you company. Go inside, trash, now!" The guard shoved another person inside the room, a scrawny looking boy, who seemed terrified of the big guard.

The boy looked at him with wide eyes and nearly jumped out of his skin when the door slammed shut behind him. He stood there for a while, looking at the ground and trembling, unable to meet Cyko's eyes.

As for the blue-haired boy himself, he was shocked. He had a roommate now? Why so suddenly? No, that doesn't matter now. The poor boy looked petrified, and he was much smaller than him, so he was probably just a young kid who really shouldn't be here.

The new boy had brown colored hair with equally brunette eyes and goodness did he look terrible. His rags were drenched in sweat and draped over his frail shoulders. The boy was shaking and his eyes were filled with tears, his mouth pursed as to hold in a sob. Cyko decided he would help him—no one deserved to be treated like that.

"Hello there," he said, noticing that he flinched at Cyko's slow approach, but didn't move away. Putting his hands on the smaller boy's shoulders, he noticed that he was nearly all bone with barely any muscle to him. Cyko almost frowned, but for the little boy's sake, he forced himself to grin.

"My name is Cyko. I can't really say anything about the terrible things they've done to you, to all of us, but... I'll try to make it as comfortable as possible for you," he said to him gently, squeezing his shoulders to offer comfort. The smaller boy, still vibrating, looked up to him.

"M-my name is Myo... U-uhh... P-pleased to m-meet you..." the boy choked out, still unable to look his new roommate in the eyes. The taller boy smiled at him, before beckoning him to sit down in one of the beds, which Myo did, his limbs folding easily as he managed to look even tinier.

"There, that will be your bed, make yourself at home... Well, as much as 'home' as this place can be, anyway," he said as he gingerly moved the child towards his new bed. A roommate, he now had a roommate! He couldn't believe it. First, he got to see his family again, then he got Snow, and then Myo appeared! Still, he couldn't help but have his suspicions for the reasons of him being there. He obviously wasn't a new kid.

"Ahh, uhh... Thank you..." he said, his shoulders hunched. Cyko looked at the little boy and sighed. The poor thing was feeble and meek, the type of person that would attract bullies in a normal life, and he could only guess how much the experiments affected him. He looked terrified even being in the presence of that guard.

Wait, of course! Snow! He knew animals could help a lot in relieving stress, and Snow was precious, and has helped him a lot these past few days, just by being there to rub herself on him and allowing him to pet her until he felt better.

Crouching down on the ground to retrieve Snow from her hiding spot, he took the little feline in his arms and gave her a few scratches on the head while holding her close to calm her down. It earned him a small lick on the nose which made him chuckle; the white kitty would cheer Myo up.

Myo was still looking down, seemingly too nervous to do anything but stare at his hands, which were on his lap. He hadn't said anything and was just trying not to be a bother to his new roommate. He didn't want to cause trouble on his first day here, or ever. His previous roommates already complained enough about his crying, and he didn't want his new one to do the same—

"Hey, Myo, I would like you to meet someone!" Cyko said, startling the brunette and causing him to turn towards the older boy... who was holding... a cat?

"U-uh?" was Myo's intelligent reply, earning a chuckle from Cyko.

"This furry little girl here is Snow, she snuck her way into this prison, and now lives here with me, with us! C'mon, Snow, say hi!" The feline meowed in response, looking at the new boy who was transfixed by her.

"Would you like to hold her? Don't worry, she is harmless, and surprisingly clean for something down here!" He held the white cat towards the boy who was astounded at Cyko's friendliness.

"C-Can I? Is it all right?" the boy exclaimed, earning another nod from the taller boy.

"Of course, go ahead!" he said as he handed over the kitten. Myo took her in his trembling, thin arms. Snow meowed as he put her in his lap and rubbed herself on his stomach, making purring noises. The boy's tense shoulders relaxed and his eyes filled with wonder and amazement as he fell in love with the feline, and Cyko knew it.

"I'll tell you right now that she is spoiled and loves when you pet her. Expect her to bug you whenever you are here," the blue-haired boy commented, making Myo look up at him and then back at the purring feline. The boy reached a hand towards her and pet her, much to the white cat's joy, as she nuzzled against his hands playfully.

Soon enough, the boy was smiling from ear to ear and he started to pet and play with her with more gusto, occasionally letting out quiet giggles. The scene made Cyko smile; it seems his plan worked, the kid definitely needed to have some way to have fun and release all of that bad energy he was getting, and Snow was the perfect candidate to help him.

Myo reminded him of little Starry, with how shy and sad she used to be at the orphanage. With help from everyone, she opened up to the others and even tried to help around the house despite her young age and small size. Just like Starry, Myo also needed help, so he decided that he should introduce the small boy to his family next time they meet.

As he watched his new roommate play around with Snow, he noticed more things about him. He really *was* paper thin, but the question was, why? He should be receiving at least as much food as Cyko was, and as disgusting as the meal could be, it still was plentiful enough to leave him with a full belly after he forced it down, even when he shared it with Snow. And, he received the paste three times a day. Maybe they were starving him on purpose? Cyko had to suffer through a week of starvation once, but he never lost enough weight to become that thin though. Maybe they were keeping him without food for longer? He didn't know, but he was certain that it was despicable to do that to a person.

"U-Uhh..." the boy started, looking up hesitantly at Cyko. "Th-thanks for letting me play with her, I-I really needed it," he said with a smile, his hands still occupied with petting the little Snow who was now snoring peacefully in his lap.

Cyko shook his head, his eyes glistening at Myo. "Don't worry about it! She loves you already, and now that you are living here with me, you can play with her whenever you want!" His smile widened as he saw the boy's face lighten up. Really, he looked much better smiling than trembling in fear.

"Th-thanks!" he exclaimed, looking down towards the snoring kitty and going back to petting her.

Cyko needed to ask *the question*, even if it made him feel bad.

"If you don't mind me asking, Myo, do you know why they sent you here? I mean, you don't look like you are new to this place." He watched as the younger boy's face changed, but he didn't stop petting Snow.

"I... I guess it's because of my... results in the experiments. I'm not really the strongest person or most useful person, you see," he said, making a frown appear on Cyko's face.

"Of course not, you are what? Five? Six? We are kids, we can't be expected to be this powerful, especially if we haven't awakened our powers yet," Cyko said, which made the younger boy's eyes fill with tears.

Myo sighed before explaining, "I'm seven, a-and the thing is... I do have powers already, they were awakened on the very first... experiment... they did on me, but... They proved to be completely useless, and dangerous." His voice was laced with regret and sadness. Cyko's shoulders fell, and he pursed his lips.

"What can you do?" he asked in the gentlest way possible. *Those inhuman, evil scientists, making such a young kid go through such trauma...* he thought.

Myo looked up at him, his lips still curled downwards. "My power is based on the Earth element. I can weaken solid structures and make them brittle... But that is it, that is all I can do," he murmured softly. Cyko, however, was amazed.

"But, but that is wonderful! If you can make anything solid frail, then... Then that would greatly help in our plan to escape this horrible prison!" he exclaimed, making the younger boy's eyes widen.

"Th-there is an e-escape plan?!" he asked, although after seeing Cyko's shushing motion, he noticed his mistake and closed his mouth. Hopefully, none of the guards would be paying attention to this particular room at this particular moment to hear them.

"Yes, there is!" Cyko said with a grin, then proceeded to tell him about the day of the socialization time where they had been allowed to talk with other children in the big gymnasium. Where they had met the telepathic girl who inspired them all and of course, telling him about the determination to escape she set within them.

"She asked us to think of ways we can help. I still don't have powers yet, but with yours, escaping will become much easier!" His body was buzzing with excited energy and he smiled at Myo's surprise. "See, if you can make things easier to break, like this door, or the walls, or even the ceiling, escaping will be a piece of cake! We won't have to expend much energy breaking down those thick steel doors they have everywhere!" he explained. The boy nodded.

"I... I see..." he said, his brain numb. Cyko smiled and continued on.

"Your powers may not be useful to them, but they are useful for us. Together, we can escape this hell, Myo. Trust us, we can do it!"

Myo looked almost happy at the thought before deflating and looking down guiltily.

"Sorry... I don't think I'll be able to help much... Y-you see... I, I have a sickness," he declared as Cyko's smile disappeared from his face, "th-the guys in white, scientis, scienti... scientists, call it myopathy, a sickness that makes my muscles very weak, and it's true. I've always been very thin, even when I eat a lot, and I have next to no strength at all." He sighed sadly.

"I understand..." Cyko said with a frown. The poor boy, now he had even more of a reason to get him out of here.

Myo exhaled. "Sometimes, my muscles give me horrible cramps, and what is troublesome... Whenever I use my powers, the worse my sickness gets. It hurts, too. It's horrible..." Tears began to gather in his eyes, which worried Cyko. He got up from his bed and sat down next to Myo, putting his hand on his head and patting it like he would for his younger siblings at the orphanage.

"It's all right, it's all right..." He whispered to the boy as he started to sniffle. Snow had woken up and was now rubbing herself against him in an attempt to comfort the younger boy. "The situation we got ourselves in is terrible and we all are suffering through the same thing, just because those evil scientists want to make us into super soldiers or something. But there is still hope, Myo, don't give up," he said as he removed his hand from the younger boy's head and put it around his shoulder, pulling him closer to a one-armed hug.

The little thing continued to sob, taking all the comfort from both Cyko and Snow as he could. This was the first time someone ever offered a friendly shoulder to him, and despite the sadness and despair that he was feeling about everything, Myo could feel himself beginning to calm down. His breathing started to slow and soon enough, he moved away from Cyko, wiping the tears from his eyes.

"S-sorry about that, a-and thanks. You are the friendliest person I've met so far; my old roommates didn't like it much when I cried about this, hah," he said with a hand over his face to hide his smile, though his eyes gave him away. Cyko on the other hand was trying not to frown. *What the heck was wrong with his previous roommates?! They were all together in this, weren't they?* he thought angrily. No matter, he could help the boy now.

"Well, now that you are here, you can cry as much as you want, don't keep anything in!" Cyko put a hand on Myo's head, and started messing with his hair gently, making the other boy blush in embarrassment. "Because, Myo, from now on, you are my new little brother, and I'll take care of you!" He declared with a big grin, once again surprising the little boy who looked at him with big eyes.

"B-big brother?" He brightened.

Cyko nodded. "Yes, I came from an orphanage, and we all used to treat each other as family, and now you'll be part of this family too, Myo. You can count on me, and I'm sure the others would love to meet you, too."

At this, Myo blinked back tears that fell onto his smiling lips.

"Y-you would do this much for me... W-we just met..." he said, earning himself a more vigorous hair rub, which made him let out a yelp of protest.

"Dummy, all of us, all the children are together in this miserable place, we should be able to trust each other, to comfort each other when we can. Be ready, I may sometimes come back here in tears myself. So, can I count on you, little bro?" he asked, to which Myo furrowed his brows and nodded.

"Y-yes! Of course, you can, big brother!" He said, elated to have someone need him for a change. He had family now, a brother, an older brother! Someone who would look after him, someone who would comfort him, someone he could talk to.

This... ever since he awoke to this nightmare, this was the nicest thing that had ever happened to him. Cyko smiled at his reaction and Snow meowed, rubbing herself against the boy's stomach.

"Welcome little brother, let's do our best from now on."

7

Cyko was being escorted to another experiment session, but instead of being resigned, he was walking as tall as he could, determined to withstand whatever torture they would inflict on him today. He hoped Myo would be all right by himself though, the poor boy had just returned from a session when he was called out, and he was a mess. At least Snow was there to comfort him, he hoped it would be enough, at least until he came back.

Face set with a determined look, he got in the corridor alongside the three guards assigned to escort him. Previously, it was just one. They must be serious about him awakening his powers shortly. He smirked at that thought. Soon he would give those fools what they deserved.

"What are you smiling about, rat? Don't tell me you're getting cocky?" The large guard hounded him again. Cyko willed his smile away and steeled his resolve, not answering the guard's question. The guard let out an annoyed gruff, and slapped his hand onto Cyko's head, pulling his hair.

"Remember, if you try anything, we will put you down. Others have tried before you and do you know where most of them are? Either red and blue in their little rat nests, or six feet under." Cyko started to wince in pain from his grip, but would not allow himself to show discomfort; he would not give this evil man the pleasure. "Understand? Stay in line and I won't have to put a bullet in your skull." The guard removed his hand from the blue scalp.

Cyko hoped he would get abilities that were useful for combat because he would love to put that particular guard through what he had experienced. Seeing the elevator door open, he shook himself from his daze, it was time to face this experiment head on. What would it be this time? The blasted shocks? Drowning? Beatings? Gravity? The oven? Whatever he would face, he would endure.

As he entered the room that the experiment would be conducted in, he noticed that it was a bit different. In the middle was a tank full of a green looking fluid with tubes coming out of it, he frowned. Drowning it would be, then, but why did it look different from the usual tank they conducted the water experiments in?

Two scientists were near the machine, holding some sort of strange equipment that looked like a mask and a cylinder. *What is happening?* Since these guys always seemed to like answering questions, he decided to ask as the guards escorted him near the contraption.

"What are those?" Cyko asked, his face still set in the serious expression, not allowing his fear and apprehension to show. The bearded torturer smiled at him, like a teacher answering a smart student's question, *how disgusting.*

"This, Subject 444, is breathing equipment. Today, we won't be experimenting on your ability underwater, no. This is special equipment that makes use of the fluids and electricity to give detailed reports about your hidden gene. This particular test is given to subjects who are near awakening, and today, it's your turn. It works like the electric therapy you have undergone a few times," he explained like it wasn't a torture machine he would be put in, but some curious scientific artifact.

Cyko's eye twitched. *Great, more shocks,* he thought, that means he would be convulsing all the way back to his room and probably for a few hours after that. He hoped Myo wouldn't get too worried about the spasms—they made his limb twitch and move like crazy afterwards.

The blue-haired boy nodded stoically, it was better to get it over with than to resist it. He learned that a long time ago. Besides, the guards loved to tell him tales of kids who thought of resisting during the experiments and got an additional bruise or two for their troubles. He'd rather not deal with more than what was necessary.

The scientists smiled at his cooperation as they stripped him of his clothes and put the breathing gear on him. "You've been really cooperative, Subject 444. This is nice and allows us to do our jobs as effectively as possible and saves you more suffering than what was necessary. Very few subjects willingly cooperate with our procedures after all." Cyko had to resist punching the guy in the face. *More suffering than what was necessary?! What the heck?! Why did they even have to go through this in the first place?!* he thought, allowing his brows to snap together and his eyes to narrow.

The scientist with the glasses approached him and placed several stickers on his body. "These will connect to the tendrils you see inside the tank—they will be used to both administer the shock therapy and monitor your condition more closely. Remember to breathe as often as you can through the mask and don't worry, we'll be monitoring the oxygen levels as well," he said in a pleasant voice, as if this would be painless. What was wrong with these guys? They acted as if experimenting and putting children through terrible pain was a normal thing to do.

Shaking his head, he saw that the two idiots had finished strapping him up with the strange equipment. "Now, please proceed to enter the tank, the treatment will begin shortly."

Huh, that was new. Usually they called what they did 'experiments,' this was the first time they called it a 'treatment,' he mused to himself. Unable to resist his curiosity, he decided to ask about it.

The scientists smirked at his question and the guards standing near them face-palmed as if they had heard it many times before.

"Why, the experiments are used to determine your worth and whether the hidden genes inside you are useful. The treatment, however, is used to help activate them. Once you are awakened, you'll receive new experiments in accordance to what powers were hidden within you," the bearded scientist explained with a smile on his face, pleased to clarify the terms they use. Cyko nodded at the answer he received.

So, this treatment should allow him to activate his powers, huh? Finally, one step closer to freedom.

Entering the tank, he noticed that the green fluid was rather viscous and felt strange against his skin. He positioned himself in the middle as the tank was sealed from the top. From where he was, he could see all the three guards and the two scientists that were working on him. The one with glasses held up an open hand to him, and slowly began to descend his fingers one by one, the experiment would begin in three, two, one...

Several tendrils rose from the bottom of the tank and connected themselves with the stickers they put on his body, and after that... *pain.*

"MHHHRGHH!" He could feel the electricity entering him via the tendrils, and thanks to the strange water, it spread to his whole body, making his muscles twitch in uncontrollable ways.

"RRrrrgnn…" Still, it was weaker than the jolts he received in the shock therapy, so he at least could maintain some coherence. He remembered that he needed to breathe, forcing out even breaths. He could bear it, he would bear it, and he would not let this pain overwhelm him.

Willing his spasming muscles to still, he opened his eyes and glanced outwards, the scientists seemed to be discussing something, and despite the fact his vision should normally be cloudy due to the water, he could still see perfectly well. The scientists had smirks on their faces and one, the bearded idiot, even nodded at him. If he could, he would've flipped him off, but currently, he was focusing on keeping his limbs as still as he could, unwilling to let the torture get the better of him.

Resist. That is the only thing he could do right now, resist and keep resisting until the day comes where they would finally strike out against those morons, when they would finally be allowed their freedom from this place. But first… He would really like to hurt them.

Yes, hurt them for what they did to you, hurt, hurt them for what they did to your family, hurt them for the twelve missing brothers and sisters, hurt them, hurt them all, hurt them for what they did to Myo, hurt, hurt, hurt, hurt hurthurthurthurthurthurthurt! His brain repeated over and over again.

So focused was he on his thoughts of revenge, that he didn't notice that his face was set with a bloodthirsty sneer and that his pupils had dilated beyond their normal range. All that Cyko could focus on right now, was the hatred he felt for those that were responsible for this awful fate. Unnoticed to him, his body and eyes had begun to emit a soft, blue glow. He felt powerful, like he could do anything.

It was like a dream, everything turned into a haze of loathing and anger, yet, he didn't feel like going out on a rampage, no, he could barely think straight as the images of pain to his captors invaded his mind, teased him with the possibilities of what he could do. It was like the tank had melted away and, in its place, a path of blood stood; everything was red.

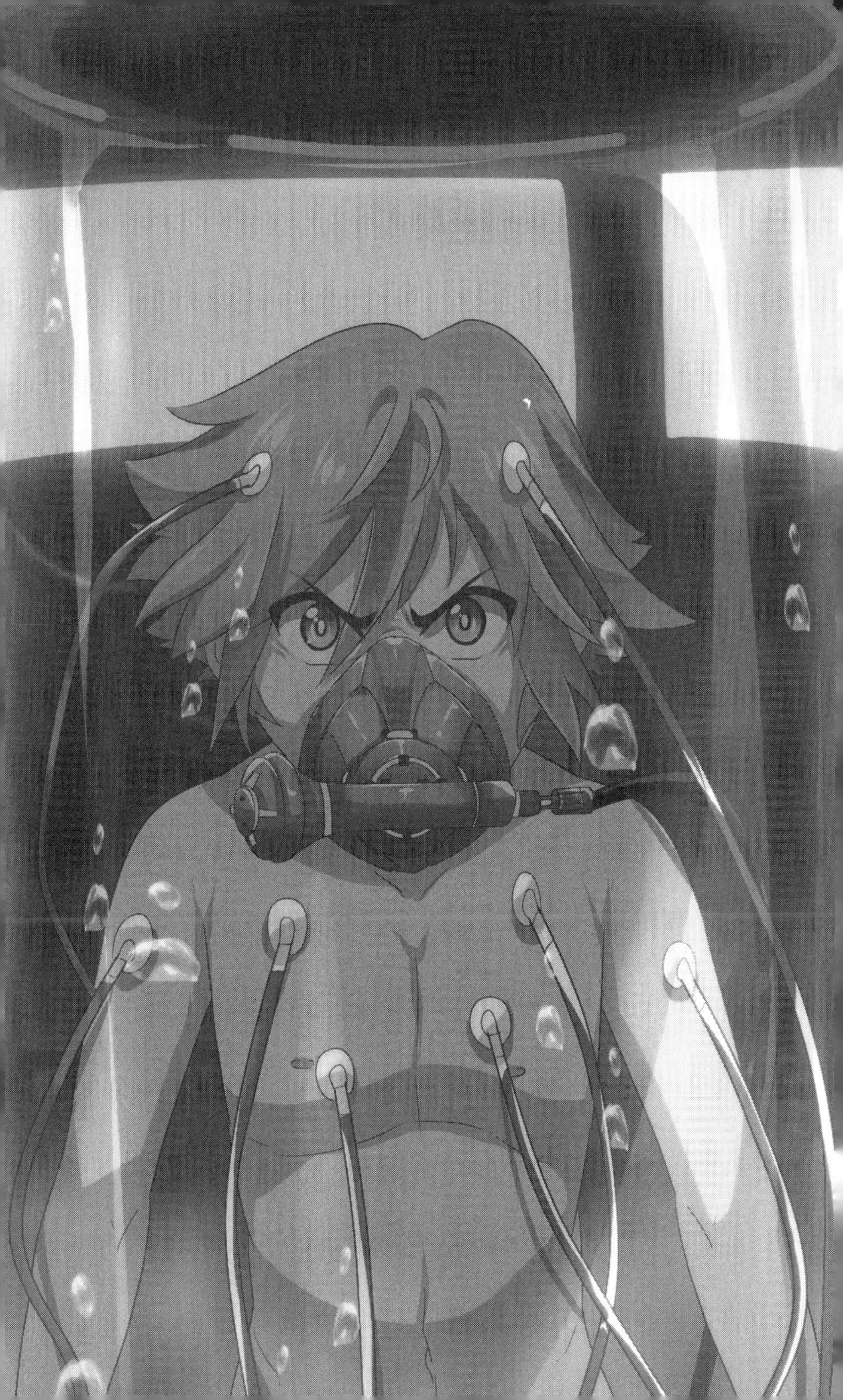

Eventually, he noticed that keeping his muscles still had become easier, and that he couldn't feel the electricity anymore. Clarity returned to his mind and he could now see the scientists discussing something and pointing at him while the guards had their weapons raised towards him. How much time had passed? He could barely remember it.

And then, after a while, the shocks stopped altogether as the tendrils left the stickers and the water began to clear out of the tube. The scientists approached the tank as the top cover opened.

"Can you get out using your own power?" the idiot with glasses asked, making Cyko turn to look at him. Of course he could, even if he was still feeling slight spasms. His control now was much better than before. Easily climbing out of the tank, he waited as the scientist removed the equipment and began to dress himself. At least his clothes weren't drenched in water or sweat this time.

"Congratulations, Subject Number 444. You're officially awakened now. Your hidden genes were successfully activated on your first try, which is rare. Rejoice, for now you have powers beyond most human beings." The bearded scientist stroked his chin while Cyko's eyes widened. He awakened?! He had powers now?!

He looked at his hands and noticed the blue glow that seemed to surround him, how much detail and how much farther he could see, and how little pain he was feeling after what was likely hours of receiving that shock. He felt so... light, like he could do what Torch did and jump to the ceiling of the gymnasium and back effortlessly, maybe even more!

The scientist beckoned one of the guards to approach, holding a thick metal bar which he handed to Cyko. He blinked and looked questioningly at the bearded idiot, what the heck?

"Go on, try to bend that with your own strength," he said, voice still holding on to his optimism. Doing as he said, the blue-haired—and now blue-bodied—boy took the metal bar with both hands... and bent it as easily as he could fold paper. He almost let the thing fall down to the ground in shock, he was so strong now! He did that so easily!

Deciding to experiment, he tried to make a knot and was surprised at the ease he did that with. He wrapped the metal bar around itself into a ball and crushed it with both hands. The power he could feel running through his veins was nearly maddening, a rush of excitement that almost made him want to jump around and shout, like he could do anything in the world, including destroying this facility single-handedly.

But he knew what happened when Torch tried that—he managed to down several guards but was eventually suppressed, either with overwhelming numbers or some sort of drug in the bullets, he didn't know. What he did know, however, was that he could use this power to help in the escape plan, at least, as a fighter.

"You are an Enhancer, Subject Number 444. That means you got a massive boost in strength, speed, reaction time and endurance as long as you maintain your energy circulation throughout your body. To turn it off, just simply will it, like you were flipping off a mental switch," the bearded scientist explained, making Cyko take his eyes off the compressed pile of steel and look up to him. The boy really wanted to shove the steel he was holding down the scientist's throat and make the blockhead swallow it, but he knew it wouldn't help much. Now was not the time to go crazy—he could always do that later.

Nodding, the orphan closed his eyes and imagined a switch that connected to his newfound powers and flipped it off. Instantly, the rush of energy and excitement left his body, making him feel like a lightbulb that was shut off. Shaking his head at the weirdness to it, he looked back at the scientist who was smiling like he was proud of a project gone right, smug idiot.

"See? You now have the great potential to be a savior of humanity! If only all the other subjects were like you… Now, you may return to your ward. Next time, we'll make a few tests in regard to your enhancing powers, due in three days from now. Be sure to rest and clean yourself well." With that, the scientist turned back and walked away, making some notes on his tablet. The scientist with the glasses walked behind him as they left the room, leaving Cyko with just the three guards.

"Yeah, you're powerful now, rat, but don't get any funny ideas. Don't forget, there are a lot of us out there. Now get moving!" The giant brute shoved him towards the door to walk back to the dormitories. Cyko barely felt it, even in his unpowered state.

Oh yes, you giant dimwit, he thought. He would love to give him his when the time comes, and it would be bloody, it would be painful, and the guards and scientists would regret ever coming to work in this place. They would be free, no matter the cost.

8

The door closed behind him with a loud bang, startling Myo and Snow as they continued to look at him. Well, Myo was, Snow was busying herself with rubbing her head against his leg.

"Big brother! Are you all right?!" the small boy asked in concern, making Cyko chuckle. He could tell he would enjoy living with him. They met only yesterday, and he already worried over him, such a nice person he was.

"Yes, I'm more than all right, look!" He grinned as he willed his power to run through him again, making both his body and eyes emit a soft blue glow. Myo looked at him in shock at first, then with amazement.

"I-is that your awakened powers?!" He squirmed from his perch on the bed.

Cyko nodded, grinning at his new roommate. "Yes! Now, I am finally ready to help the plan along! From what the scientist guy told me, I am an enhancer type, and can get more powerful due to my energy or something. It feels awesome, Myo, I wish you could feel it, too."

"That's great! I'm happy for you, big brother! What will you do now?" he asked, raising one eyebrow at him.

To answer, Cyko let the power die down. "Now, we wait and endure. We need to discuss plans for the next time we meet the other children in the gym. Don't worry, now that I have my powers, everything will be all right," Cyko said with a smile, earning himself one in return from his little brother.

Going back to their usual routine of talking about random stuff, mostly about stories of their old lives, and playing around with Snow, Cyko had time to think about what had happened those last few days. First, the socialization, then he got to meet a stray cat that somehow found her way down to this place, and after that, he got a new roommate and brother, Myo.

Today was the day he got his powers, the day that would mark the beginning of the rebellion they were planning against the people who created this place. Those geniuses all thought of themselves as brilliant—because they were children, they would be harmless and cause minimal trouble, hah!

When the time came, he would show them what happened when you made children suffer, he would enjoy hurting them, he would enjoy inflicting on them the pain they inflicted upon him and his family!

As Cyko now stared at the ceiling, preparing to sleep, he wondered when he started to have such bloodthirsty thoughts. He wasn't like that before coming here, and much less when he still lived with his parents. He never entertained the thought of hurting someone else to the point he was thinking of hurting those responsible for this terrible place. Hatred was a perfect answer for this. Hatred for putting his family and so many innocent children in this place, hatred for what they did, for the lie of a better place that turned out to be a nightmare.

Still, thinking about that would resolve nothing. He couldn't act on his hatred, not now at least. He had to wait until they had a working plan to go off of, something that would leave the fewest of them hurt, but hopefully also making as many of the guards and scientists hurt as much as possible. He knew he could trust his family, and his gut told him he could also trust Tela to come through with her encouragements. The children from this place are now more likely to work together for a greater cause than before.

As he closed his eyes, he wondered, what if he received a power that allowed him to multiply himself? To create weapons at will? He would be a one-man army and would greatly help in freeing everyone. A dream of a child who wished for freedom, that he had more power than he was given, so he could achieve his goal faster and with fewer difficulties.

As he nodded off to dreamland, the boy saw himself wielding some sort of strange, laser weapons, shaped like arrows. He could swear he had seen them somewhere else before, but they were blurry, and he couldn't see them well, but he *could* tell that they fit like a glove, almost as if they were part of him. Then, he saw himself turning into many blue-haired boys wielding the strange weapons, running up to meet against an unknown army, an army that was shaped curiously like the guards at their location.

Unnoticed to his sleeping self, his body began to emit a soft glow, one not unlike the one that indicated his activated powers, and, for a brief moment, a ghost image appeared above his body, almost like a clone of himself. As quickly as it appeared, however, it was gone. Myo, who was sleeping, never saw the strange event, nor did the boy notice when Snow left his side and jumped over to Cyko.

The feline started to rub herself against his sleeping arm, then stopped and looked at his sleeping form, her animal curiosity showing itself as it looked at the glowing aura the boy was emitting. Then, after a few moments, the cat curled up next to him and closed its eyes, preparing herself for another cat-nap.

Cyko's body continued glowing in the night as he dreamt of freedom and bloodshed.

CHAPTER 2

CATALYST

1

It felt like electricity was coursing through his body; not in a bad, painful way, but in a pleasant, exciting way. It seemed like he could do anything, like the world suddenly became much more detailed, like everything slowed down so moving fast became easy. His stamina seemed endless. This power running through his veins, it was his.

As such, he couldn't keep the grin off his face as he smashed another robot to pieces with his fists, dodging the shock rods of another three by leaping back several meters in an instant, then immediately jumping forward again, putting his small palms in the drone's neck and smashing it like a tomato, sending sparks everywhere.

Just like the scientists said, this was an experiment, one meant to test his newfound powers, and sure enough, it wasn't very different from a normal one. He had to face an army of cheap mechs equipped with shock rods and flamethrowers. He was pretty sure it would hurt as much as a normal experiment if he let himself get hit, but then again... he was allowed to fight them to his heart's content.

Ducking from a thrust by one of the robots, he grabbed its appendage and ripped it off, causing sparks to explode from the machine. Cyko immediately used this new weapon to break the enemy apart, before jumping away to dodge a small wave of fire sent at him.

That was another interesting part of his newly awakened powers. He somehow knew how to fight, which was weird, considering he never really practiced any martial arts before. The blue-haired boy remembered expressing the desire to learn to his parents, but he never got the chance to try it, because they felt that it was better he grow up a little bit first, and then the accident happened.

But now, he somehow knew the best way to move around his opponent's attacks, the best way to use their attacks against them, and the best way to take their blows should he be forced to get hit. It was like he had trained his whole life, but he could also tell that his attacks had no form to them—it was all a frenzy. Wild attacks, like that of an animal, of a raging predator ready to tear his prey apart.

Yet even a raging predator had awareness of its attacks, instinct.

Grunting as one of the shock rods hit him, sending painful tremors throughout his entire body, Cyko merely shrugged the attack off and punched the offending robot in the face, breaking it apart and making the mech fall like a sack of potatoes. He was more durable now, a shock like that merely made him uncomfortable, and he could swear it used to hurt much more before he awakened.

Still, what was the current experiment? Fight a horde of them. A mass of a thousand of those trash cans. How in the world they had both the numbers and space to fit them all, he had no idea, but what they wanted from him with this was very clear, even to his young mind. They needed to know how durable he was, how long it would take for him to go down.

They had literally thrown him inside the large area and told him to fight for as long as he could, but for once, Cyko didn't mind. He also wanted to test his limits, to know how long he could fight, to know how useful his newfound power would be in freeing them all.

That brought to mind whether it was wise to actually let the scientists know what his true limit was, but right now he didn't care. The rush of battle was addicting, the frenzied blood running through his veins made him euphoric, a feeling that the boy was starting to appreciate—as it made fighting that much easier.

He was surrounded on all sides by the cheap, silver robots, flamethrowers and shock rods at the ready, but it was fine, he could take them all, he would take them all!

Jumping towards the ceiling, narrowly dodging a jet of flame that melted another robot down, he leaped back towards the fray, crushing several of the tin cans with the impact of his landing. Looking around, he noticed that another wave of robots was lining up to replace the ones he destroyed, he *tsk'ed*, annoyed.

He had destroyed over a hundred of those things already, he lost count around 140, and it seemed like there was no end to them! The walls on the far side of this room had several doors, with dozens of them coming out all the time, did they have an entire factory just to make those things?!

He wondered how the machines stacked up against the guards, if they were weaker or stronger, but he figured it was probably the former. It would be a terrible idea to face guards that were weaker than the machines that super powered children could destroy by the dozens a minute. He wasn't stupid, there had to be more defenses in this place than just the guards, and even then, they were enough to take down Torch. In fact, Cyko wouldn't be surprised if the same tin cans he was beating down into rubble were also a part of the security system... a very expendable one.

Still, it would be annoying to deal with so many while fighting the guards and whatever other defenses this place had. Cyko decided that he should bring the issue of the 'training drones,' as the scientist called them, up to Tela when he had the next chance to meet her, which would hopefully be soon.

Getting up from the remains of another crushed robot, he looked at the never-ending pack. They said there were a thousand total. *A thousand of them just for him, or a thousand overall?* He didn't know, but he would certainly do his best to show them the damage he was capable of.

He was pretty sure he had destroyed over two hundred of them by now, and he was just getting started. With a grin, he picked up the destroyed robot's shock rod and wielded it like a baseball bat.

"C'mon you little suckers, try to get a piece of me!" he shouted as he jumped back towards the army of fragile steel, smiling like a madman.

2

Cyko was panting hard as he was escorted back to his room, he really had given his all today, and managed to destroy the thousand strong army of robots that the scientific jerks had thrown at him. He had proven himself this day, he was strong enough to take as many enemies as he could.

The bearded fool had congratulated him, saying something about his value increasing by several levels thanks to his results, and that once the experiments were over, he would be one of the elites, the strongest of the army they were amounting to "protect the world," he had said. The nerve!

Still, it had been good exercise, and Cyko could tell that if push came to shove, he could handle several hundred more, so at least the scientists didn't know his exact limits yet. Sure, they had said that he was probably near exhaustion at that point, but in the end, it didn't matter. With this strength, he would help free everyone—his family, and of course, his new little brother, Myo.

Oh Myo... His situation worried him. It had been three weeks since they met, and each time the younger boy was called for an experiment, he came back looking miserable and much weaker than before. It was obvious even to a young kid like him that his power was more of a curse than the 'blessing' the scientists said it was supposed to be.

Cyko himself wondered... *would the same be true for me?* Would his own power eventually reveal to have fatal downsides, ones that would possibly get in the way of the escape? No, he shook his head. He wouldn't allow himself to fall into despair, he was strong now, stronger than all those guards, he just needed the perfect moment to—

"What you waiting for, rat? Get inside, now!" He was shoved inside his and Myo's shared room, having only now realized that they had arrived. He looked back to glare at the guard, the same giant as always, and noticed the position his weapon was in. He blinked.

As the door closed, he gave a small grin towards the gigantic guard. He hoped it unsettled him, since he couldn't really tell under that helmet he wore, but his message was clear. *I barely felt that.* As he noticed that the idiot had actually struck him with his weapon rather than push him inside, and true enough, he hardly felt the impact and simply registered it as a shove. Things were going to change pretty soon.

Turning back from the door, he looked around his small room and noticed that Myo wasn't there. With a frown, he called out as he made his way to the bathroom. "Myo? Are you in the bath?"

The bathroom door was open, no one was inside, which made Cyko's stomach knot up in worry and anger. Darn it! They had taken Myo away again, after what he had gone through just yesterday! And worse, even, he couldn't do anything about it! Sure, he could probably break out of this room with brute force alone, but it would only be a matter of time until he was overwhelmed by the prison's defenses.

Sighing to himself to try and calm his beating heart, he grabbed one of the two towels on the hanger. As much as he hated it, there was nothing he could do about it, and after the fight, his body was really in need of a good shower... Even if this prison's facilities were anything but good.

A few minutes later, he walked out of the uncomfortably small bathroom and went to sit on his bed. He looked around again and sighed, Myo had yet to come back and until then, he would continue to worry about him. The poor boy was always terrified when he returned, he could only imagine—no, feel—whatever torture they were putting him up to.

He grunted, the only thing he could do was wait ... Shaking his head, he decided to do something productive with his free time.

"*Tela, can you hear me?*" he asked with his eyes closed. And sure enough, he heard a *PING* like sound in his mind and felt someone observing him as he listened to the telepathic girl's answer.

"*Yes, loud and clear, is there something you want to say?*" Hearing her sweet and reassuring voice eased his tension up somewhat, making it easier for him to concentrate.

"*Yes, the geniuses did more experiments on my powers today,*" he thought to her, smirking as he felt a sense of amusement from the redhead at his name for the scientists. "*They made me fight a robot army, a thousand of them to be exact. It wasn't exactly easier, but lately, the experiments they are doing on me are less painful and scary, and more like... like...*" He struggled to find the correct word.

"*Like they were analyzing you?*" She guessed the word, and Cyko nodded, although he was pretty sure she couldn't see that particular action.

"*Yes. This is the third experiment they did to me since I activated my powers, and like I told you, the first time they had me run as fast as I could, and the second, they made me carry a bunch of large blocks* around. This is actually the only time since then that the experiment had anything painful involved," he explained to Tela, and he could somehow tell that she was listening intently to his words.

"Yes, this is something they do to the awakened ones," she said with a strained voice. Cyko could feel the displeasure she was emitting. "From what I managed to pry from them, the torture they make us go through for months on end is what makes us activate our hidden genes. The life or death situation, the struggle for life, the desperation to survive is what, according to them, awakens our hidden powers. Just like a tale of a character breaking their limits to unleash unfathomable power... this can only be activated during our childhood," she explained to him in distaste, and Cyko actually could share in her anger. Making hundreds of children go through hell just to make themselves an army...

"It gets worse," she continued, "this is how they actually are managing to keep the awakened children from rebelling for so long. Their treatment gets better the more they progress through their plan—the better you are, the more important you are to them, and gradually, they'll make you feel important."

Cyko now could feel the sadness in her words and for some reason, he really wanted to comfort her, but... their treatments get better?

"It doesn't seem like that for Myo, my new roommate. He's had his powers longer than me, almost two months already, and he always comes back terrified, hurt, and in a gradually worsening situation..." he said to her in a guilty voice, and suddenly, he could feel a warm sensation of comfort around him, as if he was being hugged.

"Myo... Is that the name of your new roommate?" she asked him gently, to which Cyko nodded, before remembering that she can't see him.

"Y-yes, I kind of became a surrogate brother for him... He is just seven years old..." he said in an anguished voice, making him remember his other family members... And how several of the ones that are missing weren't more than seven.

"Please, be brave, for him. We still need to meet each other again so we can all discuss the start of our plan. I know it's hard, and I wish I could do more for you, for him, for everyone..." she said in a sad voice, but still she hadn't let up on her comforting aura in the slightest. Cyko smiled, she really reminded him of his older siblings with how caring she was.

"Please, you are already doing a lot for us, don't blame this on yourself... Blame it on those villains who put us here. They don't even keep their word, they told us we would be able to meet each other again soon, but it has been three weeks since then!" he exclaimed, trying to comfort her with their mutual anger for the people who put them here.

He could feel Tela giggle, somehow, which sent a ticklish feeling down his back. This was another thing that was unique to her telepathy, the feelings that she could transmit to the people she spoke with, which really made Cyko want her to meet Myo. She would undoubtedly be of great help to him.

"I know what you are trying to do but thank you anyway! I certainly do blame them for everything, and I won't let myself forget that!" He could feel her smile, and it somehow made him smile as well, she was back to her encouraging self. "Remember, everything they do is with a purpose. Either they lied to try and make us depressed, or they ran into some problems. Chances are that we'll be having another socialization time soon enough, hopefully," she said with a little optimism in her voice, which Cyko couldn't help but feel as well.

"It's always nice talking to you, heck, I can't imagine how many people try to talk to you each day!" he exclaimed, which earned him a feeling of amusement in return.

"Oh, it's certainly a lot! It's a good thing I can partition my mind. Right now, I'm talking with you and about fifteen others at the same time," she declared, which made Cyko nearly jump out of his bed.

"*You what now?!*" he said with wide eyes, which earned him a pause from the telepathic girl.

"Uhh, I'll explain it later, but don't worry, the feelings I am transmitting to you are genuine. On that note, you haven't told me your name yet, and you talk to me nearly every day," she said with some humor in her voice, to which Cyko simply chuckled. Well, she had a unique ability, and if it allowed her to plan better, then it was all good.

"Well, it's just that I want to tell it to you face to face. And so you can meet Myo as well," he said to her honestly, to which he felt a sense of approval.

"Don't worry, I'm not offended, I was just curious. Anyway, can you tell me how the experiment went? Were you hurt badly?" she asked with genuine concern.

Cyko laughed slightly, trying to send her the confidence he was feeling over what had happened earlier. *"Nah, if anything, I loved to be able to lash out as much as I did today. Sure, I got some scrapes, but somehow, I am not hurt at all. A little tired and sore, but all they used on me were shock rods and some flamethrowers,"* he explained with pride, which earned him an amazed feeling from Tela.

"Flamethrowers?! Are you sure you aren't hurt? How many did you destroy?" she asked in amazement, which made Cyko feel even more proud of himself for his accomplishment.

"All one thousand of them. The geniuses told me to fight against a thousand robots to see how long I'd last... I turned all of them into rubble!" he told her with pride.

"You are amazing! To destroy all of those robots... Even I couldn't do that! That's so cool! I really want to meet you personally now!" she said happily, and somehow, her feelings of amazement were rolling off him in waves, making him blush.

"Aww, you are embarrassing me!"

"Hah, sorry, sorry! It's just... With each passing day, dozens of children contact me to comfort them, and very few are as determined as you... With your help, I believe that we are one step closer to our freedom. I'll be counting on you," she said with a smile that somehow Cyko could just *feel* was there, and it warmed his heart, as well as filled him with more determination.

"Thank you, Tela, I promise I won't disappoint you," he thought to her with that determination, and once again, he felt a warm sensation around him. He was about to say more, before he heard the door to his room open—it was Myo!

"Tela, I'll talk to you later. Myo is back," he said hurriedly to her as he got up, which earned him an understanding feeling.

"Very well, please, comfort him as much as you can, you are a good big brother, I know it. Till then." Giving him one last wave of comfort, Cyko felt the connection fade away, just in time to catch Myo, who was harshly shoved inside by the tall guard, who closed the door with a loud bang.

"Myo, Myo! Are you all right?!" he asked in concern to the younger boy, who simply looked up at him with terrified eyes and then, wrapped his arms around him and started sobbing in his chest. "B-big brother...

I-I-I'm sorry..." the little boy managed to mumble as he burst into tears. Cyko's arms circled the boy and brought him into a comforting hug.

"Myo... There, there... It already passed... You'll be all right, trust me..." he whispered as he tried to comfort his little brother and as he did so, he felt the hate for the people of this prison increase even more. Myo was the living proof that what they did here was wrong, that they should pay for their crimes, that no child should be subjected to this.

The young brunette's cries slowly diminished in strength and eventually stopped all together, although his body was still trembling as he let out the occasional sniffle. Cyko picked him up in his arms, gently, and moved to put him in his bed.

"Myo... Don't worry, rest for now." He saw something white jump in the bed. It was Snow, and she started to rub herself on the smaller boy, making Cyko chuckle slightly. "And where have you been, huh? Hey, Myo, look, Snow is here!" he said gently, and sure enough, Myo slowly moved his neck to gaze at the beautiful white cat. He pet her with a smile.

"Are you all right now?" Cyko asked gently, to which Myo gave a small, embarrassed laugh. "Sorry, big brother... It's just... they made me do the gravity test again... But this time, there were those two drones... They could fire electricity... I had to either run or fight them... I-I couldn't... do... either..." he said in a small voice, looking as though he was about to cry again, but Cyko placed a hand on his arm, giving him a gentle squeeze.

"Myo, don't think about it, it wasn't your fault! You don't have to feel bad about being weak, or about being afraid... Because I'll be strong and brave for the both of us!" he said with determination, reminding himself of Tela's encouraging words. His surrogate brother looked at him with admiration and tried to blink the tears away.

"B-big brother... Thank you so much..." he said with a big smile. This had become a routine for them these past few weeks. For some reason, the scientists deemed themselves to pick on Myo as much as they could. Whereas Cyko would only be called for experiments about three times per week at most, Myo would be called five or six times, and he could tell that it was beginning to strain the poor boy.

With each passing day that he went to an experiment, his condition, both mental and physical seemed to worsen. He would have nightmares often, would sometimes break down in tears and at other times he would simply stare into the distance for hours on end. Cyko was trying his best to keep Myo optimistic and happy, but...

He didn't know how long the little boy could hold out. For his sake, he would keep trying, and he would help Tela as much as he could, that was for certain.

3

Cyko and Myo looked at the large metal doors before them, the former with confidence to encourage his surrogate little brother and relief at finally being allowed out of their rooms and having the chance to meet his family once again, the latter was both nervous and afraid. Nervous at what was going to happen, even with his big brother there, he held his hand, afraid of the guards behind them who were just waiting for an excuse to lash out.

Cyko was well aware that as much as he hated the adults from this place, he was glad for this opportunity and hopefully, the nut brains won't lie to them again just to make them feel miserable for days on end!

"All right, rats, you should know the drill by now. Cause any large-scale confusion, and we will fill your tiny bodies with bruises. Now, get moving!" the large guard yelled at them as the metal doors finished opening, leaving the children to eagerly run inside the huge gymnasium, both to get away from the guards, and to find the friends they made the first time they had this meeting.

However, as they made their way inside, Cyko immediately noticed that something was different... *The doors that are opening... were different?* he thought to himself with a frown, having a bad feeling about this, he looked around and saw that the other kids from his corridor didn't seem to notice it yet.

What does that mean? he wondered as he looked around. Then he remembered what Tela had told them all last time, about how many wards exist in this prison, and that not all of them had been allowed out to meet each other. Does that mean...

"*Hey, Tela, can you hear me?*" Cyko said in his mind, concentrating on the feeling he got whenever he talked with the telepathic girl, and after a few seconds, he felt the familiar feeling of observation wash over him.

"Yes, ahh, sorry, I'm in the middle of an endurance experiment right now..." Her voice sounded somewhat strained, and he could feel a bit of stress leaking through.

This worried him, but more importantly, it meant she wasn't there. "Tela... We are having a socialization right now," he said to her, looking around as children started to pour out of the new gates, and just at taking a single glance at them, he could tell they were new faces.

"W-what?! Are you serious?" she exclaimed in surprise, to which Cyko nodded, before shaking his head and replying with a single word.

"Yes."

Walking forwards alongside the other children of his ward, Myo still holding his hand, he made his way towards the center of the gym to get a better look at the new kids.

"From what I can see, these kids aren't the same ones that went last time," he said while looking side to side, and then at Myo. The younger boy was nervous, that was obvious to tell as he was frantically looking everywhere, his eyes never landing on one thing for too long.

"Ahh... I see, then I was correct about them holding so many others here," she said to him, both sadness and worry could be sensed from her tone. "Unfortunately, my ward doesn't seem to have been invited this time around, so I won't be of much help. If something happens, please keep me informed," she said sadly, her current stress still being transferred via the mental link.

"All right, I will. For now, please take care of yourself," Cyko said with a worried voice, knowing that she was likely going through something very unpleasant right now.

"Don't worry about me, it's not as bad as when I first arrived here. I'll survive," she said sincerely, a surge of reassuring warmth enveloping his body in response to her words, making him smile again. She was definitely someone to look up to.

As he arrived at the center, he looked to Myo, who still appeared frazzled. He glanced at the other children from his ward, and he could see that they all seemed confused, which was understandable as the new children arriving from the gates were all fresh faces and not a single one of them, from what he could tell at least, were in the previous meeting.

Wait, what? He blinked and stopped as he looked towards a particular gate on the leftmost side of the gym. Coming through was another large group of children, but... they were different; very, very different. Myo, sensing his pause, looked up at him in confusion before eyeing the direction that he was staring. The smaller boy's pupils widened, and he immediately hid himself behind Cyko's back.

Other children from his ward and even from the others also paused and gazed in shock at this particular group for they are all *different*, very different and most importantly... intimidating.

Some were standing on two legs, some on four and some on multiples from different animals—there were furry legs to scaled ones to tentacles. Very few of them had any similarities to a human. They were beings of animalistic visages; a beast given form.

A two-meter tall brown bull with a muscled humanoid torso and legs; a feral looking werewolf with razor-sharp fangs and claws whose steel-like gleam could be seen from a distance; a lion-man with a rigid gaze and hard muscles; a massive bat-like creature that took flight, displaying its enormous wingspan from the ceiling, where it was joined by two other bat-like beasts... Several such creatures streaked forward to meet the *normal* group of children.

However, the most striking one was the beast that was walking in front of them all, like he was their leader and demanded such respect. Standing at a massive five meters, the beast looked like it could single-handedly crush the gates it had come through. The only piece of clothing it adorned was the brown rags that covered its lower body, showing off its muscled chest which was covered in soft yellow scales that shifted to green as they made their way out to the extremities of its body.

Giant clawed hands twitched as its yellow, reptile eyes glared at the children, who were looking up at it in fear and shock. Massive wings, curled up behind his body, expanded to their full length, making the daunting figure even more intimidating. Its head was that of a dragon, a narrowed shape that seemed to originate from the most dangerous area of the world.

A dragon. It was a gigantic dragon-man, and he was glaring at them all with barely contained hostility. Even the commanding and intimidating beasts walking behind him seemed scared by the display of powerfulness their apparent leader displayed.

The group of children from many different wards joined together to look at the new beings, and needless to say, some were very scared. The ones that had awakened were on the verge of activating their many powers in case a fight broke out, but even those were clearly frightened of the gigantic creature.

Myo was shaking, hard, and refused to come out from behind his brother's back. Cyko was looking at the giant dragon with wide-eyes, from both shock and from a tad bit of fear... as well as anger. *Those beasts... those beings... they used to be children? Children like them?! What the hell happened to them all?!*

"Tela... We have a problem," Cyko said in his mind, hoping that the telepathic girl received the message, and just as he felt Tela's attention turn to him, the dragon beast opened its mouth.

"I am Drago, the mightiest of the mutant ward." His bellowing voice echoed through the entire gymnasium; the pressure he was exuding caused many to fall on their knees in terror. "Known that I am the strongest of all, I used to be weak, but the scientists from this facility strengthened me, they gave me power... They gave us all power." He gestured to the many beasts behind him, some flinched at his words, as if in fear.

"I can see many of you who are trembling before my might. Pathetic little weaklings! Have you no pride at all?! Look at me! I used to be no different, but now, I am strong." He raised one of his massive arms and flexed it, making arcs of electricity run down his powerful limb. "Tell me, don't you want to be as powerful as I?" He lowered his arm and snorted, clouds of smoke coming from his nostrils and mouth.

"Know this. Only the strongest will survive this test of endurance. Those who are too weak, too pathetic... They will meet a miserable end. And if *any* of you ever try to do something to stop this glorious ascension to power, I will *personally* end you!" he bellowed once again, making many of the children flinch at the volume of his voice. Then, the giant dragon made his way towards one of the ends of the gymnasium.

"...Hey, hello! Is everything all right?! I could detect many large auras near you all, including a truly massive one! Are you all right?!" Tela asked him frantically in his mind, likely being able to sense his current

emotions. Cyko snapped out of his daze, recognizing the worry in her voice and took a look at Myo, who seemed petrified at what he just witnessed.

"Dang it!" He took his little brother in his arms and walked as fast as he could away from the gigantic dragon and the other mutants. *This has gone horribly wrong! He wanted Myo to meet his family and Tela, so he could gain some confidence, but this brute just had to appear! Now the poor boy will be even more traumatized!*

"It's bad, really, really bad," he thought to Tela, whom he knew was still worriedly waiting for his answer. *"Those monsters… If it was not enough to make us go through that torture! Listen, Tela… One of the gates, the one in the leftmost corner, near a bench full of workout equipment, the… people that came out of that place… They are no longer human,"* he said to her grimly, his young mind struggling to fully comprehend what had happened to the children from that ward.

"W-what?!" she exclaimed in a shocked, terrified voice. *"What do you mean?!"*

"Exactly what I said," Cyko thought with a frown as he gently placed his little brother on his feet, to which he immediately fell to his knees. He still seemed paralyzed by what he had witnessed earlier. *"Those people… The biggest one referred to themselves as 'mutants,' are basically animals in human form, but much bigger and meaner looking, mostly. There are some I saw that are less feral and more human-like, but…"* he paused, unsure how to phrase what he would say next.

"Mutants… Half-animals?! Oh no…" From the link the two shared, Cyko could feel a lot of sadness coming through. *"This is terrible… I knew some children whose powers allowed them to transform into animals, but to actually be permanently warped… This is too cruel…"* she said with sadness in her voice, making him wince in sympathy even as he tried to calm Myo down.

"It gets worse, though… There is this massive… dragon-man that has made himself their leader, and he looks very powerful," the cyan-haired boy said with a tense voice, *"… and he seems to support their methods. From what he told us, he values only power, and nothing else. I find it hard to believe that he ever was a normal child. He is dangerous, all the non-mutants and even a few of them are terrified of him,"* he explained

to her with hands trembling. Myo was still afraid but seemed to be responsive as he latched onto Cyko and began crying.

"... *Not only warping us, but brainwashing as well... This makes things... much harder for us, but...*" The sadness in her voice and aura changed to something else: determination. Her resolve was back with full force. "*I will not allow this to stop us! We will all escape this prison and we will be free! This cruel project... it will be stopped!*" she declared with determination, even as both her willpower and her sadness started to mix together.

"And I promise I'll help you out as much as I can. No, I'll definitely help you out. We'll escape this and punish those cowards!" Cyko affirmed as he held Myo close, determined to help everyone out of this place, even if he had to go through that massive dragon-man in order to do it.

"*Thank you. I really need to know your name now,*" she said with a slightly cheerier voice, giving him a feeling of warmth. "*If anything else happens, please, tell me,*" she requested with a gentle tone before going silent. Cyko focused back on Myo and separated from the hug to look at him.

"Hey, how you doing, little bro? Are you all right?" Cyko asked in concern towards the smaller boy, who was still trembling and had watery eyes, but he was not crying. He was terrified, but not crying.

"I-I'm scared... S-someone like him... is much stronger than me..." he said in a small, horrified voice. Cyko, who was grasping his shoulders comfortingly, could tell that his trembles were only getting stronger. "H-h-he is s-so big... s-so... scary... He... *likes* this place... He said the weak will die... I-I'm so scared..." He grabbed the older boy's wrists in a vice grip, and even if Cyko could barely feel the strength behind his hands, he could tell how fearful he was.

"Myo, Myo! Look!" Cyko said as he put his hand in front of the scared boy and willed his power to flow through him, giving him a blue aura. The smaller child let go of his right hand at the display and instantly he stopped shaking, looking at the blue glow that covered his hand in wonder.

"I will NOT let that big, hulking bully hurt you—you are my little brother! And look, I am strong too, Myo," he said with a confident smile, before descending his hand into the hard ground faster than Myo could see, earning a surprised squeak from the boy. When Myo looked down at the area his big brother had punched, he was surprised to see a small crater. The ground was supposed to be very hard to break!

"Big brother…" he said in awe, because he sure as heck would be completely unable to ever accomplish that. He really, really admired the person he had come to know as his big brother over these past weeks.

"I swear to you, I'll use these powers to get all of us out of this prison, and I will not let you get hurt!" Cyko declared as he put out his palm, now lacking its blue glow, and began to rub Myo's head gently.

"Th-thank you… Sorry for always crying…" Myo said with a small smile. He really admired the bravery and determination of his surrogate older brother, and many times, he wished he could emulate them. Cyko, for his part, tilted his head.

"What you talking about, lil bro? You are not crying at all!" said the older brother with a small, proud smile. Myo looked confused, before touching his eyes and adopting a surprised face. "If anything, Myo, I'd say you are getting stronger! You used to cry a lot when we met, remember? You don't need to be a butt-kicking hero, though, leave that part to me," he said, taking his hands off Myo's head and standing up, his little brother following his actions.

Truth be told, Myo didn't really feel all that much braver, but… It made him happy that his big brother said he was getting stronger. As they began to move around the gym, avoiding the areas with the mutants and looking for anyone familiar, Myo made himself a promise… that one day, he would help Cyko in a vital way, even if he had to give his all for it.

As they walked around the gym, Cyko stopped abruptly. The younger boy looked up at him before realizing he was staring at someone. He turned to look in the direction he was observing… And saw someone walking up to them. She was a girl, she was just a little taller than him and just like everyone, she was wearing rags, the most notable part was her long, pink hair and a mole under her right eye. She was looking at Cyko with a smug smile on her face.

"Nice to meet you, my name is Magy," the pink-haired girl said with a grin, before offering her hand to Cyko.

The blue-haired child looked at her suspiciously for a second, before smiling and taking her hand. "I am Cyko and this is Myo, my little bro."

Nice to meet you," he said in an easygoing manner. Myo looked up at her, the corners of his lips turning upwards.

"Aww, he is so cute!" she said, before leaning over and pinching his cheeks, making him yelp in pain. Cyko seemed amused at the scene, but Myo definitely wasn't!

"S-stop it!" he protested, earning himself a happy giggle from the older girl, who continued pinching his cheeks, much to his chagrin.

"It's so nice to meet someone who likes him, he was really afraid of that big brute from before," Cyko commented, turning to glare at the giant dragon, easily visible even from this distance. The pink-haired girl stopped her teasing before turning to look at Drago, adopting an expression of distaste on her face.

"That idiot thinks he runs the place. If I'm not mistaken, he's just been here for a little over four months now. He is a weakling, that's what he truly is, a weakling that hides behind that huge frame of his and terrorizes those scrawnier than him. It makes me want to... hurt him, badly," she said with a frown, glaring at his form in the distance. Myo froze at her words. Did, did that girl honestly think she could go up against that giant?! She was barely taller than himself!

"How long you have been here, then?" Cyko asked with curiosity, but also a bit of sadness in his voice.

Magy looked at him and gave a small smile. "A year already. It feels like I've been staying here forever. My powers have already been awakened for a long time now," she said with a voice that sounded nostalgic, freaking Myo out a little and making Cyko raise an eyebrow.

"It must've been hard, being here that long, I mean."

"It *was* hard at first. I was alone and scared, and the pain, the torture... I am a traumatized child, I know that, but eventually... I learned to like it," she said, wrapping her arms around herself.

"Y-you what?!" Myo exclaimed in surprise.

Like it? How can anyone like the torture they were going through?! It made no sense! Cyko thought to himself. However, he didn't seem as shocked as Myo, which made the younger boy worry a little.

Magy looked serene. "After a while... You find ways of coping with things that are making you sad, even if it seems weird to others. I am happier that way, well, as happy as I can be in this place anyway." She sighed and turned to glare at the giant mutant again. "However, if there is one thing I can't forgive, it is to make others suffer against their consent. That is cruelty and I hate it," she declared with fervor, causing streaks of black lightning to run across her body, surprising both of the boys because of its intensity.

Cyko stared at her, his brow furrowed, before nodding to himself. He calmly touched her shoulder, making Magy turn to him, confused. The blue-haired boy simply gave her a smirk, his body giving off a blue glow. "Actually, Magy, I have something to talk to you about. Do you know this girl called Tela?"

4

In a large surveillance room, several scientists watched through cameras the events that were happening in the 'Socialization Area' as they opted to refer to it in the current phase of their preparations. Amongst them, Dr. Gacha was making several notations in his tablet.

"Sir, was bringing the mutants into the mix really a good idea?" a scientist wearing glasses that concealed his eyes, said in confusion.

The head scientist took a moment to look at him, before returning to type information into his device. "It was an experiment. Previously, we only allowed non-mutant subjects to experience a single socialization. Purposefully lying to them about the frequency of their meeting would instill enough stress to accelerate the process of awakening. However, many of those recently awakened had decided to… try to escape with their newly acquired powers," the head scientist explained, his voice analytical and his expression neutral.

He turned his tablet off and opened his coat to drop it in the pocket. "As such, I deemed it necessary to instill some greater feeling for consequences. At this point, subjects are already used to pain… However…" He gestured to the screen that was showing the massive form of Drago, who was sitting in the far north corner of the gymnasium, surrounded by many other, large mutants. "They are not used to terror. As you all know, it was fortunate for us that much of the mutant ward grew to respect power and strength. Their very genetic structure is completely overwritten when they awaken, and as such, they are no longer human. Their DNA now matches many of the monsters encountered in the wilderness, on the most dangerous places of this planet. Whatever humanity the subjects who turned into these great beasts had, is dead, and as such, they respect the power we gave them and have no wish for it to stop. The mutants would be the ones that would defend Project R.N.G. the hardest and their great stature and power can be very… intimidating," he said as he kept looking at Drago with a blank stare.

"Wouldn't that cause further unrest between the subjects?" another scientist, one with a beard, asked curiously.

Dr. Gacha shook his head, turning away to look at the other screens. "Drago is far from being the strongest subject, or from being the most important, however, it is true that he is the strongest mutant and that very few others would have the courage to stand up against him… Granted, they aren't motivated by something, however, the might of the loyal mutants plus our security measures should be more than enough," the head scientist declared, earning a nod from the two that had questioned him. Any doubts would be swiftly answered, there were no secrets amongst the scientists working in the deep levels, after all.

"On that note, sir, fifty more subjects have awakened this past week, the reports will be sent to your office for analysis. As it stands, only a few dozen are yet to have their hidden genes unlocked, but current data indicates that it's only a matter of time," the bespectacled scientist said as he began typing on the console in front of him, "we've been conducting the experiments and the treatments at an accelerated pace these past weeks, but it appears that there has been no drop in efficiency."

"Excellent. We should soon be ready to start the next phase then. How are the preparations coming along?" Dr. Gacha said blandly, while turning to look at the bearded scientist, who was still gazing at the subject's interactions. He then switched his stare to the head scientist, giving a smile.

"Things are progressing smoothly; the subjects are bonding well with each other. And if I were to say, the introduction of the strongest mutant will only strengthen the connection between the non-mutant ones. We will continue the preparations as planned," he said while stroking his beard.

Dr. Gacha nodded. "Very well."

Soon, everything will be set in place. The next phase is important, as current experiments are not enough to determine the usefulness of their awakened powers. If everything goes well, we'll soon have an army capable enough to take over any nation, an army good enough to protect the whole world, the head scientist thought to himself as he looked at the many screens, his face still in the mask of neutrality he always wears.

He knew what hangs on the balance, what was necessary to ensure safety. The danger they were preparing for is not to be underestimated, for Creators are the most dangerous creatures of them all, but if there is something humans like him are good at... It is to surpass the dangers they face, no matter what methods are used.

5

It felt like the weight of a thousand elephants was weighing him down, making every single muscle in his body hard to move, yet... he could still walk at a rather normal pace, even if it took a lot of effort to do so.

Today he was to be the subject of another experiment to test his powers, and once again, the coated jerks had put him in the gravity room, except that this time, they told him to make use of his enhancement to resist the increasing gravity as much as he could, and that was what he was doing.

His previous limit of eight times the planet's gravity? That was left in the dust. If his prior endurance was already great for a non-awakened child, then his new endurance—now that he had his powers—was much, much greater.

"Current gravity setting is at eighty times that of the planet's. Subject Number 444, how are you faring?" the voice of one of the two scientists monitoring him asked via the intercom. Cyko looked at the window glass that separated him from the control room where he was sure the idiots were observing him. He gave them a small smirk, the blue aura around his body providing him an intimidating visage.

"Well, we'll keep the gravity at this setting for now. For the next part, we would like you to run a few laps around the room," the voice said, making Cyko give them an 'Are you kidding?' look.

"We assure you, this is serious. From now on, all the experiments we will subject you to will be to help you strengthen yourself or to make an accurate analysis of your limits," another voice spoke from the intercom, likely the bearded idiot that always accompanied the four-eyed jerk.

Grunting to himself, Cyko nodded in affirmation and got himself in position, before breaking into a fast jog around the room. It was large, so he had plenty of space to run at least. As for the activity itself, it was hard, but the electricity running through his veins was making it easier and if he was honest with himself… he liked this challenge, the opportunity to train and better himself for their eventual rebellion and escape from this imprisonment.

Panting from the effort he was making, Cyko continued his laps as he thought about the events of yesterday. The giant dragon mutant, Drago, a possible obstacle on their way to freedom, someone he would not hesitate to strike down, even if he used to be a child just like the rest. That child was far gone by now.

The better part of the socialization was meeting Magy, the serene girl who seemed to have found her peace inside this facility. Yet, she still hated it enough to despise the dragon mutant for bullying the weak into following him and that the scientists of this place didn't care if you had no desire to be part of those experiments.

He had told her of their plan to start a rebellion to escape their prison, and how someone with strong telepathic powers was leading them and organizing things. She was cooperative, even adding that should the giant dragon get in their way, she would help to slay him.

She seemed to be looking forward to the eventual bloodshed that would happen—if her chilling smile at his words of rebellion were any sign. Still, after that, they had hung out and talked about some other things. Myo even seemed to have taken a liking to her even if he was also a little intimidated by her way of coping.

As for the small boy himself, well, he appeared to be in a much better mood when they had come back yesterday. Meeting Magy had been a positive experience for him even if he had to go through that giant brute of a dragon's presence to enjoy it. The sad part was… he would still need to endure the experiments as usual, and Cyko didn't know if he would come back terrified and traumatized as always, and that worried him.

"You now have a record of ten laps," the intercom voiced, breaking Cyko out of his thoughts and making him notice he was slowing down.

He gritted his teeth; the pressure was increasing and his jog became more tiring; he was reaching his limit.

He shook his head and took a hard, deep breath and concentrated on feeling the electricity run through his body and suddenly, he felt better. Running around while feeling that heavy though, was still a problem, but he would not stop, he would get stronger no matter what!

Grunting to himself, he felt his muscles starting to burn and his breathing get heavier. He was tired and exhausted—he had arrived at his limit in this test of endurance. But even as he now knew his true potential… Somehow, somehow, he felt like he could continue on, continue running with this heavy weight on his shoulders for a long time yet, even if it hurt him in the process.

Slowing down, he allowed himself to fall to his knees in exhaustion, his body drenched in sweat. He felt thirsty; his body demanded that he consume water, but still, he ignored it. He felt the pressure on his shoulders lessen and sure enough, it soon disappeared completely.

A thick metal door near the glass panel opened, and from it, the two scientists that always seemed to hound him stepped forward, accompanied by three security guards, one of them being that giant brute. He spared a moment to give the guard a glare before returning his focus towards the two smug scientists.

"Subject Number 444, your current record is fifteen laps total in eight minutes. Your performance is excellent for your power group, as is your endurance. Current results show you have a positive growth in efficiency," the bearded scientist said as he raised his eyebrows. Like always, both seemed optimistic with his performance.

"Hah… Next time… I'll beat that record," Cyko said with determination, earning a chuckle from the hairy crook. The scientist threw something at him, which Cyko caught with ease. Blinking, he realized he was now holding a cold bottle of water. A bottle, of water. What? They never gave him water.

"What?" the blue-haired child asked in confusion, to which the bearded imbecile laughed again.

The one with glasses then took out a tablet and took notes on it. "Drink, it's mineral water. Your body needs to replenish what it lost with your sweat," he said in an uninterested voice.

"Okay, but why?" he asked in confusion, but still opened the bottle and took a big, large gulp from it. The refreshing coolness entering his throat felt like heaven, and he couldn't help but let out a satisfied sigh as he finished. He was still a little thirsty, but at least he felt better now.

The bearded scientist waited until he was finished before replying. "The experiments were hard, but it was a necessity to integrate you into our project and awaken your dormant powers. All subjects that show even a little promise will receive better treatment and accommodations. We all will work together to protect this world," he explained with a sneer, earning a nod from the one with glasses.

Cyko just stared at them before looking down. "I see. Thanks, I guess," he said in a neutral voice. He was fighting hard to not lose it right then and there. Those jerks, how dare they!

They implied, no, confirmed that only the strongest will receive better treatment, while the weak and unwilling will continue to suffer! What about Myo? What about his poor little brother, who was so weak and scared he always returned to their room in tears? Did those fools have no compassion? Did they enjoy making small kids suffer to the point of despair?!

He wanted to go loose on them, to teach them to never touch a child again, but he couldn't—he shouldn't. Both because he was exhausted and wouldn't put up much of a fight, and because that would only create difficulties for Tela, who was meticulously organizing everything in the background.

"For now, go back to your dormitory and rest. Tomorrow you will have another chance to socialize with your friends. You did well today. If you keep up your current progress, you'll get the opportunity to be put in a position of leadership," he explained as Cyko got up from the ground and looked at him. Saying nothing and giving him a nod, he made his way back to his room, the three guards from before ensuring that he would try nothing on the way back.

Another socialization time tomorrow, huh? If that man was not lying, then that would prove to be an important opportunity. He hoped that this time, he would at least get to meet his family again, and Tela too, he wanted to talk to her after all this. Maybe if he was lucky, he would even get to see Magy again. He knew he could get along well with her.

Still, as he tried to think about the future, he wondered how his little brother was doing... He was called for an experiment before Cyko was and he worried for Myo. No matter, he would try his best to comfort him once again, that was what an older brother was supposed to do.

6

As Cyko made his way inside his room, he was so focused on the feeling that something was different that he missed the bang of the door closing behind him. He kept staring for a minute until the source of his curiosity looked up at him with a serene smile.

"Your poor brother was a mess when I arrived here. He was crying hard and didn't even see me until I comforted him," the pink-haired girl, Magy, said to him in a gentle voice, indicating to Myo, who was sleeping in her lap while her hands patted his head. "This little lady also helped a lot to calm him down, I can't say I would have been very successful without her," she explained, pointing to Snow, who was sleeping in the bed near Myo.

Cyko blinked in confusion. Magy?! Why was she here? "Not that I'm unhappy to see you again, but why are you here?" he asked in a low voice in order to not disturb his sleeping brother although he was surprised that the banging door didn't wake him up.

"I asked to be transferred to your dorm," she said with a small smile, earning a surprised look from Cyko, "I like you two, and Scythe told me that a lot of important events will happen around you soon and I want to be there when it happens," the pink-haired girl said with a larger smile, making Cyko blush a little. She asked to be transferred to their room just for them? That was flattering.

"Wait, did they just grant your request?" he asked in confusion. Why would they even entertain transferring her there just because she asked? It didn't help that Magy kept smiling, continuing to look at him in a way that was making him squirm.

"The scientists in this place treat those with high potential well... It helps that I am very cooperative with their experiments. I've grown to enjoy them, even when they are painful, especially when they are painful. My favorite is when I get to play with the robot army although

I wish I got to beat up those guards too," she said smiling, making Cyko look at her closer.

That was what she meant by coping? he thought incredulously.

"So, you are saying you enjoy pain?" he asked in confusion. As someone who also enjoyed the rush of power through his veins, he could understand if this was the same feeling that she was experiencing now. Magy nodded in response to his question and giggled a little.

"Scythe says I'm too young to enjoy these feelings, but it's true. This was before I got to meet my dear Scythe—I was a traumatized and suffering girl who only wanted her parents to save her... Even now, I feel sad when I think about those times—oh, I'm all right Scythe, thank you very much," she said in a way that confused Cyko. Who was this Scythe she kept talking about?

"I thought to myself, *'what if I enjoyed the pain instead?' 'What if I smile instead of cry?' 'What if I asked for more instead of begging for it to stop?'* and somehow... it worked. Before I knew it, I was enjoying the pain they were putting me through. You should've seen the look on their faces! Hah, it freaked the scientists out the first few times!" Magy said, her voice chipper, reflecting her fondness of the first time she enjoyed the torture.

Cyko himself stared at the girl, his brain scrambling to make sense of her. Sure, he liked the adrenaline and using his powers, but... Was she all right? Should she even have to think such things? No, it was obvious Magy was broken and had kept going despite the terrible situation she was in, and she had been here for a year. Would the same happen to him or Myo if they continued?

"Magy..." the blue-haired child said as he walked over to her. He sat down on her side, opposite of Myo, and took her hand to offer comfort, noticing how small and frail she looked. The girl looked at him with questioning eyes. "I'm sorry this happened to you... That they forced you to learn to like the pain... it is too cruel," he said with a frown, distressed at the thought of more children breaking like she had. Even that monster, Drago, was another victim of this twisted place.

She gave him a melancholic smile and entwined her fingers in his. "Don't pity me, Cyko, you are in the same situation as me. Scythe tells me you too will change because of this nightmare," she said in a small voice, looking at their hands. She shook her head and gazed into his eyes with her serene stare. "Even broken people need friends. Can I be your friend?" she asked, her eyes wide and sincere even amongst her messed up psyche.

Cyko kept looking at her, thinking about the words she had spoken. He had noticed he was changing, just like she said. Using his powers seemed to give him a rush of violent feelings, and lately, he had been dreaming of slaughtering all the scientists and guards in this place... Such a dream would make a little kid scream in terror, it would be a nightmare... But for him, he felt like they would be good dreams, somehow.

He didn't want to lose himself, but for the sake of escaping... he knew he couldn't do anything about it. It would forever change them all because of it so he might as well have people he could trust. Magy seemed honest, despite her apparent craziness, and he could also sense a hint of loneliness in her gaze. Did she get along with her roommates if she had any? No, that didn't matter anymore, she requested to move to their room, so the least he could do was trust her and welcome her.

"Of course you can be my friend, Magy. We are in this together, and I know I can trust you, somehow. Welcome to the family. If you ever feel sad, I'll be there for you," he declared solemnly, watching as a grin emerged on the pink-haired girl's face. She looked relieved for a moment before returning to her serene expression.

"Thank you, Cyko. That means a lot. I promise, when the time comes, me and Scythe will give you our full support."

"Thank you, Magy," Cyko said with a smile. He could already tell he would like her, and with her here, Myo would have a better time since she seemed to care for him.

Although he wondered, "If you don't mind me asking, why did you approach us, Magy? And who is this Scythe person you keep talking about?" Magy's smile widened, before she took her hand from his and put it near her chest, close to her heart.

"I guess I'll answer that question in reverse, my friend. Scythe is the wonderful spirit I met when I awakened, she is the main source of my power and my dear companion that has been helping me ever since she first appeared," she declared with a fond smile, surprising the boy. *A spirit?!* His mind raced.

"A spirit? Your power is to have a spirit by your side?" he asked in surprise, to which she shook her head.

"No, unlike other spirituals, as the scientists call us, mine is linked to my soul. Scythe is part of me, and I am part of her. Here, let me show you," she explained before inserting her hand inside of her chest. He worried that she might've hurt herself before realizing that there was no blood and from where her hand entered, a small tear could be seen.

From inside her chest, she pulled her hand back out, and alongside it, a big handle came along before revealing a beautiful blade. It was a scythe; a beautiful, purple scythe with a chain attached to its end that connected to the tear in her chest. Magy looked happy at seeing it and began to caress the weapon.

"This is Scythe, she is my dear friend, my mentor, my weapon, my soul. She takes the form of two scythes but the other half is still inside me. Her name is what she is, but I don't mind. She is my friend, and I love her for always being there for me when I need her. You can't hear it, but she talks to me, gives me advice, teaches me how to fight…" she said in a fond voice, looking at her scythe with sparkling eyes, before hugging it.

"Wow… she's beautiful," Cyko commented, for it was true. The happy smile and positive emotions she showed towards her scythe—her soul and the source of her power—were heartwarming to witness. Magy slowly separated from her weapon, looking at her friend with a happy smile.

"Did you just compliment me?" she asked, her eyebrows raised, earning a blush from the boy who looked at her with a dumbfounded expression. She giggled. "Thanks! I also believe she is beautiful, does that make me a narcissist? I don't know, and I don't really care," she said with a smile before adopting a contemplative look.

"Would you like to touch her?" she asked, her voice soft and open, making Cyko blink at her question, before realizing the trust she was giving him. This was her soul and her closest friend.

"Are you sure? I mean, we just officially became friends…" Cyko looked at her with wide eyes. Magy smiled before handing the weapon towards him.

"Scythe says friends should be able to fully trust each other and she tells me you'll be important in my life, so…" she said with a small, shy

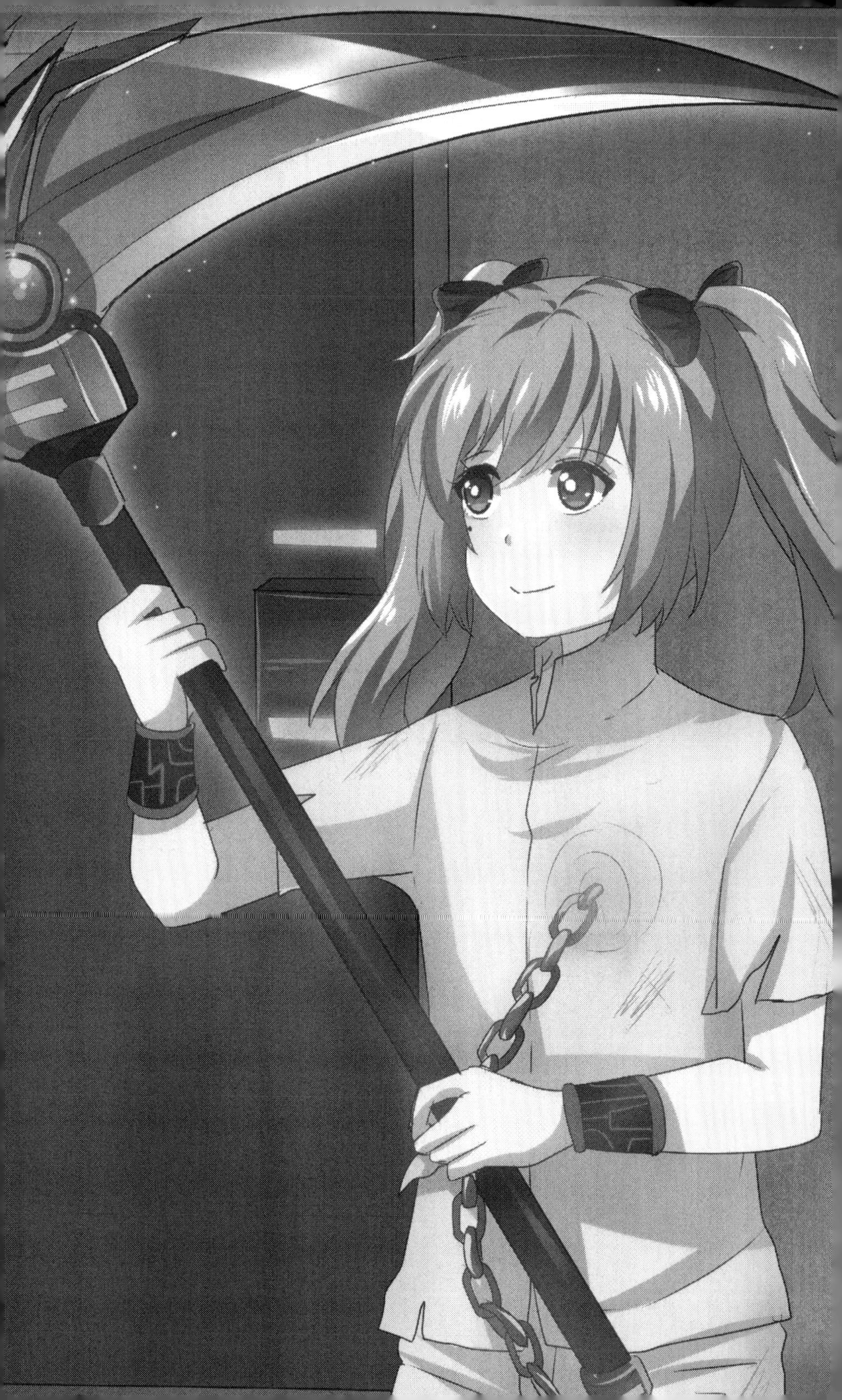

look. That shocked Cyko. How come a spirit can make such predictions without even knowing him? Still, her show of faith was touching, and if one thing was true, it was that he knew he could trust her.

Extending his hand, he touched the weapon. Its handle felt smooth but firm. It fit into his hand as if he'd been holding it this whole time. And then, he felt it... Something looking at him, something feeling him out, analyzing his own soul... But not in an uncomfortable way, it felt like someone he knew for a long time was looking out for his safety.

"Can you feel it?" Magy asked. "Scythe calls it the Smile of Death... Such a scary name, but it feels so nice and so right... She says only a few people can be blessed by Death, and you are one of them, Cyko. She says she can feel the weight of your importance, that you will be central to future events, although she cannot yet determine how," she said, her hand still holding the handle of her weapon alongside Cyko's. The boy seemed confused by her words.

"Why me? Was that why you sought me out?" he asked in curiosity, to which she nodded in affirmation.

"Yes, Scythe told me that something big may happen soon and that you'll be in the center of those events, somehow. She can't see the future, but she can determine someone's importance, so I trust her... and... I wanted friends. I was alone before in my room; all my roommates had disappeared in their first few months of being here." She looked to the ground and paused before smiling again.

"I'm glad Scythe encouraged me to meet both of you, and once again, I promise I'll help you when the time comes. Even if I like pain, I don't want to see this suffering continue." Her brows furrowed, her steel eyes looking at Cyko who took her words to heart.

"Don't worry, it won't... And you too will be free from this place... Even broken people deserve freedom, right?" he said with a smile, looking into her eyes. Cyko let go of her weapon, which Magy somehow managed to store back inside her chest. "You know, you look younger than me, but you are great with words," he said with some amusement, earning a giggle from the pink-haired girl.

"Scythe teaches me a lot more than just how to fight," she replied in amusement.

That day, the two kids spent their time talking and getting to know one another, speaking about everything from their powers to some curious things they have noted, such as how it seemed like the bearded scientist and the one with glasses were always near each other, or how the large guard from this ward tries too hard to be intimidating.

Myo himself woke up to a big surprise, seeing both Cyko and Magy chatting with one another, their faces bright and animated. He got over the shock and thanked her profusely for helping him out in his moment of sadness, to which she put his head in her lap to continue patting it.

They had a lot of fun talking that night.

7

It was the day after, and this time, the scientists had kept their promises and called them to have a socialization meeting once again. Cyko, Magy and Myo were walking side by side, trying not to get lost amongst the other children of their ward.

Yesterday had been a good day, since both Cyko and Myo got to know Magy rather well, and even if they had just met her for a while, they both felt like she was part of the family already. And Cyko felt an even greater need to introduce the two to his orphanage family members and talk with Tela if possible.

Cyko hoped that the mutant ward didn't make an appearance today. It's hard enough they have to deal with the constant experimentation, but he also could see how nervous Myo was, even if both he and Magy were holding his hands. If another encounter with that giant dragon happened, it would only traumatize the poor boy further.

Shaking his head, he saw they were standing right in front of the giant metal gate that separated them from the gymnasium. The large guard who always seemed to hound him walked forward to press a button which began to slowly open the gate. Just like always, he pushed them hard inside the space.

"Hmm... It's not the same doors as last time and the mutant ward gate is also not opening," Magy said after a single glance, her expression being a neutral one. It seems she herself was also nervous about who they would meet this time although she hid it well enough that Myo didn't notice.

Cyko could tell that the gates that were open now differed from before, and there were no dangerous beasts appearing from them... He sighed when he noticed that the gate that led to his family's ward was closed and it didn't seem like it would open. He would have to go a little longer without seeing them, and that made him a bit sad.

Still, he noticed one particular gate open and a group of children came from it and in front, as if leading the group, was Tela. She was looking at everything with analytical eyes, counting who she knew and who she didn't out of the groups that were arriving. He made his way towards her group alongside Magy and Myo, followed by the rest of the children from his ward.

Tela, the redhead who had inspired him to not give up and to fight for what he believed in was once again walking towards the center of the gymnasium, although this time, a lot of children were walking up towards her, likely eager to hear what she had to say. It confused the ones who had never seen her, which was the case for Myo, and Magy was just looking at her with a smile.

"She is important, too," Magy acknowledged as she gazed at the girl who was now closing her eyes, likely in preparation of whatever she would say. Myo seemed nervous, but curious as to what she was doing. After a moment, they all felt someone observing them, the feeling of something in the back of their minds.

"Interesting..." Magy murmured as she looked at the girl, Tela seemed to be deep in concentration, but after a few seconds, she opened her eyes and looked around.

"Hello again everyone, to those of you who know me already, I'm glad you are still with us despite everything, please, keep having hope, we'll help each other out," she said to their minds, a smile appearing on her face. Magy looked intrigued at the words being spoken into her head while Myo looked scared, but after a moment, he calmed down as a feeling of warmth and comfort grew inside him.

"Many of you here don't know me, so let me introduce myself... I'm Tela, a girl with telepathic powers. I have been here for a long time, and I can say with sincerity that I know what each of you is going through right now, we are living in a terrible place..." she started her speech, the same charismatic talk she had given to Cyko and several others the first time around, one filled with emotion.

Cyko could feel it all again, her determination, her sadness, her comforting aura taking a hold of many of the children present, whether it be the ones who have met her before or newcomers. Tela's speech was great in effectiveness, as he could see many people nodding along with her, their eyes watering as they regained their hope of one day escaping from this horrible residence.

Even Myo, who was severely affected by both the terror of the experiments and from the dark aura of the mutant dragon, was looking at the redhead girl with awe and admiration, his eyes filled with something rare...

Hope.

Magy's expression was one of happiness, like she found something or someone worthy of following, of fighting for. She had already promised to help Cyko fight for their freedom, but it seemed like physically meeting Tela had made her even more determined to help those who are suffering against their will.

Tela's speech continued on, declaring her plan to organize an escape, to make those who wronged them pay for their crimes, to never give up hope and always hold on to their determination. She was a kind soul; she finished by saying that her mind was always open if someone wanted to communicate to her, even if just for the sake of a talk.

Cyko sighed, letting the feelings she projected on them all wash over him and fuel his determination and desire for freedom, to save his family from this hell, to make the monsters who put them here pay... He desperately wanted to talk to her, even if that might be hard, considering how popular she was right now.

Still, it didn't hurt to try.

"Tela, can I talk with you later? I am here too," Cyko thought to her and faster than expected, he felt her attention shift to him, just like whenever they talk, but this time, she herself also moved to face him from the crowd of people around her who were talking about many things.

"You are here!" she exclaimed in his head, the sensation washing over him and making him feel warm at her excitement, she looked around the crowd she was in for a moment, before turning to him again. *"Just a moment, I'll be there soon!"* she said with sincerity before turning and talking with those around her.

Cyko wondered if it was just him imagining things, but she seemed to have taken a rather fast liking to him, as she always wanted to know his name ever since he started talking to her every day, though he kept insisting he wanted to meet her in person for that. Maybe he had made her curious by doing that? He wouldn't know, but he always appreciated her words of support and comfort, as she always had some to spare, even when he could tell she was sad or having a bad day, indicated by her voice being softer and lower in his head.

She was a good person, and her goal was one worthy of following. Turning his head to Magy and Myo, he spoke, "What did you guys think of her? She is the one who motivated us all to work together." Myo looked happy at his words and Magy gave him a nod, a serene smile present on her face.

"S-she is great! I don't know what she did, but I... I feel a lot better now!" Myo declared with a big grin on his face, earning a giggle from Magy, who patted his head, much to his discomfort.

"I'd say she will be a great leader. She possesses natural charisma and her telepathic abilities directly translate her motivations to us. Hmm, I believe that having someone comfort you, even when they don't know you, is a very nice feeling. I like her already," the pink-haired girl said with a smile, earning a nod from Cyko.

"Yeah. Before I met her, I would say I had less determination to escape this place. Sure, I hated the scientists and still wanted to get out, but I had kind of resigned myself to be here forever, I didn't even believe them about the powers until one of my brothers showed me his," Cyko said with a small smile. Meeting Tela had been a turning point in his and likely many other children's lives. He was certain she could get through to the children from the wards that haven't seen her yet. He hoped she did, she might even get through to Drago, but he was ready in case she didn't.

"Big brother... She must be a really great person, then..." Myo whispered, feeling excited at the chance of meeting her—clearly the boy was already idolizing her just like he looked up to his surrogate brother.

Cyko chuckled and patted his head. "Yeah, I owe a lot to her, and I wanted you to meet her, too."

It didn't take long before Tela untangled herself from her group of followers and made her way to Cyko's small party of three with a smile on her face. Cyko separated himself from Myo to move towards her, extending one of his hands forward when they met.

"Hello there, Tela. My name is Cyko, and the two behind me are my little brother, Myo and my newest roommate, Magy," he said with a big smile, glad to talk with her face to face.

Tela took his hand and greeted him with a smile of her own. "I'm glad to finally know your name now, Cyko! You sure liked the suspense, huh?" she said, earning an amused chuckle from him.

"Well, it made you interested in me at least," he teased, to which the redhead let out a soft giggle. She then walked towards both Magy and Myo. The pink-haired girl stepped forward, with Myo hiding behind her back. She had a serene smile on her face as she also offered her hand for Tela to shake.

"Like my dear friend Cyko said, I am Magy. Scythe has a lot of good things to say about you. You are trustworthy and charismatic, I can't wait to follow your lead when the time comes," she said, her eyes glistening.

Tela seemed amazed at her words. "I can see you are powerful, Magy. I'll be counting on you when the time comes and tell Scythe I give her my warmest greetings," the redhead replied, surprising Magy who gave her a happy nod.

She then turned her attention to the small boy, Myo, whose eyes were darting back and forth between the two, hiding behind Magy's back. Tela gave him a kind smile and offered her hand for him to touch, to which he reached towards, but winced in pain and gripped his own hand.

"Myo, what's wrong?!" Magy worried as Cyko hurried to move to his side as his hand convulsed. Tela herself looked worried for him and reached out to touch his shoulder. Myo felt himself relax a little more, but his hand still hurt, which made the redhead sigh to herself.

"I'm sorry, I can't heal whatever is happening to you." She said, her voice pained.

Myo shook his head. "I-it's not your fault…. I-I have a disease, that makes my body hurt sometimes… It gets worse when I use my power…" He said, shaking his head. It pained him to admit being useless, even with powers that should help him get stronger.

His surrogate big brother crouched down next to him and began to massage his affected hand, making the boy wince in pain, although it helped his muscles relax a little. He sighed as he felt the comfort and warmth from earlier increase. It was nice.

Tela put a hand on his head, tousling his hair as she looked at him with a frown. "You have faced horrible treatment in here, haven't you? The scientists don't take well to weakness… But don't lose hope, it's okay that you're not the strongest, you were not supposed to be a fighter, you were supposed to be a happy child living a normal life…" Her quiet words comforted the young boy.

"However…" she continued with sincerity, "don't give up, even if it hurts, even if it makes you cry, don't lose hope! We'll get out of this prison, together, and find our place in the world, some place where we won't have to go through this kind of hell again. You can leave everything to us, little Myo, we'll bring that hope to you," she said in a determined voice and once again, Myo experienced a surge of willpower wash over him, making him feel like he shouldn't give up, that he should try to resist as much as possible until the promised day of their freedom.

"Th-thank you… Th-that means a lot…" the sickly boy offered, letting the feelings and emotions coming from the older girl empower him. The pain in his hand subsided and he could now shake her hand in a greeting even though he wanted to give her a hug for being so nice.

"You are welcome, little Myo," she said in a kind voice, still nuzzling his head, "I'm available always if you need me, you just need to think in your head as if you were talking with me. I'm sure I'll notice you," she said with a smile, earning a large grin of gratitude from the small boy. She removed her hand from his head and turned to look at Cyko.

"They are nice roommates to you, I can tell that much. I'm glad you got to meet them and be a part of their lives," she acknowledged, earning grateful nods from all three. She narrowed her eyes.

"I'm afraid, however, we must discuss more serious matters. Even now, I can sense the turmoil inside many children, especially those who went with you to that meeting a few days ago. Drago, the self-acclaimed 'Mutant Lord' will be a serious problem. I haven't met him yet, so I can't tell, but if he is as twisted as you say…" She took a deep sigh as if what she would say next was very painful. "If that is true, we might not have any way of saving him," she admitted. For her, not being able to save even one of the children whose warped future resided here… was painful.

"He deserves pity." Magy's lips curved downward. "No matter what kind of child he used to be before, he is now nothing more than a monster who preys on the weak. Scythe says even other mutants are afraid of him and his power, especially the weaker ones," she scorned, causing Tela to let out a sigh of sadness. Cyko put a hand on her shoulder.

"Tela, don't worry about him, he is likely beyond saving... For now, we should focus on helping those that we can, and we need you for this. Can you tell me how many children you have... tagged so far?" he queried, hoping to take her mind off the giant dragon mutant, even if only for now. The redhead shook her head to dispel her negative emotions before focusing on the blue-haired boy.

"As of now, I've probably tagged the souls of two-thirds of all children in this place, if my memory of which gates were open now and before is correct. That means most of the children I still don't know about are likely the ones that came to the last meeting you mentioned to me, and maybe a few others who may or may not have met yet... And the mutant ward..." she said with a serious face, explaining to them what she had already accomplished.

"Then, we are close to having everyone know about this... What about plans? Do you have any in place, Tela?" Cyko asked, hoping to get information on how they would go about this. The redhead shook her head for a moment before putting her finger on her lips in a 'silence' motion.

"It would be unwise to talk about this out loud, at least for now. As for what I'm doing, I am mentally cataloguing the types of powers we possess. I'm using the labels the scientists created for us, and so far, my result are as follows." She took a deep breath and once again thought to them, *"About 30 percent of us have physically enhancing powers, like yours, Cyko, where you get stronger in one form or another. Another 30 percent of the children possess elemental affinities, where they gain control of the elements in various ways, sometimes obtaining extra senses in the process. They label those two as Enhancers and Elementals respectively and right now they are the most common type of powers to be unlocked through the experiments,"* she explained, her eyed searching the group to ensure they understood.

"There are people here that fit into the same category as me, the Mental type. People with mind related powers, such as telekinesis and emotion sensing. But those are very rare to appear, with a measly five percent of our total numbers so far. Some of them also possess abilities such as clairvoyance and mind reading. They are few but have been a great help in scouting this place." She looked at Magy, who was hanging on her every word. "If Scythe is what I think she is, then you fall into the Spiritual category. These are curious cases, because they can make contracts with spirits, usually elemental ones, who can grant them powers related to the elements their spirits belong to. They are rare, being about only ten percent of us. These spirits have been helping me as much as they can, considering that the prison is heavily warded against spirit action. Spirituals are only able to interact with spirits when the scientists call them for experimentation," she explained as Magy raised her eyebrows at her.

"I see, then I guess I'm an exception to this rule," she thought to Tela, who channeled it to the boys as well, "Scythe is a part of me, so I'm always in contact with her. She is a representation of Death and takes the form of an actual scythe when I call her forth as a weapon. She also allows me to channel dark energy. The scientists treat me well because I'm both powerful and cooperative. I'll tell you more later." She sighed. Tela cocked her head towards her, her eyebrows raised.

"That's fantastic news! Then... then can I count on your support? If Scythe can scout the prison, even just a little bit... It would help the plan out!" Tela squealed and Magy nodded at her, grinning.

"I can do that for you, although she can't go very far from me yet, but I'm sure she'll be useful, Scythe has never failed me before," she admitted, her hand touching the center of her chest.

"I'm glad to have you on our side then, Magy." Tela smiled before pursing her lips. "Now, there are two more types, and while they may seem the same, they differ greatly from each other. At first, I thought the Mutants didn't really exist or were another way of saying Shapeshifter, but it's actually completely different. The former, the Mutants, I discovered after you told me of their ward and their... leader, yesterday. From what I gather, their form and personality is now changed and warped into something else, like a demon or a curse from old stories. Shapeshifters are people able to change their form into something else at *will, some even being able to turn into creatures of legend. According to my calculations, Mutants should represent about fifteen percent of the children present in this prison, while Shapeshifters are slightly rarer at ten percent. I had to re-estimate after that disastrous encounter with the mutant ward, though,"* she disclosed.

"If you are wondering how I, as a child, did all this? Well, I was a prodigy before they brought me here... And the scientists will do small favors to subjects they deem important or cooperative. I asked them to give me books on basic education, to continue my studies, which includes math... It was hard, but I managed make those numbers and organize everyone who wanted to help," she said, shrugging as if it was easy. *"Thankfully, you weren't the first ones to ask me about how things were going, which I think is favorable for our cause."*

Her explanation awed Cyko. She was organizing everything so well! Even he, forced to mature faster than the average kid, could not make such a structured force of action! "You are amazing, Tela!" he said out loud, before quickly realizing his mistake and going back to the mental conversation. *"To do something so grand in such little time, you are amazing! I am even more confident in following your orders now!"* he thought, beaming with pride.

Tela's face turned red as she looked down and chuckled. *"Thanks! I am trying my best, and I'm glad you think it's good enough! However... don't let your guard down,"* she said, giving them all a look of warning. *"They think we are too dumb or too scared to do anything, especially after that display from Drago. They are trying to instill the Stockholm effect on us, by gradually treating us nicer until we feel like we belong in this place... Don't believe in them, don't let them make you think any of this is right!"* Her words grew louder and louder, her hands clenched at her side.

This brought to mind the way those two scientists are treating him now, Cyko thought. They were being nicer than usual, and while that confused him at first, it made sense now. They were trying to brainwash him! He would not let them get their way!

"Oh, don't worry about that. No way I'll let those absolute jerks think they can sweeten me up!" Cyko fumed.

Tela smiled in return. *"Then, please, don't forget these words. I'll be counting on you when the time comes."*

Magy and Myo looked at her with clear admiration, as did Cyko. She seemed to be the perfect leader for them, and they hoped that everything went well. Tela had been taking all that she could into account, and they respected her for it.

The blue-haired boy, however, couldn't help but wonder how she was doing, health-wise. After all, she had given him his hope back, the least he could do was give her emotional support if she needed it.

"And you, yourself, Tela? How are you doing?" Cyko asked in concern, out loud, which earned him a confused glance from the telepath, "I mean, with everything going on, how are you feeling?" He pointed to his heart. She looked surprised at his question before giving him a grateful look.

"Aw, you don't need to worry about me!" she thanked him, "I mean, there are some things, a lot of things that make me sad every day but… I need to be strong, I can't let my sadness get the better of me, no matter what. There are people that are counting on me, but… Thanks for worrying, that's sweet of you." Cyko could feel her warm smile wash over him, making him giddy all over.

"You are welcome Tela!" he said with a big grin, before gesturing towards both Magy and Myo, who were watching the exchange with curiosity. "We are all friends here, so if you need someone to talk to, either me, Magy, or Myo can help you!" Cyko declared, earning a big smile from the redhead.

"Thank you so much, I will remember your words!" She beamed. "I must go back to the others now, there are people wanting to talk today, and I need to continue making plans for everything. It was so nice to finally meet you!" She stepped forward and gave the blue-haired boy a hug, making him blink in shock and turn red at the sudden contact. She separated and gave both Magy and Myo hugs, earning one back from the pink-haired girl and a tomato-colored blush from the younger boy.

As she walked back towards the group she left earlier, they waved goodbye to one another. Yes, Cyko thought, meeting Tela had been worth it, and he could tell that for Myo, it had been a great experience. To feel the comfort, the warmth and the charisma of the telepathic girl that wanted to help free them all seemed to have lifted their spirits again.

For the rest of the socialization time, Cyko, Myo, and Magy mingled around the gymnasium, talking and trying to have fun as they watched the redhead talk to many, many people. It was moments like these that gave Cyko the impression that everything would go well, and that they could get the freedom they were striving for.

Judging from the look on Myo's face as he stared at the ceiling that night, it seemed he took Tela's offer to talk to heart. It made Cyko happy to see his brother in such a good mood considering all he had gone through.

Both boys fell asleep with smiles on their faces.

8

Dr. Gacha watched intently as the girl known as Tela walked around the gymnasium, talking and interacting with as many people as she could, gaining friends and followers everywhere she went.

"Tell me, what do you think she is doing?" the head scientist asked one of the others with him in the surveillance room.

The bespectacled scientist pushed up his glasses and looked at the screen. "It seems she is trying to make connections, sir. That particular subject is one that is very important, and she was always cooperative in the experiments," he answered with precision, gaining a nod from his superior.

"Her impressive ability with telekinesis and emotional manipulation makes her a powerful asset in our army... However, just the same, she can also be a great danger to the safety of Project R.N.G. She is just a youth, but children can also be... rebellious. Be sure to keep an eye on her, don't let her know we are suspecting her of something, we still need her cooperation." Dr. Gacha mused, gaining a nod from the scientist with glasses.

"I will do that, sir. We will increase security in her ward and install hidden cameras in her room to keep an eye on her at all times," he said in a matter-of-fact tone. Dr. Gacha nodded and went back to watching the interactions of the many subjects present today.

"If you allow me to ask, sir," the bearded scientist said, earning a nod from his superior, still with his head glued to the screens, "what of... them? The subjects in the highest security ward, and especially our most precious subject. Should we allow them in the next socialization?"

Dr. Gacha stood silent for a few moments, contemplating his answer. The subjects from that ward were some of the most dangerous ones... Dangerous for the project, as most of them had powers that could increase their chances of either escape or rebellion, still... It would be beneficial to see how they would interact with their peers.

Preparations were going smoothly; the subjects were trusting one another to share their burdens and one of them even requested to be transferred to the same room they had sent that inevitable failure to. At this rate, everything would soon be in place and they could prepare for the next phase of their project... The part that would determine if they were as useful as they seemed or if they were failures.

"Dr. Gacha, sir!" one of the scientists present called for him. He turned his head towards the speaker, to show he was paying attention but refused to take his eyes off the screen.

"Mr. Whale would like to speak with you in his office," the scientist spoke, earning a nod from his boss.

"Very well, I'll be there shortly," he said with no indication to his feelings, finally taking his eyes off the screen to head towards the office of the person that was financing his project. It was a pity, he hoped to observe for a while longer, but he is a busy man.

A small part of him, though, was wondering about something unrelated to his project, something that had disappeared from his office a while ago that worried him. He didn't mind though, she knew how to take care of herself, and he was sure he would find her, eventually. After all, he had raised her to the best of his ability.

As his mind shifted towards this as he made his way out of the room, he didn't notice a scientist mutter to himself, "Why do I feel like I'm being observed?" before shaking his head and going back to work. The walk towards Mr. Whale's office would be a rather boring one, and even as self-disciplined as he is, his mind couldn't help but find something to do to pass the time.

9

"There, there, everything will be all right now, Cyko," Magy said as she stroked the blue-haired boy's hair, who was resting his head on her lap and blushing at her treatment.

"Big sis Magy is so kind, isn't she? A bit scary, but I like her!" Myo, who was sitting on the other bed and playing with Snow, said with a smile.

The reason for Magy trying to comfort him? He had just gotten back from an exhausting experiment, which combined the last two they had thrown at him. That meant he had to fight a robot army whilst being held down by heavy gravity levels, the same intensity they had used on him last time.

Nothing like pain to make him fight for his life even when held down by gravity, as he still destroyed all one thousand robots for his test… He had exhausted himself today, and thanks to the pressure, he was hurt many, many times by both flamethrowers and shock attacks. Luckily the rags he wore were fire resistant, otherwise he would rather die than go back to his room naked.

When he arrived back, both Myo and Magy had already returned from their respective experiments. Magy could barely keep her eyes open as she comforted Myo, but from the look in Cyko's eyes, he had put on his bravest face yet. They both looked at him and his wounds with concern but said nothing as he made his way to the shower.

When he came back from cleaning himself, both gave him quick hugs, and Magy dragged him towards her bed and made him put his head on her lap while his face burned red with embarrassment. But if he was honest, it was calming, and after the stress he went through in that lab, he could use some relaxation.

"I-I'll be fine!" he said sheepishly. "What about you guys? How are you doing after today?" he asked, looking first at Myo, who was still playing with Snow, and then looking up at Magy, who was smiling softly.

"Myo was a very brave boy today. His experiment was hard, but he refused to cry. I think meeting Tela yesterday was a beneficial experience for him. I gave him the treatment I'm giving you as a reward." She continued to stroke his hair. Still blushing, she turned his head to look at Myo and Snow, who was rubbing herself against him. "The cute kitty has been a great help too, she seems to know when we are sad and in need of comfort."

"What about, Magy?" he asked as he turned his head to look up at his friend, she smiled at his question.

"I'm fine, as I said, I seem to like the pain some of those experiments bring me. Today has been a little rough, so it was a rather enjoyable experience. Scythe says it will get better as I get older though I'm a little afraid of getting too addicted to pain." She continued pampering her newest friend.

Cyko's face, although still flushed, looked at her with concern. Sure, she said she learned to like pain to cope with her suffering, but... Magy noticed the way he was looking at her, and her lips curved downwards. "Does that make me weird, Cyko?" she asked in a sad voice, making the blue-haired boy's eyes widen.

"No, no! It's just... It's sad that you had to do that at all to find any enjoyment in this life. You are not a bad person for enjoying pain, just be careful not to hurt yourself too much, okay?" he said, concerned. Her frown turned into a smile at his words, and she resumed stroking his head.

"You are a good friend to me, Cyko. But like I said, I'm fine, I don't suffer emotionally from those things anymore... Only when I see others put through it, which is why I'm helping you all right now," she said, reminding Cyko of her promise. "I wouldn't mind being experimented on forever, as long as the ones who don't want this could be free." She smiled sadly.

"Hey, please, don't say that! You will be free along with all of us, and then, you can decide when you want to feel pain rather than have it decided for you!" Cyko said, aware of how weird that sounded, but the look she gave him as an answer was worth it.

After a few minutes, Magy released Cyko from her warm, calming hold to eat as their food had arrived—the same disgusting porridge it always was. Magy even commented on it, citing that "Even if I like pain, I can never like this food," earning herself a snicker from both boys; it was a happy moment for them.

They were further surprised when a second bang resonated on the door followed by the burly guard ordering them to get ready for another socialization. This confused them, they had one yesterday! Now they were being called for another one?

They did as they were told and got themselves ready for the meeting. Cyko hoped they would get to meet his family again this time, he missed them and wondered how they were doing, or if they had gained their powers. Now, though, Cyko decided on doing something else... He would bring Snow with him! Magy seemed hesitant at the idea, but Cyko really wanted to let the others meet her if possible, both because she was an adorable kitty who always helped comfort them, and because he felt like she should take a walk after spending so long in their room.

As they made their way towards the gate that led to the gymnasium, Cyko took a moment to look at the other children from his ward. He hadn't had the chance to speak with them much, but he at least knew some of them in passing. Before, they all had looks of despair or sadness, but after that first meeting with Tela, most of them seemed a little more hardened, a little more determined or at least not on the brink of giving up anymore. This brought a smile to his face. Maybe, just maybe, they had a chance.

The gates were opening, and once again, Cyko looked at the many doors around the large gymnasium. He noticed that Tela's gate wasn't opening this time around, but as he scanned the area, he noticed that the one that led to the ward where the rest of his family resided was opening! Grinning, he urged both Magy and Myo to follow him, not noticing how Magy briefly stopped to glance at one of the gates, her mouth opened slightly, before shaking her head and following Cyko.

As the many children from his family's ward broke off to walk in different directions, likely to mingle with people from the other wards they had gotten to know previously, Cyko could see his family members forming into a group of their own. Starry, his youngest sister, saw him from the distance and tugged at Anna's clothes to get her attention. They all turned to where she was pointing and when they saw him, they all began to sprint towards him.

"Cyko! Big brother!" they exclaimed as they reached him, pulling him into a group hug that made him yelp in surprise and Snow, who was tucked inside his rags thrashed around.

"Ouch, ouch, ouch, ouch! Snow, stop!" he shrieked as he hurried to take the feline out of his shirt before she tore his belly apart.

"A kitty!" Starry cried as she looked at the struggling feline that Cyko had unveiled. His brothers and sisters separated from the hug to give the boy and his cat a surprised look. After a few seconds, he managed to calm down the wriggling kitty.

"Whew, you can be a handful, you know? Anyway, guys! It's been so long! Here, meet Snow! She is a kitty that somehow found her way inside this place and I took her with me because I was feeling lonely. Here, do you guys want to hold her? She is sweet!" he said as he handed the feline to Sara, who was nearby him.

The blue-haired girl cooed at the kitten who began to purr at the attention she was receiving. They all sat down on the ground to play with her. Sara handed Snow to Starry, who was giving heart-eyes to the little cat and immediately snuggled her, making the older members of the family smile, and Torch blush at the adorable sight.

Magy and Myo caught up to Cyko, who looked behind him to smile at the two. "Myo, Magy, I would like to introduce you to my family from the orphanage I lived in before being… here," he said, turning to his siblings who were now paying attention to him while Snow was being gently pet by Anna. "Everyone, this is Myo, my new surrogate little brother, and Magy, my friend. These two are my roommates, and I can sincerely say that I like them both very much." Myo and Magy blushed at his honest words.

"Hello there, you two! I am Anna!" the blonde girl introduced herself with a smile, before pointing to Geon, who was grinning at them.

"Hi, I am Geon, thank you very much for taking care of Cyko," he said, pointing towards Sara, who got the hint.

"I am Sara, pleased to meet you!" the blue-head said and pointed to the person next to her. Henry.

The smart boy nodded, offering his hands for them to shake, which they did, smiling. "I am Henry, I hope we can get along well with each other," he said, motioning to Matthew.

The boy gave a small bow, letting some embers escape from his mouth to show off his fire breathing power. "I am Matthew, but you can call me Mat! I hope Cyko has been good to you!" He nudged Torch, who had been playing with Snow alongside Starry.

"I am Torch, and one day, I'll help us all escape this place!" he said with determination, earning a giggle from Magy. To her, it was obvious how much he cared for the little girl he was playing with, and how much he wanted to protect her. She could see the same thing in Cyko and herself towards Myo.

Starry looked a little shy at being the center of attention but spoke too. She wanted to know the two people that were keeping her big brother company. "I-I am Starry! I-I can make stars, nice to meet you!" she rushed through her introduction and placed both her hands in front of herself and created a dark star which made both Magy and Myo look at it in awe.

"That's very interesting, little Star! I can feel your soul being translated from that pretty thing. Just like you, I'm also dark natured, so I can sense those things better than most," Magy complemented her, causing the little girl to blush in embarrassment.

"Th-thank you, miss!"

"Y-yeah, it's so pretty… I wished I could do something like that instead of… Never mind, but really, it's pretty!" Myo offered, awed at the beautiful little star she had created. Starry's blush intensified, which brought out a small chuckle from the boy.

Cyko let out a sigh of relief that both Myo and Magy were getting along with his family. Even Snow was receiving attention from meeting them, which made him feel wholesome and truly happy. If there was anything good about these meetings, it was this, these moments of happiness rather than moments of tension like Drago wanted to inflict.

They moved to sit at one of the many tables present in this place, one large enough to fit their group of ten children plus a cat so they could have somewhere more private and comfortable to discuss the events of past weeks. Cyko began with the topic he was most interested in…

"Everyone, it has been too long, how are you all doing, after all this time?" he asked in concern.

Anna was the first to speak after a few seconds of silence. "Well… all of us have powers now, although, I only know the ones we went over last time and those who are in the same room as me, so maybe we should recap everything?" she recommended, to which they all nodded in agreement.

"Well, since I suggested it, I will start. I can do this!" she exclaimed before putting her left arm on the table. They all watched in awe as her arm turned into a futuristic looking cannon. "I call it the A-Buster! I can do this with both my arms so far, the scientists say I'm classified as a shapeshifter, because I can shift my arms back and forth into those robotic cannons. They are very strong, too! I can fire either weaker automatic shots or charge my cannons for greater damage. They tire me out after a while though." She smiled and then frowned. "I almost used them to blast the scientists who were experimenting on me, but… I contained myself at the last minute. They congratulated me for it. I like my cannons, since they can be useful for our escape, but I would still prefer to not have them if it meant never being here…" She bit her lip, making Cyko grit his teeth at the sadness on her face.

"As many of you know, I can breathe fire like a dragon," Mat said, letting out an ember from his mouth. Putting a hand on Anna's shoulder in an attempt to comfort her, he continued his explanation, unaware of her grateful smile. "My ability has gotten stronger since last time, as the area and duration of my breath increased. They made me do many, many exercises to increase the length of my fire by making me survive underwater as long as I could without breathing. At least they allowed me to pull up when I started to run out of breath…" He crossed his arms but grinned and let out a small breath of fire towards the ceiling, surprising them all at the flash of heat that rushed to their faces.

"I will help everyone out when the time comes," he promised, the embers in his mouth slowed and stopped.

Geon, who was sitting next to him, volunteered to speak next. "I said it before, but my power is to cause localized earthquakes. I can also feel vibrations from the ground in such a way that if I closed my eyes, I can tell where in this room you are and who you are based on the level of your vibration." He smiled, before pointing his hand at the table and making it shake, which made Snow, who was napping on the table, jump up in a panic.

"Oops, sorry Snow! Anyway, I've been helping Tela create a map of this place. She said she is using the aid of as many people as she can, those who have special sensory abilities such as me, to make the most accurate map possible. I've practiced seeing if I can feel vibrations in the air, although so far, that has been a little hard to do." He shrugged and returned Cyko's grin.

"That's amazing Geon! I knew your power would come in handy!" He chuckled as his older brother rubbed the back of his head in embarrassment.

"I awakened myself a week ago. My power is to control water!" Sara spoke up, putting both of her hands in front of her in a cupping position.

From nowhere, a small puddle formed in her palms. "It feels so… natural to me. I sometimes spend longer in the shower than I used to, because I love water so much now… Also, I don't need to hold my breath underwater anymore, I can breathe!" She smirked, something uncharacteristic for her.

"I can also do this!" The water in her palms began to float up into the air and take an elongated shape, which then instantly froze into a spear of ice. Cyko, Myo, and Magy looked at her small stake of ice in awe, as did the others. "My elemental powers are very good, I'd say… But I'm weak to dryness, as I found out very painfully during one experiment. Still, I think I am powerful enough to be helpful in our escape."

"You guys know what Starry and I can do, but I'll say it again for the newcomer's sake. I can strengthen myself with fire, like this!" Torch said as he turned his power on. Magy and Myo were impressed at his transformation: his hair caught on fire and his body and eyes gave off an orange glow. "I'm very strong! And these last couple of days, I've been getting stronger. My current record with that robot army is seven hundred. They say if I was a little older, I'd be able to defeat the whole army by myself," he boasted and gestured for Starry to talk.

The girl, shy to speak so much about her special powers, simply made another show of stars appear before them, making them dance in different patterns. Magy smiled at the beauty of her show. She finished and beamed at everyone before looking at Henry, who had yet to explain his abilities.

The boy put one of his hands on the table… and from it, a small, yellow flower emerged. Everyone at the table was silent, watching the flower grow. He smiled as he explained his powers. "I can make plants grow at any speed I want, and I can also create seeds from the earth. It's useful if I want to capture someone or create obstacles. Making seeds tires me out quickly, though, so I would prefer to have actual seeds with me rather than make ones from scratch. Right now, I have about twenty seeds with me." He frowned in contemplation. "I don't know how useful my powers will be, but I'll try my best. I can think of some strategies to adopt using them, and I've been discussing with Tela if they can be of any use to our plan."

After hearing everyone explain their powers, Cyko grinned at the awesomeness of it all, his brothers and sisters are great! Now, it was time for him to show them he wasn't going to be left in the dust!

"I also have unlocked my powers recently, and if I were to compare, mine are like Torch's. Look," he said as he activated his enhancing power. The group gasped as the blue aura covered his form. "It makes me much, much more powerful than I should be... I have defeated the entire robot army with relative ease." He looked out to his family, only to be met by wide-open mouths and admiration in their eyes, especially from his young brother, Torch.

"No way, Cyko, that's too cool!"

"All one thousand of them, that's impressive, Cyko!" Geon complimented, followed by the rest of his family, which made the boy blush at the praise.

He giggled. "Thanks guys!" His blue aura faded away.

"Well then, I guess I should explain myself..." Magy said, grinning from ear to ear. "Scythe is the spirit that is also a part of me, she takes the form of a scythe and gives me power over darkness." She watched the shocked looks from everyone, except Cyko and Myo, as she put her hand inside her chest, and retrieved Scythe. She let everyone inspect her beauty before storing it back inside herself. Cyko's family seemed surprised and fascinated by her power, especially Starry, who looked at the weapon with stars in her eyes.

After she finished, everyone looked at Myo, who pursed his lips and sighed to himself. "I... I can weaken structures, and that's it. Things become frail and brittle when I use my powers, but... It also affects my muscles, making them weaker. It hurts a lot, the e-experiments... I really, really dislike them..." He looked down. Cyko's family patted his back and murmured words of encouragement to him.

"Myo..." Anna said with a sad voice, representing what everyone was feeling right now. Pity. Pity for what he had gone through and is still going through, and anger for the same reasons.

Myo looked at them, his eyes welling with tears. "I... I am a crybaby, but ever since I met Tela last night... I-I feel like I can change, I don't want to be a burden anymore..." he said with a sigh, before blinking as a tiny star appeared and danced in front of his face, and his breath evened and he felt calm.

"Myo... cheer up!" the small Starry said, making the star dance around him, much to his delight. Everyone smiled at her successful attempt at cheering Myo up, and they all decided on something... They should, they would get stronger, if at least so that children like Myo can get away from this nightmare.

The group of them continued talking and discussing their abilities and ways they could use them, although they all agreed that they shouldn't say much out loud in case the scientists were listening.

After a few minutes, they heard footsteps approaching them, and turned their heads to see two children walking towards their table. One of them was a short, thin girl with bright green hair and an infectious grin on her face. Just like everyone, she was wearing rags... But what surprised them was the red-haired boy that was accompanying her. He was wearing clothes that could only be described as a robe of some sort, and the aura they were feeling from him was strong.

Magy's smile dropped in an instant. Seeing this, Cyko prepared for trouble, while the rest of his family looked at each other, trying to determine how to react.

"Hello there! Ah! I knew I heard a meow when I entered this place! See, Reddox, I told you I heard a cat! Look! An adorable little kitty!" The green-haired girl talked in short bursts of exclamation to her companion, who merely nodded at her words.

"Greetings, I am Reddox and this airhead by my side is Ellyn. We hail from the high security ward and met the moment we came out from our cells. For some reason, she wanted to hang out with me," the short boy said blandly, and still the girl chuckled and swatted at him.

"That's because the wind around you says you are an interesting person to know! I mean, we came from the same place; it's lonely! Don't you want friends?" she teased, which only made the boy sigh in resignation.

"I suppose you are right," he said in a low voice although Ellyn still heard him and grinned.

"Anyway, I heard a cat sound when we got here, and I wanted to see if it was an actual cat! Ah, she is so cute!" Ellyn exclaimed with hearts in her eyes as she admired Snow.

Everyone at the table was at a loss for words. Cyko and his family were trying to figure out the eccentric girl and her apparent connection to the wind, while Magy, however, was looking warily at Reddox.

Cyko opened his mouth for a second before speaking, "My name is Cyko, would you like to pet her? She is friendly." He thought it wouldn't hurt to have more friends after all, plus, Ellyn lurched forward to meet the feline.

"Ahhh! Can I? Can I? Thank you so much!" She pet Snow's head, who woke up and looked at her. After a while, the white kitty rubbed her head against the green-haired girl, who could barely contain a squeal at Snow's cuteness.

She didn't resist and picked the small kitty up and gingerly cuddled her to her chest, giggling at the purring sounds the cat was emitting. After a few seconds her eyes welled up as she set the cat back down on the table.

"Thank you, thank you so much… I really missed the warmth of a pet… That meant a lot to me, thank you." She offered a smile that Cyko returned with ease.

"Hey, don't worry! You can pet her whenever you want if we meet again, I'll bring her next time." He touched her arm lightly.

"I already like you, Cyko, would you like to talk more? We, from the high security ward, don't get to talk with other kids a lot and—"

"Attention all subjects, socialization time is over. Proceed to the gates you entered from to be escorted back to your quarters," the cold voice came from the intercom, making everyone blink in surprise. Was it time already?

"What? But I could have sworn we still had half an hour left…" Henry muttered to himself before shaking his head. They couldn't do anything about it now. Ellyn, on the other hand, visibly drooped, her face wrestling to contain her tears.

"But we just met…" she whispered, taking one longing glace at the white cat who was now licking her paws unaware of the sadness surrounding her, which made Ellyn want to cuddle her again.

Reddox sighed, unable to get a word out, either. "My apologies, it seems we will have to talk more at a later date, if possible. Come, Ellyn, we shouldn't hold them back, the guards will punish them if we do." He touched Ellyn's back as she reluctantly allowed him to lead her away.

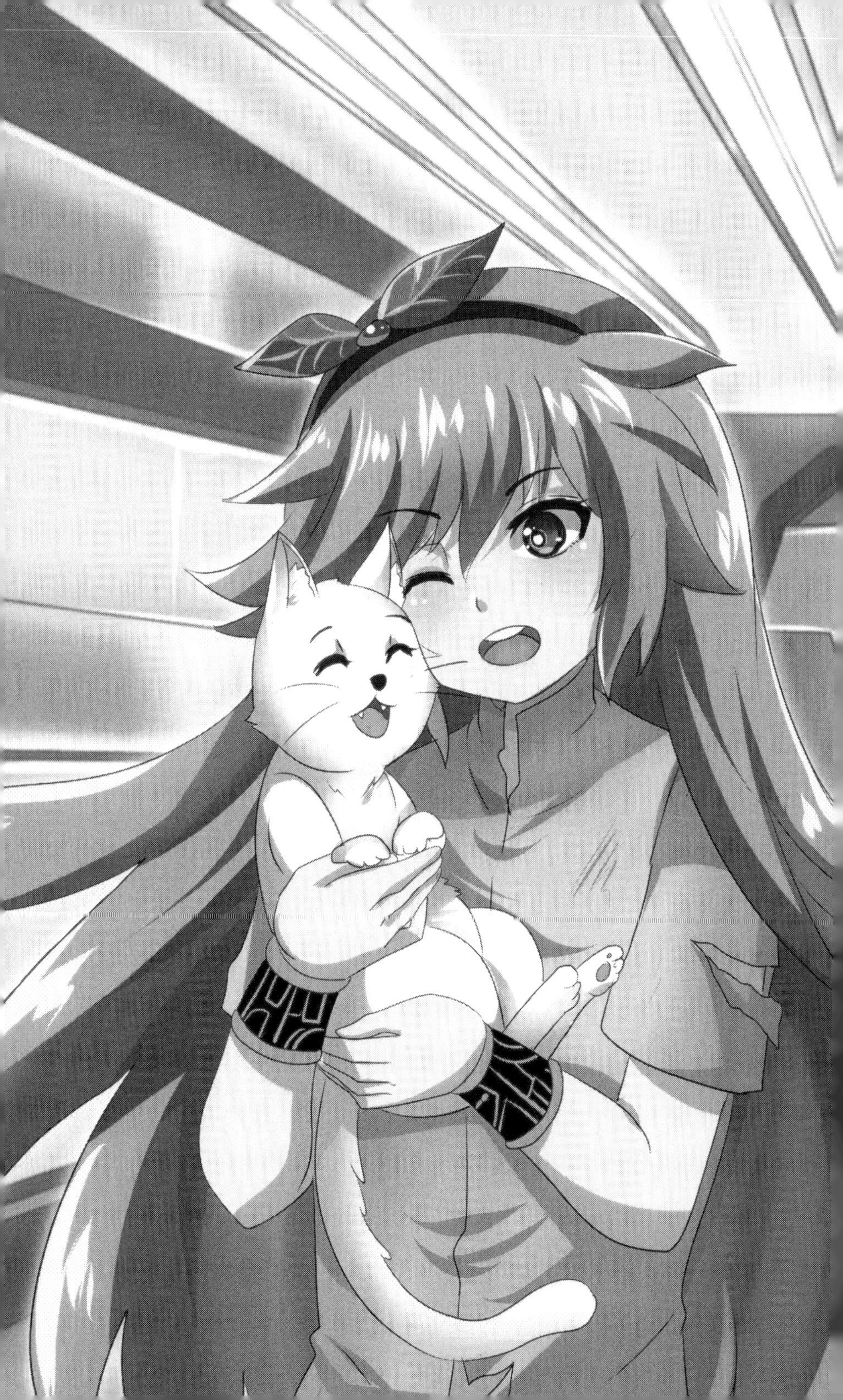

"I understand... Let's go." She turned back towards them. "Once again, thank you very much for letting me hug her, I hope we can meet again."

Cyko nodded to her, holding a frown back from the early call to return to their dorms, but it couldn't be helped. "You are welcome, I hope we can meet again, too," he said with a smile, waving his hand as they made their way back.

Magy stayed quiet as they were escorted towards their ward. She kept her silence even as they had gotten up and prepared to leave, Cyko picking Snow up and hiding her under his shirt. "Did you guys notice? His clothes were nicer than ours. Maybe it was just the favor he asked from the scientists, but... Scythe tells me he is powerful, very powerful." Magy frowned, surprising the others.

"I did notice his clothes, they are cleaner than ours, but it also couldn't mean much. He seemed nice, to make friends with that eccentric girl, even if he was a bit serious," Henry, the smart boy, said with a hand on his chin, "maybe we should just wait and see, he doesn't seem like that Drago fellow you told us about. Maybe we should give them a chance? Try to recruit them?" he suggested.

"... Hmm, I think it may be a good idea, Scythe suggested this too. Okay, but I still feel danger around him." Magy frowned, before shaking her head as if to dispel her thoughts. She realized they had arrived at the point they had met before, just in front of the gate that leads to Cyko's family's ward.

"Well, guys... I guess I'll see you next time." Cyko pursed his lips at the thought of when he'd be able to meet them next.

Magy, adopting her serene smile, looked at them with tears filling her eyes. "I also am glad to have met you all, Cyko was right when he told me you all are nice people, Scythe also speaks highly of you." She wiped away a small tear that had escaped.

Myo's bottom lip quivered. He had made so many friends these past few days! He couldn't believe they treated him like one of them, they were so nice! He would miss them, but it wasn't like this would be the last time he would see them, right? "I-I'll miss you guys too, it was nice meeting you all..." He lowered his head as to not cry again.

"Don't be like that! I'm sure we'll see each other again soon!" Anna promised as they all reunited for a group hug.

"You take care of each other, you hear me?" Mat said with a smile as they separated.

"Don't worry, we will!" Cyko called out as they walked in opposite ways to return to their dorm rooms.

On their way back, Cyko kept smiling to himself. Today had been a good day, he had gotten to see his family again, Myo's mood had improved more, and Magy looked happy from their talk. Even with meeting Ellyn and Reddox, he could tell, somehow, that they were not bad people.

No bad person would cry tears of joy while holding a cat after all.

"Ahh…" Cyko said as he fell down in his bed. Even if today was a good day, he was still exhausted. He looked to his side to see Myo also falling onto his bed, and Magy sitting on hers, gently petting Snow who was on her lap.

"Tired, my dear friend?" Magy asked as she played with the cat.

Cyko chuckled at her question before nodding. "Yes, we had a long day. Even if we got to have fun at the end, it was still tiring after the experiments." He yawned. Myo himself looked drowsy on his bed.

"Well don't let me stop your rest, dear friend. You too, little Myo. I'll stay up playing with this little one for a while. She is still full of energy afte- Ah!" She jumped at a loud bang on the door, startling both Cyko and Myo from their sleepy state.

"You little rats! We're coming in, make yourselves presentable and don't try anything funny!" the steely voice of the large guard barked at their door, making them glance at each other in confusion and in Myo's case, in fright.

Bursting through the door were two heavily armed guards on both sides… and one scientist they had never seen before in the middle. The man had white hair, a beard, and a dead, cold look on his face. He looked around the room before zeroing in on a particular sight…

"Ahh…" he cocked his head to the side, his face breaking from its unsettling mold to give off a large, warm smile. "My dear Shiro, I was looking for you everywhere, do you know how much you made me worry?" Dr. Gacha said as he looked at the snow-white cat, who instantly jumped from Magy's lap high into the air, where a white light covered her form for a moment.

Then, the light faded to reveal a girl half the scientist's size, who landed gently on the ground. The girl's feline ears and tail twitched for a moment as she opened her mischievous golden eyes, which focused on the scientist in front of her. After a moment, she happily shouted, "Papa!" and tackled the older man in an affectionate embrace.

CHAPTER 3

THE DEATH GAMES

1

Dr. Gacha made his way towards the entrance to Mr. Whale's office, interested in knowing what the man wanted this time. He would report to the best of his ability as everything was progressing smoothly so far.

He paused, however, as he saw something peculiar. A small desk was set up near Mr. Whale's door and sitting in the chair looking at documents was a woman he'd never seen before. He wiped his face of any emotion and made his way forward, her purpose becoming obvious to him. Mr. Whale hired a secretary—a dangerous move knowing that every single employee in this facility, even the ones on the upper floors, had to be highly trusted, and he couldn't seem to recall her being on the employee sheet.

The woman had pale, purplish hair and identically colored eyes, he noted as she turned towards him as he approached and gave him a polite smile. "Good afternoon, sir. How may I help you?" the secretary said in a professional, silky voice.

Dr. Gacha stood there, staring at her for a few moments before answering, "I am here for an appointment with Mr. Whale, I assume you are aware of that?"

Giving a short nod, she spoke, "Dr. Gacha, yes?" She straightened her posture.

The scientist nodded.

"Perfect, Mr. Whale is inside waiting for you." She motioned towards the door to Mr. Whale's office. The scientist adjusted his tie and gave her a nod before making his way inside the businessman's office.

Seeing the door to his office slide open, Mr. Whale looked up to the frigid gaze of his head scientist. For a second, he wondered if he did something to earn his wrath but remembered that the man was always like that.

"Good afternoon, Dr. Gacha. Thank you for coming on such short notice," the businessman said with a smile to which the scientist looked up at the ceiling before focusing his gaze on Mr. Whale.

"It's no trouble, however, the sooner we finish, the sooner I can go back to work," the scientist said with no emotion, which made the rotund man let out a chuckle.

"Hah! True enough! The reports I receive every day are mostly positive, which is a sign of good work, and as a businessman, I appreciate that!" he said lightheartedly before narrowing his eyes and rolling his shoulders back so they could get down to business.

"Anyway, the reason I called you here is because the shipment of material you requested has arrived and is being stored on Level 4. It was costly, but for the sake of the project, the board of directors were willing to grant the expense." Mr. Whale folded his hands together.

"Excellent, then the next phase of the project can start once everything is set up," the head scientist said with the slightest tone of approval in his voice. "By the time everything is ready, I expect all remaining subjects will be awakened, and all experiments regarding their abilities will be completed," Dr. Gacha said in a clinical voice, although Mr. Whale could tell the man was looking forward to the results of the next part.

"That's wonderful news! Now, while I have a hunch on what you have planned for the next phase of the project, I would like to discuss the details of what you are planning," Mr. Whale said in a professional tone. Dr. Gacha acknowledged this and moved to take a seat in front of the businessman.

As was protocol whenever they were to discuss sensitive material, Mr. Whale entered a simple command on his terminal which caused the walls of his office to glow with arcane symbols. A security measure set up by their team of highly experienced magicians, it should prevent anyone, physical or ethereal, from eavesdropping on their conversation.

Nodding at Mr. Whale's action, the head scientist put his hand inside his coat and retrieved his tablet, where he typed several commands before placing it atop the man's desk. From the tablet, a hologram appeared, showing the seventh level as it currently was. Several large wards surrounding the central gymnasium which the subjects used for socialization time were shown.

"All subjects have been given the opportunity to meet and form both connections and rivalries. All the wards have made contact with each other at random intervals. Considering the high-stress environment they have been subjected to, it's expected for them to form deep emotional connections and we'll take advantage of that." He swiped his hand through the image and the hologram changed, showing a drastically changed gymnasium.

"Research has shown that unlocked powers are strengthened by emotional distress and true enough, we have made sure that all subjects went through stressful situations to overcome their limits. The next phase of Project R.N.G. will serve both as an experiment on live combat against dangerous opponents and a way to further impose limits for them to overcome. In addition, to prepare for the phase after that," the scientist explained matter-of-factly.

"Oh? How so?" the businessman asked, prompting his head scientist to speak.

"After the stick, one must give the carrot. I have told all the scientists in charge of conducting experiments to treat subjects with favorable results well, and the more cooperative said subject is, the better they'll be treated. If enough favoritism is given, they'll be given the right to ask small favors. Some subjects already have been granted that."

"And what is it you want to achieve with this, doctor?" Mr. Whale's forehead creased.

The scientist's voice was flat. "Ever heard of Stockholm Syndrome? In situations where there is a person being held captive, they become attached to their captors. Small kind actions that would be scoffed at by an outsider would be of great significance to the victim, making them believe in the humanity of their captors and even wishing to continue befriending them. Some say it's a survival instinct, but it shall be of great use to us. Turning scared children into loyal soldiers should be simple. The experiments and their living conditions are hard on their physique and because of that, they will learn to love any positivity or kindness we show them," Dr. Gacha said, his face remaining expressionless despite the topic of conversation.

Mr. Whale paled at the scientist's words. *That was... a little too much, wasn't it? It was basically brainwashing the children we forced to be part of the project...* his mouth twitched at the thought. Yet, they had gone too far to be held back by morals now. They had invested too much time, too much money to stop now. It was a cruel thing they were doing, but... It was necessary.

"I... I see. Very well, Dr. Gacha. Proceed as you please. As long as the results stay positive, you are free to do as you will," the businessman said in a resigned voice, to which the head scientist nodded in clear satisfaction, although his expression didn't change.

"If that's all, then I'll be taking my leave," the scientist declared and rose from his seat.

"Yes, that'll be all for now, Dr. Gacha. If anything else arises, I'll call for a meeting." The businessman leaned back in his chair to signal the end of the conversation. The scientist nodded once again and turned to leave.

As he neared the door, he spun around to look at his boss with a deadpan stare. "Mr. Whale, while placement of employees in the upper floors is up to you, I trust you have thoroughly checked their background information," the scientist said and walked out of the office, the glowing runes on the walls deactivating after confirming the meeting was over.

Mr. Whale, however, blinked in confusion. *What was that about?*

2

In his own office, Dr. Gacha looked through several reports and documents detailing performance and recommended course of actions for several dozen subjects at once, his fingers typing at inhuman speeds on the console of his desk.

So far, everything was proceeding smoothly; fewer subjects were showing signs of rebellion after being introduced to the mutant ward whose figurative leader respected power and strength above all else, and who would annihilate any signs of revolt. Any actual violence was yet to happen, as the dragon mutant was an intimidating figure, especially to children. This intimidation factor indirectly helped curb most of the rebellious test subjects during experimentation, which increased the efficiency of research.

A sound brought Dr. Gacha's attention to the corner of his console's screen. His science team had called him to oversee today's socialization, not an unusual thing as he himself often volunteered to watch over the evolution of the subjects. He moved to turn the console off and closed his eyes, sighing.

He was a professional—a scientist dedicated to his line of work and research. He had to be. Yet, the small stinging sensation in his chest was still there, no matter how much he focused on his work, it wouldn't go away. All because of a small side project he had got attached to.

The only light in his dark life of loss and amoral dedication to science, the only thing that he allowed himself to feel any sort of attachment to, the only thing he loved after his long life of hate. His small, white cat.

A pet. That is what anyone else might think; love for an animal companion was incredibly common for a human. Yet, his cat, his Shiro, was much more than just a cat. She saved him from the depths of despair and he, in return, had saved her. To him, she had just been a pet, but now…

Shaking his head for being emotional, he got up from his chair. He wouldn't worry, he shouldn't worry. She was strong, she could take care of herself. Even the brutes they had as security guards or the sociopathic mages and scientists wouldn't harm her. He was worried though, because she had ventured out and hadn't come back, but he knew she was all right, he could still tell that her vitals were strong and healthy.

A few minutes were enough for him to make his way towards the security room where numerous scientists, particularly those specializing in psychology, observed the socializations. But while it was serious work, it had an air of casualness to it; the room was sprinkled with many scientists drinking coffee or munching on snacks as they worked on their reports for individual subjects.

While a hardworking man, Dr. Gacha found value in clearing one's mind with short breaks to refocus, so he allowed those bits of indiscipline to happen as long as they didn't affect the results of the project. In fact, coffee is a wonderful tool for a scientist who works long hours like himself.

They had, however, asked him to come here for a reason. This being to observe the interactions between subjects to see if there are issues they would need to address, and for that, he made his way to the main display board, where an overview of the entire gymnasium was shown, along with several smaller displays to focus on individual subjects.

"Good morning, sir. The subjects have already been taken out of their cells. Today will be the first time the subjects of maximum-security will be present for a socialization," a scientist with glasses said as Dr. Gacha approached the console controls. The head scientist glanced at the man who spoke to him before turning to look at the sizeable screen displaying the gymnasium.

The maximum-security ward, filled not with those who were the most powerful, but those whose powers might represent a pronounced risk to the project by calling for outside help or being overly destructive. Most of the subjects that classify under the spiritual category were placed in this ward to prevent them from contacting spirits, as the seals protecting that ward were the strongest they had.

Today would be the first time they would let these threats out of the ward without a higher security detail. As much as they wished to preserve the security they had, it was a necessity that even they be allowed to participate in these meetings in the hopes of inducing them into the Stockholm Syndrome. It was a risk they had to take.

They had instructed the guards in maximum-security to give harsh warnings for them to behave, but he doubted it would be enough. Still, should they follow the rules, then everything would be fine. As a scientist, he hated depending on luck, but that was the basis behind this whole project, so he had to try at least.

As he observed the subjects entering the gymnasium, his eyes caught sight of their most valuable asset. The subject known as Reddox, whose raw power could match a dozen of their own elite mages at age seven, he could only guess what kind of monster he would become with their help. If Reddox could match even ten percent of the Creator's power, it would make everything they worked for worth it.

Their golden ticket seemed to have already connected with a female subject. A quick search on his tablet labeled her as Ellyn, a high priority subject who had a strong spiritual attachment to wind. Her reason for being placed in the high security ward was due to her ability to talk with wind, which she claimed were spirits. Their mages confirmed that wind did, in fact, behave strangely around her. As he watched them, it seems they had connected with each other. He updated their files noting such.

As he was observing their actions, he noticed that they seemed to be wandering about, chatting with only each other but as if they were searching for something. *What could it be?* he wondered. *Did the wind tell her of something interesting?*

"Dr. Ferdinand, focus a camera on Subject 100. I'd like to observe his movements," the head scientist said to his colleague in charge of the cameras. The bearded man nodded and worked on his console, causing one of the smaller displays to focus on Reddox.

Continuing to watch their movements and taking notes on his interactions with the green-haired subject, he noticed that she seemed to be the more talkative of the two, while the redhead seemed mostly stoic, although he appeared to tolerate her. He realized that they were walking towards a small group of children, and with a quick search, it was revealed that most of them came from the same orphanage.

His eyes widened as he saw something on the screen. Is that...

"Strange, how *did* a feline get inside the gymnasium?" the scientist with glasses asked, his eyes wide as he stared at the screen alongside the bearded man, who hummed in thought.

"Hmm, maybe it's a shapeshifter? I don't think we have records of one turning into a domestic cat though. They would be labeled as a failure almost immediately, although, we may use them for espionage," he said with a stroke of his beard, not noticing how his boss's face changed from stoic to a hint of surprised.

"Today, the socialization will end early," the head scientist's cold voice cut through any lighthearted emotion left in the room, making the two scientists look at him in shock.

"Sir? Is that advisable? We still have one hour to go. Besides, today is the first time we can observe Subject Number 100 interacting with others." The scientist with glasses frowned.

"Yes, for that reason, we need more time to review his current interactions so far." Dr. Gacha's mouth set in a hard line, curving downwards at the very end. The two scientists still seemed confused, but nodded; they trusted their boss to know what he was doing.

The head scientist activated the microphone and spoke his orders to the subjects below, indicating the abrupt end of the socialization period. Many of them looked confused at the suddenness, but still complied, knowing the consequences if they were to refuse his orders. The guards had disciplined them well.

After, he looked at the group with the small feline, inspecting them carefully. Noticing that a blue-haired kid was hiding the cat inside his clothes, he searched for his information on his tablet. Subject Number 444, name: Cyko. A subject with high enhancing powers who was sharing a room with two others, one of them was one of their most cooperative subjects, while the other was a failure.

"Take care of things here," Dr. Gacha said as he turned around and headed towards the exit, his jaw set, "I must go back to work." Upon exiting the floor, he ordered the security guards of that ward to escort him towards a particular cell. He had work to attend to, and he couldn't wait to get to it.

3

The cat-girl, for that is the only thing Cyko could call her thanks to the feline ears and tail she had, snuggled the scientist with love, purring as the man caressed her hair.

Her clothes were in a much nicer condition than his and his roommates, comprising of a short, white fluffy hoodie that exposed her stomach and an equally fluffy white skirt. Her appearance also made her look at least three years older than them as she already had the beginnings of a developed female body.

Cyko analyzed that in just a few seconds because that was the only thing his brain could comprehend. *What, what was happening?! Where is Snow?! Where did that girl come from?!* his mind raced.

"W-what is going on?" Myo began to shake at the unexpected sight and the threatening presence of the guards. He didn't understand what happened to Snow, the adorable little cat that had comforted him on many nights after a nightmare.

"It seems..." Magy said indifferently, "we have been deceived. This pain in my heart, I dislike it," she finished, her face and posture growing more threatening, with small sparks of dark energy floating out of her body.

"W-what, no, th-this cannot be true, right? S-Snow has been... helping us all this time..." Cyko said with a disbelieving voice, watching the interaction between what appeared to be father and daughter. The scientist's face, which had been stone cold when he entered, had morphed into one of warmth, and as for the cat-girl, she was perched on his waist, just like a cat, just like... Snow.

"I suggest you cool down with that, rat," said the big security guard as he pointed his massive gun towards Magy, who they deemed as the greatest threat. She glowered at both guards and the father-daughter couple, who seemed to be unaware of anything but each other.

"B-b-big s-sis, c-calm d-d-down, please!" Myo stuttered. All the guards had raised their weapons. Magy didn't let up on her glare, her eyes boring into them.

Shiro, as the scientist had called her, turned around as if finally noticing Magy's threatening aura, and looked at her with wary eyes. "Magy, don't hurt papa! He did nothing wrong!" she said while spreading her arms wide open as protection. Magy's furious aura only increased in intensity, however... It wasn't her that exploded at this action.

"What the heck?! What the heck, Snow?! Do you know who he is? What he and everyone in this Luni-forsaken prison did to us? DO YOU?!" Cyko yelled in outrage at seeing his tiny companion defend one of those responsible for all their suffering. The scientist's face went blank as he watched Shiro, whose lips curled downwards.

"You always speak of such complicated things! Papa is papa! I wanted you to meet him, and introduce my friends to him! Why are you angry?!" She yelled back, her lower lip trembling, earning herself an incredulous look from both Cyko and Magy.

"Complicated? What do you mean complicated? What part of 'they are torturing us for their sick power plan' is hard to understand?!" Cyko fumed at the cat girl's confusion, whose frown had grown deeper.

"Because it is! Papa is a good person!"

"Snow. Don't you understand?" Magy spoke up, her threatening aura lessening as she seemed to realize what was going on. "The reason Myo cried every day? The reason Cyko is so stressed? The reason I am as I am? The reason that girl cried when she met you? We are imprisoned here against our will. They mistreat us, abuse us, starve us…" she trailed off, her eyes welling up with tears. Shiro seemed to understand, but still she looked confused, glancing from Cyko, to Magy, to her father.

"But that makes no sense! Papa is not a bad person!" she repeated.

Cyko was about to yell again when he was stopped with a gesture from the scientist, whose raised hand dropped to caress the cat-girl's head, calming her down.

"I know the nature of our research can be… harsh for some of you," he spoke in a cold voice that sent shivers down the three children's spines, "however, from this point on, we are already on the move for the next part of the project. I can assure you, your quality of living will improve from now on, as long as you keep cooperating with us."

"You think we are idiots?!" Cyko asked incredulously before looking directly at Snow, "Snow, please! Don't you see what they have done to us? Heck, haven't they done something to you to give you the power to transform into a cat?!" he pleaded, trying to reason with the first one to keep him company in his cold and lonely room.

She shook her head again, refusing to accept his words. "Papa is not evil! And I used to be a cat! He changed me and I love him for it!" Her cheeks reddened as she spat out the words, making Cyko flinch in response to the unexpected reveal.

Snow… used to be a cat? A normal cat? What?

"Shiro, that's enough. You can tell me about your friends later," the scientist's voice echoed in the small cell, making the children look at him. "It's understandable that they are shocked right now, you need to give them time to… accept all this." He turned to his daughter and allowed a small smile to show on his face.

"You worried me, you disappeared for a long time," he said, his voice kind but teasing, making the cat-girl's ears and tail drop in regret at his words.

"A-ah... I'm sorry Papa... I didn't mean to..." She said, lowering her eyes, which only made the man pet her head once again.

"It's all right, I can understand what it's like to be young and impulsive. Now, let's go," the scientist said as he took her hand in his and lead them out of the room.

"Ah, wait, Papa!" Shiro looked back at the kids and to her father with a concerned stare. Dr. Gacha tugged her arm. She glanced back inside the room and flinched when she saw a returning glare from both Cyko and Magy. She didn't understand, she did nothing wrong... Why were they looking at her like that?

"Shiro," her papa said as they walked the corridors of the ward, escorted by two guards who frightened her, "you understand why my work here is important, don't you?"

She furrowed her brows at his question.

"I know it's complicated, papa, but... yes, I do... You are working hard and doing your best to make sure nothing bad happens to me again..." she said in a subdued voice, her ears and tail dropping as she thought of her past before meeting her papa.

"That's right, little Shiro. Everything I'm doing here is for your sake. The Creator of this universe, Luni, is dangerous. There are suspicions of her getting more and more unstable and although nothing is confirmed, we need a way to defend ourselves," he reasoned, putting his hand on her cheek.

"I understand, papa." The girl perked up even if she found it hard to comprehend most of what he said. "I know how much you love me! I love you too!" She bounced in place as his hand fell from her face. He grinned.

Yes. He loved his daughter, and she loved him, they are family foremost. He knew if she understood more of what he was doing here, he would be criticized, but... All that mattered was that the project was successful, no matter the cost. He would not let this universe die at the hands of a crazy Creator and for that... The next part of the project would be essential.

"Oh, Shiro, is there anything I need to know about those three?" Dr. Gacha asked, his face back to the impassive mask of professionalism he always wore.

His daughter looked up at him, squinting in thought. "Hmm... I don't think so, they always talked about complicated stuff, so I never paid much attention." She shrugged, earning a nod from her father.

"Well, then we'll proceed as planned," he said. His plans for the next phase of the project were already in motion, and even if he was glad to have found his daughter, there was a lot of work to be done.

4

As the door leading out of their room closed with a bang, everyone stared in silence, still unable to believe what had happened. The kitty, the small companion they had cherished for so long... Was one of *them?*

"Snow... S-Snow... She... She!..." Myo stuttered, falling to his knees as the strength left his body, unable to accept that the sweet and affectionate little kitty was actually with the bad people who were torturing them every day... It wasn't possible!

"Dang it... DANG IT!" Cyko yelled in rage as he felt tears forming in his eyes. Snow was... she was... the first roommate he had, the first thing he could share warmth with in this forsaken place, yet she... She had gone away with the evil scientist without a single word of protest! "She... she didn't even try to understand! She just, she just left! Just like that!" He fell to his knees, feeling nothing but betrayal.

It felt like his heart was stabbed, like it was on fire and he couldn't do anything to stop it or the torrent of tears running down his face. To make matters worse, he could hear Myo bawling beside him. A friend, someone they had trusted, who had comforted them... had just left them, without a single word of compassion...

"Why... Why would such a thing... happen..." Myo asked between sobs. Snow had slept curled up into him every night, she always comforted him when he had nightmares or when he got back from experiments... Was that... was that all fake? Did she not love them as they had loved her?

"Cyko... Myo..." Magy crouched down near them, a few tears running down her face. Her heart hurt just as much even if she hadn't known Snow as long as the boys. "This... It's hard... She betrayed us, but... she herself said, she used to be a cat... We can't expect a... a pet... to stop loving her owner..." she said, trying not to choke between words, putting her arms around both boys and bringing them closer to her.

"But... But she... She saw what they did to us! Even if she didn't see the experiments, she saw the results... Myo's nightmares, our injuries, our tears... How couldn't she understand that?!" Cyko asked no one in particular. He allowed himself to lean into Magy's embrace. This was not fair, they had suffered too much already!

"Snow, she... I... Why..." Myo said miserably as his sobs lowered in volume, trying his best to calm down despite what had happened. Yet, it was still hard. One of his best friends, even if he hadn't known she could transform, had left them to go with that man. The small boy couldn't comprehend why this had happened.

"I... I know it's hard to accept it, but... we need to be strong. S-she used to be a cat, we can't expect her to be smart... Even if it hurts to know she loves that... man more than us. We still have each other, don't we?" Magy said in a comforting tone, while trying to find solace herself by embracing the two.

Cyko's eyes widened. "Wait... She... She was there... She was right there, all this time! Our plans, what he had planned together with Tela... She heard it all!" Cyko covered his mouth in terror. And to make things worse, Tela herself had never met Snow, so she wouldn't have any way of stopping her!

"Cyko, Cyko! Calm down! Remember, she is dumb! I doubt she could understand most of what we were talking about, and even if she were to tell what she could... She still wouldn't be able to comprehend the most important detail... We all are in this together!" Magy pulled both the boys closer. They had to overcome this, they couldn't let their grief win, Magy knew this. She wouldn't lose to despair again!

"B-big sister Magy is right!" Myo exclaimed, freeing himself from his surrogate sister and grasping Cyko's shoulders. Tears were streaming down his face, however, his expression was that of determination. "E-Even if... Even if Snow left... We still have each other, and everyone else! It hurts, it hurts a lot, and I still can't believe she did that, but... we can't give up, big brother!" The small boy declared, looking into his big brother's eyes.

"Magy... Myo..." Cyko said, before sighing and letting out a tiny giggle, "I'm glad I have the two of you. I'm sorry for causing a scene, we should... We should think of what to do next, instead, shouldn't we?" The blue-haired boy said with a small smile, using his shirt to wipe his face of tears.

"I'm glad you are both back to normal," Magy said, raising her own shirt to wipe her face, which Myo copied. They still felt sad about what happened, but they had each other... They would be fine. Exchanging smiles between the three of them, they held each other's hands.

"Scythe says we should worry about that tomorrow. We all had a long, exhausting day that ended on a bad note for us. We need to rest," Magy said as the two boys nodded, "I... I recommend we all sleep together. The warmth of those we trust... Of each other... It should help us sleep better," she proposed, a red tint blooming on her cheeks.

Myo looked confused but nodded in acceptance.

Cyko blinked at her offer which embarrassed him for some reason, but he was touched by her suggestion. "Magy... Thank you... I think we all need each other's warmth today," he replied.

They had to move their beds around, but in the end, they made it so there was enough space for all three to sleep comfortably together; Magy in the middle and both boys beside her.

They had a hard time sleeping at first, not because they were together, but because of the fresh wound of Snow's sudden departure and concern for their future... However, they would not give up, because they had each other.

5

The day after Snow's departure, they were called for a socialization. It had been hard on all three but still they slept enough to ignore the nightly disturbances from the guards. Waking up next to each other had been an embarrassing but heartwarming experience.

What was strange, however, was they were given more time than usual to prepare. Normally, the guards would intrude and demand they move their butts out, but this time the guards had given them two hours to freshen themselves up as much as they could, and advised they would not have any experiment done today. Magy said Scythe was suspicious of the extra generosity, but they made the best of it.

Two hours later, they were as presentable as they could be, considering they were dressed in rags, but they were at least clean and ready to meet their friends—should they be lucky today.

When the guards came to get them, they were more subdued, even the brutish giant of a guard that seemed to be their leader, although they were still strict. They had arrived at the gates leading to the gymnasium with minimal fuss from the guards.

"Listen up, rats. Today you'll be receiving an important announcement from the higher-ups which I suggest you listen carefully to and because of this, today's meeting will have *all* wards and it will be extended by one hour," the giant guard said with his menacing voice, although he made no threatening gestures this time.

"If you are lucky, you won't be just lab rats anymore and actually be useful. Also, I suggest you don't cause trouble. We won't be there, but that giant dragon I know you all are afraid of? Oh yes, he will be there." The guard sneered, causing several children in the crowd to shiver at the mention of Drago.

"Now, move along, it's almost time!" the guard yelled as he pushed the button that started to open their gate, which caused many of them to move inside, already used to this routine. Just as the guard said, all the gates surrounding the gymnasium were opening, including the one that led to the mutant ward.

The crowds of children stayed near their respective gates, staring at the mutant ward's gate, watching as the giant dragon, their self-acclaimed leader stepped forward, leading the mutant ward towards the middle of the gymnasium. His footsteps echoed around the large area, both powerful and intimidating.

"I hope you all are ready for what's coming. For the greatness that will be instilled upon us!" the dragon mutant bellowed out, eager for whatever it was the scientists were about to announce. "By now, all of you have unlocked great power! Be ready to join us, to join me! Under my command we will achieve greatness!" Drago said in a loud, commanding voice. Some mutants cheered for him, but everyone else stayed quiet, afraid of his wrath, however…

"You'll achieve nothing like this!" a voice yelled out in such a way that every single one of them heard it—silent in volume, but great in significance. They all knew who that voice belonged to.

"Oh? Who dares speak up against my command?" the leader of the mutants asked out loud. The glare he was directing towards all other wards was heart stopping. His snake eyes focused on a sole figure that was walking towards him from the outskirts of the gym.

Red hair waving behind her frame, the small girl looked at him with a determined gaze. "You will not subject these children to further torment. I forbid you to do so!" Tela yelled, her eyes returning the fire in his. She walked forward to stand just a few meters in front of the giant dragon, her head tilted up to meet his eyes.

"FOOL!" the dragon scoffed, leering over her, electricity pulsing through his powerful body. "Who do you think you are? To stand against the strongest of the mutants?! Know your place and stand down!" His rage caused many mutants, even the most loyal to him, to back away in fear. Tela did not waver, still standing tall and glaring at him.

"I AM THEIR TRUSTED FRIEND!" she yelled her response and her eyes shone a brilliant red and for a single, long lasting moment, everyone could feel a terrible pressure of emotion engulf them, yet, it was different for each one of them. People like Cyko, who wanted nothing more than to get out of this cursed place felt their sense of determination rising. Those like Magy, who were broken into accepting their treatment and just went with the flow, felt their sense of indignation rising, resentment of the treatment they had received against their will. Those like Myo, afraid and traumatized beyond hope, felt their faith coming back, their faith that everything would end up all right, no matter what happened.

However, for those like Drago and several mutants, they could feel terror and sadness beyond anything they had ever felt, not their own, but of all the children kept captive in this facility, tortured against their will. The weakest amongst them fell to their knees in despair at the torrent of feelings that was invading them.

Drago, despite the despair inside of him, stood tall in front of Tela, glaring at her while growing in size. "GRRRR, your powers are nothing against me! This is the power you gained from the awakening and now you are using it against your betters? You should realize that they gave us power and now, we must continue to grow STRONGER!" the giant dragon roared, the electricity in his body growing in intensity as his rage grew to counteract Tela's mental attack.

Tela stood unfazed against his threats, continuing to let out her own power in great waves of pressure. "You are delusional! Don't you see what they did to us? To YOU?! Look at what you turned into! You are nothing more than a monster now!"

"THEN YOU DESERVE TO DIE! KNOW YOUR PLACE!" Drago lashed out with his lightning covered fist, faster than the crowd could see towards Tela, who was still standing in the same place, her eyes blazed with bravery.

The punch, powered by his massive frame and strength was stopped by an unseen force, which canceled out the kinetic energy behind it, dispersing to the sides with a loud sonic boom. Tela, staring at the fist that was bigger than her whole body and just a few centimeters in front of her, showed no fear, just resolve.

"Don't underestimate me. These people, they trust in me for a reason, and I will not disappoint them!" she yelled as she raised her hand towards the stunned dragon and opened her palm. An immense force pushed against the dragon, stunning him. He could not react to the sudden power and lost his balance, stumbling back and causing several mutants to panic and scatter away from him. The dragon man fell to the ground with a massive boom.

"W-what?!" Drago said in shock as he tried to get up, but the strange force kept pressing down against him, forcing him to stay grounded. Humiliating! This was humiliating! His mind reeled. A powerful beast like him, forced to kneel to such a tiny girl! He would not stand for it! "YOU'LL PAY FOR THIS!" he yelled barely able to raise his head enough to glare at the girl, his hatred visible in his eyes.

Tela, sweating from the effort of keeping the monster down, still kept her posture. After a moment, she showed off a gentle, yet strained smile, as several children were moving to stand beside her. "I'm not afraid of you. I'm not alone. None of us are! We won't let you hurt us!"

Cyko, who had moved to stand beside her, looked at the girl in admiration. Even he had felt intimated against the giant dragon when he first saw him, but now... Now he felt like he was just another obstacle in the way and they could escape from this accursed place... if they tried. Tela caught his gaze and shot him a smile before returning her attention to the dragon who was still struggling to stand.

"FOOL! IT DOESN'T MATTER HOW MANY OF YOU THERE ARE! I'LL CRUSH YOU ALL! I'LL MAKE EVERYONE SEE THE MIGHT OF MY POWE-GHAAAH!" Drago's raging stopped as several tendrils of energy shot out from the bracelets on his wrists and covered his body, immobilizing him as his movements slowed and stopped. Drago was awake but drained of his power and could only scowl at the ceiling.

What just happened? Everyone was shocked to see such things come out of the bracelets they were wearing. This was their function?

"Subject Number 4, please, release your hold on Subject 357 or we'll take severe action. This is to ensure your own safety and the safety of all those present," a cold, robotic voice echoed throughout the gymnasium, making everyone blink as they realized that the scientists had been observing the scene. Tela glared at nothing, unable to determine where the scientists were located, and released her hold on the dragon who put himself in a sitting position as the tendrils of energy left his body to return to his bracelets.

"Now, if all distractions have ceased. I have an important announcement to give," the cold voice declared, setting the children on edge.

What would they make them do now? It had been a long time since these meetings started. Did the scientists have something planned regarding their meetings now?

"First, allow me to congratulate you. All of you have gone through severe training and rigorous experiments. By surpassing and conquering your limits, you have awakened powers beyond anything a normal human can achieve," the scientist told them, his voice just as clinical as when he first spoke, "you survived this far, meaning you all have the potential to be the defenders of humanity, our greatest protectors."

"Fool, who do you think you are...?" Cyko whispered to himself before he felt someone's hand touch his. He looked to his side to see Tela, who smiled at him.

"Don't let him get to you, we'll get through this together!" she whispered to him, calming his raging heart. He nodded back to her and was about to say something, but the scientist spoke again.

"Because of this, because you were the ones who made it this far, you'll be... compensated. Some of you might already know this, but we grant favors to those we deem worthy and to those who are cooperative," the scientist said, causing some children to blink in surprise. Most of them already knew of the favors—which might as well be called bribes to keep them in line. "You might find yourselves pleasantly surprised upon returning to your dorms, but I digress."

"Because you have progressed this far, we need to continue training you if you are to be humanity's protectors. Upon returning to your dorms, you'll find special clothing labeled with your names. Each of you will receive three outfits, which from now on, will be your official uniform while working for us," the scientist declared, voice still cold and clinical.

Cyko was getting irritated—he spoke as if they had a choice in the matter!

"As for the reason you'll be receiving the special uniforms, it will be to complete the next step in training. You all have had combat training against the robotic drones, a wave of a thousand per session. Many of you had excellent results while others did poorly, and for the sake of humanity's future, we need to... separate those that made it this far only because of luck from the talented ones," he said with an unsettling voice, shocking the children.

What did he mean? He wouldn't dare kill the weak ones off, would he? Tela's smile slipped off her face as she had a bad feeling at what he was going to say next.

"For the next part of the project, we will require you to have real combat experience. Starting next week, instead of meeting for socialization, you'll be participating in live combat against each other, selected at random every meeting. You are to fight each other with the best of your abilities, or there will be... consequences. Subjects who refuse to fight will have themselves and all their roommates denied provisions for an entire week," the emotionless voice of the scientist rang out around the gymnasium, scaring many children stiff.

Tela herself was panicking, no, no! This is the worst possible thing they could have done!

"And, the subjects we deem unworthy of future investment will be terminated. Few of you are in danger of that now, but I advise you to take the combat events seriously."

At his words, many children started to outright panic, and while still rooted in their places, many began to cry or fell to their knees in terror. They would be forced to fight or even kill each other... And if they refused, they would be killed either way! Tela could sense their terror, their despair, and she herself could do nothing but feel afraid. Her plan relied on everyone's trust, but this... This would make everyone turn against each other!

Drago, meanwhile, was smirking as much as his mouth allowed him to. A test of strength! This would be the perfect thing to separate the rubble from the diamonds; the weak from the strong! Their army would be tough by the end, and he would prove himself to be at the top! However, as he looked at the redhead girl who was paling, he couldn't help but wish he was paired to fight her—to put the insolent girl in her place would be glorious!

Cyko, Magy and Myo showed much of the same reaction, despite their different personalities: terror. They didn't want to have to hurt each other to any degree! The trio got closer and held each other's hands, trying to find comfort within their warmth. Yet, even as they looked at Tela, their leader, they found that she herself was struggling just as much as them.

"We will provide further information regarding the battles on a need-to-know basis. You'll be given one week to rest and prepare for them. Any conflict occurring outside the sanctioned battles will be handled with extreme force," the scientist said, uncaring towards the feelings of the despairing children, and just like that he stopped talking, filling the gymnasium with an oppressive silence.

"MUAHAHAHAHA! This is great! We will test our powers against each other and leave the trash out of our glorious army!" the dragon bellowed, despite the weakness induced by the bracelets. Getting up from his sitting position and standing tall once again, he glared at the redhead who knocked him down earlier.

"You see, don't you? It doesn't matter that people are with you! What matters is POWER! You said you are not alone? HAH! You'll soon be fighting your precious friends! And when our turn comes, girl, I'LL be the one to CRUSH you!" The dragon man laughed as he turned and walked away, his amused and murderous voice echoing through the entire gymnasium.

The dragon sauntered towards his gate, signaling all the mutants to follow him back inside. Some did without question while some, those who still had a mostly human body, did so with hesitation and fear. No one was in the right mindset at the time to notice that Drago could return if he wished—they had far more worrying thoughts.

Tela could feel their anxiety, their despair. She could feel it all, and it was proving very hard for her to keep her composure and try to think of a solution. They would be forced to fight each other, and the weakest of them, the most pacifist ones... would just be discarded, disappearing forever, like many people she used to know.

She wanted to save everyone, to make sure they all could escape this hellish prison and have a normal life! She didn't want to be forced to fight those who are trusting her! What... what could she do?

"T-Tela..." Cyko, who was standing near her, clutching both Myo and Magy's hands, said in uncertainty. She could see that the youngest of them was trembling but refusing to cry while Magy herself was pale and stone-faced.

"We... we need to talk. About something that happened to us yesterday... And what happened now..." he said in a trembling voice. Tela sighed before finding her determination again. They needed to do something, and fast.

And so they told her what had transpired just the day before. How Cyko had first come across Snow, the impossibility of there being a cat inside this place and finally... The reveal that Snow was in fact, a pet of one of the scientists, and that she left them for him without so much as a protest, refusing to understand that what her papa was doing was horrible. The betrayal was hard to explain, with little Myo breaking down in tears again, but they had to let Tela know.

That piece of news unnerved Tela, who asked about the risk of their rebellion plan leaking out, that this whole fight against each other thing might be the scientist's retaliation, but Magy refuted this by saying that

Snow herself didn't seem very smart and would be unlikely to understand what exactly they were planning... Yet, this didn't change their current situation.

Many children in the gymnasium were mourning what they'll be forced to do, with friends huddling together to comfort each other. Cyko could see from where he was that his family was one of those who were bunching together, with Torch doing his best to cheer up a crying Starry. He clenched his fists. This was unfair.

"I... I may have a plan on how to deal with this situation," Magy spoke up, making everyone turn towards her, "I... I've been discussing with Scythe the best course of action... She suggested we do as they tell us and fight as seriously as we can but avoid hurting each other too much," she offered in a small voice, to which Cyko looked at her in disbelief.

"Magy, you can't possibly be serious! Look at what they did to us, at what they are forcing us to do!" he yelled in anger, not at his friend, but at their situation.

Magy nodded, signaling that she wanted to say more, "Yes... We have no choice. Scythe says we should treat this as just another experiment and bear through the pain and the guilt. Use this as an opportunity to get stronger so we can escape this place together," she whispered, making Cyko, Myo and Tela's eyes widen with understanding.

"Of course! All of us... as tragic as it is, are already used to pain. If we just treat this as another experiment and avoid hurting each other too much... We have a chance!" Tela exclaimed with a look of epiphany; it was so simple! Their hope hadn't been taken away yet, they could still work together and save everyone!

"*Everyone, please, listen!*" Tela's mental voice yelled out, snapping all the children from their despair to look at their leader. Some showed hope that she had found a solution, others felt apprehension at their future, nonetheless, she beamed and broadcasted her positive feelings.

"*What we've just been told is hard. We'll be forced to fight each other just to keep ourselves alive... This is cruel, they are forcing us to turn on one another, but... We can't let them have their way! We have to stay united even as we fight each other! I have a plan!*" she declared, letting everyone feel what she was feeling... hope. "*Just like the scientist said,* we have no choice, we have to fight each other when called to it, but... We can still come out alive from this! As tragic as it is, all of us are already used to pain, we need to treat this as another experiment to resist and overcome!" she declared, making many children's eyes widen at her suggestion. Treat it as another experiment? Would that work? What about the weak ones among them? Would they be sacrificed so the rest could move on?

"No, we won't give up on the weak! I have a plan, a plan to ensure all of us survive this! We may still have to fight and purposefully hurt each other, but... We'll just have to bear it, to resist and survive until our preparations are ready!" Tela broadcasted to everyone she knew was a part of their fight, "we are in this together... And we will escape this prison! We won't let them break our spirits, no matter what!" She let her feelings transmit to every single one of them and sure enough, the kids that were previously hopeless over their future, were now slowly gaining back their bearings; their own determination and hope.

They were united in this. They wouldn't let the scientists get the better of them, they wouldn't! Many of them were helping Tela map the underground prison, many were strengthening themselves for future combat against the guards, and the rest were contributing in their own ways. They would be ready soon! They would get the scientists, the ones behind their suffering, and win!

For Cyko, Magy and Myo, who were near Tela as she did her speech, they were filled with a sense of courage, like they could accomplish anything if they put their mind to it. They would all escape together and live a much better life than in here.

6

They were shocked at the radical change their room had gone through in the few hours they were in the gymnasium. Their beds were now bigger and more comfortable, the shower had somehow grown in size, giving them room to bathe, and the strangest of all, the room had received a television set! It was a small LCD screen, but it was much more than they had ever been given!

Needless to say, they were suspicious. "Those evil men... They were right when they said we'd be surprised upon our return!" Cyko said with a frown, glaring at the TV screen, "I bet my dinner they are trying to gain our favor!" He walked over to sit on his bed. It was soft now; at least it should make sleeping easier.

"Whatever the case, we should make use of what we have. Look, there are the new clothes they expect us to wear from now on," Magy said as she pointed towards a big box near her bed. Cyko blinked as he looked around his own, finding a similar box. Myo did the same and found his although smaller.

"Huh, at least we'll have something to wear other than those itchy rags, I was getting tired of having to wear only a towel whenever I had to wash them," Cyko said as he took the heavier clothes from the box. Three sets of them were present, just as they had said.

"At least now we have better clothes to wear. Hmm… Let me go get changed really quick," Magy said as she took one of the clothing sets and went to the bathroom to change, leaving Cyko and Myo alone. The two boys looked over their new clothes, taking them out of the packaging.

The only way Cyko could think to describe it, was that it looked like armor. It had some separate pieces, like shoulder and chest plates, but the clothes themselves were comfortable. He saw that his were blue colored while Myo's were brown.

"I'm done! It does make me feel like a soldier, somewhat," Magy said as she stepped out of the bathroom revealing her own purple version of their new uniforms. It fit her form comfortably, being sleeveless with a skirt the same shade as her hair. The armored parts made her look more like an infant soldier than anything else.

"You look good, Magy! But… I don't know if that's a good or bad thing…" Cyko said with a small smile as he looked at his friend, who giggled at his praise.

"It feels good to wear this, it's much more comfortable than those rags! Scythe says the plates are good enough to protect and absorb damage from something like a bullet or a sword, but compared to what we can do, it's very basic protection. She says even the armor the guards use is tougher than this," she said with a smile as she twirled around to show off her new outfit.

"Big brother is right, you look great, big sis!" Myo exclaimed as he looked at her with stars in his eyes.

"Thanks, little Myo!" she said with a sweet grin as she made her way to sit on her own bed.

"The armor parts can be removed rather easily, I found out, which leaves just the clothes. They are made to be resistant to cuts and impacts, according to Scythe, and they are comfortable enough to sleep in!" Magy said as she went through the process of removing the armor plates of her uniform. "See? It's easy!"

"Ah, darn it, they gave out something useful this time," Cyko sighed in irritation, though he knew it would change nothing, not for them anyway.

"We'll use it in the coming weeks, I'm certain," he said as he eyed his own uniform, still inside the package it came in.

Myo was fidgeting, believing the same as them, but he was also anxious about something else. "Uh, can we see if that TV works?" he asked, making his two surrogate siblings look at him.

"Hmm, it would be interesting to know how the outside world is doing after all this time. Maybe we can find out if anyone is looking for us?" Magy asked. Cyko nodded.

"I think that is a good idea, though I doubt it. Let's check it out," Cyko said as he walked towards the small LCD screen before turning it on once he found the controller. The TV turned on, showing a news channel.

"On today's urgent news, Creator Luni announced that an extinction level event has just been averted. According to her, a massive, planet-devouring creature was heading toward our solar system posing a threat to our world. In her recent live stream, she said the beast was the fruit of a 'mad cult's insane leftover experiments' and expressed her hate for them but reassured us that everything was fine now. Governments around the world have expressed their heartfelt thanks and the desire to give her high honors for saving the world once more, the tenth time since she revealed herself to the citizens four thousand years ago…" the reporter on screen said as several more details regarding the incident appeared on the bottom of the television, including an image of the Creator herself and a depiction of the giant creature which looked like a massive, planet-sized serpent.

"Huh, and they tell us she is a threat. She has saved us ten times already! I mean, I'm strong, but I doubt I could even scratch the thing she killed!" Cyko exclaimed in awe as he watched the news intently. What would be the point of this whole thing if they were just eaten by a giant space snake? "They'll just be throwing us out to die if we stay here. Just like Tela said, we all need to work together on this," he said, earning nods from both Magy and Myo.

"I wish *she* could save us... She is so strong..." Myo said with a hopeful voice, looking at the Creator on the screen where it showed parts of the live stream she had made to address the danger.

"Yeah, it would be great, but here we only have each other. And now more than ever, we can't let these bribes win us over. We need to keep resisting," Cyko said in a determined voice. They may have gotten a lot of comfort today, but they wouldn't allow themselves to become complacent. Nothing would make him forgive them for what they did. Nothing.

And he was sure his friends and family felt the same. They would escape, and they would show those scientists just what they had created.

7

A week passed and sure enough, they had all been given time off and allowed to rest as much as they could before being called to the gymnasium, which was now a different place than the school-like gym they had been used to.

It looked like a massive coliseum now—a large arena in the center with hundreds of spectator seats surrounding it. On the ceiling, directly above the arena, was a large set of displays that were turned off.

One thing that stood out the most, however, was the circle of robed and armored figures who were sitting in the seats closest to the edge of the arena, some having quiet conversations while others stood silently as if waiting for something. They all had long staffs. Having entered through the highest levels, the children were unable to see their faces.

"I welcome you all, to the Coliseum," a steeled voice from the ceiling spoke, making everyone turn towards the large displays. They turned on, displaying the image of an emotionless scientist with white hair and a beard. Cyko's eyes widened. *It was him! It was the terrible man who took Snow away!* he seethed.

"I am Dr. Gacha, the head scientist of the project you all are a part of," he declared, making the children's eyes widen.

He was the one responsible for all their suffering?!

"The Coliseum is titled for this level of the facility, named for this part of the project. All subjects will conduct live combat experiments against each other in the arena located below," the man explained with a bland voice, the image on the screens changing to show the arena.

"You may take a seat wherever to watch the combats—either for entertainment or for studying your possible adversary's powers and abilities. The team of mages located by the lowest seats will be responsible for protecting the audience from any wayward attacks. The screens will display the names of the combatants. Further instructions will be given on a need-to-know basis. Combat will start in three minutes," the cold voice declared, before the screens changed to show an ominous looking countdown.

"I'll kill him, I promise, I'll kill him!" Cyko said under his breath, clenching his fists as many children from his ward made their way to the seats. After a few seconds, he felt two hands touching him, looking up to see Magy and Myo.

"It'll be all right, Cyko, we are all together in this!" Magy said with a comforting smile, even as her eyes showed her anger at the scientist.

"B-big sis is right! E-even if it's painful, we'll make it through together, big brother, I promise!" the smaller boy said with a sweet smile, as he trembled in fear at the possibility of fighting. Sighing, Cyko allowed himself to smile at his roommates.

"Thanks you two, I know I can count on you! Now come, we have to find ourselves some seats," Cyko said as he walked down the stairs to the seats, looking for somewhere they all could sit.

"Everyone, please remember what we discussed this week. If your opponent is weaker than you, try to find a way to let them score a win discreetly. If both of you are strong, put on a good show. Please, try not to hurt each other too much," Tela's voice rang out to everyone. Cyko heard a buzzing sound as he and many other children agreed with her. Good, they had a plan of action and they would follow it through.

"Attention to the first combatants," the scientist announced as the countdown reached zero. Everyone looked up with apprehension as the black screen started to rapidly flash names before stopping on a single name. "Subject Number 444, Cyko, will be the first combatant," the detached scientist declared, as a picture of him was shown alongside his number and name.

"So, I'll be the one going first, huh?" Cyko said in disdain as everyone turned to look at him with pity. Magy and Myo, who were both sitting beside him, touched his hands in comfort and encouragement. Soon after, the screen started to flash names at random again.

"Subject Number 105, Ellyn, will be the second combatant," the voice announced, showing the image of the girl alongside her name and number.

Cyko's eyes widened. The girl he met just before Snow was taken away? He would have to fight her?!

"All other subjects are to remain in the Coliseum. Restrooms are on the fourth level of every area. The subjects who have been called must proceed to the arena with a reminder of the consequences of refusal. The main stairs lead directly to the arena," the scientist said, making Cyko curse once again, knowing he had no choice.

"Be careful, Cyko," Magy said as Cyko got up.

"Yeah, be careful big brother... And try not to hurt her..." Myo's small voice earned a smile from the blue-haired boy.

"Thanks, I'll do my best, and I'll try to avoid injuring her too much," Cyko said before making his way towards the main stairs, noticing how the mages had sat up and were now standing in formation with their staffs in front of them.

"*Cyko, be careful. She seems to be from a ward I've never seen before. They weren't at the last meeting!*" Tela's voice rang out in his head with alarm, making his eyes widen. How hadn't he noticed it?! Too late to back out now, though.

"*They are from the maximum-security ward, I met her a week ago, she didn't seem like a bad person, maybe you can get through to her?*" Cyko asked as he made his way down to the arena.

"*I... I can try, I can see her from here. But please, be careful, Cyko!*" Tela's worry washed over him, but it made him smile, knowing she was concerned about him. It meant she cared.

"*Don't worry, Tela, I'll be fine!*" he thought to her, trying to show her his confidence. He would do his best, he still needed to kill that scientist after all.

After a few minutes, he stood on one side of the arena, with Ellyn facing him. The two looked at each other with sad, but determined eyes.

"*All right. Both of you seem to be in good standing with the scientists of this place, this means you two can fight on equal terms without worries, but please, don't hurt each other too much. Good luck to both of you.*"

Both nodded before moving towards each other to the center of the arena.

"This is quite a lot to take in, huh?" she asked as they approached each other.

Cyko nodded.

"How is little Snow, by the way? I trust she is doing well?" she asked, curious about the cat. He was dreading this question.

"They took her away," he answered with a sad sigh, "she belonged to the nasty scientist up there who was speaking a few minutes ago. Turns out she can transform into a human and was likely just curious about us," he explained, hating how the girl's green eyes shifted from curiosity to deep sadness.

"I see… Guess we can't have nice things, huh? They'll just take it away… Like forcing us to fight our own friends…" she said as she put her hand to her side, causing wind to shift around her. Cyko shook his head at her.

"Even if we have to fight today, Ellyn, you'll still be my friend. I'm sorry for any bruises I might give you now," the older boy said with a bitter smile while activating his power to flow through him, surrounding his body with a soft, blue aura. The green girl showed him a thankful but brittle smile of her own.

"Thank you, friend. I'm sorry if I hurt you also or take my frustrations out in this fight. May the best of us win," Ellyn said as the wind surrounding her hand became stronger, eventually creating a bow-like form, including a wind string. She drew the string back as much as she could before pointing her wind bow at him.

His enhancement allowed him to take in several details about her in an instant. Her uniform and armor looked just like Magy's, but with a greenish color. Her stance seemed to be one gained through constant practice, like from the robot wave experiment, and just like she always says, the wind danced around her form.

His own armor had a bluish hue and his own battle stance, rather than a martial arts one, was just the one he adapted to after many, many times fighting the robots. Now, he could see if he was strong, by fighting someone else that he believed to be strong too.

With no announcement from the scientists, they burst into action. Ellyn took the lead by launching her attack—an arrow of wind that caused a large sonic boom as it left her bow. Even with his enhancement, Cyko barely had time to dodge the attack, managing to jump away at the very last second, noticing how the arrow left a small crater in the wall that he was just standing in front of.

His mistake of looking away at this moment was clear as he heard more booms coming from Ellyn, signaling more arrows being shot in his direction while he was still in the air. Unable to dodge in time, he put his arms in front of himself to defend against the attack.

It felt like a truck struck him as the arrows reached him, making him lose his breath as he was thrown backwards, hitting the wall of the arena with a loud boom as more and more arrows exploded against his body. Gritting his teeth, he forced his body to jump away from the next barrage, running around Ellyn as she shot arrow after arrow of wind at him at inhuman speeds.

Finally he caught an opening as she stopped to correct her aim. He launched himself at her with the extreme speed from his enhancement, catching her off guard as Cyko appeared in front of her with a fist raised. However, a distortion of wind appeared between them just as he struck, slowing his attack enough to allow her to block it with her arms, making her slide back only slightly, rather than send her flying as he had intended.

Her mouth formed a circle and her eyes widened when she realized he could pierce her shield, but her brows furrowed as the surrounding wind grew more violent as she pointed her wind bow at him again. Cyko jumped away in instinct as she launched her arrow, which was much faster than before. She was taking him seriously now.

She fired at a much more rapid pace than before, keeping him busy with having to dodge left and right to avoid getting pummeled by her arrows. When he was far enough away from her, she raised her right foot and stomped the ground which, added to the force of her wind, caused small parts of the ground to break out and fly around her.

Seeing her actions, Cyko once again launched himself in her direction, hoping to land a hit, however, he was surprised when the pebbles she had broken from the ground were covered in a green aura and shot themselves at him. He dodged them by a single millimeter, thinking he was safe, but that was a mistake. As the pebbles passed him, they exploded into a gale, sending him flying away again towards the far wall which he hit hard, disoriented and unable to react as more arrows reached him, detonating against his body and carving him deeper into the wall.

Despite the difficulty of approaching her and the pain from her attacks, Cyko grinned. Yes, yes! She was a much better fighter than those stupid robots! Much stronger, much more durable! He was already enjoying this!

Smiling as his enhancements gave him more power, he forced himself out of the wall, jumping away from the barrage as soon as he was able to. He watched as another pebble was shooting towards him while leaping as far away as he could, it exploded once again in a violent gust of wind.

She must tear apart the robot army much faster than he can with those powerful area of effect attacks! She was strong, and he knew Ellyn would be a great help in the coming rebellion, but for now, he needed to prove himself—to her, to his friends, family and to Tela, who was no doubt watching their fight.

He tried to approach her again, but this time, moving in a zigzag to throw off her aim which seemed to be working, though she had to take a moment to correct her aim, and her automatic pebble shooter was running out of ammunition. Barely managing to outrange another blow, he managed to position himself in front of her, up close and out of range from her bow.

Ellyn's eyes widened as Cyko launched a powerful kick at her, breaking her wind shield once again, which only slowed half of its momentum. The attack was enough to send her flying away, in which he gave chase to her soaring body.

Stopping her flight with her power over wind, she managed to barely evade a mighty punch Cyko sent her way. Using the opening it provided, she used her wind bow as a club and struck out at him using the gale force it contained, staggering him enough to jump away and

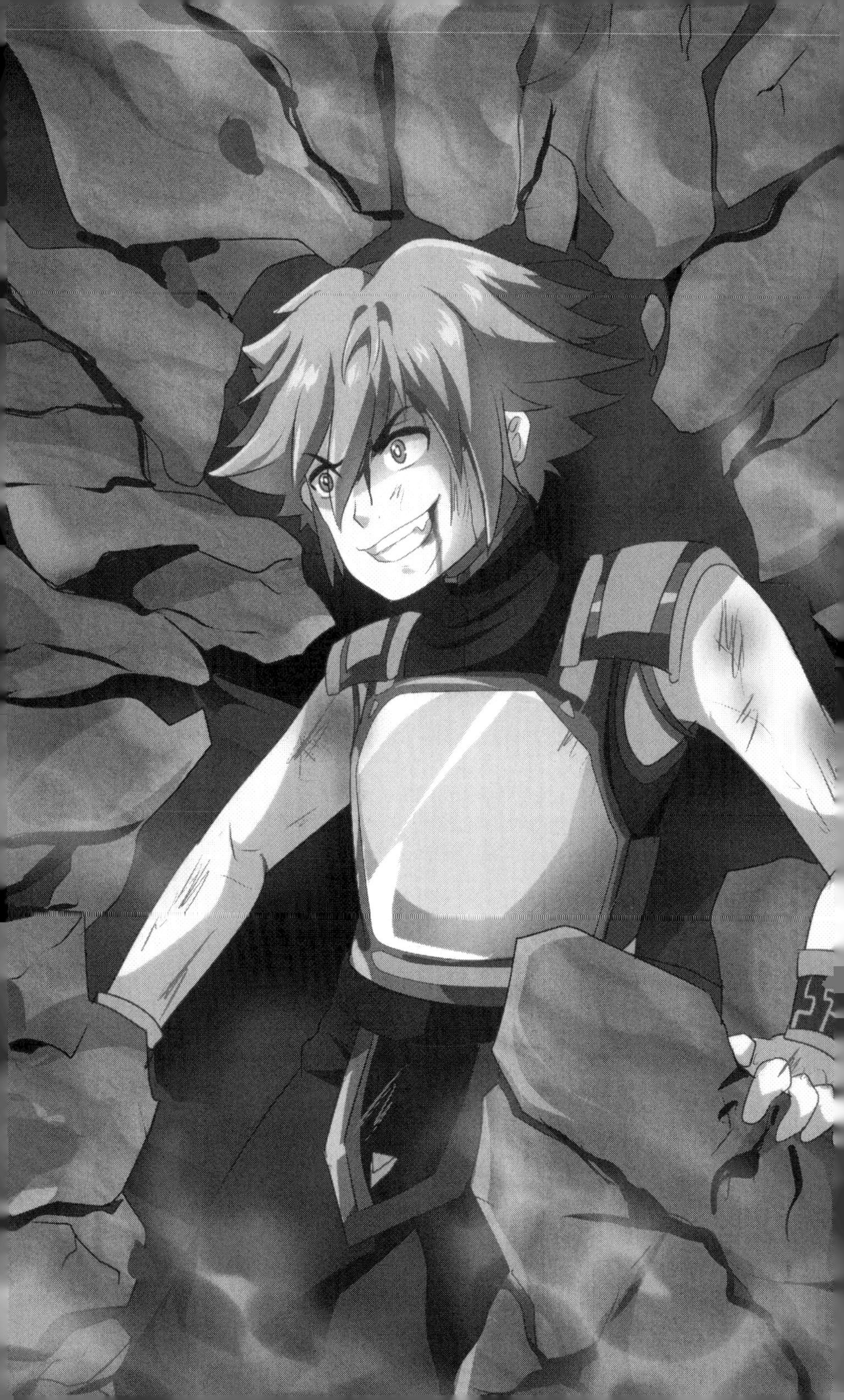

send more spirit-possessed pebbles at him, which exploded in a powerful tornado as he flew away from her.

Ellyn knew Cyko was a powerful enhancer; he barely seemed hurt by her powerful gale attacks, and if anything, the difficulty to approach her seemed to motivate him. What's more, his attacks *hurt*, she thought as she winced and tenderly touched her left side. It would be a bruise in the morning. If she wanted to beat him this fight, she needed to keep piling the attacks on until his stamina ran out—she needed to pressure him!

She exhaled, shaking her head to concentrate. The abilities the scientists unlocked in her allowed Ellyn to communicate with the wind—the spirits that were invisible to most people—and therefore, control it to her will, which meant she allowed it to guide her to the best path possible. It also gave her sharp eyesight and increased speed and reaction time. She needed the best of each of her abilities if she was to win and guarantee her survival!

"Oh, wind spirits, I beg of you, guide me in this moment..." she prayed as she sent more gale pebbles to keep Cyko at bay. Wind power covered her body as a targeting mark appeared in front of her right eye, signifying the usage of her full power. Pointing her wind bow up rather than at Cyko, she began to prepare her attack. She knew there would be a barrier that would prevent harm from those watching, and the wind told her the screens were unprotected, which meant they could be used as a weapon, but that wasn't her intention... She needed her arrow to be as high as possible now.

"Oh Wind, guide my arrow... Tempest Spirit!" she pleaded as a green aura covered her bow before launching it upwards towards the ceiling where it stopped just before it reached the screen. The green arrow expanded and conjured up powerful winds around it before turning into a full-blown tornado that covered the entire arena. A translucent barrier appeared in front of the mages sitting in the first row, a protection against wayward attacks.

The wind grew stronger and Cyko was having trouble standing on his feet without being sucked into the massive tornado. His smirk had grown in size, this was awesome! Ellyn was so strong! He really wanted to beat her now! However, his sneer disappeared from his face as several gale pebbles appeared next to him, bursting and adding to the force of the wind. Sent flying by the explosion, he couldn't stand against the powerful gusts.

Ellyn started to fire her arrows rapidly, all of them hitting him while he was helpless. He was forced to take it all, trying to use his arms to defend himself. He could see Ellyn in the center of the tornado, spinning alongside him with a small whirl of wind at her feet.

Dozens of pebbles appeared next to him, exploding and sending him flying away like a rag-doll towards more rubble that was blasted. He would lose if this kept up! He needed to do something, but what?

Grinning despite his predicament, he found the answer just as more pebbles flew his way. He needed to find a way back to the ground so he could disorient her! Pushing his enhancement once again, he took hold of several pebbles and, just before they exploded, pointed them diagonally with his palm open in the opposite direction of Ellyn. The powerful explosion of wind sent him flying downwards and despite the strength of the tornado, it was still enough to plant him on the ground, which while very painful, he was able to take it.

Positioning himself to get up and not be sent flying away by the wind again, he saw that Ellyn was close to him and had a panicking look in her eyes as she pointed her bow at him, but he was faster, and before she could launch the arrow, he jumped up with his fist aimed towards her stomach.

"A-ahhh!" Ellyn grunted in agony as the punch was powerful enough to bend the plate covering her stomach, pushing her to her knees. The wind quieted down and dissipated as she vomited on the ground, her hands covering her stomach in anguish.

"Gah... Gah..." She panted in pain as she tried to get up, but her body hurt too much. "I... Gah... Can't fight anymore... it hurts..." She gasped out as tears of pain fell down her cheeks. Cyko regretted it after seeing the state he left her in and allowed his own enhancement to fade away.

"Ellyn! Oh, my Luni, Ellyn, I'm so sorry!" Cyko exclaimed as he knelt down next to her and tried to comfort her, even as he winced in pain from his own bruises.

Ellyn let out a pained laugh. "Ah... Ugh. C-Cyko... Gah... Th-that... Ahh... Really hurt..." she said between gasps and sobs.

"This round of combat is concluded. Both subjects are in excellent standing. You may now return to your seats to watch the remaining battles," the uncaring voice of the scientist rang out, signaling the end of their fight, much to their relief.

"I'm so sorry, Ellyn…" Cyko said again as he cradled the shaking girl's head to his chest.

She laughed, then winced. "Ahh… B-being… Ugh, hugged by a boy… Gah… Is worth it…" she said, blushing.

"You don't need to get yourself hurt for a hug!" he said in a worried voice before sighing again. This girl was eccentric as ever, and he really hoped he didn't hurt her too badly. "Is there anything I can do to make you feel better?" he asked, still feeling bad for what he did.

"Aha… Urgh… W-well… I-if you… ouch… Carry me like a princess… Ahh… To my seat… I-I'll forgive you…" she asked between sobs, looking up at him with a mischievous smile, despite her pain and tears.

Cyko blushed and nodded his head. "I can do that. I don't think you can walk by yourself yet," he said before positioning her better and lifting her up from the ground. Despite not being enhanced, she felt light as a feather to him, even with her armor.

"O-ouch… Th-thanks…" she said with a grateful, pained smile before grimacing as more tears built in her eyes, "ahh… It hurts so much… D-don't… Ahh… Mind me… I-I'll just c-cry for a while…" she said with a smile before turning her face into his chest to hide her tears.

" It hurts so much…" Ellyn sobbed, panting and gasping as the pain from Cyko's attack throbbed. The boy just looked at her, wanting to comfort her in some manner, but he knew he wouldn't be able to. The way he was carrying her was comforting enough for Ellyn, but Cyko knew… only being free from this hell, where they are forced to hurt each other, would truly put her at peace.

"You two did great, I'm sorry that you had to go through so much pain. Please, keep working together," Tela said in their minds, her voice sad, but relieved at them being alive. *"Rest up as much as you can, I'll be keeping in touch,"* the redhead said before going silent.

After they were out of the arena and walking the main stairs, Ellyn painfully directed him towards her seat, which he followed as best as he could, finding an empty seat near Reddox, whose face was impassive as ever, although a wrinkle in his forehead showed that he was worried about her.

"Thank you for bringing her here. I can take care of her," he said as Cyko set her down next to him. She got herself into a more comfortable position, still holding her stomach in pain.

"Th-thank you, Cyko… Ah… L-looks like the next fight already ended…" She said as Cyko turned towards the arena. It seemed the next battle had already started and finished in the time it took for him to take Ellyn back to her seat.

The winner's body was covered in spikes dripping poison, whilst the loser's had turned into metal, though he was on his knees, panting. "Combat concluded. The winner's standing has risen, averting elimination. The loser's placement remains good," the scientist announced, making the spike girl fall to the ground, crying out in relief before panicking and helping the boy heal from her poison.

"Th-that plan… of that girl… is really working, huh?" Ellyn commented with a smile, making Reddox turn to her in confusion, while Cyko smiled and nodded.

"Yes, she is doing her best to ensure none of us are… eliminated… by those sick men," he said bitterly, directed at the scientists who were watching them fight for their own twisted amusement.

Seeing the look of confusion plastered on Reddox's face, Ellyn turned to him and strained out a smile. "D-don't worry, I-I'll explain it you later, ugh," she said, though at least she could breathe now. She looked up at the blue-haired boy and beamed at him.

"D-despite th-the pain… It was a good fight… Th-thanks for helping me."

It had been a great fight, much more challenging and real than fighting those stupid machines they were forced to spar with. Waving at her one more time, he made his way back towards his own seat, where Magy and Myo were waiting for him anxiously.

"Big bro, that was amazing! You are so strong!" Myo exclaimed with a grin before grimacing, "I feel sorry for Ellyn… Do you think she'll be all right?"

"I think so, at least, her friend said he could help take care of her. I hope I didn't hurt her too much," he said as he sat down between the two of them.

Magy put her hand on his own, looking at him with a comforting smile. "Don't worry, dear friend. Scythe says her wind spirits will help her heal, and I loved the performance you two pulled off. I should feel bad, but… I'm kinda looking forward to my own fight," she said with a serene smile, making the boy sigh, although he smiled nonetheless.

"I know you are, I loved fighting Ellyn, even if I hurt her more than I intended to," Cyko said, grimacing before looking up towards the screen as two more children were called forth to fight against each other. The names on the screen made him seethe in anger, but he knew he had no control, at least not now.

The third combat of the day turned out to involve one of his youngest siblings, Torch, against a child whose power was to turn himself into a cloud of locusts, strong enough to eat through metal. It had been a… unique battle, for despite the threat of the locusts, Torch kept the fire around him going at maximum potency, which made the insects unable to approach him. In the end, Torch won the combat by burning half of the locusts into dust, causing the other boy to shift back to his human form in agony. Being a shapeshifter, the defeated combatant would soon heal from these burns, but the scientist put a stop to the battle before this could occur. Torch was worried he might have gone too far, but the other boy, despite the pain he was in, told him that he was fine.

The next chosen to fight that day was another member of his family, Sara—one of his eldest sisters. Her opponent was someone who could use her mind to disorient and confuse her opponents. It was a hard fight for both of them, because Sara's control over water was nearly as good as Ellyn's own control over wind, and the mind-powered girl had to rely on her powers of confusion to make Sara miss her attacks. In the end, Sara froze the entire floor, thus immobilizing her opponent as the girl's feet got stuck in the ice. It seemed she would win, having prepared a large water bullet to knock her out, but her opponent's mental disruption ability proved too much for Sara and she dropped unconscious just as she was about to launch her attack.

The next battle set everyone on edge, as it involved someone from the mutant ward, an adult sized werewolf with steel claws and teeth, and a girl who was trembling with fear at the beast's predatory gaze. From his position, Cyko could see that Tela had a panicking look on her face.

It seemed the flaw in her plan had emerged. The mutant ward consisted of inhuman monsters who listened only to violence, and it didn't seem like the werewolf beast would follow Tela's plans.

The girl that was fighting him, however, had the ability to control sound waves, which included a supersonic scream. Despite the ferocity and strength of the werewolf who was clearly not following any specific strategy, she still won against him. Just as his body had transformed, so did his senses. Her control over sound turned out to be his weakness, allowing her to emerge from the fight with only a deep cut in her arm.

Tela told everyone that if the mutant children refused to cooperate, they should fight to the best of their abilities and she would indirectly help if things got bad. Hopefully, it wouldn't come to that.

After that fight, Magy was chosen to fight. Her opponent would also be one of the mutant ward children, a girl whose body turned translucent and head and hair turned into that of a jellyfish. Smiling serenely at the words of encouragement from both her friends, she made her way towards the arena.

"My name is Medusa. As you can see, I'm a jellyfish," Magy's opponent said openly as she arrived. Magy tilted her head at her comment. "I'm not in favor of that mean dragon... I just want a big ocean to float away in," she said with a wistful smile as she got into a ready stance.

"All anyone wants is to be free from this prison, right?" Magy leveled, as she put both hands inside her chest, taking out her twin scythes. She winked as her opponent's eyes widened.

"Eh... That's a nice trick! I wish I could do that!" the translucent girl said before shaking her head, causing her hair to stand up and move like snakes, "but my tentacles are just as good! Be careful, though, a sting from them really hurts!" she warned in a playful tone as her waist-length hair waved around.

"Oh, I look forward to it, then!" Magy said with a small grin on her face as she got ready. "I just so happen to love pain, I'm sure we'll get along great!" Magy let the dark energy cover her body and launched herself at a surprised Medusa, who barely had time to dodge a cut from one of her scythes.

Thinking fast, the jellyfish girl sent her hair towards Magy, who evaded by jumping up in the air and—by concentrating her dark energy into her scythe—sent a crescent wave of darkness towards Medusa, who once again used her enhanced reflexes to dodge.

"Oh! So close, so close!" she said in a panic as she landed on the ground.

Magy wasted no time in using her dark energy to make a burst behind herself, propelling her towards the jellyfish girl, who panicked for a moment, before sending her hair straight towards the approaching reaper. With a smirk, Magy dodged at the last second, using her energy burst again to propel herself to the left. In quick action, she struck out with her scythe, passing right through the jellyfish girl, who let out a pained gasp, before lashing out with her leftover hair. Magy was unable to move in time.

"Ahhh!" the pink-haired girl cried out as the tentacles hit her, sending agonizing pings through her body. Medusa was right, her stings hurt, a lot. And it felt great.

Rolling backwards away from the jellyfish girl, Magy got into a crouched position and looked at her, licking her lips in anticipation. "That felt great! I can't wait to feel more! Come at me, I'll make you feel great too!" Magy declared before using her darkness to propel herself at her opponent, this time much faster than before.

Medusa didn't have time to react, so she covered herself in her hair hoping to block the scythe, but was surprised as—just like before—the weapon passed right through her, sending an uncomfortably cold sensation through her body. Shocked by the attack, she was unable to respond as Magy slashed her again and then, using a dark-enhanced kick, sent her flying a few meters away.

"My scythes can pass through any physical defenses, your hair won't help you," Magy said with a smirk as she approached the fallen mutant who was struggling to get up. "Each time my weapon cuts you, you get one step closer to death. But don't worry, I'm not evil! I'll just knock you out now," Magy raised one of her scythes up high before frowning as her arm began to tremble and it became hard to move.

"S-so scary, b-but I'm not done yet!" the jellyfish girl said as she got up, grimacing in pain. "M-my stings inject a paralyzing venom. Soon, you won't be able to move anymore!" The girl smirked, even as she panted from the weakness she was feeling.

Magy let her arm fall down. She could barely move her arm.

"It seems I've been beaten. I didn't expect actual poison. You are a jellyfish, I should've thought you'd have some venom," Magy struggled to speak, "if you are going to beat me, I don't suppose you could allow me to... feel your sting again?" she lowered her voice, which embarrassed Medusa.

"U-uhh, the poison could be dangerous!" she exclaimed in nervousness, though she raised her hair again.

Magy's smile didn't leave her face. "Oh, but it also would knock me down faster, wouldn't it?"

"Very well, I'm into that weird plan of yours, so, I'm sorry," she said as she sent her tentacle-like hair towards Magy, covering her in them, bringing her closer so she wouldn't struggle too much.

"Ahh! Ahhhhhhh!" Magy cried out in agonized ecstasy as she felt the burning sensation all across her body. It hurt and yet she loved every second of it, but...

"I... GOT YOU!" Magy screamed out as darkness surrounded them both. Before Medusa could react, it exploded out in a violent wave of blackness, making the jellyfish girl cry out in pain. The pink-haired girl, seeing her opponent's agony, felt herself lick her lips in enjoyment, even as she felt the pain of the tentacles still attached to her. Ah, so she liked to inflict pain as well... this place has truly broken her.

Letting the dark energy dissipate, both she and the jellyfish girl fell to the ground, her opponent lying on her back in pain, she on her knees in exhaustion. "It seems it's my win, new friend." Magy smiled at the groaning girl on the ground, whose hair had retracted back to herself.

"It... Ouch, seems that way..." Medusa replied with shortened breath, rolling to her back and trying to get up.

"Combat concluded. Winner is in great standing, loser is still in good standing. The next combat will start soon," the cold voice announced, causing Magy to sigh in resignation, getting up off the ground. The jellyfish girl stared at her in shock, how could she already move?!

"Oh, me? Scythe here takes care of my body. If I get poisoned from your venom or even from food, she'll be focused on curing me. It was a daring plan, but I'm glad it worked!" she said as she walked over towards the mutant girl, offering her hand, which the downed girl took with a grateful smile.

"H-haha... Ouch. I-it's hard to think, ever since I turned into this, but you got me," Medusa said, wobbling on her feet before sighing.

"Well, I must go back to sit with the others. See you, Magy," Medusa said with a smile, waving at the pink-haired girl, who returned the gesture. At least now they knew not all mutants were bad people, they were just scared of the giant dragon. Magy herself would love to teach him a lesson.

Arriving back at her seat, Magy beamed with pride at the congratulations given by both her brothers, although she wondered why Cyko was blushing. Still, it felt nice to fight someone else that could pose a challenge to her, even if it was forced. Sitting down on Cyko's side, she rested her head on his shoulder. The fight left her tired.

The next several fights were interesting and showed off everyone's potential. Geon, Cyko's older brother, showed the might of earthquakes by causing a shapeshifter's wings to vibrate so strongly they fell flat on their face. One kid with mind reading powers could evade all the attacks from someone who could launch strong, steel projectiles from their fingers until they dropped from exhaustion. Then, two large mutants, a rhino and a bull, showed just how powerful the mutants were, as they engaged in a vicious physical showdown, with the bull coming out as the winner.

Following this, the scientist declared a fight that left Cyko's stomach in knots. Tela was called to fight and right after that, her opponent was revealed. Leo, another member of the mutant ward, but not just any other. He was a lion mutant, sitting right next to Drago, from what Cyko could see. The mutant rose with a challenging roar and, while nowhere near as large as Drago, he was still much taller than even the adult guards in their bulky armor.

"*Tela, please be careful...*" Cyko whispered in his mind, which caused the girl who was far away from him to turn towards him with a smile. It filled his body with warm feelings as she made her way towards the arena.

"*Thank you, my friend. Leo seems unlikely to cooperate, but I'm not defenseless either,*" she said in his mind, transmitting her own feelings of determination and confidence to him. Cyko nodded at her. She would be all right, he trusted in her, after what he had seen her do to Drago.

She arrived at the center of the arena, looking at her opponent who towered over her. Wrapped in a massive version of their armor uniform, he looked very intimidating.

"Grr... I am Leo, the second strongest of the mutants! I can't believe how lucky I am to beat the *child* that made our illustrious leader fall to his knees!" the lion roared as he watched Tela approach him, a fearless and determined look on her face.

"So, you'll also stand in our way? You'll also try to stand in favor of this continued torment?" Tela asked with a hard voice, glaring up at the lion who roared out a laugh.

"Torment? This is great, girl! I have earned this power by surviving their trials and now I can fight and crush enemies with my own two hands!" he yelled as he spread his arms, causing the ground below him to disintegrate and form a cloud around him.

With a loud snap, the dust formed into a giant hammer in his left hand and an equally intimidating axe in his right. More dust floated up from the ground, surrounding his body and with another loud boom, formed into a massive rock armor, giving him an even more daunting appearance. Tela stood still, unfazed by his powers.

"GRAAAA! I would have preferred to fight our so-called leader one-on-one, to show him who is the strongest. But by fighting you, I'll prove to him my power and become the king I was born to be!" he roared as more dust rose around him. "Now choose! Either be sliced by my axe... OR BE CRUSHED BY MY HAMMER!" The lion dashed towards Tela with both weapons raised high.

"So be it then..." she whispered under her breath before raising her hand towards the charging beast, her eyes shining with power. Before the lion could comprehend what had happened, he was pushed back, all his momentum turning back against him as she sent him flying, crashing hard against the far wall, opposite from Tela.

"Your own abilities will prove to be your undoing...!" her words came out between her clenched teeth. She raised her other arm and made a crushing gesture with both. Still stunned, the lion roared in pain as he felt his rock armor start to compress against his own body, threatening to squash him from the insides.

"As if that would be enough!" Leo roared in opposition, using his earth control to disperse his armor, momentarily freed from Tela's hold, allowing him to launch himself with much greater force than before, his axe raised and ready to slice her in two.

The redhead, however, was faster and used her telekinesis on the raised weapon, dragging it down to the ground just before it reached her, causing a great crash. With her other hand she sent a strong kinetic push against him, sending him flying away once again, which made him lose hold of the axe.

Immediately, she took hold of the giant axe and willed it to spin with such speed that it resembled more of a saw. With a gesture, she sent it towards the staggered lion who looked up just in time to block the attack with his hammer, destroying the axe.

"Using my own weapon against me… YOU WILL NOT GET AWAY WITH THIS!" he screamed with hatred as he willed his power to take hold of the entire ground. Large clouds of dust formed in the air around Tela, whose face stood unfazed at his display.

"Be crushed!" he yelled as he willed the dust to form into large spikes that rained down on her. She raised a hand upwards to stop the spikes and another one to stop a giant stone cannonball from hitting her. She blinked as she saw Leo appear in front of her, with his hammer raised, ready to strike.

"DIE!" the great lion roared, bringing his sacred hammer down on the redhead.

It struck the ground, causing a large boom to resound through the arena. But, as the worried children looked on, they found that Tela had somehow gotten herself on top of the hammer, arms still extended to show she was holding both the spikes and the cannonball. The lion glared at her form before trying to raise the weapon from under her, but it seemed a thousand times heavier.

"Mind over matter!" Tela yelled as she made the cannonball hit him in the head, stunning and disorienting the beast, leaving him wide open for Tela's final move. With a snarl, she brought her raised arm down, which caused the many rock spikes floating in the air to shoot towards him, impaling and piercing his entire body, only missing the vital areas.

"GRAAAAAAAHHHH!" the beast roared in pain as his skin was assaulted and pierced by his own spikes. The stakes continued to rain on his defenseless body until there were none left in the air.

Bleeding profusely from the stab wounds, the lion's eyes rolled to the back of his head as he fell to the ground, unable to fight any longer. Tela looked at his fallen form with a pitying but fierce look on her face.

"I'm glad I was the one to fight you, and not a defenseless child. Learn your lesson; the path of violence and thirst for power won't get you anywhere," Tela said softly before turning away from the fallen beast, ending the battle without a single scratch on her body.

"Combat concluded. Winner is in excellent standing, loser's standing remains good; however, he'll be taken for medical treatment. As this session's combatants have damaged the arena beyond quick repairs, today's battles will end. The next session will be in three days. All subjects will return to their dorms," the scientist declared as a team of mages made their way towards the fallen beast to extract him.

Cyko stood in awe at Tela's performance. She absolutely demolished that giant lion, all while making it look easy! She didn't even break a sweat. The message, he knew, was clear... Anyone from the mutant ward who continued to support this atrocity will have to answer to Tela. And from the look of absolute rage on Drago's face, it seems he also got the message.

"Tela, by Luni, you were amazing!" Cyko thought to the redhead, his admiration for her growing even more. He knew now how powerful she was, even he would have had a lot of trouble against that giant lion! *"You made it look so easy, and you don't have a single scratch on your body!"* he praised her with a big smile as she turned towards him.

"I don't enjoy violence, but it was necessary. Still, thank you, my dear Cyko," she replied, winking at him. The blue-haired boy was once again filled with warm feelings, courtesy of Tela, making his smile widen. Magy, who had been watching the fight intently, giggled.

"Our leader is very strong, isn't she? Scythe says we would have a hard time even getting close to her if we had to fight against Tela. Her power and, uh, c-charisma was it? It makes me optimistic on our chances of getting out of this place," Magy said, earning an agreeing nod from little Myo.

"Yeah! Big sis Tela is so strong! She'll save us, I'm sure!" the smaller boy piped in, making Cyko chuckle.

Yes, Tela was powerful, and he was sure they could trust her to pull through. But... Even if the battles had been stopped for now, he knew this would be the first of many fights to occur in the next few weeks. Cyko was half looking forward to it, half not.

8

The three days of rest from combat passed too quickly for Cyko's liking. During that time, they didn't have much to occupy them, except take advantage of the TV. There was only so much they could plan for ahead of time.

They had discovered that the company behind their current situation was sending aid, technically money, in order to help the authorities with the case of the disappearance of many children. This had been going on for a couple of months already, and they were no closer to finding them, the reporter said. Cyko cursed when he saw the news report; the jerks were making themselves out to be heroes!

Still, Tela had contacted everyone again, not too long after her fight with the lion mutant, and declared that mutants whom she couldn't convince to work alongside them were to be met with full force.

"Leo didn't think for a moment to hold back against me. If I was anyone else, his attacks would have been lethal. We can't allow that to happen!" she had said, and further encouraged any other child with mental powers to run interference alongside her, in case of another match with a violent mutant.

And so, they found themselves once again in the Coliseum, nervous and preparing for the possibility of fighting either a friend or foe. Cyko, Magy, and Myo had somehow got their seats around the same area they were in last time, but that was little comfort for they knew there was still much left to happen today.

For round two's first match, little Starry was the first child called, much to Cyko's ire. She was only five years old, darn it! Still, he could do nothing as the scientists once again chose a random opponent for her. It was another girl who wasn't from the mutant ward, thankfully.

The little girl seemed nervous. Her older opponent seemed guilty at what was about to happen, however, both smiled at each other moments later. Cyko guessed that Tela must have said something calming to each of them, and after that, the battle began.

It turned out Starry's opponent was a shapeshifter who could create extra metallic limbs on her body, which took the form of a battleship's cannons with power to match. Starry would fly using her own dark energy and shoot her black stars in varied and beautiful patterns while her opponent would fire her main guns at her. Due to Starry's small stature and agility, though, she ended up making it very hard for the ship girl to hit her, only being able to graze her at times. Cyko almost jumped out of his skin when one of the girl's shells struck the barrier right in front of them, but thankfully it held.

Starry ended up winning, for despite the ship girl's strength, she was rather slow, which allowed Starry to pelt her with black stars until she couldn't take it anymore. After the battle, both girls were friendly, which brought a smile to his face. The battle was destructive and hectic, but at least they were friends now. That's how it should be, they were forced to fight but not hate each other.

After the fight, some mages walked towards the arena to make quick repairs and the next combatants were called. Henry, his oldest brother, and a mutant girl were called out to the arena. The girl herself had the lower body of a snake but otherwise didn't seem inhuman or even feral like the bigger ones.

The lamia, as Magy said that is what her species is called, smiled and waved at Henry as he approached her. It seemed she was a friendly mutant which was good for everyone. They talked for a bit before the battle began, too far away for Cyko to hear.

The lamia girl proved to be quick with her snake-like movements, but Henry knew how to catch her off guard with his plant powers. His seeds exploded into many vines to capture and strangle her, but the girl revealed to have another ability on top of her mutation... Singing. After evading Henry's vines, she sang with a vibrant, beautiful voice.

Henry's movements had gotten sluggish as he felt more and more sleepy. Even as he tried to trap her into a forest of trees and vines to drown out her voice, it was useless as the effect was already successful. Too sleepy to do anything, he fell to his knees, unable to stop the lamia girl from approaching him and wrapping her snake half around his body.

The scientist announced that she had won, and while Henry's standing stayed good, the girl's own increased enough to avoid being...

discarded. Cyko could see that she was crying in relief, just like the girl from the first day. She whispered something to Henry who smiled and let himself fall asleep. She carried him back to an area with empty seats, and refused to let him go until he woke up, which Cyko and Magy found hilarious.

"The next combat will be between Subject Number 100, Reddox, and Subject Number 444, Cyko. Both subjects may proceed to the arena," that awful voice echoed around again, causing the boy to sigh in annoyance. He had been called to fight, again?

"Good luck, big bro!" Myo whispered to him with a smile as he got up.

"Yeah, dear Cyko, take care of yourself." Magy smiled briefly before she narrowed her eyes. "Scythe says he has a lot of power inside him. So much it made me unnerved the first time I met him. Please, Cyko, be careful."

Cyko nodded and forced his lips to turn upwards. He would be careful; he didn't want his family and friends to be worried about him.

As Cyko arrived to the center of the arena, he felt someone's eyes on him and instinctively knew it was Tela. *"All right, both of you are in good standing. You can fight to your heart's content, but… Once again, please, try not to hurt each other too much, and remember. We are all in this together. No matter how hard or how badly either of you loses, no hard feelings, okay?"* she said with a gentle voice, to which both nodded in agreement, before looking at each other.

"Cyko," she narrowed her eyes at him from across the arena, *"I actually had some trouble convincing him to help us. Apparently, the scientists value him and his power of magic, a unique category so he is treated well by them, despite being subject to the horrible experiments we all were, at first. Thankfully, Ellyn managed to convince him to help us. Be careful, however, if what he says is true, then he is even more powerful than me,"* Tela said in a worried voice.

"Thank you Tela, don't worry, win or lose, we are all in this together, aren't we?" he replied with a smile, hoping it would get through to her.

"It seems we will be opponents for today," Reddox said as he crossed his arms.

Cyko nodded to him in respect. "Yes, I'm sorry in advance if I hurt you too much. On that note, how is Ellyn? Is she doing better?" the blue-haired boy asked in worry, causing the redhead in front of him to smirk.

"That airhead is fine. She complained of a bruise on her stomach, but by now the mark is mostly faded. If she is called to fight later today, she should be able to give the same level of performance," he said, the serious expression on his face barely changing.

The blue-haired boy let out a sigh of relief. "Good, I'm glad she is better now." He got into a stance and let his power flow through his veins, covering him in a bluish aura.

"Again, no hard feelings," he repeated, earning a nod from the redhead who let his own power show: crimson lightning streaking across his body. Several red-covered books came out of his body.

"Yes, no hard feelings. Although, I may get you back a little for punching my... friend." Reddox let the full pressure of his power flow out of him. Cyko was sweating—Magy was right, he really did have a lot of power running through his body! Is that the power of an awakened mage?

"I wouldn't have it any other way!" Cyko chuckled as he forced more of his power to flow through him with a grin, increasing the intensity of the blue aura around his body. This was bound to be fun.

They stood there, looking at each other, waiting for an opening... And then, before Cyko could realize what had happened, he found two large beams of red energy streaking towards him at an alarming speed, launched from two of the six books flying around the redhead. Barely able to react, he dodged the beams by crouching low to the ground and rolling away after he saw another tome charge up and fire in his direction.

Noticing the deep crater it left, he cursed, although the grin didn't leave his face. He could see Reddox's lips moving quickly and before he knew it, a large pentagram appeared below him followed by a torrent of energy jumping out of it, paralyzing him in place.

Pushing his enhancement to the limit once more, Cyko used all his strength to break free of the binding Reddox had placed him under, jumping away just a moment before the large beams of red energy roasted him.

Finding his footing on the ground again, he used the same strategy he did with Ellyn, by zigzagging towards Reddox to avoid his arcane bullets. Arriving in front of him, he prepared to deliver a powerful punch, but a book appeared and shot a potent beam of red energy, which covered him entirely. Reddox exhaled as the attack ended, but noticed something weird. There was no sign of Cyko anywhere.

Appearing behind him, Cyko took advantage of his momentary distraction to send another punch against him, aimed at the back of his head, putting all of his strength behind it, in case there was a barrier, like Ellyn used. As expected, a shield appeared to stop his attack, but it shattered from the impact of his fist, only slowing him down a bit.

Reddox was surprised and had no time to react to the attack which launched him across the ground, rolling uncontrollably. Not wasting any precious seconds, the blue-haired boy rushed to follow him, intending to knock him out before he could recover. He needed to take advantage of this opportunity!

Just before he could reach him, something happened. One moment, Reddox was still rolling on the ground and the next, he was gone and Cyko found himself wrapped up inside the pages of a book. Still dazed at the suddenness of it all, he couldn't brace himself as they all exploded.

"Ghhk!" he grunted in pain, burns showing on his exposed skin and torn clothing, but he was able to dodge another large beam of crimson energy that shot past him. He found the redhead on the opposite way of where he had launched him, and he seemed no worse for wear—he even had a challenging smirk on his face, which Cyko mirrored. This guy, he was good!

Deciding to test something, he concentrated on the feeling running through his veins and once again launched himself at Reddox, who was ready this time, employing the use of a barrage of projectiles followed by giant waves of energy from his books. Cyko avoided some, but was engulfed by one of the larger waves, vanishing from Reddox's vision.

Once again appearing behind the redhead, he prepared himself to lash out, but Reddox was ready and a book appeared in front of Cyko, ready to engulf him in red energy. The blue-haired enhancer managed to avoid the attack and appear besides Reddox with his legs raised, ready to strike.

As he was about to hit the redhead, however, another strange occurrence happened. Once more, Cyko found himself far away from Reddox, with all six of his tomes around him, charging up and leaving no escape routes. The enhancer's eyes widened as they all fired against him at once, causing a large pillar of red energy to form where the attack occurred.

To Reddox's displeasure, he found himself face-to-face with Cyko, again. He had a mad grin on his face despite almost being pummeled by six books. He was clearly enjoying himself in this fight. Once more, reality changed before the enhancer, and he found himself paralyzed, wrapped up in book paper, and all of Reddox's grimoires aimed right at him.

"Overkill much?" he asked with a smirk at seeing all that Reddox had aimed at him.

The mage returned his smirk. "You are strong, I need to take this seriously," Reddox's lips mouthed out words as if he was charging up his spell books. All at once, they fired against the struggling enhancer, which also caused the paper books wrapped around him to blow up.

For good measure, Reddox created several floating pentagrams, which started to shoot dozens of projectiles both in the direction Cyko was immobilized before, and all around him in varied, hard-to-dodge patterns. Yet again, however, Cyko appeared mostly unharmed beside the redhead, a toothy grin on his face.

Just as Cyko raised a fist to strike against Reddox, he suddenly felt weak, which gave Reddox plenty of time to summon his tomes back and launch an energy wave against the enhancer which hit him head on this time.

"Ghaaah!" Cyko exclaimed in pain as the arcane energy engulfed him.

As the debris around them dissipated, Cyko was revealed, standing, his body covered in nasty burns, grunting in pain as he tried to get up. Eventually, he sighed and decided that it would not be wise to continue this fight. Reddox had gotten him this time, despite the new trick he discovered.

"You were caught in a hex, a strength draining one. I'm still learning how to use them effectively, but the one I used was good enough to slow you down enough for my last attack," Reddox explained as he approached the downed enhancer who smirked at his words.

"Hah, Magy was right, you really are powerful. And versatile too, I doubt even those mages over there can hold a candle to you," his opponent said grinning despite his loss before trying to get up to a sitting position.

"Combat concluded. Winner remains in perfect standing, loser's standing rose considerably. The next combatants will be chosen shortly," Dr. Gacha's voice hung around the Coliseum, making Cyko groan in distaste. When would these fights stop? Sure, he might enjoy it, but others certainly don't.

"You did well, Cyko, the battle was amazing! You also seem to have unlocked a new ability, congratulations, I'm so happy for you!" Tela exclaimed in his mind, sending warm and prideful feelings. She always knew how to make him feel better.

"You were strong too, Cyko. Had I not mastered a special ability, you would've likely bested me at least two times by now. Let me take care of your wounds," Reddox said with respect before pointing his hand at Cyko, who blinked as he was covered in a reddish energy. Slowly, the burns on his body disappeared.

"That's... That's amazing... You can cure wounds like these?" Cyko asked in amazement as he rose, looking at the redhead in awe, causing the boy to look away in embarrassment.

"Yes... I actually used to have cancer before awakening my powers. I was close to death. I was able to use my magic to cure myself." He looked around as he spoke as if he didn't want anyone else to hear. Cyko's eyes widened.

"Cure cancer... By yourself... H-hey, do you think you would be able to cure a disease that makes a person's muscles weak?" Cyko asked, voice trembling in hope as he contemplated the possibility.

Reddox frowned. It would be hard, but if he had enough time to study it, maybe... "Possibly, I would need to see them first," he answered in honesty as Cyko smiled so big it looked like his face couldn't stretch any further.

"C-come with me, then!" he exclaimed, grabbing the startled redhead by the wrist and dragging him towards the main stairs.

"Hey! Some warning would be nice, first!" Reddox exclaimed uncharacteristically as he was dragged off by the excited enhancer. Cyko wasted no time moving towards his seat, where Magy and Myo were watching with amusement and confusion, respectively.

"Magy! Myo! Remember Reddox? I just fought him!" Cyko offered, which made the pink-haired girl let out a giggle at his words.

"Of course, we were watching it! What a great battle, both of you!" She smiled at them with praise, almost completely covering up the hint of worry in her eyes. She had nearly jumped out of her skin several times during the past twenty minutes.

"Yeah! You two are so strong!" Myo bounced in his seat, which caused Reddox to turn towards him with a speculative glance.

Magy's smile turned upside down as she watched his reaction. "Is there something wrong with Myo?"

Reddox shook his head.

"Is this the one you wanted me to cure, Cyko?" the redhead asked out of politeness as Magy's eyes widened.

"C-cure? You can cure him?!"

"Perhaps, if I have enough time to study his disease," he answered her before turning back to Myo, whose forehead wrinkled. His eyes brightened as he realized what they had said. A cure!

"I-is that possible?" he whispered in uncertainty, looking up at the red-haired mage, who nodded his head.

"Possible, yes, but I won't lie. Depending on how serious it is, it may be difficult for my current level of skill. Let me take a quick look," Reddox offered as he raised his hand and pointed towards the smaller boy, who flinched as his body glowed with a reddish aura, "hmm... muscle degeneration, it seems. I can give you a temporary strengthening boost to mitigate the effect for now, but an actual cure will take some time to engineer." Reddox looked towards Cyko, who had tears in his eyes.

"Th-then... It's really possible?!" Cyko exclaimed.

"Indeed, like I said, it'll take some time, but I should have a formula ready in a week at most," he explained.

"M-my weakness... Can be cured? I... I..." the small child stuttered, his voice and eyes full of emotion. Magy herself looked very hopeful at his words. If he could heal Myo, then... he should be able to perform well in the experiments and reduce his chances of being discarded!

"Yes, don't worry, I'll just ask that you all work hard with making your escape plan succeed in return for my services. For now, let me give you this," the redhead said as he reached out to touch the boy's shoulder.

Myo felt a sensation of pure energy and strength enter his body, blinking in surprise. He felt much more powerful now!

"This is a strengthening charm. It'll reinforce your body for a few hours. Should come in handy if your name is picked," Reddox said with a smile before turning back to Cyko, "if that's all, I'll be returning to Ellyn's side." He bowed slightly as a show of respect, earning a nod of gratitude and a bow from Cyko, who watched as he departed.

After Reddox went away, the combats continued, with another one of his sisters, Anna, called to fight against a brown-haired boy. Her opponent had the ability to control earth, similar to the giant lion the other day, but instead of turning earth to dust, he could control it directly.

It was an interesting fight as Anna's plasma blasts were blocked again and again by thick earth walls raised by the brown-haired elemental. He tried to crush her with them several times, but her charged shots always managed to carve a way out in time. They had to hold back to not hurt each other too much, but in the end, Anna managed to pierce his defenses by using an explosive blast that knocked him out.

Matthew was the next called to fight—the last of his orphanage family members to be summoned. His opponent was a blue-haired girl who, in opposition from his own powers, could breathe arctic blasts. She first tried to freeze the entire arena with her breath, but Mat melted it immediately. After that, they clashed their powers against one another, hoping that either extreme heat or sub-zero cold would turn the match in their favor. They both ended up panting on the ground, short of breath. Their battle ended in a draw, neither of them suffered a loss of interest from the scientists, who considered their abilities incredibly useful.

"Subject Number 443, Myo, will be the first combatant of the next match," the scientist's clinical voice announced and Cyko could feel Magy stiffen.

It was his opponent that made them panic.

"Subject Number 357, Drago, will be the second combatant for this match. Both subjects may make their way to the arena," the ominous voice of the head scientist called out. Cyko, eyes wide in terror, turned to his little brother.

Myo's face was one of shock, but at the same time, the enhancer could see determination brewing behind it. Myo was called to face the strongest of the mutant ward, and from the way he was breathing, he knew... Myo would not back down, no matter how frightened he felt. Even still, the terror and despair in Cyko's heart was twisting his stomach, because as he turned to look at the enormous dragon, he could see only a predatory smile on his face.

9

Dr. Gacha watched as the two polar opposite subjects made their way towards the center of the arena. Drago, in his massive form, jumped from his seat towards the middle of the Coliseum and waited for his opponent with an impatient look in his eyes.

It would be a swift match, he decided. Unlike the other subjects in the previous battles, 443 showed no promise. His hidden ability, while useful, crippled him to a point where he would become disabled in the coming months if he kept using it. It was a good thing his little Shiro decided to go back to his office to nap at the conclusion of the last match, for he was sure that 443 would be demolished.

The entire science team—from analysts to experiment managers—was present in the security room overseeing the Coliseum at the moment. These live battles allowed them to collect precious data that they would use for future versions of Project R.N.G. Simulated combat with drones could only get them so far, and subjects they previously thought would be useless proved themselves to be valuable enough to justify the costs.

However, he doubted that Subject 443 would be able to raise his worth. Dr. Gacha was a scientist foremost, and he needed to abide by the results of the coming battle to decide whether Myo should be discarded.

Sitting at his sides were Doctors Ferdinand and Ivanovski, two of his most trusted scientists. They were both conducting an analysis of potential in real time, allowing them to measure the worth of any subject in combat at any given moment. As Dr. Gacha was looking at the screen, observing as 443 was making his way towards the arena, he didn't notice the frowns on both doctors' faces.

"Dr. Gacha. If I may, shouldn't we have someone else face 357? Subject 443 shouldn't be able to survive with the data we have gathered so far," the bearded scientist said, earning a nod from the bespectacled one.

"Indeed. 357 is too powerful, while 443 is too weak. I recommend we make another random selection," he complimented his partner, causing Dr. Gacha to close his eyes.

"Should we just discard him then?" Dr. Gacha asked. Subject 443 had no use to them, in fact, if they could study his body and recreate his ability without the drawbacks, he would be a far better advantage to them.

"Excuse me sir, but I would like to object to discarding 443," another scientist, who was working on the post-combat analysis spoke up, causing the three scientists sitting at the main screen to turn to him.

"Is that so? May you share your reasoning?" the head scientist questioned. He noticed that Dr. Ferdinand and Dr. Ivanovski nodded their heads in agreement with the other scientist.

"Maybe there is still some value we can extract from him?" yet another scientist who had been working on the slow-motion camera for details, said, making the head scientist blink.

"Yes? If there is, may I know what?" Dr. Gacha asked, exasperated. His science team should know by now that he doesn't take suggestions without well-developed reasoning first.

Another scientist rose from his workstation. "Perhaps we can find a way to cure his disease and counter the negative effect his ability poses on his body?" he suggested.

"At this point, we would need to make an autopsy to avert that particular effect for the future," Dr. Gacha spoke, his frown deepening. What was making his team defend a worthless subject? More scientists rose from their seats and spoke against the discarding of 443 with random ideas and guesses. It was nothing like how a professional and respected science team should behave.

"Uh, sir, what's going on?" one of the few scientists who *wasn't* defending the boy spoke up. Dr. Gacha noticed that only certain members of his science team were not speaking up and seemed confused by the reasoning of the other advocates.

"Sir, maybe we could just let the rat go?" a *security guard* spoke up, causing the head scientist to snap his head towards him. Something was wrong, he knew it, but he could not figure it out. Were they compromised? Was someone from the outside using a sort of mental interference against them?

He could understand their reasoning though. Subject 443 was *mostly* useless to their project, but if they were willing to spend some extra time on research, they would surely find a way to use his unique abilities of degeneration.

"Very well, I accept your reasoning, call off the-" Dr. Gacha's eyes widened as he felt a hand on his shoulder. It was one of the magical researchers, whose face was grim.

"Sir! We are under mental interference! I'm ordering the mages to place this room under a lockdown!" the man said before turning back to a group of assistants who now had staffs in their hands, "Activate mental blockades, now!" The researchers nodded their heads and started their chants.

Watching the room regain their bearings as the mental interference subsided, the head scientist frowned. Someone had tried to interfere with the combat experiments. He would find out who it was and how they did it, but for now, the team must return to work. He turned back towards the main screen, noticing that 443 had arrived to the arena and was looking up at Drago as the screen turned black and the lockdown commenced. This room would be isolated until he could be certain they were safe from a mental attack. It would be a pity, but there were cameras that would record the combat for future analysis. Regardless of what would happen now, the combat would continue.

10

"*No, dang it!*" Tela yelled into Myo's mind as he made it to the point of no return—the entrance to the arena. Myo was scared stiff, but Tela reassured him and told the young child to walk as slowly as possible towards the arena and she would try to make them cancel or change the match.

"They did something... I can't reach the minds of the scientists I had tagged anymore! I'm sorry, little Myo... Please, just hang in there as much as you can!" Tela said in desperation. He nodded, looking to the ground.

"So, they are going to make me fight a kid? A weak-looking child with barely any meat on his bones?!" the giant dragon scoffed as he glared down at Myo, who had arrived at the arena. Myo trembled under his gazed.

"At the very least... I'll get to rid our future army of a pathetic, unworthy weakling like you!" the dragon roared as he uncrossed his arms, standing tall to intimidate the boy.

He was enormous, powerful, and scary. More than anything else, Myo wanted to be back in his mom's arms, where she would tell him everything would be all right and—

"PAY ATTENTION, FOOL!" the beast yelled as he stepped in front of Myo, casting a dark shadow on him. Before Myo could react, the mutant delivered a powerful kick against him, embedding his body into the far wall.

"G-GHA!" Myo screamed in agonized pain as he spasmed from his muscles cramping. No, no, not now!

"If you can't even fight, I'll just end your pathetic life here!" Drago snarled as smoke emitted from his mouth. Myo opened his eyes in pain, looking up at the dragon about to roast him alive.

However, as he prepared to launch his attack, he suddenly turned to the side and sent a wave of flames that way instead.

"Myo, quickly! Me and the other mind users are trying to cloud his perception! Get out of the wall!" he heard Tela's voice scream in his head. He was a burden, wasn't he?

Groaning, he activated his power and used it on the walls surrounding him, weakening them enough to get out of the wall. Falling to the ground in pain, he blinked as he noticed something. His muscles stopped cramping! This was probably thanks to the treatment he had received from Reddox earlier!

Looking up at the giant dragon who seemed confused at what had just happened, Myo lifted up his hand and pointed at his head before freezing. No, he wouldn't, he shouldn't! He focused his palms on the dragon's legs.

The dragon snapped from his confusion as he felt a stinging sensation on his legs as if his muscles were slowly burning. Snarling, he turned his head in search of the culprit and located Myo, whose body was enveloped in a sickly brown aura.

"I don't know what you're doing, weakling, but it's not working!" he yelled as he pointed to the boy, causing a bolt of electricity to shoot towards him.

"Gaaaah!" Myo yelled as he was struck by the bolt, triggering his already weak muscles to spasm and cramp once again. Drago walked forward with a snarl on his demonic face.

"I don't know what just happened, but it won't work again. The attack I used against you is one of my weakest, yet, for you to be reduced to such a state, it's pathetic!" he said in disgust as he raised his arm to squash Myo, but something weird happened.

To the dragon, it felt like the boy was in one position and suddenly in another, which he corrected accordingly and crushed the weakling underneath his fists. In reality, he missed Myo by several meters, though the impact was enough to send him rolling.

Forcing himself to get up, Myo cowered in fear. He knew Drago was barely trying, he was just playing around with him! But he didn't want to die!

I... I need to weaken his muscles... No, not the muscles, the bones, I need to make them brittle! he thought to himself as he focused on the legs of the giant creature. Instead of trying to weaken his musculature, he focused on degenerating his bones.

Drago growled and groaned in pain as he felt a sting in his legs, but this time, it felt deeper, even more painful. His bones, he could feel them eroding away!

"Stop running away and accept your fate, weakling!" the dragon yelled as he turned towards Myo, who had a look of terror in his eyes as the giant beast walked towards him, seemingly unbothered by his disintegrating bones.

"No... No, no, no! Stay away from me!" Myo forced his frail power to work harder, increasing the pain in Drago's legs, which only made him angrier. Snarling, the dragon swiped at the little boy, ignoring the confusion he felt for a moment and clasped his hands around Myo's thin neck.

"YOU JERK!" a voice yelled from the seats, making the dragon turn his head to see a blue-haired child bashing against the barrier, a blue aura covering his body, "STOP! YOU ALREADY WON! LET MYO GO!"

"Oh? So, there are people who care for you, huh, you little ant?" Drago whispered, lessening the pressure around Myo, who breathed relief before the beast started to squeeze him again, strangling him.

"CURSE YOU!" Cyko yelled, forcing his power to deliver stronger attacks against the barrier, but it still held.

One of the mages turned back from the fight to look at Cyko with a sly grin.

"This barrier is made to withstand such attacks, you know. Your pleas are falling on deaf ears," she said as Cyko's rage increased, knowing he was powerless.

A scythe blade flashed across the mage's face and caused her to pale in fright and look back to Cyko's partner.

"This barrier can't block Scythe! I won't let him continue to hurt Myo!" Magy hacked against the barrier, making deep gashes that were repaired as soon as she could leave a new one.

"Muahaha!" Another mage who turned back to look at them, laughed with crazed eyes. "This barrier is made to keep people in… AND OUT! And before you think of doing so, the arena entrance is also sealed!" he spoke as if this was pure entertainment, not children getting hurt.

Out of nowhere, black stars rained upon the barrier, followed by concentrated plasma shots, giant vines slapping against it, twin streams of white-hot fire, a powerful blast of concrete-breaking water, and finally an earthquake localized at the base of the barrier that made it hard for the mages to stand.

"Myo is part of our family, too! We won't let him get hurt!" Anna yelled from her seat, firing plasma shots against the mages, whose faces started to look panicked.

"I'll help Myo!" Starry yelled as she increased the number of falling stars against the barrier, followed by stronger attacks from all eight of the orphanage siblings.

"Reddox, help out too! We can't let him hurt Myo!" Ellyn yelled from her own seat, using her wind bow to send shots. The redhead nodded and out emerged all six of his grimoires to start raining arcane spells against them.

"Everyone... Thank you so much!" Cyko thought to Tela, who broadcasted his thought.

"Ha! HAHAHAHAHA!" Drago laughed maniacally at the number of people trying to help. "So many powerful fighters, all trying to save a weakling! Pathetic! ONLY THE STRONGEST WILL SURVIVE!" he yelled in glee as he brought his arms up, ready to use all his strength to throw and crush Myo.

"No... No... I... I don't want to die here! Mom... Daddy... Cyko... M-Magy... Please help!" Myo screamed in his head, body filled with agony by the beast's grip, but just as he was about to be thrown on the ground... Drago's grip went slack, letting him fall to the floor, which, while painful, he survived.

"GRAAAAAAHHHH!" Drago yelled in pain as a skull-splitting headache sprung in his vision, filled with excruciating, negative emotions from all those present in the Coliseum.

"CURSE YOU! DON'T INTERFERE WITH MY JUDGEMENT!" the dragon yelled, putting both of his hands against his head.

Myo, who had crawled away, took notice of what was happening. Drago, yelling in pain while clenching his head, big brother Cyko, big sis Magy, and several others using their powers against the barrier... Why... Why would they go so far, for someone as useless as him?

"Myo... Don't give up! We are all in this together, remember? We won't abandon you! I promise!" Tela whispered to only him, filling him with warm feelings to combat his self-loathing. Why... Why was she being so nice? Tela started to help, encouraging as many children as she could to start helping out and using her own telekinetic powers to put enormous pressure on the barrier. Soon, cracks started appearing, causing the mages to put more power into it.

"AUGH!" Drago shouted as the pain in his head and his anger increased, "ALL MUTANTS! RUN INTERFERENCE AGAINST THE NORMALS! NOW!"

Many of the beastly mutants who were watching the commotion with eager eyes howled and roared in bloodthirsty anticipation, ready to feast on the blood of their leader's enemies before launching themselves at the other children.

The entire Coliseum was in chaos—the non-mutants fought against the mutants, while many others, human and mutant, were scared and tried not to get hurt in the brawl. This was, however, to the relief of the mages that needed to maintain the barrier, as fewer attacks were focused on them.

"*No*... NO!" Cyko and Magy yelled simultaneously as they were pulled away from the barrier by the giant lion mutant Tela fought on the first day. He attacked them with both his stone weapons and projectiles, giving them no choice but to fight back.

Drago, upon seeing the chaos, laughed as the pain in his head lowered to a manageable level. "HAHAHAHA! NO ONE! NO ONE DEFIES ME!" He turned to a shell-shocked Myo, who was looking at commotion with wide, terrified eyes.

"See, weakling? All of this caused because of a pathetic, weak child like you! Now, not only you will have to die today... BUT SO WILL ALL YOUR LOVED ONES!" Drago mocked as he took a step towards the paralyzed Myo.

For the first time in his life Myo felt rage... Rage at the scientists who put them here, rage at the guards who tormented them every day, rage at the fight his friends and surrogate family were in, risking their lives to try to help him... Rage at this giant dragon for being one of the main people responsible!

The murky brown aura that had been covering him shifted into a clear, golden tan glow with several markings appearing all over his body. He looked at the approaching dragon with a new sparkle in his eyes and pointed at his leg, willing it to disintegrate.

Drago, who was about to laugh at another feeble attempt to harm him, widened his eyes in shock as he felt the bones in his leg suddenly turn to dust.

"GRAAAAAHHH!" Drago roared as he fell to one knee. Impossible! How could this brat, who was so weak just a few moments before...

"I WON'T LET YOU HURT MY FAMILY!" Myo yelled in opposition as he ignored his own pain and pointed at Drago's other leg, forcing the bones inside to disintegrate, causing Drago to scream in agony as he fell over, his legs unable to support him.

"FOOL! DON'T THINK YOU'VE WON!" Drago shouted as electricity ran across his body and before Myo could react, launched a stream of lightning at him. Myo's entire body spasmed, but he refused to scream. Using all of his strength, Myo pointed his shaking palm at the arm Drago was using to send the lightning stream at him, and willed the bones to degenerate into dust.

The dragon bellowed as his arm fell uselessly to his side, stopping the electricity from flowing towards Myo who grunted and gasped, but refused to go down before his opponent, who glared at him.

The downside of his powers was that his own muscles degenerated the more he used them. The stronger he willed something to disintegrate, the stronger the backlash would be. Already, he could barely feel his legs, but he would not go down!

Screaming in defiance, Myo willed the bones on the giant dragon's only remaining arm to disappear into dust. The dragon fell to the ground completely. The young boy smiled at last. He had done it... He had defeated the strongest mutant!

Meanwhile, Cyko and Magy had just finished off the lion mutant who collapsed to the floor like a puppet with its strings cut. They were about to return to their previous work of destroying the barrier when suddenly, their bracelets activated, trapping them in tendrils of energy. The enhancer felt his body grow heavy, he could feel the tendrils sucking his energy away and paralyzing him. He struggled with all of his might. He would not leave Myo alone at a moment like this!

Then, with his tired eyes, he saw that Myo was doing well against the dragon, bringing him down with his willpower alone. Eyes widened in shock, he could only think that Myo, his little brother, had really come a long way. From a scared, traumatized boy to the hero he was now, Cyko couldn't be prouder. Yet, he felt nauseous, as if something, anything, could happen to Myo if Cyko couldn't break free from his bindings to save him.

Cyko's eyes widened as he saw the dragon raise himself from the ground, launching himself at Myo.

"MYO! WATCH OUT!" both he and Magy shouted at him.

"*MYO! BE CAREFUL!*" Tela's voice suddenly invaded his mind, making him turn his head towards Drago too late, as an enormous fist made contact with his frail body, sending him flying.

"To be pushed so far by an insect like you... So humiliating!" Drago grunted in hatred, glaring at Myo, who was pulling himself from the crater he landed in, "if you wanted to defeat me, you should have aimed at my head or my heart! I am a DRAGON! A disintegrated bone is just a trivial wound for me!" The giant dragon was using a single leg to support himself, the arm he used to punch Myo bent at an odd angle.

"Gah!" Myo coughed into his hand, grimacing as he tried to stand up. Looking at his hand, he saw blood. His insides felt like paste and he couldn't feel his legs anymore. His arms were intact, but even then, the backlash had degenerated them to a point where it was hard to move them without feeling horrible cramps, but he tried to persevere through it.

The dragon was approaching, painstakingly using his regenerating limbs with hate evident in his eyes. Myo let out a small laugh. It seems... he really was too weak. If he had been willing to kill Drago, to use his powers fatally... he knew what would happen. He would die. He would never see the outside world again, he would never be able to laugh at big brother Cyko's jokes, he would never be able to receive big sis Magy's affections, he would never again be able to talk to Tela... But if he couldn't stop Drago now, that's exactly what would happen.

"*No, no! Myo, get up, please, get up!*" Tela yelled in distress, trying her best to cause interference against Drago as she resisted the strength draining tendrils. He withstood her mental attack, but she kept trying.

"*Myo, please! Get up! Fight back!*" she begged in desperation, tears running down her face as she looked at the battle with hopeless eyes.

"*Tela... Please, tell Cyko and Magy that I love them... I love you... and everyone else...*" he thought to her with sincerity, letting his feelings of love and gratitude flow, even as he glared down at the dragon approaching him.

"*Yes... Yes, but you can come tell us that yourself!*" she tried again.

"*I'm sorry...*" was the only thing he could tell her as he focused his power deep within him. The only thing he could do was degenerate things and make them frailer. If he so wished, he probably had enough strength left to degenerate either Drago's heart or brain... but at the cost of his own life. He had already pushed himself too far. Any more and he would die.

But... as he glared at the dragon who had arrived in front of him, he knew he had to do something, even if it would be fatal to himself. Raising both fists in the air, he spoke out.

"We'll be free! No matter what! WE'LL ALL ESCAPE THIS PLACE!" he yelled with a resolve he had never felt before in his life. His eyes shone gold with power as he yelled out in determination.

"YOU'LL NEVER ESCAPE! ACCEPT YOUR FATE, WEAKLING!" the leader of mutants roared as plumes of smoke escaped his mouth before letting out a white-hot stream of fire against Myo, whose entire body was engulfed and enveloped by the dragon's fire of hate.

Yet... even as he felt his body burning, his senses slowly leaving him, his vision turning black, he kept reaching out, willing his power to reach as far as it could, with as much strength as his dying body could allow. Even as his body burned in the fire, even as it gradually turned into cinders... Myo never gave up, reaching forward... Until the end.

Drago's stream of fire stopped, revealing the only thing left...

A small stain of black ashes.

Myo was nowhere to be found.

The dragon stood to his full height, tall and proud before letting out a mighty roar of victory.

But for those watching, this was anything but. The only thing they could do was stare in horror and despair as the dragon mocked his opponent.

A scream from the seats echoed around the entire Coliseum. "MYYYYYOOOOOOOOOO!!!!"

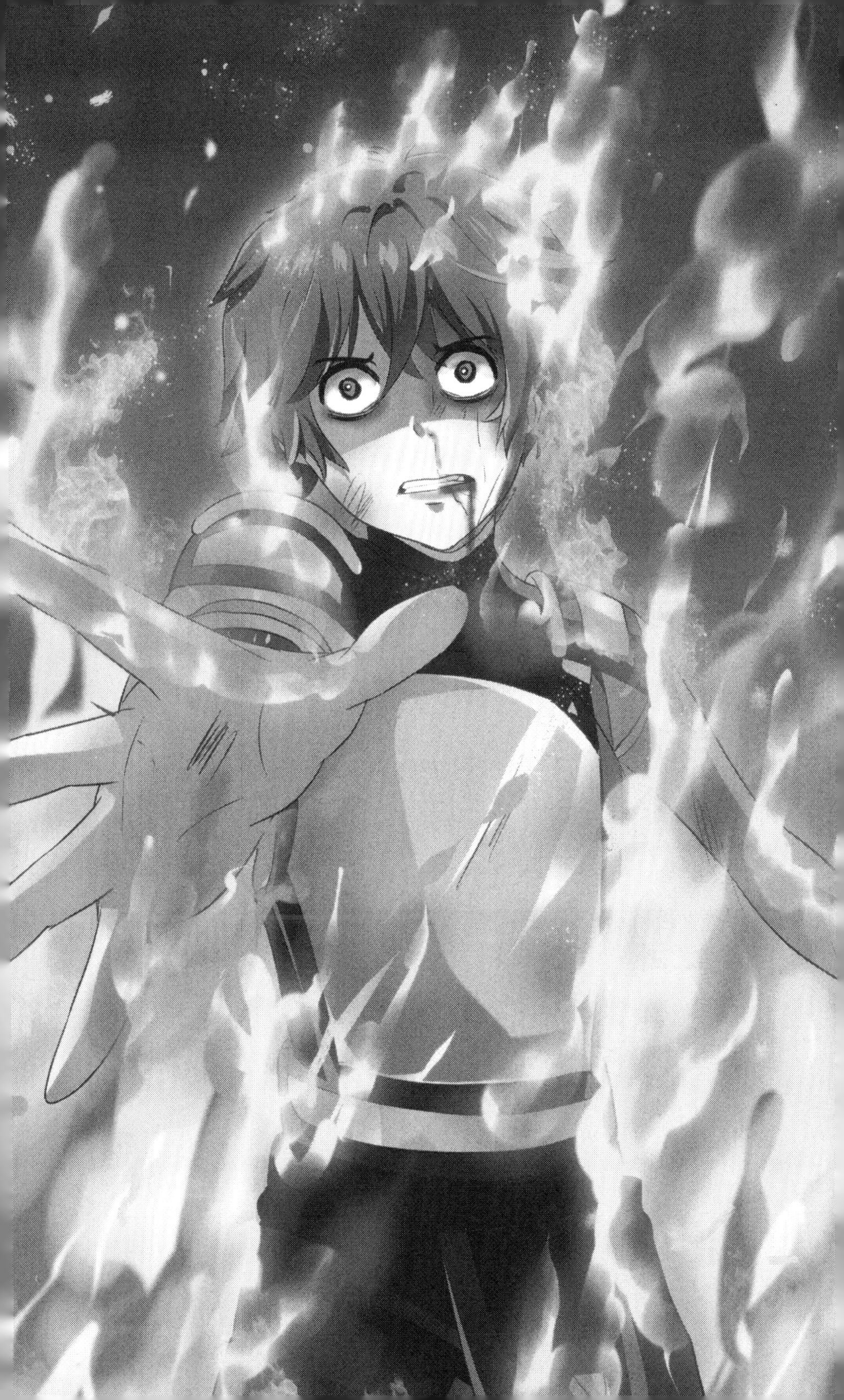

CHAPTER 4

AWAKENING

1

There were several emergency protocols created during the long initial phase of Project R.N.G. to protect research data and essential staff in situations of crisis, like the one happening now. Here, all rooms, corridors and laboratories in the facility can be sealed off, both physically and magically, to help protect against a non-physical invasion, whether it be magical or mental.

However, one disadvantage of such methods is that it cuts them off from the outside world. Soon the room was enveloped in darkness, lasting all of one second before the emergency lights, which depended on their power sources, kicked in and a faint, red glow illuminated the area.

In cases where such a thing was to be evoked, both the third-floor security ward and all guards near the affected room would be notified of the emergency and instructed to prepare countermeasures, tighten security, scan for possible leaks and, if possible, counter them to restore normal levels of order. Dr. Gacha was sure that, at this moment, a large team of guards and mages was outside the door, scanning for any traces of the mental attack that was cast on them.

Looking around the dimly lit room, the head scientist saw the status of his staff. Many seemed visibly unnerved that they were caught in such a way, including Dr. Ferdinand and Dr. Ivanovski, who were stiffly conversing with other mages to find out what they had felt during the mental control. Dr. Gacha couldn't blame them for feeling this way, they were brilliant scientists and there were few things people like them valued over their own minds and intelligence. To know someone had tampered with them in such a way as to act completely out of logic and reason was unnerving.

Making a mental note to have both himself and all affected staff in the room checked for any traces of further mental corruption, he turned to look at the guards and the magical researchers. Some guards were also exhibiting anxiousness, visible even through their full body power suits, thanks to their constant twitching. The mages, however, had a look of professionalism, typical of those who were trained to act in such situations, as expected of elite researchers in their field of specialization. While the guards were professional in their own right, they had no way to defend themselves against mental attacks, so that job fell to the mages. Dr. Gacha made another note to assign at least one mage to all critical areas.

Soon after, the mages were walking around, searching every nook and cranny with their diagnostic spells to define the nature of the invasion, and determining if any effect of mental control remained. This was good. They needed to lift the seal as soon as possible to counteract more disorder from happening, but he could tell it would still take a while.

Deciding to hasten the process as much as he could, he walked towards the magical researcher who had freed him from the mental hold. The man, who had been directing the other mages, noticed him and nodded respectfully at his boss.

"Sir! All personnel under mental control have been freed and at the moment, we are securing the area to make sure no remnants of mental interference remain. Results are promising. The room should be unsealed within ten minutes," the man said in a professional tone, gesturing towards the researchers walking around, glowing staffs in hand.

"Excellent work Dr. Myers," Dr. Gacha praised, his mouth curving upwards ever so slightly to show his approval. "There is much to be done, both now and when the seal is lifted. Can you tell me what you know about the mental attack?" the head scientist inquired, earning a nod from the mage who after a brief look around the surveillance room, turned back towards his boss.

"At first, nothing was wrong. Activity in the surveillance room during the matches was proceeding as normal, even when Dr. Ferdinand and Dr. Ivanovski objected to allowing the latest match to proceed, we didn't suspect foul play until we noticed more and more scientists were speaking up to stop the match," Dr. Myers replied, gesturing to the scientists who were still discussing the situation amongst themselves. "Mental interference was confirmed both when a guard, of all people, objected to the match and when we ourselves felt our mental shields being attacked. I acted immediately and after making a quick report about the situation, I initiated the emergency seal."

As expected of the team he personally assembled, the man could adequately react to a situation that fell within his jurisdiction. Dr. Myers' expertise lies in magical research, specifically the research of the mind and magical powers related to it. Normally, he stays in the soft labs conducting research on the numerous samples provided by the experiments on subjects with mind-related abilities, but he made an exception to watch the live combats, wanting to witness the powers he researches.

"Do you have any suspects in mind?" Dr. Gacha asked the man, who shook his head in denial.

"At the moment, we have none. All subjects that have recorded mental abilities lack either the range or control to pull off something like this, or they have shown no ability of mental control," the mage said before gesturing once again to the rest who were scanning the room.

"We still don't know how the attack got past the usual protections for this kind of situation. The magical wards show no signs of being tampered with," the researcher continued, earning a nod from Dr. Gacha. "Normally, such attempts would leave a trail but... So far, no traces of the attack have been found. We suspect this is because of the hidden genes' unique properties—if the attack came from a subject." Dr. Gacha's face slipped into the slightest of frowns.

He already knew powers gained through hidden genes would be different, but to leave no trace of its uses... A chilling, but exciting thought. If they could find out who was responsible for the attack and... correct them, they would gain an enormous advantage in the spying field, for he knew even a Creator would have a hard time finding someone powerful enough to leave no trace.

Now, however, it was an inconvenience, one they would be better off without.

"Dr. Myers, starting tomorrow, all scientists will be required to undergo a medical examination to determine if they have been compromised physically or otherwise. I will need you to assemble a team of members with medical knowledge for this. I will send any further details and schedules to your personal workstation," Dr. Gacha said, making sure to emphasis the importance of this. What happened here cannot happen ever again.

"Understood sir. This may affect research speed, but we will make sure the impact is minimal," Dr. Myers answered with a nod before turning to a mage walking towards them.

"We finished scanning the perimeter. While no evidence of the attack is left, we have determined that the area is secure from any remaining mental control," the man said.

"Stay on standby and be on the lookout for any more possible attacks," Dr. Myers said, earning a nod from the mage who walked away to inform the others. He turned towards Dr. Gacha, who was waiting for more information. "It seems the area is clear, sir. We can now lift the seal and move on to further the investigation."

"Waste no more time," the head scientist declared as he moved back to the center surveillance console. While the isolation cut off all power and any incoming signals, it would be foolish to have no way to remove the seal from the inside and as such, small terminals were located in key areas of every room and corridor, of which every higher-up scientist and mercenary were made aware of. Said terminals were made specifically to deactivate the isolation field, both physically and magically, as it was connected with the magical wards.

Crouching and reaching under the main console, the scientist felt around the floor for a small hole in the ground wide enough to fit four fingers and deep enough for a good grip. Finding it, he pulled, causing the tile to slide towards him, revealing a glowing, holographic screen. It worked in a manner similar to the emergency lights where its battery charged as long as the room was connected but would activate once a full seal was confirmed. It had enough power to last for a full week, but in case of a power loss, there was an additional manual lever just under it.

The screen showed information regarding the room—temperature, oxygen levels, battery duration, structural integrity—mostly useless information that becomes useful in a crisis. In the middle was a glowing green button the size of his palm. Tapping it, the screen changed to a confirmation message, and after pressing again, a 'please wait' request appeared.

After putting the tile back in place, Dr. Gacha stepped back to wait, watching how the equipment went back online as the seal was lifted. The staff who had been quietly discussing the situation amongst themselves went back to their previous positions. Dr. Ferdinand and Dr. Ivanovski joined him at the console.

"We apologize for our behavior, sir," the bespectacled scientist said as he sat down and worked on bringing the system back online.

"Yes, we should have expected something like this would happen sooner or later," the bearded scientist said, mirroring his colleagues moves.

"It's no fault of your own. Even I was affected by the mental attack, which is why we should work as quickly as possible to find out how our defenses were breached," the head scientist said as he typed on his console, "the surveillance cameras will be back online in a few seconds. I suspect the last match already ended, therefore, we will conclude today's battles and proceed immediately to investigations." He moved his head towards the screens as the live feed from the Coliseum went back online. His eyes widened.

"W-What?!" The two scientists beside him exclaimed at what appeared on their screen, many others around the room jumped at what they were seeing. Chaos, it was pure and complete chaos.

From the large screen in the surveillance room, a bird's-eye view of the Coliseum emerged, and everything was in disarray. Besides the current match, which was still ongoing despite their expectations, all the subjects present were engaged in a massive battle royale which, Dr. Gacha quickly noticed after his initial shock, seemed to be the mutants against the other subjects.

"What's going on?! Why has no security guard stepped in?!" Dr. Ferdinand asked in confusion, watching the battle proceed.

"... That's because no security guard stayed inside both the gymnasium and the Coliseum. The only mercenaries present are the mages holding their barriers," Dr. Ivanovski replied with a frown, realizing the mistake made during planning.

"The mages need to stay still to maintain that high-level barrier, and this room is the only one with access to surveillance of the Coliseum. We were careless; we never expected an attack," Dr. Gacha explained, his face back into a mask of cold focus. Examining the fight, he noticed how some subjects, two in particular, were desperately trying to attack the barrier where Drago was playing with his opponent.

"Activate the bracelets of all subjects in the Coliseum except for the two in the middle of their match. We need to put an end to this rebellion now!" Dr. Gacha ordered, forcing his staff to snap out of their shock and work on his orders. Soon enough, all subjects, human and mutant, were covered in the restrictive tendrils, except for the two supposed to be engaged in combat.

"Order the ward guards to move in and subdue any subjects still struggling. After the match is finished, everyone will return to their dorms," he ordered, keeping his eyes firmly on the screen. Normally, he would restrain everyone and cancel the combat in case of a crisis such as this, but whoever tried to control them wanted to save that useless subject currently in battle. If he could make them desperate enough to tip their hand, they may discover who is responsible.

For the moment, however, as the doors to the Coliseum opened and guards poured in, it was time to wait until the suspect made their next move.

?.

The battle was over just like that. Despite his best efforts, despite everyone banding together to save him... Myo was still defeated. No, much, much worse than that. He was dead, reduced to ashes in the fiery storm of Drago's wrath. Cyko's scream of despair snapped the children back to reality and hopelessness set in.

Reddox stared weakly at his friend as he tried to resist the restraints. Ellyn's body was shaking with sobs as she whispered to the boy who used to be. She didn't know him well, but she felt the loss. Guilt settled inside Reddox's cold heart; he could have done more, he should have done more. He was the strongest subject according to the scientists—he should have been able to save a simple life, like he saved himself so long ago.

His own guilt was nothing next to the sadness that those who knew him well were feeling.

Close to him was a group of siblings, who had also tried their best to help their new brother... but it was not enough. A little pink-haired girl was on her knees, wailing as another child, a redhead, was crawling towards her to provide comfort, even as his own tears streamed down his cheeks.

Their older siblings felt torn, their tearful gazes alternating between their siblings and the arena where their new family member had met a tragic end. Despite their improvements, despite their teamwork, they couldn't save Myo... They failed him as his new family and as older siblings. They could do nothing but watch as the great dragon continued to laugh and proclaim that all who were weak would perish, just like Myo did.

Even those who had never personally met Myo were feeling the tragedy of what happened as they all tried to help the little boy. They had joined in bombarding against the barrier, remembering Tela's words about how they all should work together to escape, many even trying to fight against the mutants who were sent to run interference, but it was not enough.

In particular, a small group of children was feeling guilty for not being able to save Myo. His previous roommates, who had never treated the little boy well, were crying at his death, knowing now they'd never be able to make amends for their horrible treatment, and feeling they should have helped him and stuck close rather than driving him away. The shame of what they did and did not do... would stay with them for the rest of their lives.

And then there were those who had lived with Myo, who talked to him and gave both comfort and encouragement in his darkest hours. Magy and Cyko stood on their knees next to the barrier, the former crying her eyes out and holding her twin scythes in a death grip as she struggled against the binds, yelling Myo's name out to all who could hear. Magy admitted to loving pain, but the kind she was feeling right now was far from pleasant, the hurt she wanted to avoid the most.

Cyko, however, was the opposite of the pink-haired girl. After shouting Myo's name, he shut down, staring, his eyes cloudy and unfocused, towards the arena. Tears rolled down his cheeks, his emotions feeling like a hollow pit of hopelessness as his thousand-yard stare bore down on the blackened remains of his little brother.

To make matters worse, the barrier mages, who had already deactivated their obstruction, were mocking the two children, laughing and taunting them about how useless their efforts were, how painful it must have been for Myo to die the way he did, and about how they made it worse by giving the boy hope. Even as they panted from keeping the barrier against the earlier onslaught, they were exhaling an aura of superiority, basking in the two's sadness.

And Tela... Tela could feel it all. The emotions coursing through the crowd, both hers and the others, were very strong. She usually takes measures to not be overwhelmed by the feelings of sadness and despair of the other children she interacts with, but... this time, she let it course through her body.

A long time ago, she took upon the mantle of a leader and a source of hope for the children present in this prison. Her powers were suited for the role and ever since she awakened them over two years ago, she had been planning the best way to break them free and stop this accursed project, training and honing her powers in secret. As far as the scientists knew, she had some ability of telepathy, but it was restricted by eyesight since it was a mere secondary ability to her main one: telekinesis.

It was difficult. She hardly managed to catch a glimpse at other subjects during that time, but the few she did... She had to work hard at trying to convince them to join her, and now they were the people who helped her the most. When the socialization was announced, she jumped at the chance of being able to talk with everyone at once, to know who was who, to unite everyone under a single banner, and to save themselves.

She had been overwhelmed at first, feeling all their hopelessness at once, but she persevered and let her emotions propagate to them, doing her best to convince them that there was hope for them, that as long as they could work together, everyone could leave and be free. And it had been working. Over several meetings she created loyalty, both to her and to each other as they worked together, everyone using their abilities in any way they could to help. She already had a map of the two floors she could access and had several plans in the making.

But she had failed, in the most terrible of ways. She had failed to save Myo, the cute little boy who had looked up at her with such admiration. Even with her heart hurting through the pain of others, the knowledge of failing the boy who talked to her nearly every day since they met, whom she comforted whenever he had a nightmare was…

"Myo… Little Myo… I'm so sorry… I'm so sorry…" She wept, her eyes focused on the cold, harsh floor. She felt all the emotions and suffering the poor boy felt during the battle, how scared and terrified he was at first, how confused and hopeful he got when they tried to help him in the fight, how angry he was when Drago ordered the mutant ward to harass them… his despair at knowing he would die, and the determination mixed with agony and desire to live during his last moments. She could feel his soul moving on and leaving his body as he died. A single instance of utter incomprehension, a mixture of regret, peacefulness, relief, warmth… and then nothing. Her connection with him was lost forever… Myo was now truly free, in the most tragic way possible, and it was all her fault.

To make matters worse, she had acted out of desperation in her attempt to save Myo. She had tried to implant the feelings of aversion to letting him fight Drago into the scientists she had tagged in her time here, but the speaker didn't cancel the match so she got desperate. She tried to do something she never had before: using her mind tendrils to snare whoever was in charge and force them to stop the battle. But, she never tagged him, so she was forced to involve any other minds she could feel at random, which is what caused the room to be sealed off for security, severing her tendrils and whatever control of the situation she had.

The staff would be more vigilant now, especially with those who had mental powers. Their future escape would be much harder than before. It was all her fault. Because of her, Myo was dead, and there was nothing she could do, except cry her heart out and endure the stabbing feeling that hundreds of despairing children, two in particular, were piercing her soul with.

She didn't deserve to be a leader.

3

Emptiness. That was the word Cyko would've used to describe his current state of mind if he had enough awareness to do so. He had tried everything. It wasn't enough. Myo was dead, slaughtered by a giant monster.

He wasn't thinking anything; he wasn't feeling anything aside from the wetness on his cheeks. The only thing Cyko knew was the blackened stain that was left where Myo used to be, the image burning itself in his mind, not allowing him to even notice the stinging of his unblinking eyes.

And then images appeared in his mind's eye, overriding all his senses, all his thoughts and even despite that, the image of Myo's remains overlapped anything that appeared, anything he felt.

Cyko slipped into his own memories...

The door suddenly opened, revealing the same large guard who was looking straight at him. "Listen up, rat, your days as a loner are over. From now on, you'll have another rat to keep you company. Go inside, now!" The guard shoved another person inside the room, a scrawny-looking boy, who seemed terrified of the big guard.

The boy looked at him with wide, frightened eyes and nearly jumped out of his skin when the door slammed shut behind him. He stood there for a while, staring at the ground while trembling, unable to bring himself to meet Cyko's eyes.

The black ashes shone in the Coliseum's bright lights, staining the memory of their first meeting. Myo had looked so fragile, so desperate for a kind face... Cyko couldn't help but want to take in the poor boy, to guide him, protect him...

"It's all right, it's all right..." he began to softly tell the boy as he started to quietly sob. Snow had woken up and was now rubbing herself against him, seemingly in an attempt to comfort the younger boy. "The situation we got ourselves in is terrible, we all are suffering through the same emotions, just because those evil scientists want to make us into super soldiers or something. But there is still hope, Myo, don't give up," he said, removing his hand from the younger boy's head and putting it around his shoulder, pulling him closer to a one-armed hug.

"Myo... Is that the name of your new roommate?" she asked him gently, to which Cyko nodded, before remembering that Tela couldn't see him.

"Y-yes, I kind of became a surrogate brother for him... He is just six years old..."

"Please, be brave, for him. We still need to meet each other again so we can all discuss the start of our plan. I know it's hard, and I wish I was able to do more for you, for him, for everyone..."

He was brave, he made sure to be. No matter the situation, he tried to show Myo that he could always count on him. Thanks to him, Myo didn't give up hope, he had been getting stronger...

"Your poor brother was a mess when I arrived here. He was crying hard and didn't even see me until I comforted him," the pink-haired girl, Magy, said to him in a gentle voice, indicating to Myo, who was sleeping in her lap while her hands patted his head.

"I asked to be transferred to your dorm," she said with a small smile, earning a surprised look from Cyko, "I like you two, and Scythe told me that a lot of important events will happen around you and I want to be there when it happens."

When they met Magy, the poor girl likely never thought for a second that one of the important events would be this... She had fallen for Myo at first glance, treating him like a little brother, constantly doting on him, and protecting him when he had nightmares; she had been a perfect big sister for Myo.

"Don't give up, even if it hurts, even if it makes you cry, don't lose hope! We'll get out of this prison, together, and find our place in the world, some place where we won't have to go through this kind of hell again. You can leave everything to us, little Myo, we'll bring that hope to you."

He had loved Tela instantly, her charisma and comforting aura made it seem like everything would be all right. He knew his little brother talked to her nearly every day, and he knew Tela loved him just as much... But in the end, they all failed Myo. They were supposed to protect him, to give him hope of a normal life, but... they couldn't.

"Snow... S-Snow... She... She..."

"Magy, don't hurt papa! He did nothing wrong!" Snow shouted.

Blackened stains covered the face of the cat-girl in his memories, making the once pristine white turn into a charcoal black. The small kitten he had met and taken in, who had comforted Myo numerous times, turned out to be a traitor... He remembered how much Myo was hurt when that happened, how much they all hurt by her defense of the monster who put them all here.

And because the man she defended wanted power so badly, because he made them fight against each other... Myo... He—

Dark blotches clouded his vision, a kaleidoscope of memories filled his senses. Everything turned into a single whirlwind of black ashes as the world disappeared around him.

In a world of chaos, everything was turning dark, stained by the remnants of his dead brother, a black memory that threatened to consume him. Unable to even blink, the ashes covered him, drowning his soul in a sea of despair.

Myo

Myo

Myo

Myo

Myo

Myo

Myo

MYO.

IS.

DEAD.

4

He was sinking, that was the first thing Cyko noticed when he opened his eyes, the second being how dark this place was. Darkness as far as the eye could see, never ending, inviting him to join its depths. He could feel the ice-cold water in his bones as he couldn't help but shiver.

For a moment, he thought he would drown, but he realized that he could somehow breathe just fine. He tried to wiggle his arms and propel his body upwards, but he couldn't tell up from down in this dark abyss. Frowning, Cyko gave up and accepted that he would stay here for a while.

How did he end up here, anyway? The boy couldn't recall any moment in his life that would have brought him to this, the last thing he could remember before waking up here was...

With a shocked start, his eyes widened as he looked around in desperation. Nothing, he couldn't recall anything! The only thing in his mind was his name, Cyko, but other than that... Nothing. A void where the memories of his life should have been.

His frown deepening as he tried not to panic, Cyko focused hard in his mind to remember something, *anything*, about his life, but he realized that the more he tried to remember, the more his head hurt and, to make matters worse, the smell of burnt flesh invaded his senses, allowing him to think of nothing but the sickly aroma.

"Gah!" he shouted in pain as he grabbed his head, feeling tears forming in his eyes. He looked around, but he still couldn't see anything, nor could he recall where he was. The burnt smell was getting stronger by the second and it was making him even more anxious.

Unwilling to stay any longer, he swam in a random direction, attempting to go in the opposite direction he felt he was sinking into. Trying his best to ignore the lack of light surrounding him or the confusing lack of direction, he swam with all his might for what seemed like minutes and eventually, hours.

"What... Where am I?" Cyko whispered as he stopped, swimming around himself to see something, anything. He had swum for what seemed like several hours, but there wasn't a single change in his surroundings. The smell of burnt flesh seemed to be following him, getting stronger by the second.

"*I need... I need to remember... Why am I here? What happened before I ended up in this strange ocean? Did I die, and this is Hell? Why can't I remember anything about my life?*" he mused to himself with a frown, trying to see if he could find any logic at all. "*Maybe... Maybe I should try to swim towards where I felt I was sinking?*" he considered, before shaking his head. His priority was to remember his life and what happened before he was brought here.

Bracing himself, Cyko closed his eyes and concentrated. He closed off all unnecessary thoughts, trying to ignore the coldness and the sinking feeling, concentrating only on his memories. Soon enough, the pain he felt earlier came back, but he squeezed his eyes tighter, trying to break through it.

With the horrid smell growing almost unbearable, the image of a black stain on the ground, *burnt ashes*, he realized, appeared in his mind's eye. A second after he saw it, he felt an unbearable pain in his heart, an ache so great that it drove him to tears. Why did seeing that image hurt so much?

And then, something changed. The surrounding water pushed him forcibly as the previously non-existent current made itself known. Unable to resist, he was carried away by the strong tides, the smell of burnt flesh overwhelming his senses for a moment.

Struggling, he tried to withstand the current, waving his arms and legs as much as he could, but it was useless, no matter what he did, he couldn't fight it. Thankfully, he could still breathe.

Somehow, he knew he was on the right path, remembering that the black stain on the ground made this happen. He should try to conjure it again, even if it brought unbearable agony to his heart... He needed to know why this made his heart ache so much, just by looking at it.

Focusing his mind on that image, he faced the pain that was blocking his memories. More, he needed to know more, to know about his life, about the pain that made him cry and made him happy...

The smell of burnt flesh disappeared and the violent current ceased as the answer came to him, making his eyes widen in horror. His body fell to the ground that wasn't there before, the pain registering in him as his memories returned. He knew exactly what that black stain represented, and where it had come from...

Myo...

He almost wished that he could go back to oblivion, but... he knew he couldn't, nor should he. Myo was dead because he had failed to save him and that was something he couldn't run away from... That pain, that anguish, was something he deserved to suffer from. His little brother, his sweet little brother, was no longer alive...

What could he do now? He had it thrown in his face that he was pathetic, unable to pierce the barrier those mages created and because of his weakness, that tragedy occurred. He couldn't even guess what Magy must be feeling. No, he knew she was blaming herself as much as he was.

Useless. It was always useless to fight, to resist. That giant dragon proved that only the strongest, the ones with the most will and desire to fight and to become strong, would thrive in their environment and survive to the end. Those that were too inadequate would perish... just like Myo did, because he was feeble and unwilling to hurt anyone, even the monster who killed him. Myo had many opportunities to kill Drago, if he had just aimed at his head, but... his little brother was a sweet soul, he could never bring himself to resort to that, even against a monster like the mutant leader. His compassion, his pure soul cost him his life.

Someone so sweet, so innocent... shouldn't have to suffer like he did. He shouldn't have been forced to fight for his life, knowing he would die anyway... He shouldn't have been forced to make a kill-or-be-killed decision... It angered him that he had to lose another family member that way.

"B-but what can I do? Myo is... Myo is... AAAAAAAHHHHHHH!" he bellowed out, no longer able to hold his grief any longer.

Already on his knees, he shifted to a fetal position as his cheeks became wet with tears. "Myo... I'm sorry... I'm so sorry! Myo... Myo... MYO!" he yelled again. It felt like the world around him was growing darker by the second, filled with the feelings of loss and anger.

Then, he felt a hand touch his shoulder, jerking himself up, he looked at the person who had touched him. Crouched in front of Cyko was a pale face with cyan-colored hair and equally blue eyes, dressed in the rags they used to wear. A mirror image of Cyko was looking at him through tears of his own, but there was a fire in his eyes that Cyko lacked.

"It'll be all right," the mirror Cyko reassured, looking into the real Cyko's shell-shocked eyes. The figure put his other arm on the real Cyko's shoulder, clenching it tightly, but he was not in pain. "We can't... We cannot bring Myo back. But we can avenge him. Make those responsible for his death pay... IN THE MOST PAINFUL WAY POSSIBLE!" the mirror Cyko yelled with pure loathing, his tearful eyes glowing.

Cyko was mesmerized. Who was that person? Why did he look exactly like him?

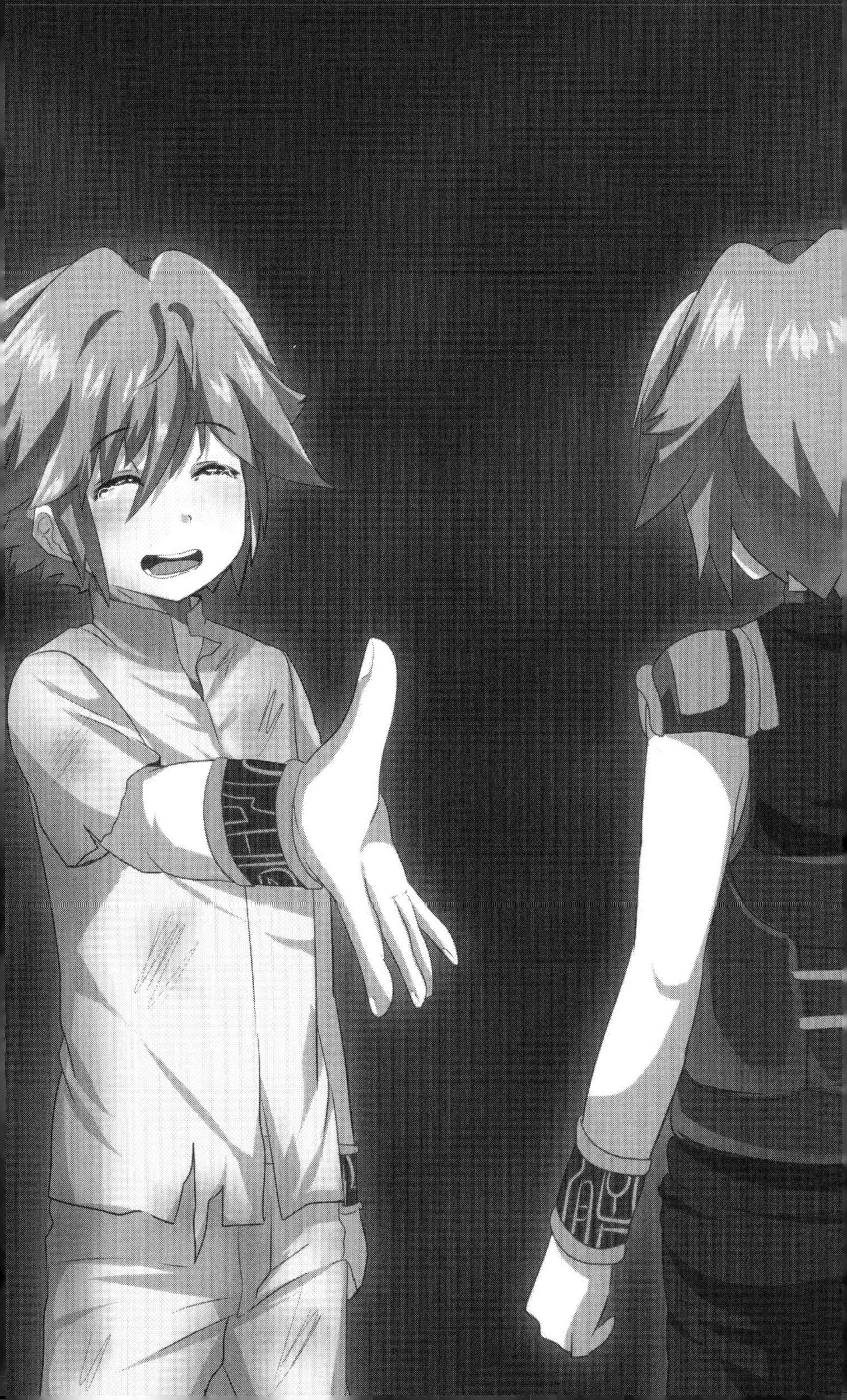

"W-who are you…?" the boy asked in confusion, causing the mirror's angry visage to shift into a gentle smile.

"My name is Cyko, just as you are. I am a representation of the path you are being forced to walk. For simplicity, just call me that, Path." The mirror image used his sleeves to clean the tears away.

Standing up, Path offered him a hand, which Cyko accepted. Helping him to his feet, his mirror image stood there smiling, as if waiting for a response.

"What do you mean, a representation?" Cyko asked, tears flowing from both of them once again.

Path smiled sadly, pointing at himself. "We always knew we would change because of the evil place we are stuck in. Even more, I am a representation of your powers, Cyko," he answered, causing Cyko's expression to morph into one of contemplation.

"The power we unlocked when those geniuses shocked us is unique, much different from the powers of, say, Torch, who is also labeled as an enhancer. You may not have realized it, but our abilities don't just allow us to become physically stronger but accomplish many other feats that are normally impossible. You realized it during our battles against Ellyn and Reddox, right?" Path explained, earning a nod from Cyko, who seemed pensive.

"If our powers are so unique… why couldn't we have saved Myo? He didn't deserve to die!" Cyko exclaimed in anguish, causing Path's anger to magnify.

"You are right, he didn't! Myo was just a sweet little boy who wanted to live, to be happy! And that chance… was taken away from him!" Path yelled in a rage, tears threatening to fall from his eyes, but he evened his breath.

"Yes, we weren't strong enough then. Chances are, if everyone wasn't working together, then even if we commit to this, it still wouldn't be enough, but… But…" the mirror Cyko exclaimed with snarled teeth, a mix of rage and sadness visible in his eyes. "We can avenge him! We can make sure that this doesn't happen again to another child! All we have to do IS KILL THEM ALL!" Path's face burned red, his teeth clenched, and his eyes were full of fury, shocking Cyko, but somehow, he did not mind it that much.

"But… it doesn't change the fact that we are weak, and Myo died because of it!" Cyko said with a sob, voice cracking from the weight of his emotions. "What hope do we have?! Even Tela and Magy would be disappointed in us!" he yelled, feeling the proverbial knife in his heart twist further with each passing moment.

"Then we CHANGE!" Path yelled, grabbing both of Cyko's arms, making the original boy's head snap up towards him. "If we are weak now… Then we change! Become stronger and merciless! They want us to be perfect killers? THEN WE GIVE IT TO THEM!" his mirror image declared in a vicious, yet desperate voice. Path sighed and took several steps backwards.

"If we… If we change… what will happen to us? Will we be able to help Tela? Protect Magy? Protect our family?" Cyko asked in desperation, looking at his mirror image, who was gazing at the ground. Path looked back at him, his eyes narrowing.

"Do you remember that feeling? That rush of bloodthirstiness we feel whenever we use our powers? The joy whenever we defeated one of those robots, or even Ellyn? The rush of adrenaline and how *good* it feels?" Path asked suddenly, causing Cyko to blink in surprise before he remembered.

Yes, whenever he activated his enhancing powers, he always felt a rush of pleasant feelings, the desire to crush his enemies, to bathe in their blood. Heck, ever since he activated his powers, he often caught himself daydreaming of slaughtering the guards and scientists of this cursed prison, sometimes imagining a glorious and bloody battle. What did this mean?

"You remember, then. I'll be honest, if we commit to this path, if we become one… We'll no longer be the same person we used to be. We'll no longer be you, but we'll also not be me," Path explained, his voice lowering as Cyko's eyes widened.

They would turn into something else? But… "How would that make us different from… from *him*?" Cyko wondered, unwilling to say the mutant leader's name, it would madden them both.

"The difference would be that we would know who to protect, and we would be stronger from it!" Path said, before sighing, "I am the representation of your powers. I am your desire to fight and to kill the people you hate, which is why I get angry so easily. You are the original

Cyko—cheerful, friendly, protective... caring. Our personalities will mix and from that... Something else will be born," the mirror image explained.

"Then... who—*what* will we become? How will it feel? Will we still have our memories?" Cyko questioned, wary of the possibilities that could go wrong.

Path took a deep breath before replying. "For all intents and purposes... It's a deal with the devil. But ever since we ended up here, we were doomed to change one way or another. It will be a gradual thing, but from the start we will notice the differences, everyone who knew us will, but that can't be helped. If you want to know what will happen to us... just say our names together," Path replied with a grave voice, causing Cyko's eyes to narrow.

"Our names together? Cyko and Cyko...? No... Cyko and Path... Cyko... Path... Cykopath..." His eyes widened as he realized it.

"Psychopath..." he whispered under his breath, earning a nod from his mirror image that made his knees feel weak. It was funny, how their names combined perfectly for the definition, a pun on the word for a ruthless and maniacal serial killer...

"It may be some cosmic joke that our name, when joined with the path we will walk into, compares us to a deranged psycho who kills only for pleasure," Path said, before shaking his head and looking at him with a serious expression.

"No, we still will be ourselves, to an extent. A psychopath doesn't feel emotions, but I'm sure we still will! Our bloodthirstiness will increase a hundredfold as will our love for bloodshed. Whatever may happen, the new us will be responsible for the person we will become," he said with an affirmative nod.

"Still... it is such a big change... Will we ... be able to be friends with the others? Won't we turn on Magy? On Tela? On our siblings?" Cyko asked fearfully, afraid that if he took this deal, he may end up hurting his loved ones even more than their prison stay ever did.

Path shook his head, sending relief through Cyko's veins. "No! We will be doing this to protect them, to save them! To avenge the fallen! We may no longer be the person they used to know... But we won't hurt them, no matter what!" the mirror Cyko exclaimed with certainty, causing the real Cyko to let out a breath he didn't know he was holding in.

"But in the end... The choice is yours, as you are the original Cyko. Do you want us to turn into another being, to gain the power to avenge Myo and protect our loved ones at the cost of our sanity? At the cost of our very being? Or do you wish to remain yourself until the end, staying the person you are now... At the price of not getting any stronger and possibly failing to save our friends and family once again? Which will it be?" Path asked, his eyes searching Cyko's.

Cyko sighed and took a deep breath. The darkness around him began to change, turning into a greyish void that seemed infinite, swirling around like smoke. He felt like he was in an abyss, a zone where, once a single step was taken forward, there would be no turning back. A great weight pressed itself on his shoulders. This was it, he had arrived at the point of no return, and he had to decide.

Letting his tears of sadness fall for a few more seconds, he inhaled and used his arms to wipe off his face. Was he willing to throw himself away? To give up the chance at a normal life... so he could help others have a chance at one. Possibly turning himself into a monster... just so he could fight the actual monsters.

Fight fire with fire, an eye for an eye. He already lost so much of his family and just now, he lost Myo because he was too weak... Those monsters were responsible for this, for putting them up against each other!

Even Snow... She defended the mastermind, thought of him as a father even after knowing how much they suffered every single day.

He felt the wrath burn within him. He already knew his choice. Those scientists wanted a monster, a super soldier who could wreck entire armies by himself? Then they would get it. Oh, would they get it.

As for the traitorous cat, he would deal with her when the time comes, but she would *pay* for taking the side of those *monsters*. He will make sure that *anyone* who sided with the scientists paid for their crimes, for every single child whose life was lost, whose chance for happiness was stripped away! He will kill them all... and enjoy it!

By now, the world around him had turned into a brighter gray, with a glimmer of light blue coursing through it like veins of some sort.

Stepping closer to his mirror image, who opened his eyes when he sensed his approach, Cyko opened his mouth.

"I've made my decision," he said in a determined voice, heart heavy but eyes gleaming and free of tears.

Path nodded. He could feel the certainty coming from his reflection, Cyko's entire soul could, too.

"Then... what have you chosen? What will become of us?" the mirror image asked as a confirmation of his resolve, despite the world around him already telling him of Cyko's choice. The original took a breath as if to steel himself, but let his emotions run free.

"We will become Cykopath. We will be strong enough to avenge Myo, to avenge all fallen children! We will become strong to slaughter all the ones responsible for this torture! We will become the monster... SO NO ONE ELSE WILL HAVE TO!" Cyko yelled, his voice making the world around him shake at the weight of his choice, causing his mirror image to smile and nod.

"Then, it's decided. We will become the angels of death upon the real monsters," Path said as he extended a hand, which Cyko clasped firmly, not looking away from his eyes.

"Let this moment be burned in our souls as the point where we chose who we wanted to be, rather than let it be chosen for us. We are one, we are Cykopath," Cyko's mirror image said with a smile, to which Cyko returned the vicious, predatory grin.

The world shifted once again, in a much more drastic manner than before. The cyan-colored veins running through the grey smoke got brighter and bigger. Soon enough, he was squinting against the strong light, but it wasn't uncomfortable... In fact, it felt like he was being born again from the ashes of his despair. He could feel hope, anger, and anticipation.

"Yes..." Cyko said, just as the light was engulfing both him and his mirror image. "Even if this choice was forced upon us... We will walk this path—we will change so we can create change! We are Cykopath!" He smirked and then both boys' forms were engulfed in a brilliant, aqua-colored glow.

The shining world, no longer resembling grim despair, shifted, a maelstrom of energy consuming everything. Any life present in such an environment would be destroyed... before being born anew in a great explosion of pure, cyan energy.

5

Magy had stopped struggling, instead submitting herself to feeling powerless. His death had hurt more intensely than any experiment, than any torture those jerks had ever inflicted upon her, and it was far from the pain she loved. No... she hated feeling like her heart was stabbed, like she would die from sadness alone.

Scythe had been trying to console her, but even her trusted companion was feeling the anguish. Her friend had been emitting melancholy ever since the dragon had ordered the other mutants to interfere with their efforts to help Myo... It only increased when he died.

It was not fair... He was so innocent... He was like a brother to her, someone she would fight tooth and nail to protect, and she did, but... It wasn't enough. And Cyko... Poor Cyko... Even amongst her own internal turmoil, she could see how much he was hurting. Her dear friend had been rooted on the spot ever since he screamed Myo's name, looking forward with an unblinking stare as tears flooded down his face. He looked so... so broken. Magy wanted to do something, *anything* to snap him out of it... But with her own suffering, and the restraints, she couldn't do anything.

"Cyko..." Magy managed to whisper before feeling another wave of despair hit her.

"Myo..." she murmured between sobs, doing her best to ignore the jeering of the mages, whose laughter intensified as she cried.

"Stop your weeping, rat!" Magy heard someone bellow from behind her, before something whacked her on the back of her head. She fell to the ground. Sniffling, she looked up at the perpetrator, and stared at the glaring visage of a guard.

"The robed guys over there told me you are responsible for this mess! I hope you are ready for a beating, fool!" As she rose, Magy noted that the whole Coliseum was brimming with security guards, stomping around, beating children up and yelling at them. The mutants, however, were being treated with caution rather than outright abuse. It was a nightmarish scene and Magy could do nothing to stop it.

"I DIDN'T SAY YOU COULD GET UP!" the guard yelled before kicking the pink-haired girl in the ribs with his armored boots.

She let out a strangled gasp as the sudden pain hit her.

"You'll stay down until I'm done with you!" he shouted at her before kicking her in the leg this time.

"Gah!" She let out a loud cry, making the guard even angrier so he kicked her again. Pain, physical pain… This was something Magy could deal with, but in her current state, even that couldn't take the suffering from her heart away.

"Urgh…" she moaned as the guard grabbed her by the hair and brought her up to his eye level.

"Trash like you doesn't deserve to live! You all should sit like the lab rats you are and just stay in line!" the guard yelled, punching her in the stomach. The girl gasped as the air in her lungs was forced out. After watching her for a second, he grunted and threw her in Cyko's direction, landing near him. Coughing, she looked up as the guard approached.

"This rat is also responsible for this mess, is he not?!" the guard questioned, making Magy's eyes widen.

He wouldn't… He is going to hurt Cyko! And unlike her, he is in no position to take the pain! He can't even brace for it!

"N-no! Don't hurt him, I was the one who started it!" she begged in desperation until the guard stopped and turned towards her.

"Hah! She is lying!" one mage said with a sneer.

"That blue haired brat? He is the one who sparked everything by attacking the barrier! Thanks to him, it was a lot of work to keep things from spiraling even further!" he seethed. Magy had to say something quick to save Cyko…

"Oh, is that so?" The guard raised his eyebrows, approaching Cyko and lifting his armored fist. Magy's eyes widened again. She had to act before—

"NO!" she screamed just as the guard landed a hard punch.

"CYKO!" She yelled, straining herself to move closer to him, but the guard grabbed her by the hair.

"I don't like being lied to, rat," he said between gritted teeth before crouching down and driving her head into the ground.

"YOU'LL LEARN TO RESPECT YOUR BETTERS!" he yelled before raising her head again and striking her against the ground.

"DON'T LIE AND DON'T YOU EVER MAKE A MESS OF THIS PLACE AGAIN!" The guard bellowed, slamming her head against the ground at each word, causing a small crater to form before lifting her head and using his other hand to grab her by the throat.

The blows hurt Magy's face, but only a few bloody bruises were present. A plus from having awakened her powers, but that didn't lessen the pain she was feeling in the slightest. She would have normally loved it and even mocked the guard to make him continue, but the emotional turmoil of losing Myo and from seeing Cyko hurt made the pain less pleasing and more agonizing. She let out tears of agony for what was happening to her, and to everyone else, too.

"You lab rats sure are stubborn little roaches. I'll have fun with you, girl, before making you witness me beat your little boyfriend up like a punching bag!" he mocked before standing up and causing her to hang from his hand by her throat, making it hard for her to breathe. The guard brought his free hand back into a fist and tightened his grip on her neck, making her choke and struggle in his grip. She closed her eyes, not wanting to see his fist meet her face repeatedly. She had to endure. If he got tired from beating her up, then maybe Cyko would… would be safe from him.

"L-let…" a voice spoke up from under them and Magy's eyes widened. The guard looked down to see Cyko's glowing eyes glaring up at him with contempt.

"Let her go, you jerk!" the enhancer demanded, somehow causing the guard to feel intimidated, however, it only made him snort.

"Oh yeah? What if I do this?" the guard teased before tightening his grip on Magy's neck, watching with a grin as she gasped as the oxygen was cut from her.

"Yeah… I thought this would be the case. I made the right choice then…" Cyko's voice got louder, which the guard and the mages ignored in favor of mocking and laughing at them. However, the moment Cyko's eyes raised to meet the guard's, the man froze as a massive wave of hate enveloped the room. He slackened his grip on Magy and she fell to the ground and coughed, gasping as she tried to regain her lost breath.

Turning his face to look at the child, he met his eyes. They were wide open, glowing stronger than they ever had before. His face, an expression he had never seen before in his fifteen years of mercenary work, was an expression of murderous intent so strong he could almost feel it.

"I'll kill you all," Cyko said before a large sphere of blue energy engulfed him. There was a loud snapping sound and, as if he had never been there, the sphere of cyan energy disappeared.

Suddenly, standing tall and strong on his feet was Cyko, but he looked different from before. Body glowing with cyan-colored energy, his presence made the guard nearest to him cower in fright. More terrifyingly, he was free from the restraints and their broken remains were scattered on the ground, vanishing from lack of magical energy.

His hair, which was never quite tame, was tousled as if he had just escaped a tornado, but that was not the biggest change...

No, the biggest change was in his face, where an expression of psychotic and murderous intent could be seen beneath two wide, glowing lines that went up and down on his cheeks. Small bolts of lightning flashed across his body as he surveyed the surrounding scene, his shining eyes scanning the room like he was looking for victims.

Then his hands went to his sides as if grasping for something. Lightning appeared on his palms and in a flash, two weapons materialized in his hands. They were shaped like arrows but with every part, aside from the handle, made of blue light.

Twin holo swords.

He looked at the guard who had been hurting Magy and was now pointing his gun at Cyko with his whole body trembling.

Cyko grinned.

"S-STAY AWAY YOU RAT!" the guard yelled. Those eggheads had assured them that in case of emergencies, the blasted bracelets would act as handcuffs and restrain them! How did this happen?! How did that brat get free?! Even the giant, bulky mutants couldn't do that! Someone yelled from his right, making him look up to notice two other mercenaries had joined him, weapons aimed at the glowing enhancer.

"R-Right!" The guard rose to stay in formation with the rest of his team, aiming his large weapon at where the brat was... well, used to be. Where did he go?!

In the seconds he took to notice this, he heard two thuds on both sides. He shifted towards his left, eyes widening underneath his helmet. He whipped around to see the same scene on his other side.

Death.

Both soldiers who had arrived to back him up were dead, gushing blood through their armor! How?! Those things were designed to take a lot of punishment!

"Hey, maybe you should pay more attention to your surroundings," a voice said from behind him, causing him to jump and turn towards the source, before he felt a terrible pain in his stomach.

Looking down, he saw the large blade the boy was wielding before he disappeared again. It had passed right through him, and it was covered in blood. He tried to turn towards the boy, to say something, but both the pain and the pressure he was exerting was too much. The boy chuckled maniacally at his feeble attempts to free himself.

"Looks like those idiot mages are trying to set up their barrier again. Pity, I wanted to play with you more for hurting Magy, but I guess it can't be helped… Instead… I'll give you the privilege of bleeding out on the ground!" Cyko gave a sly grin before kicking the guard off his blade and sending the man tumbling to the floor, where he twisted and gasped in agony at his wound, trying to stop the bleeding.

Turning towards the mages, he could see many pale faces trying to erect the barrier they use for the battles. Even with his newfound strength, Cyko knew he wouldn't do much against that by himself, and so… he decided to kill them before they had time to cast their first spell.

Taking a step forward, the enhancer vanished from sight, surprising those who had been looking at him. The mages continued chanting the spell required for the arena barrier, which would keep them safe from the killer's attacks long enough for reinforcements to arrive. But because they were only looking at the direction he used to be, they didn't notice Cyko appearing behind the farthest mage on the opposite side of the Coliseum. They only noticed something was wrong when that person gasped in pain and fell to the ground in a loud thud.

Before they could even scream, the mages who were closest to him got cut down just as fast, their bodies falling to the ground like puppets with their strings snipped. By now, most of the mages were aware of the sneak attacks and stopped chanting for their barrier, knowing it wouldn't work without their full numbers. Instead, they focused their magical energies on both defensive and offensive spells. After all, they are elite mages of one of the most prestigious mercenary groups in the world!

Magical projectiles of all elements streaked across the arena, racing towards the last known position of the enhancer who had just finished off another mage and had looked up just in time to see a particularly large fireball approaching his face. The explosion of energy engulfed the area in a large cloud of smoke. As the mages were about to breathe a sigh of relief, several of their numbers let out death hails as they fell down, their hastily erected magical defenses not even slowing down Cyko's blades, who had appeared behind them.

"Hey now, I can't just let you guys interfere," Cyko scoffed, giving off a bloodthirsty grin as the mages all turned towards him with fear in their eyes. "I have business with big, green and ugly down there… And you guys are in the way, just like you were when I tried to save Myo," Cyko said pointing a finger towards the leader of the mutants, who had long since stopped gloating and was now watching Cyko's every move.

"J-Just because you got some of us, doesn't mean you can take us all! We are elite mages!" a robed female threatened in a fearful rage, using her staff to create a large magical circle in front of her, to which Cyko raised an eyebrow. With a shout of desperation, she activated her spell, causing a beam of light to soar across the Coliseum towards the enhancer, whose smirk still hadn't left his face.

The spell hit with full force, causing a huge, spiraling dome of light to form as the energies of the beam expanded in all directions, vanishing after a few seconds to reveal a massive crater in the place her spell hit. The mage who had cast it was left panting, her magical energies almost depleted.

"Hey now," a voice she wished to never hear again spoke in her ear, causing her and many of her colleagues to turn around in terror.

The boy pursed his lips in annoyance. "That was dangerous. You put the kids behind me in danger. Thankfully, I managed to save them all just in time. Can't say the same about the guards, however." Cyko's eyes twinkled for a moment before he vanished.

"Oh, and just so you know," the enhancer said, his voice back in the female mage's ear, "just like with Myo... No one can save you," he whispered before she felt a piercing pain in her lower back.

Leaving the woman to bleed out, he giggled and threw himself towards the other mages. It was a one-sided slaughter. The mages' elite status meant nothing when they were drained from a long day of barrier maintenance, proving to be their ultimate weakness. Weaving around them in a dance, Cyko dodged their desperate attempts to put him down. The mercenaries had long since given up casting non-lethal spells and instead tried to hit him with everything their exhausted bodies had. One tried to end him with powerful orbs of dark energy, but Cyko tricked it into killing a dozen of his colleagues instead before finishing him off by surprise. Another tried to slow him down with weakening hexes but found himself dead before he could even properly finish his spell.

In the end, only three mages, huddled together in horror, remained from the large group that had maintained the barrier, the corpses of their colleagues staining the ground of the Coliseum in blood. The pained moans of those still barely alive hung in the air, diminishing by the second as they took their final breaths. Amidst this show of blood stood a child, covered in crimson, beaming like it was Christmas morning.

"S-STAY AWAY, YOU MONSTER!" the mage in the center shrieked. His hood had fallen down, revealing a grey-haired man in his forties. "O-ONE MORE STEP AND WE WILL KILL YOU!" the man yelled in fright, trembling alongside the other two who were holding their staffs in a feeble attempt to appear intimidating.

Cyko smiled mockingly at them. "Oh? You and what army? Oh wait, I think I already took care of them," he said with a smirk, enjoying the fear he could feel from the man and his two remaining friends. He stepped towards them, watching with satisfaction as they took a step back for each one he took forward, the terror in their eyes increasing by the second.

"S-STAY AWAY!" The grey-haired mage tried again, bringing his staff up to protect himself. Cyko's smile widened, making him look even frightening to the trio.

"AAAAHHHHHH!" The middle mage, finally having snapped, made a desperate move, using all that was left of his magical energy to snare his two surviving colleagues in imprisoning magical sigils.

"H-HEY! WHAT THE—" one of the mages cried while the other tried to free himself. Cyko raised an eyebrow at the grey-haired man's actions, curious how he would get out of this alive.

"I WILL NOT DIE HERE!" the man sobbed as he covered himself in blood-red energy, causing the two paralyzed mages to spasm in pain as their forms also turned into pure crimson energy.

With a shout, the man willed the energy to move towards him. In the place where the two mages had been snared, only skeletal remains were visible.

Cyko blinked in surprise, what did that fool do?

"Converting organic life into pure vital energy, a spell that was outlawed a long, long time ago in this world… But, with this, I CAN KILL YOU!" the man's wild, deranged voice shrieked as he willed a dome of red energy to surround him. He fired off blast after blast of intense magic at the enhancer who dodged his attacks with a grin on his face.

"DIE! DIE! DIE DIE DIE! AHHH!" the man yelled with increasing desperation, raising the frequency and potency of his spells. When he felt an experimental attack on his barrier coming from behind him, he snapped again and fired off in all directions with projectiles and beams of magical energy, causing Cyko to let out an annoyed growl as he saw himself having to save many children who were in the way of the mad mage's attacks. Nevertheless, Cyko took satisfaction in seeing the guards, who were busily getting into position to shoot him, run for their lives and still get incinerated for their troubles.

The Coliseum was chaos. With the guards deciding to leave to get reinforcements and children yelling and crying in fear of being hit, there was no time to think. Cyko made sure that not a single child got hurt, even if he had to block the attacks himself, which, he noted, were not that strong. Soon enough, the man's spells were less intense, eventually stopping altogether. Finally! Now he could finish off that bumbling idiot and move on to the real business.

Approaching the man who had fallen on his knees in exhaustion, he could see that the mage was sweating profusely and seemed much thinner than a minute ago.

"Oh, is that all? I almost believed you would actually cause me trouble," Cyko mocked.

"N-no... Nonono! Please... don't kill me! Have mercy!" he said between gasps of air, struggling to stand. The mage cursed at his own idiocy. He had wasted too much energy in his desperation!

"Hmm... Let me think about... Nah, I want to kill all of you. For Myo." He shrugged before raising his arm up high as the man's whimpers increased until he was outright wailing... Then, he was silenced as the sound of a blade cutting through his flesh echoed around the Coliseum. All mages who had formed the barrier and stopped them from saving Myo, along with several guards, were dead.

"Now..." Cyko said as he surveyed the arena, looking right into the eyes of the dragon leader who had been silent until now, glaring at him, "it's time to avenge my little brother." The enhancer's face conveyed his hatred louder than his voice did.

As for those who had witnessed Cyko fighting, their reactions were many and varied. Some were afraid at how easily he killed those people; others were surprised at his newfound strength. His siblings from the orphanage had been watching him with both awe and sadness. Their brother had finally snapped, and they could only hope he remained the same person he used to be.

Magy was looking at the carnage Cyko had caused. On one hand, she was happy that her dear friend could avenge their little brother, bringing justice to him, but... Scythe told Magy that Cyko's soul changed, that he was no longer the same person he used to be—in exchange for his increased power. She only hoped that her friend would be all right.

Tela, however, stared at Cyko with heaviness in her heart. Even as weakened as she was by the restraints, she could still feel what he was feeling... His desire to kill was much stronger than before, a change in his soul that signified the complete loss of his innocence. He would never have a normal life ever again... and it was all her fault. Tears of regret slipped down her face as she thought of what he was forced to do, and what he was forced to become, and she promised herself she would support him and help everyone so such a thing would never happen again!

Still, she couldn't help feel that the mages and guards that died in his rampage deserved it. Others may call her sweet and friendly but even she can feel hate even if it hurt her heart. She could see that Cyko was moving to confront the mutant leader and if he could take him out, then everything would be easier. She only hoped that her friend would be fine, that he wouldn't suffer the same fate as Myo... He deserved to live, just as much as all the children trapped in this prison did.

6

In front of Cyko stood the mutant leader, Drago, in all his glory, looking no worse for wear despite the punishment Myo managed to inflict upon him. The dragon had been watching Cyko intently since he broke free of his restraints, not saying anything even as he killed those around him—just glaring with his serpentine eyes.

"So now you stand in front of me," the dragon drawled out his words, "do you see now? The power you have gained? How easy it was to crush those considered strong by the outside world? This is the power they are granting us! Power to overcome even the strongest!" Drago yelled with pride, baring his teeth.

"That... 'friend' of yours was nothing more than an ant compared to our strength! Unworthy of the privilege of being part of our glorious army! In this world, only the strongest thrive, by trampling over the weak! Swear loyalty to me, and the world will know our might!" Drago thundered, his deep voice heard all across the Coliseum.

Cyko, whose hair had been covering his face, looked up at the dragon, eyes full of emotion. For a moment, the reptile thought the boy would accept his offer, becoming the first non-mutant to join him, but alas... Cyko started to laugh.

In shock at being chastised for his offer of power, the dragon stood dumbfounded as he watched the blue-haired boy catch his breath.

"Hahaha... Through the eyes of madness, I see..." Cyko said in a voice just loud enough for Drago to hear, looking at him with a full-blown mocking grin. "You are nothing but a *cheap villain of a cliché children's cartoon!*" he declared, causing Drago's eyes to widen in shock.

"Oh yes, the big dumb dragon that believes he is a hotshot. What? Did you hear those lines you keep spouting over and over and *over* in some sort of cartoon, thought they were cool and felt like it would be a good idea to repeat them?" Cyko mocked, relishing in the look of indignation on the mutant leader. "Let me guess, you used to either be a bully or be bullied and now that you have power, you feel like the strongest thing in the world? What now, big guy? Want me to hand over my lunch money?" the enhancer continued, pleased at how Drago seemed to be losing his cool.

"INSIGNIFICANT CHILD! YOU DARE MOCK ME?! I AM THE STRONGEST OF THE MUTANTS!" Drago bellowed, uncrossing his arms and letting them hang at his sides, fists clenched.

"I CAN EASILY CRUSH YOU, JUST LIKE I DID WITH THAT WEAKLING YOU CALLED A FRIEND!" the reptile said, bolts of lightning running across his shaking arms with each word.

Cyko however, looked at him and sighed, a smirk still in place. "Look at you, you are so dramatic—you flaunt too much! Acting all high and mighty while spouting lame lines about power and survival of the fittest, blah blah blah blah!" Cyko said with a sneer.

"I'VE HAD ENOUGH OF YOU! IF YOU WON'T JOIN OUR SUPERIOR ARMY, THEN YOU SHALL PERISH LIKE THAT BABY DID!" Drago roared, the lightning over his body even brighter than it was before. He charged towards Cyko, punching the ground where he was seconds ago, leaving a crater the size of a boulder in his place. Removing his arm from the ground, Drago snarled and turned around to find the enhancer, whose gaze was turned towards the ground.

"You are just a child. A monster, but still a child. A spoiled brat that needs punishment," Cyko whispered, although Drago's enhanced senses still managed to pick up his words. His head snapped up, revealing a murderous expression on his face, a look of loathing so strong it made Drago pause for a second. "Say, how about we bring the child out from inside you? Give you a nice dose of REALITY!" Cyko disappeared.

The mutant leader's eyes widened before he instinctively brought his massive left arm up to protect his head, just in time to intercept a slash from Cyko, who left a deep gash in his scaled arm. The dragon roared and launched a wave of fire at the airborne enhancer who was engulfed in the fiery cloud with nary a reaction.

Already aware of his tricks from observing his fights, Drago, once again, chose to sacrifice a limb, his right arm this time, to block another slash.

This time he reacted much faster, reaching out with his left arm before Cyko was able to react, strangling him, causing the enhancer's eyes to widen in surprise. "YOUR TRICKS WON'T WORK ON ME!" he yelled before sending a powerful charge of electricity down his arm.

"GHHHAAAAAHHH!!" Cyko screeched as the electricity, much more potent than any charge he received during the experiments, coursed through his body.

"I-Is that the b-best you can do, you oversized gecko?!" he asked before his body's blue aura increased in intensity. With a loud snap, Cyko freed himself from the dragon's grasp, breaking all the fingers on his hand in progress.

"AGH CURSE YOU!" Drago choked, grasping his broken left hand with his right, glaring as Cyko landed on the ground.

The enhancer snarled at him before vanishing once again, this time appearing right behind Drago's head, ready to cut it off in his moment of distraction.

Cyko let out a surprised shout as a massive object slammed into him just before he could attack, sending him crashing to the ground. He barely had time to realize he had been hit by the dragon's tail before he had to dodge a torrent of flames, courtesy of the irate dragon.

He clicked his tongue; of course, he wouldn't be as easy as the mages were.

The dragon rushed at Cyko's airborne form, left arm raised ready to strike. Thinking fast, the enhancer deactivated his holo blades and brought his arms in front of him in time to protect most of his body from the massive fist, though he was sent reeling in the opposite direction. Not letting up, Drago charged with speed betraying his size, stopping just in front of the flying child, ready to strike, this time with his now healed right hand.

Unable to turn around in time, Cyko took the full brunt of the attack with his back, ploughing to the ground like a meteor, a huge cloud forming at the point of impact. In a show of viciousness, Drago launched a wave of white-hot flames towards the crater, causing the heat of the entire Coliseum to turn up several degrees as the ground around the point of impact melted into lava.

Stopping his stream of flames, Drago fell to his knees in pain, the heels of his feet having been slashed by a grinning Cyko, who had appeared behind him on the ground, still looking in great condition despite the punishment he received. The same could not be said about his armor, however, as it looked dented in several places.

Cyko and Drago fought for what seemed like an eternity. Regardless of how deep Cyko cut him, Drago was a fast healer, and Cyko was running out of creative ways to hurt him. The dragon wasn't fast enough for Cyko, whose biggest strength in the fight was being able to disappear and reappear elsewhere. They were a perfect match, neither one of them able to fatally injure the other.

Meanwhile, in the stands, those watching the fight had varied reactions. Both Magy and Tela had felt their hearts almost leap out of their chest at some of the stunts Cyko had been pulling off, and how outright suicidal he was progressively getting, running straight into fire, taking the mutant's lightning attacks head on, all just so he could inflict more damage on him, damage that healed itself in seconds! Magy wished that her dear friend would be all right and could avenge little Myo. Tela, while desiring much the same, was more concerned with Cyko's state of mind, being able to feel his emotions of hate and elation during the whole fight. She was concerned by how thrilled he felt whenever he hurt Drago.

A particular pair, however, was watching the fight with great interest. Ellyn had long since stopped crying, ever since Cyko broke free of his restraints and massacred the mages, she had swallowed her sorrows for the time being and had focused on observing the fight, trying to understand what the wind was telling her.

"Can you feel it, Ellyn?" Reddox whispered as he too was glued to the fight. Being more intimately connected to energy, the mage could feel something very different in Cyko, something he didn't have during their fight.

"Y-yes... It feels like something changed within him, I mean... more than just his increase in power or a new personality..." she said in a small voice, wincing as Cyko took another fireball to the face without hesitation just so he could land a deep gash on the dragon's chest, which only earned him another punch to the face.

"Ever since he broke out, his energy levels skyrocketed. I would've preferred to be less restrained to run a better diagnostic but…" Cyko had stopped trying to dash directly at the dragon and was now evading his attack as he analyzed him for an opening. "I believe he may, in fact, be in the same category as me," Reddox whispered, observing how Cyko seemed to be in deep focus, the glowing aura surrounding him increasing in intensity.

As for the said enhancer, he had long since figured out that no matter how deep a wound he caused, or how fast he tried to inflict them, they would always recover by the time he made another. Even when he tried to aim for areas that caused more pain, or try to cut deeper, it was never enough to take the dragon out long enough to aim at his true vitals: his neck and head. Sure, he had cut into the mutant's throat, getting covered in blood as a result, but that wound had since healed.

He needed to think about what to do, something other than just running ahead, taking his attacks and cutting himself apart. Cyko was sure he could keep doing this for hours, but he didn't have hours. He knew how many guards could storm the place at any second. He needed to kill that monster *now* or he might never again be able to avenge his little brother.

Grinning, Cyko knew what to do after a moment of focus. Ever since Cyko and Path fused, he had gained an extensive insight on how his powers worked and how to do many things he thought he could not. This was how he got his holo blades; they were a part of him all along, first manifested by that dream he had on the day he awakened his powers… And since he is also Path now, he knew exactly what he could do to finish this. He had been playing around too much.

First, he had been fighting as Cyko would have, then, he fought as Path would… Now, it was time to fight like *Cykopath* and slaughter his enemy. It was time to let his anger, his bloodthirstiness run its course… It was time for a massacre!

"I hope you enjoyed your five minutes of fame, you ugly lizard," Cyko said as he dodged another tongue of fire, "because NOW is when the fun starts! Prepare to get slaughtered!"

"The damage you've been doing is nothing more than irritating, you can't possibly think of defeating me without an army!" the dragon retorted with an air of superiority, not a single scratch present on him. Even the bloodstains from the countless wounds Cyko had inflicted on him had evaporated from his constant use of electricity and heat. Meanwhile, the enhancer looked rather ragged, armor dented in several places, parts of his clothes either torn or burnt, and his skin was scratched and bruised. It was only a matter of time until the annoyance in front of him ran out of stamina, and then, Drago would show him who is superior!

"An army huh…?" Cyko said with a smug grin on his face before his form wavered, like when a pebble hits water. With a maniacal look on his face, the blue-haired enhancer started to laugh, causing Drago's eyes to narrow at him.

"HAHAHAHA! I'M GLAD YOU ASKED!" the boy yelled as mirror images of himself appeared all around the arena, their forms coming forth with a small flash of light.

Surrounding the mutant leader was a small army of Cykos, every single one of them sporting the holo blades and the same, bloodthirsty grin on their faces. They were technically hologram projections, one ability the boy learned about when his two halves fused, something that would give him the upper hand in any combat situation. They looked solid and their attacks were just as powerful as those with his real holo blades. The clones couldn't talk or follow complex tasks, but they only needed to follow one order, anyway. Attack; attack without stopping!

Drago spun around, eyes wide and mouth open, unable to comprehend what the enhancer had just pulled off. How did he do that?! The brat didn't have this power in his previous battles, or even just a few seconds ago! Had he… had he been holding back?! The thought of that was humiliating! Growling in a rage, the dragon turned around to glare at the original, but he could no longer tell who amongst the sea of clones was who.

The dragon roared in fury, spreading both arms and sending waves of lightning and a stream of flames from his front, slowly spinning as he did so. In response to his attack, the clones, as one, charged towards the gigantic mutant leader, the voice of Cyko's mad laugh echoing amongst them.

Many clones were destroyed trying to get closer to him, as they fearlessly charged head on, but for any five that were devoured by flames or destroyed by lightning, one or two managed to get through and attack the giant, causing several gashes. Legs, arms, knees, chest, tail, wings... No part of Drago stayed safe from the reach of the clones, for even as he destroyed them, Cyko just created more and more.

Growing tired of the increasing pain from his wounds, even as they healed, the dragon used his limbs to attack, block, swat away, and crush the clones. A swipe of his arm sent ten clones flying away, but it opened the way for three to use their blades to cut up his arm before they were destroyed by the lightning covering his body. Flailing his tail, he kept a dozen of them off his back, but two slipped through and created deep slashes close to his wings.

As for the original, Cyko knew his back was the most vulnerable area of his body despite the danger of his large, spiked tail so he kept himself concealed, waiting for the perfect chance to attack. His clones were slowly managing to overwhelm the dragon's fast recovery, as wounds were created quicker than he could heal, and it was beginning to show as Drago's attacks got increasingly more desperate and rasher.

And then, just as the reptile's tail crashed into the ground, destroying another five of his clones, Cyko found the perfect opening and took advantage of it. Laughing madly, the enhancer launched himself towards his now vulnerable lower back, blades raised and ready to strike.

"GRAH!" Drago yelled in agony as he felt enormous pain on his lower back, losing strength and control of his legs and falling forwards, trying to support himself with his arms. Cyko cut deep enough to sever the dragon's spine, crippling him and turning the fearsome beast into a sitting duck for his slaughter!

Now! Now was the time to cause real damage! Mentally ordering his clones to overwhelm him, he jumped from his position to join the others in causing damage all over Drago's body, ordering several of them to continue cutting his lower back at the slightest sign of regeneration. He wouldn't recover this time!

"GRAH!" Drago continued roaring in pain, trying to keep the clones at bay but failing, quite miserably.

"Look at yourself, you oversized gecko. Oh, how the mighty have fallen," Cyko mocked, standing in front of him so the dragon could see his tormentor. "Just like the cliché villains you like to imitate, you are about to have a pathetic end. Someone you called weak, the brother of the person you killed, is about to kill you… *slowly*."

"No… NO! You can't do this! I AM THE MIGHTY LEADER OF THE MUTANTS!" Drago yelled, launching a powerful wave of fire at Cyko, who vanished, appearing on the other side of his vision. The reptile glared at him, eyes full of hatred and behind that, fear. "I AM DESTINED TO LEAD THEM TO GREATNESS! I AM THE CHOSEN PROTECTOR OF THIS WORLD!" he bellowed, sending another wave of flames at Cyko, who once again dodged them, appearing back in his previous spot.

"Don't you *get* it? You will *die,* you cannot heal fast enough, and without being able to move, you can barely fight. You are going to die as the pathetic, worthless monster you always were! No one is coming to save you!" Cyko said in a cruel voice, face twisted and vengeful.

"No! NO! NO!" The blood loss made Drago feel dizzy and cold as panic set in. He would not die, not like this! He is the destined leader of the army! He will not… HE WILL NOT BE DEFEATED BY THIS HUMAN!

"GRRAAAAHHH!" the dragon roared with all his might, concentrating all his energy into his manipulation of electricity. With another powerful boom that made Cyko stumble, a great explosion of lightning occurred with Drago at its epicenter, launching the enhancer several meters away and destroying all clones that were closest to him.

"NOW YOU'LL DIE AS THE PATHETIC INSECT YOU TRULY ARE! FEEL THE POWER OF A DRAGON'S ROAR!" Drago's voice bellowed. Recovering from his shock at the reptile's last-ditch effort to survive, Cyko looked up to spot the dragon flying several meters up in the air, near the ceiling and just in front of the displays used to announce the matches. He was badly cut and bleeding heavily but was also slowly healing. His eyes were wide open and fearful as lightning streaks traveled across his entire body, emitting a strong, white light of pure energy from his mouth.

In the stands, those who could feel his power widened their eyes at the potency of the attack that Drago was preparing. If he were to unleash that on the arena, chances are that the whole Coliseum would go up in ashes! It could kill everyone here!

Reddox, Ellyn, Magy, Tela and several others started to struggle against their restraints so they could do something, anything to stop that catastrophe from happening.

Cyko stared at the dragon with wide-open eyes as he racked his brain for something to do.

Calming himself, Cyko went deep into thought. It would be risky to rely on his newly strengthened powers to help kill him, since he was still getting the hang of them. He dismissed his clones—they would not be useful for targeting something several meters up, even if they could jump that distance.

The enhancer closed his eyes and concentrated, feeling the world around him slow down. Deep inside him, he accessed the well of power that represented his abilities, now much stronger than they ever used to be.

When he opened his eyes, they were glowing a pure cyan color, the blue aura that covered his body increasing in intensity, showing just how much energy he would put into this. As the light from the dragon's mouth got brighter and brighter, Cyko knew this would be his only chance. He focused as much as he could, increasing his own perception of time tenfold to spot the perfect moment to strike... There!

"GRAAAAAAAAAAAHHHHH!!!" Drago let out a thunderous roar, throwing his head downwards as he launched the beam of energy from his mouth, its shine tinting the whole Coliseum white.

Just as the attack had reached halfway to the Coliseum floor, a spinning blue projectile covered in a great aura of cyan rose to meet it, colliding with the white sphere of destruction and stopping it in its tracks as they competed for dominance. A threshold was reached when the great ball of energy gave out and exploded like a supernova. It had a wide path of destruction that thankfully was too high to hit anyone, even as the shock-waves traveled through the air, knocking the displays off their strengthened supports.

As Drago looked at the explosion with hope, he saw something that made his heart skip a beat.

"AAAAHHHHHH!" The scream of a psychopath covered in blue, cutting through the explosion and the air at an astounding speed, the tip of the blade on his right arm leading him forward. Unable to get over his shock of his strongest attack failing, Drago's exhaustion from the long battle against the enhancer worked in Cyko's favor.

Drago opened his mouth to scream, but only a torrent of blood came out as Cyko struck the ceiling and, using his momentum to temporarily stand upside down, he looked towards the falling dragon, grinning as he spotted a large hole in the middle of his chest.

Letting himself fall back down, the blood covered child struck the ground moments after Drago, who was in a crater the size of his body. Drago was twitching, still trying to hang on to life… But his wound was not healing. Either he had hit a vital spot, or his body was too exhausted to heal him, but he was not getting better.

"No… this… No… I don't… want… to die…" The dragon whined, trying to stand up, trying to will his body to fix the hole in his chest, but it was useless. He was too drained, too weak… too defeated.

Cyko approached him, dismissing his holo blades, as they served their purpose for now.

"I don't… want to die… I am… supposed… to be… great…" Drago whimpered in pain, coughing blood as he stared at the ceiling, trying in vain to survive.

"You killed Myo—this is what you deserve. This pathetic end, whimpering and begging for your life, is all your own doing, the consequence for your actions," Cyko said coldly.

"You wanted to play the tyrant, guess what? Tyrants are always overthrown in the end. Now die, knowing you never amounted to anything but a pathetic brat who was a slave for scientists who saw you as nothing but a zoo animal," the enhancer said, watching as tears of despair flooded out of the dragon's drooping eyes, as he was losing strength to keep them open.

"I… I don't… want to… die… I… miss… my… family…" Drago whispered, trying his best to keep his eyes open, sobbing as he felt his life leaving him, unable to do anything to stop it.

"I'm… just… seven… years… old…" he said in a whisper, his voice child-like for the first time since Cyko had met him. He let out one last wracked sob before closing his eyes forever. Cyko stared at the now dead mutant, eyes hard and cold as he let his hatred pulse through his veins.

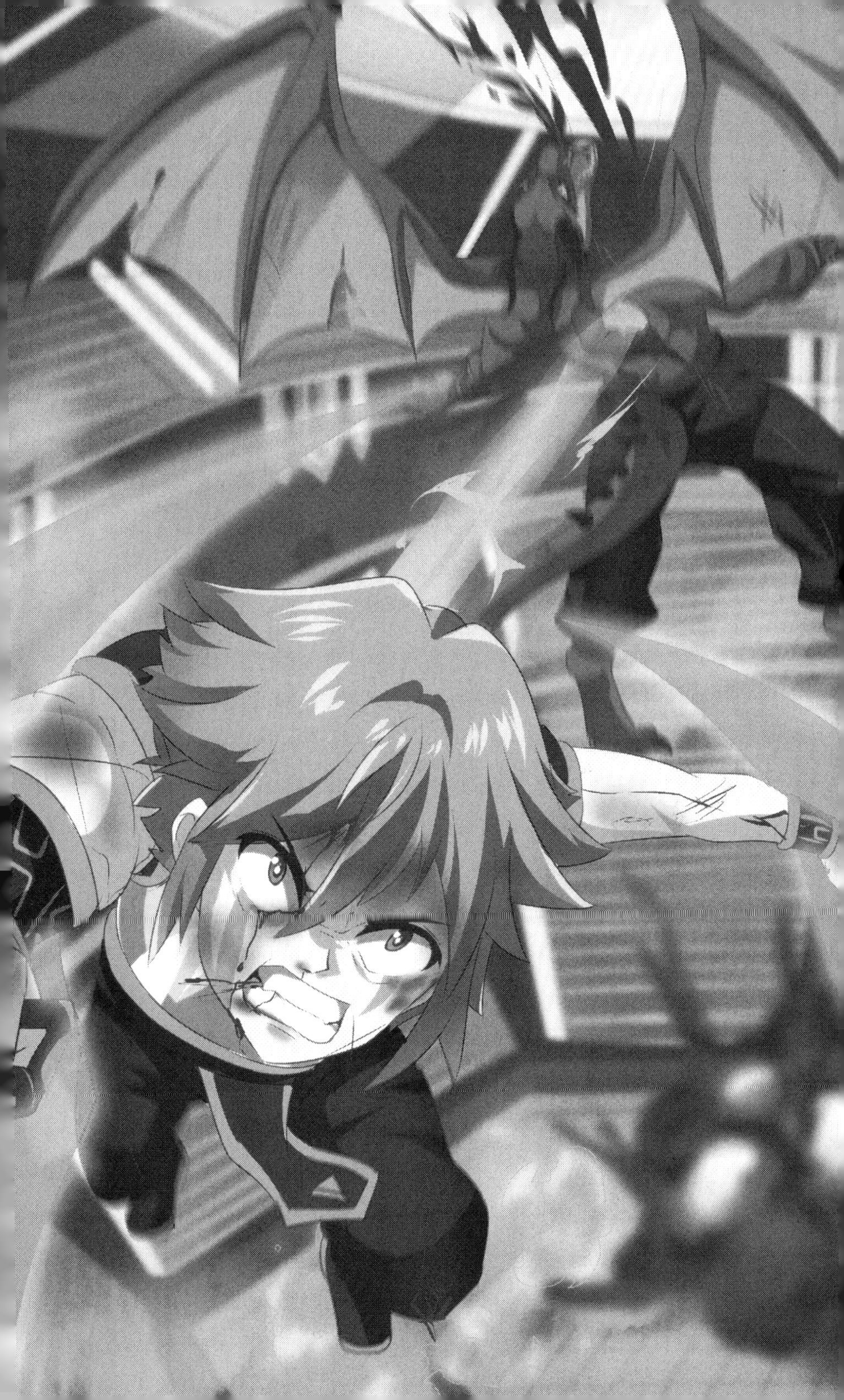

"Myo... I avenged you," Cyko whispered to himself, his face softening. Killing Drago wouldn't bring his little brother back. Nothing would. "I'm sorry for failing you, I hope you are somewhere better now," the child said in a small, sad voice, letting tears run down his cheeks as he turned towards the stands of the Coliseum. As the battle between him and Drago finished, a torrent of guards entered the arena, taking position to shoot at him.

There were a lot, but Cyko still had the energy to fight. If he could take as many of them down as he did before... then maybe that would make things easier for Tela and for the others. He didn't know, but part of him was itching to try, to let out the psychopath once again and cause a bloodbath amongst those cruel beings. The war would never end until they were free. The moment he realized this, however, was when he felt a pair of eyes on him.

"*Cyko... Please, don't do anything, don't fight anymore,*" Tela thought to him, her voice one of extreme sadness, surprising him as he had never felt his friend that depressed before. However, before he could voice his protest at wanting to keep fighting, another wave of sadness hit him, stopping the enhancer in his tracks.

"*I don't care about the guards, about Drago... I care about you! If you continue fighting, they may be forced to take you down for good! But if you surrender now, they should let you live because of your power. Please, Cyko, don't keep struggling, not now!*" Tela begged him, crying as she was forced to stand up by a pair of guards who began to escort everyone out to deal with Cyko alone.

The enhancer surveyed around him, counting the number of guards he could see. Around a hundred, without counting the number that were taking the other children away, presumably to their cells. Standing in the level the mages were in, right next to their corpses, the guards all pointed their weapons at him, waiting for him to make the slightest move. Cyko paused, analyzing the situation, his powers begging him to kill them and bathe in their blood, but he couldn't get Tela's pleas out of his head.

"Attention Subject Number 444, surrender and stand down. If you comply, we can guarantee you will not come to harm," the cold voice of the wretched scientist who started this all was heard from somewhere above him.

"Subject Number 444, surrender and stand down, we promise to not take harsh action against you if you cooperate," the head scientist repeated, to which Cyko scowled.

"Please Cyko... We can fight another day! Please don't throw your life away, I don't want to lose you too... not more than I already have..." Tela whispered in his mind, her feelings of loss, sadness and regret bleeding over to him, causing the enhancer's own eyes to waver.

Cyko realized how hard this must have been for Tela. She once said she could sense what someone else was feeling, so if she could also sense what Myo had felt in his last moments and what he himself had felt when he changed...

"Tela... No matter how crazy I become from here on out, you haven't lost me yet," Cyko replied to her, hoping she could feel the reassurance he tried to send her alongside his loyalty and friendship. Looking around the Coliseum one more time, the boy sighed before willing his power to fade away. His glowing eyes and blue aura vanished. He was not giving up. No, he was just going to survive today so he could continue helping his loved ones out.

Raising his arms in the universal sign of surrender, he could feel enormous relief passing through him, likely from Tela, before a feeling of warmth covered him like an embrace.

"Thank you..." she whispered in erratic relief, not wanting to see another child who she had sworn to protect, and a friend, die in front of her while she was helpless.

The boy smiled, watching as the guards descended towards the arena, approaching him from all sides with their weapons still aimed in his direction.

7

Magy sat in Myo's bed, hugging herself with her arms. The room felt huge, too big to be comfortable. The sweet little boy's scent still hung around the covers, the pillows, and the bed itself. It reminded her of how innocent, emotive and lively he was, how much he wished to be free, to have a normal, happy life even with the disease he had. She hadn't spent as much time with him as Cyko had, but she still thought of him as a little brother, wanting nothing more than for him to be happy and safe... but he was dead.

To make matters worse, after Cyko surrendered himself to the guards, they took him away somewhere unknown to do who knows what. She had tried asking Tela about his whereabouts, but all she had gotten was a sad *"I don't know..."* explaining that her connection with him had been severed.

That was 3 hours ago.

Myo's death was still fresh in her mind and heart, the pain from losing him tearing her apart and pressing on her soul like the weight of a thousand rocks. She feared losing her dear friend, Cyko, on the same day. Fresh sobs wracked through her body, making the pink-haired girl clench her arms tighter in a useless attempt of self-comfort.

She felt a hum coming from the depths of her soul, calming her down a little. Scythe, her closest friend, her heart and determination, was trying to reassure her that everything would be all right, that Cyko was strong and would come back. Magy wanted nothing more than to believe her, but it was hard, with how much her heart was wavering.

Then, the loud bang of the door opening brought the girl out of her depression long enough to stare at the intruder, spotting the giant guard who seemed to be in charge of their ward. The man said nothing and shoved a blue-haired boy inside, snapping the door closed.

Cyko, it was Cyko! He was okay!

"CYKO!" Magy leapt to her feet and rushed towards him, eyes still full of tears as he waved a tired hand in her direction.

"Hey, Magy..." the boy managed to say, not resisting in the slightest as she clung to him, pulling his trembling body into a tight embrace.

"Myo... Myo is... and you were..." she sobbed out, emotions in disarray now that he was safe. She was glad and relieved to see him again, but on the other hand, her heart was still hurting from losing Myo—not even the death of Drago and those mages were enough to relieve her.

"I know, I know. Let's sit down." Cyko led his friend towards the bed she was at... Myo's bed. Magy started a new round of sobs, to which the boy wrapped his arm around her in comfort, as his own heart hurt with her. The satisfaction and vindication from Drago's death was short lived.

"He was too innocent, he didn't... He didn't deserve... to end up like this!" she cried into his shoulder, sobbing as the sadness struck her again, holding onto her friend for dear life.

"I avenged him, I killed him, Magy! I killed that monster who took Myo away! But..." Cyko's voice cracked as he began to cry into Magy's shoulder, unable to contain his emotions. "It won't... It won't bring Myo back! It won't make this suffering go away!"

As they cried into each other's arms, the pair remembered all the moments they had with Myo, both good and bad. Their first time meeting him, introducing themselves to him, comforting him when he cried or got scared, slowly motivating him until he became the brave boy that stood against the mighty beast, his moments of sweetness and innocence... They were all gone forever. Both Magy and Cyko shared their sadness, venting and crying for what felt like hours.

However, they knew they couldn't stay that away forever, they had to do something else, even if it felt impossible to forget the sadness of losing Myo. They would mourn, they would mourn for a long time, but they had to be functional. There were many others who still needed their help.

After dinner—which had arrived without either of them noticing—they climbed into the same bed, facing each other with sad, tired eyes.

"Your face is a little different now," Magy whispered as she brought her right hand up to Cyko's head and began to trace the markings his face had gained from his change.

The boy seemed confused. "It is?" he whispered back, his voice just as tired as hers.

"Mhm," she affirmed, fingers grazing his cheek next to the blue mark on the side of his face, "not just those markings, but... I could feel it, Cyko, I could feel the change in your soul when you broke free of those restraints. Scythe... Scythe told me you are no longer the person you used to be... I could see part of it when you fought those mages."

What she said surprised Cyko. *She noticed?* He knew Tela had noticed his changes because of her mental abilities but... No, that's not what matters at the moment. Yes, he did change, and he'll likely keep changing for a while until he's unrecognizable, but... he promised himself. Putting his hand on Magy's, he clenched it, giving his friend an understanding smile.

"Yes, it was the price I had to pay to gain the power to avenge Myo… and to stop something like this from ever happening again to the people I love. Which includes you, Magy," Cyko answered, causing the pink-haired girl's eyes to widen. "I'd pay any price to keep you all safe, even if it means becoming a monster myself," he added.

"Cyko…" Magy whispered, tears forming in her eyes. His words made her happy. Moving herself closer to him, the girl wrapped her arms around him, finding comfort in her friend. "You'll never be a monster to me…" she offered, smiling as she felt him wrap his own arms around her.

"Thank you, Magy."

That night, both friends slept in each other's arms, finding comfort from the tragedy that happened that day. They would never forget their sweet little brother and how he met his tragic end. They made a silent promise to each other to kill as many of them as they could during their escape, but for now… Now was time to rest, to find comfort, and to mourn.

8

Dr. Gacha examined a sample he had collected from Cyko, using the advanced equipment in his personal lab to analyze it from as many angles as he could, both in the realm of science and of magic. If he could find the source of Subject 444's sudden change and power increase… it would advance their research of the hidden genes by over two hundred percent

He glanced towards his desk at the small, white kitten asleep on top, unaware of the events that happened a few hours ago. If she were to learn of the death of one subject she got attached to, he knew she would be saddened. He had not expected Drago to go that far.

The whole chain of events from the mental attack to the riot, to that child managing to break himself free with a sudden raise in his energy levels, slaughtering a security guard and dozens of elite mages in two minutes before proceeding to kill the strongest subject of the mutant ward… was a lot.

During the fight, his team had made several protests of allowing the battle to continue, but Dr. Gacha had been adamant in allowing it to proceed. They had an anomaly, one never seen before.

Subject 444 had exhibited new abilities that didn't match with the ones they had recorded. Besides enhanced strength, speed, endurance, and reflexes, he had shown the ability to vanish and procure a weapon from thin air, and create several copies of himself.

When Drago had gotten desperate enough to use his strongest attack, which he had been explicitly forbidden from using, his team panicked. Even Dr. Gacha himself would be lying if he said he had not felt scared, terrified at losing all their subjects at once, which would mean a catastrophic failure for the entire project, but the blue-haired subject kept his calm and countered him, resulting in the mutant's death.

At that moment, Dr. Gacha knew he needed answers, and needed them immediately. As soon as the guards had him surrounded, he sent explicit orders to not shoot him or antagonize him. The head scientist was pleasantly surprised when he acquitted to his request and asked the guards to *gently* escort him to a room in the soft labs before taking a small team of mercenaries to his destination.

During his interrogation, Subject 444 proved himself cooperative, even giving explicit details as to the reason of his rampage and increase in power: hatred and the desire to avenge the subject known as Myo, which the child referred to as his little brother. He blamed himself for his death and promised that he would kill Dr. Gacha if he ever got the chance to.

Thankfully, he stayed calm for the whole interrogation, answering every question with honesty—according to the mages. However, Subject 444 was too emotionally compromised to be convinced of the scientists' innocence regarding the death of his brother, and thus had to be released. Dr. Gacha asked him to give them a small sample of his blood alongside a few strands of his hair, to which the child agreed with a drained glare.

Watching as his innovative equipment analyzed the samples, the scientist thought about the future of Project R.N.G. If all subjects experienced this enormous power increase and addition of new, unexpected abilities, they would have an enormous advantage in their army. Their efficiency and capability to protect the world would increase tenfold. This made Drago's sacrifice worth it, as now, all Dr. Gacha had to do was to figure out how to replicate the results and make it work, preferably with an injectable solution.

Walking over to his desk, he stopped to pet his sleeping kitten, his mask of indifference cracking to show an affectionate smile. He reached over to his tablet, which was beside many drawings the feline had made today to pass the time. Opening it, he typed a message with top priority to his superior, Mr. Whale, informing him of his plans to cease combat simulations and move forth for the final phase of Project R.N.G.: Loyalty.

As he walked away to continue typing his message, he didn't see one drawing in particular was near where he took his device from the table, as preoccupied with the project as he was. A detailed depiction of Cyko, Magy, Myo and the artist herself, all smiling happily. Their names were written on top of their figures, several small hearts and cat paws covering the edges of the drawing, giving it a heartwarming atmosphere and at the top were the words, 'Friends Forever.'

CHAPTER 5

AFTERMATH

1

"Dr. Gacha, my friend, would you care to tell me what happened down there?" Mr. Whale asked in a strained voice, face set into a hard frown in contrast to the head scientist's emotionless one.

Mr. Whale waited a moment before launching into his spiel.

"Over a hundred mercenaries killed, many of which were elite mages. Some at the hands of a rogue child and the rest by one of their own, who decided going berserk would be the best choice. Before that, we had a revolt and a mental attack on nearly the entire scientific team, which got through our many, many expensive security measures!" The plump man hit his desk with his clenched hand, face morphing into an angry scowl.

"Because of these deaths, the Neon Lunatics have *doubled* their monthly fees, which were already costly enough! One of our most successful and loyal subjects is dead and now the psychologists say that the chances of rebellion are much, much higher! And to make matters worse, we may already be compromised from that mental invasion! Do you *know* how hard it will be to explain that to the Board? They are expecting results, not failures!" He concluded his rant and retreated into his chair.

After a few deep breaths, his voice returned to its rational tone. "I apologize for my strong response." Mr. Whale noticed that the scientist's face hadn't changed since he yelled at him. "But you must understand, everything was going so well before that, to have a crisis arise so suddenly… It's a bad sight for business. We've come so far to have our plans crash and burn, and you want to cancel the remaining combat simulations to rush ahead to the next phase? Can you tell me why?"

The scientist closed his eyes for a moment, thinking about his next words. "Maybe it was a stroke of luck, but most of the subjects with the highest potential had already been tested before this happened. We have valuable data on potential live combat scenarios that can be used for future training. But what really brought up the need to skip to the next part is twofold." The head scientist brought up his right hand, one of his fingers raised.

"First, the subjects are divided amongst mutant and non-mutant, and a hatred towards the staff originating from the second faction. They all are expected to work together, both with each other and with us, so divisions on that scale will only lead to further conflicts which may lead to even more loss of lives, money, and time," Dr. Gacha explained, before bringing up another finger.

"Second, a great discovery was made during this fight that may prove the losses suffered were inconsequential. Something that, once fully understood, could increase the efficiency of each individual subject up to 200 percent or 300 percent." He watched how Mr. Whale's expression changed during his explanation, eyebrows knitting together in contemplation.

Reaching inside his coat, Dr. Gacha took out his tablet, clicking and swiping through the menus. "The first reason is obvious enough, but the second requires more substantial evidence. Here is the recording of the scene, shown from multiple angles. You can make your own conclusions, Mr. Whale." The head scientist leaned back in his chair to wait.

As Mr. Whale took the device and played the recording, he mentally prepared himself to witness chaos and the loss of life. From the start of the video, the situation rapidly evolved into madness as the two subjects attacked the barrier to interrupt the fight in the arena. Dr. Gacha had told him that at that point, they were already under attack and could not put a stop to the turmoil that followed. More and more children joined in, their many powers and abilities crashing down against the mages, threatening to break the barrier until the dragon roared his orders for the mutants to interfere. That was when things escalated into a free-for-all.

When the bracelets activated, it brought the combat to a full halt, restraining even the strongest subjects. Sheer strength was useless, elemental manipulation was voided, direct transmutation of the bracelets nullified, shape-shifting reared pointless, and even intangibility couldn't pierce through the shackles as the soul-bonding technology made sure that the bracelets would stay on their bodies, no matter the form or lack thereof.

However, when the battle of the two subjects in the arena resulted in the death of the small child present, Mr. Whale had to take a minute. He knew that sacrifices had to be made, knew that children died in the experiments and that they suffered during their stay, but it was hard not to be affected by the violent death of a child so small.

"Doctor, why didn't you stop the match when you could? Surely that boy didn't have to die," the businessman asked with a sigh, knowing that the man in front of him only cared for one child, his own.

"That *subject* was the lowest on the priority list. While his powers could be useful, the side effects would have been too expensive to justify," the scientist said, pausing before he concluded the harsh truth. "Whoever targeted us wanted to stop the match to save him. I allowed the fight to go on hoping to catch the perpetrator or at least, get closer to identifying them. Whoever they are, they didn't try again," The doctor explained, his voice as cold as always.

"Was his death necessary? Surely you could have arranged for the fight to end just before Drago took his life, remember what we did with many of the children that didn't make the cut?"

The scientist shook his head slightly at the suggestion. "While yes, that option was available for him, it was before the mental attack happened. The importance of discovering the perpetrator outweighed the subject's life and while the gamble failed, you understand that many sacrifices have to be made for the greater good, Mr. Whale. He was not the first and likely will not be the last to die for the sake of humanity's own future," the scientist replied matter-of-factly, to which the businessman nodded in reluctant acceptance.

As Mr. Whale resumed the recording, he wondered if he'd ever be able to have children of his own and raise them without thinking of all the ones whose lives were ruined.

Turning his attention back towards the recording, he saw what he expected. Children fought and broke away from the main battle at hand. He still couldn't figure out the cause for the deaths and chaos that followed. What had happened down there?

His frown hardened when the guards entered the area to physically and verbally torture the children. It was his own permission that allowed the science team to use the guards to further torment the children. He shook his head as the guilt was strong now.

Clearing his thoughts, he had noticed that one child, the blue-haired boy who had struck the barrier first, had risen from his position on the ground.

From that moment, Mr. Whale witnessed what could only be described as slaughter, a scene ripped right out of nightmares. The child who had been restrained somehow broke the bindings and slew the mercenaries near him and all the mages that had been maintaining the barrier. How was that possible?! Not even the strongest enhancer could break them, they were supposed to drain strength from the prisoner's soul—the magical engineers had assured him of that!

And then, the video showed his brief fight with the last mage who, in desperation, had used forbidden magic and blasted everything around him, other subjects included. After finishing the mad mage off with ease, the rampaging child moved on towards the dragon. The blue-haired subject and the dragon fought, and fought, and continued to fight even when he thought they'd have been done for.

The boy and the dragon seemed to be evenly matched, keeping up with each other blow for blow and with every advantage one had, the other had a way to make up for it... Yet, somehow, the blue-haired child always stayed one step ahead of the giant dragon, provoking, mocking, and hurting him with indifference. It wasn't until the end that the boy showed any desperation when Drago resorted to his strongest attack.

Mr. Whale almost choked as he watched what happened next. If that child hadn't stopped the dragon's roar, most of the children would have died in the following explosion, just how close to complete failure was this work of years and billions of gems?

Still, that scenario didn't come to pass, fortunately enough. They still could salvage the situation from what he witnessed... Using his own tablet, Mr. Whale checked the now outdated information regarding Subject Number 444. A simple enhancer type with heightened strength, agility, endurance and reaction time. He was nothing better than all the other enhancers, but now...

New abilities had been awakened in him. Possible teleportation used for surprise counter attacks. Weapon creation of excellent quality, as they could cut Drago's scales, which were supposed to be as tough as titanium. The ability to create mass clones of himself, duplicates able to fight and act near independently from what he could observe, being able to dish out just as much damage, if not being able to take as much punishment. These powers were all coupled with the noted increments of his own base strength... If they could find the source of his powers and make it so all children could be as strong as he was now...

"I must admit, Dr. Gacha, you have me interested in your proposition. I even have one of my own," the businessman offered as he handed the device back to the doctor, who nodded at his words. "My feelings on the catastrophe that almost happened down there are mixed, but that discovery outweighs them by a large margin... If we can reap the benefits, that is."

"Ms. Allure, could you please bring in a few refreshments for us? And clear my schedule for the next two hours," Mr. Whale spoke into the intercom connected to his secretary's desk.

After a few seconds, she spoke back to him, "I cleared your schedule, Mr. Whale. I'll be right in with some refreshments." The secretary's light, cheery tone made the businessman smile. He had made the correct choice in hiring her.

He looked back at his head scientist to notice the man looking at him with a raised eyebrow.

"I have a feeling we will be here for a few hours, Doctor, might as well talk business over refreshments," he said lightly, his previous anger and exasperation left behind.

After a minute, a request for entrance appeared in Mr. Whale's terminal. Once granted entry, his secretary opened the door and paused enough to give her boss a respectful nod, entered, elegantly carrying herself even as she balanced a tray full of snacks and drinks for the two men.

"By your leave, sir," she said, raising an eyebrow and winking at him, to which Mr. Whale replied with a nod of gratitude. Turning to leave, she looked at the scientist who had been watching her like a hawk the entire time.

"Doctor," she said in the same polite, friendly tone, nodding at him before slipping out. Turning his attention back towards his superior, he noted how the man seemed more relaxed after seeing the woman.

"Well, let's get down to business," the scientist said as he poured himself a cup of soda. "As you know, the great discovery I referred to was about Subject 444's incredulous increase in power and I believe I'll be able to find the source of his newfound strength. Despite his claimed hate for us, he was willing to give genetic samples for us to study," the doctor explained, taking a sip of his drink.

"After having a look, I arrived at a hypothetical conclusion that the creation of a 'Limit Break' serum would be possible, using the same enzymes and substances present in his blood that weren't there before, to force a state of being like what he experienced, hopefully increasing the target's own powers," Dr. Gacha said, waiting to see if his boss had questions about his explanation.

"Can this method apply to any child that has already awakened?" Mr. Whale asked.

The scientist shook his head. "It's too early to make assumptions, for all we know, it might only work on him. More in-depth studies are necessary, but so far, I am optimistic in finding a useful application for this discovery," Dr. Gacha explained.

"I would like you to direct as much personnel as needed for that line of research. Dr. Gacha, your reasoning is sound, and I like the direction this project will take if your research proves fruitful." The businessman set his empty cup down on the table. "We have much to gain from that possibility, can you imagine the monsters those children will be once they reach their full potential? We'll have an army that could single-handedly take over the entire world and even the Creator would have to respect that."

"Now," Mr. Whale continued, "I have a proposition, one I've been contemplating since the project started and we saw results, but it always stayed a low priority... until now."

"Concerning genetics, science is not my area of expertise, I only really know the basics, but what do you think about the possibility of mass cloning? Starting with clones of that child, you could make it so they are already awakened and in possession of that 'Limit Break.' We could completely skip the first phases of the project and go straight to the most important ones, wouldn't we save a lot of time that way?" Mr. Whale asked, which made Dr. Gacha blink in surprise.

"Hmm... I must admit, Mr. Whale, sometimes an outsider's perspective can be useful," the head scientist said with approval, face still neutral as he pondered his boss's suggestion. "If we can find out how to properly clone each of the strongest subjects... If we resort to cloning, the secrecy of the project would be kept, the loyalty of the subjects would gradually increase as more and more trustworthy ones are born, not to mention it would be much easier than to start from scratch every time." The scientist's face changed the slightest into one of wonder as he considered the possibilities.

"Very well. I will officially request a small increase in budget for the creation of two additional science teams. A smaller one led by me, whose focus will be on engineering a special serum that should, in theory, give the same level of power boost that Subject 444 experienced, and a larger group whose task will be set on researching the existing subjects' genes to make an embryo with those powers activated, and engineer cloning facilities to facilitate the study and production of future clones," Dr. Gacha said, earning a nod from Mr. Whale, who had started typing on the console in his desk.

"Put this larger budget to good use, you may do as you wish as long as you get results, for now... We need to discuss the next phase of the current project, I have ideas on how we can try to get the children on our side..." Mr. Whale said, beginning his own plans for the other topic of their meeting. Dr. Gacha listened intently to the man's explanations, adding his own expertise when he felt it needed it or asking questions when necessary. They already had a plan down for the next step, but it never hurt to be extra prepared.

2

After Dr. Gacha excused himself to focus on his own projects, Mr. Whale exhaled as he pondered the fate of Project R.N.G. At first, it used to be a mere fancy of thought, an increasingly desperate worry about humanity's future, but nothing much he really could do about it. Until he met Dr. Gacha, that is.

It had been several years ago, way before Project R.N.G. was put into motion.

Mr. Whale was a wealthy businessman, part of the worldwide GACHA Conglomerate, however, at an area unrelated to his current one of top-secret scientific research. The GACHA Conglomerate is a huge company, having stakes in businesses all across the globe.

Mr. Whale had climbed all the way up the entertainment sector of the company, working tirelessly so that he maximized the company's earnings and the citizens got the best entertainment money could produce. Movie theaters, amusement parks, film production, video game consoles, virtual reality, investments in cultural festivals, music and even more... exotic, but still within the law, forms of entertainment. He had dedicated himself to make sure his area of the company excelled, and he liked to believe that he did a great job as he landed himself a position on the Board, which consisted of the owners of the GACHA Conglomerate.

However, even as he was living a happy, fun, and wealthy life, he still couldn't help but worry. As a child, he was told about the Creator, Luni, the beautiful but powerful being that lived on the moon who had created and protected their universe. Many revered her as a goddess even when she declared that praying to her was a waste of faith as she could not hear prayers.

As he grew up, many class lectures focused on everything humanity knew about their Creator, how she came to be, how she introduced herself to the world, the times she saved humanity from great catastrophes and, her personality—how not to offend her and what Luni liked and disliked. Because of those classes, Mr. Whale always held a fear, deep down, of her turning on them and destroying everything the humans worked for.

And it would be easy, too, for even the strongest human being on their planet knows they wouldn't stand a chance against her, even if they threw all their technological might, their armies, their weapons of mass destruction, their strongest mages and super humans and even creatures of legend… It would do nothing but annoy her further. It was a sobering thought to know their combined power would amount to next to nothing against her if she ever got rid of humanity.

He had studied her behavior over the last few millennia, ever since she had revealed her existence to the world in a historic occurrence that had marked the start of the New Age. Back then, she had been pleasant and often came down to explain many things to humanity—amongst them, the laws of science and a few universal truths. It was interesting to Mr. Whale that she always matched her clothes with the current fashions so her clothes during those first appearances seemed much more divine and regal than the casual set she seemed to prefer these days.

Many gods and goddesses had foolishly challenged her during the first century, claiming that she was nothing but a farce. They were all put in their place. For most, a simple display of power, the sheer might of a Creator was enough to persuade them. Others, however, blindly tried to kill her and were met with their own doom. It surprised the humans that actual gods—beings so far above them that the very nature and laws of the world obeyed them—had no chance against Luni, either.

That was another interesting piece of their history. Humanity had always believed until then that the gods were beings of ultimate power who were immaterial and almost never graced the world with their presence, and when they did, it would be with some physical medium, like an animal or plant. The sudden appearance of the ultimate being, plus the many gods who challenged her and got destroyed had been a turning point for civilization. Many religions disappeared, many countries rioted, and some went to war over the mere existence of a being so powerful.

Many humans had, during this chaotic period, tried to beg the Creator for aid in their wars or to stop it somehow, but she had declared that she would never interfere in wars between citizens, saying they needed to rely and have faith in their own strength rather than relying on hers. She would protect them against cosmic threats they had no chance of beating but would not interfere in wars.

When the battling ceased, thanks to many treaties and exhaustion, the world finally knew peace. Humans and the many other species lived in harmony for the past four millennia. There were many, many times where the world came close to its end and the wars started all over again, but some way, somehow, everything always turned out all right. During those periods of peace, Luni made many appearances, almost always to provide entertainment.

They soon discovered that she loved to amuse people—making them smile, laugh, and struck speechless in awe for her. For over two millennia, she dominated the entertainment sector of the world. Most people would rather expect her next move than think about their own lives, it was a source of escapism for many and Luni always had a huge grin on her face when performing her shows.

To the keen historic, however, they would quickly notice a pattern in her behavior. As the years went by, many conflicts happened because of her existence and involvement. People would openly discuss her, both in favor and against, and as humanity's own technology and imagination grew, Luni's presence in entertainment seemed to lessen. Other species who were content with staying connected with nature and only using human technology as a necessity flocked to the human cities to see newer forms of entertainment.

That seemed to frustrate the Creator despite knowing her mere existence kept her in the top level of popularity, both good and bad worldwide. With the Internet, she soon created blogs and humanity had access to what was essentially a diary of her life, and the true reason for her increasing frustration was clear to those who cared to search for it.

Her job was not just the creator of their world, the protector of a single planet, but rather, of the entire universe. Humanity learned early on that the universe was a very enormous place, which was a severe underestimation. Luni's attention was always turned to the most distant corners of the universe, as she had once declared in a post about what her 'job' entails. Whenever she described a massive threat, she always sounded angry and agitated, which is even more obvious during her video posts.

There were many posts where she is in a good mood, many of them discussed her personal assistant, the succubus known as Lilith, while the rest described games, ideas, philosophies, and new creations she thought would be useful for humanity. However, the number of those positive posts were decreasing in relation to her neutral or agitated ones. To make matters more worrisome, it had been roughly five years since she last made an appearance. She used to appear regularly—going to festivals, visiting hospitals, beaches, game events... Now she spent all her time rolled up on the moon.

For someone like Mr. Whale who is deeply fearful of the Creator, that was a bad sign. A normal human might snap, yell, break things and in the worst of cases, become physically violent. He always tried to make sure his employees had plenty of downtime to avoid this happening and he was generally successful in preventing stress tantrums. Imagining what a Creator might do if they snap from stress, however... It was a frightening thought.

He started reaching out to others, both on social media and in his private and business life. On his own blogs, he occasionally made posts showing concern for Luni's state of mind and what would happen if she were to ever snap from stress. In his private life he tried searching for countermeasures, reaching out to the government, business rivals and even mercenary companies to see if anything could be done to stop her if she ever went on a rampage.

When those approaches yielded nothing fruitful, he reached out to the other directors of the GACHA Conglomerate, knowing full well that if anyone had any countermeasure for a rogue Creator, it would likely be the military-tech branch. That meeting had resulted in some other directors laughing at him, calling him paranoid, but once he presented his proof, likening it to a normal human and how probable it was for them to snap once a certain threshold passed, this thing became more serious.

To his disappointment, however, all that it had accomplished was ruining everyone's day. The military branch leader declared that even with their strongest weapons they couldn't even scratch Luni. He had explained that the best they could hope to accomplish was a battle of attrition: throwing everything they had at her and hope it bought enough time to evacuate civilians and hopefully bring the Creator back to her senses. Even with powerful mages, the chances they had of surviving against a Creator's manipulation of reality were very slim.

That meeting had ended with a somber tone, everyone praying that something like that never happened. It had left a bad taste in Mr. Whale's mouth, knowing that the entire universe's continued existence depended on the ultimate being's mood swings.

It should have been easy for him, since he was in charge of the entertainment branch of the company, to come up with ways that Luni could relieve her stress, but aside from the occasional blog posts, she had ceased contact with the people.

What was strange was that Luni's assistant also stopped answering messages. In the past, when Luni wasn't available to manage her social accounts, the succubus often took care of it instead. She maintained her own social media, filled with provocative content, including running a small side business of love advice for couples. Lilith had a very large fan base of her own, mostly because of her nature and openness to share just about anything.

Lilith had made succubuses famous, the previous stigma and hatred towards the demonic species was completely gone by end of the year 1500. She was known to be even more social than her master. The fact she went silent as well only added to his worry that something was deeply wrong and would eventually reach them.

He bought a large plot of land and prepared for the worst even though he knew it would amount to nothing since Luni's inevitable blowup would impact the whole planet. It was one of the darkest periods of his life. Because he could not find a way, any way to counter the Creator in case she went mad, he resigned to a life of anxiety and expected the worst. It was like nothing he did mattered anymore; all of his accomplishments were just a temporary relief from the certain doom that soon would claim their world. However, even in the pits of his depression, he never gave up his search and eventually, something miraculous happened.

Dr. Gacha came into his life.

It had almost seemed like a joke; a mysterious scientist with their company's same name appearing out of a dark alley and offering him the opportunity of a lifetime: a way to stop Luni, a countermeasure, a way out. All that the proclaimed scientist required was access to ridiculous amounts of funding, staff both professional and amoral enough to not care about any experiments done, and a facility to work his theory out.

As proof for his concept of 'hidden genetic power,' he presented Mr. Whale his pet, a white kitten with gold eyes. The businessman was doubtful of his claims, but the stone-faced doctor merely replied that his daughter, as he called the cat, could defeat entire armies on her own, easily equaling and eventually surpassing the strongest warriors of the world.

Then the cat turned into a feline-girl and made lightning surround her body. That convinced him that the doctor's vision had truth to it, but he needed to test it out first—you never accept a business deal without insurance and so, to ensure that the doctor was not just an overly proud dad, he went to the strongest mercenary band he knew of, asked for their twenty strongest members and told them to beat up the feline.

The mercenaries laughed and asked if he was serious, despite the large sum of money he offered. They thought Mr. Whale had finally gone insane from his paranoia but complied. They met the cat, Shiro, in her animal form and laughed again. When she transformed and fried the first mercenary with a bolt of lightning, they didn't find the situation very funny anymore.

The demonstration ended as the last mercenary fell to the ground, writhing in pain. The girl smiled triumphantly at her father. She hadn't even broken a sweat, in fact, it looked like she was just getting started. The mercenaries had resentfully given the girl their respects and retired with their money.

Dr. Gacha then explained the rest of his reasoning. His plan was to make an entire army of hundreds of thousands of people who had undergone the 'awakening' as he seemed to call it.

Mr. Whale used the large plot of land he had bought for the initial lab where Dr. Gacha conducted his beginning experiments, funding it with his own money. After results began to pour in, he presented it to the director's board, got even more funding and the rest is history. The gigantic facility that is the HQ of Project R.N.G. is proof of the efforts they went through to get the positive results they did... Regardless of the means they used to arrive at them.

If everything worked out as planned, then they would have the means of possibly stopping the Creator when she eventually snapped, they could protect not just humanity, but the entire world, possibly even the entire universe. No matter the costs, they would be successful. The future depended on them.

3

It had been a month since that meeting occurred after the revolt in the Coliseum, and true to his word, Dr. Gacha created two, new specialized teams to conduct the proposed projects, one led by himself and the other by a scientist of his choosing. On the fifth floor, both labs had acquired new, cutting-edge equipment for engineering and conducting research.

The 'Duplicate' project was expected to produce over a hundred clones per week, but for now, it would be a place to test suitable cloning with the equipment for dealing with failed experiments or defects.

The 'Limit Break' project was ready for their new assignment the day after the meeting with Mr. Whale. Using his personal office, which was already a highly specialized lab for personal tests, the team consisting of him, Dr. Ivanovski, and Dr. Ferdinand immediately went to work analyzing Subject 444's samples.

"Dr. Gacha, sir, we have finished today's experiments," the bespectacled scientist said as he approached Dr. Gacha, accompanied by his bearded partner.

Dr. Gacha looked up from his console, nodding as the man handed the document to him.

"I never expected to find the exact components that caused the abrupt transformation in that subject, let alone discover a way to make it work for others. But I believe we finally made a breakthrough. Once you read the report, I'm sure you'll understand, sir," the bearded scientist said with enthusiasm.

"You may be done for today. Good work." Dr. Gacha glanced over the paper.

At first, the trio had thought it would be hard to find what exactly caused the sudden increase in power, but with the new equipment and technology they had access to, it had been relatively easy. By the end of the first week of research, they had found the source and the substances that triggered the 'limit break' in Subject 444. However, it was one thing to know the source, and another to trigger 'limit breaks' in different subjects.

For the basis of Project R.N.G., they had created a series of steps that would ready a subject for the eventual awakening of their genes. They had defined stress, adrenaline, suffering, desperation, and hope as the essential conditions required for the awakening, but too much would either cripple a subject's emotions, make them vegetables, or end in death. Thus, the shock therapy was born.

Requiring just the minimum amount of a harsh environment for each subject, the treatment forcibly awakened the genes thanks to a combination of electric shocks and a special fluid, engineered using genetic information of each individual, which guaranteed the awakening of the hidden genes in just a few sessions, many of them on the very first one.

The scientist noted as he read over the report from today's latest breakthrough in their project; they had been partly successful in integrating the new source with his daughter's blood. The report noted that a few more adjustments would be necessary for the blood sample to seamlessly integrate with the source, theoretically making the perfect serum for his Shiro.

She always offered to donate blood for testing the moment she heard they needed some, wanting to please him in any way she could.

"Papa, are you finished for today?" his beloved daughter asked as she walked towards him in human form.

He smiled. "Of course, my dear Shiro. Thanks to you, things are progressing much faster now." He set the report aside as the girl took a spot on his lap.

"Yay! I'm happy to help you, Papa!" Shiro exclaimed joyfully, purring at her father's praise. Few things could cause him to laugh, but his daughter was one of those things.

"How about you, my child? I heard you kept the doctors busy today," he asked in a kind voice, causing the girl to tilt her head towards him.

"I had a good workout! I beat my record at the robots by a whole ten seconds!" she exclaimed, causing the doctor to chuckle and put his hand on her head.

"You did great, my daughter. I'm proud of you."

Unlike all the subjects in the facility who had been forced to train their powers, Shiro did it out of her own will. Ever since she awakened, she was charged with an enormous motivation to protect him, and for that, she had to get stronger. One of her favorite pastimes was to train herself and master her own abilities, willing her body to become stronger, faster, and more resilient with each exercise session.

In fact, she was the one who recommended the use of their current training facilities. A gauntlet against a thousand robots, enduring the force of crushing gravity, resistance against elemental attacks, holding one's breath to its absolute limit, ultimately forcing the body to adapt and evolve. She tested and trained in all of them, making sure her body was as strong as it could be. Of course, also being a cat, she loved her rest hours and often took cat naps to re-energize.

He noticed that she stopped purring and had a worried look on her face. "Shiro, is something wrong?" he asked the cat girl, causing her tail and ears to stand up in surprise, she turned to him with an awkward smile.

"It's nothing papa, I'm just… worried about them. I know you said I shouldn't be, but they are still my friends…" the girl mourned, causing the scientist to sigh.

His daughter's friendship with those subjects was problematic. She had disappeared for a long time, making him worried that she might have been caught in something, but he knew she could take care of herself. Even Drago was nothing compared to his daughter's strength. When he had found her in that room with the other children, on friendly terms, he explained to her the importance of this project.

He had told her that if she were to find a subject, that she should not, under any circumstances, get attached to them. She did, and they now likely hated her for her association with him. To make matters worse, Subject 443, Myo, had perished during the pandemonium. He had yet to tell her of that fact, so whenever she asked how they were doing, he changed the subject.

"It's all right to worry about people you are close to, my Shiro, but remember… They only met you as a pet, a cat, not as the person you truly are. They expected you to comfort them like a pet would, they didn't expect you to have a family," he explained to her, gently rubbing the tip of her left ear.

She sighed, purring slightly, but still looking down. "You always speak in hard words, Papa, but I get it... I was just curious to see them, the soldiers who would one day help protect everyone. I still want to be friends with them," Shiro said, her eyes glistening at the possibility.

She saw how sad and angry they seemed to be most of the time. Being a cat made things harder to understand, but even then, she could still see they were unhappy being there, especially in Myo's case, who would sometimes hug her against his chest whenever he couldn't get to sleep. As a cat, Shiro did whatever she could to try to comfort them, and for a while, it worked, but... When they learned of her true identity and who her father was, affection turned into shock, and then hate. They hated her father, and it hurt her a great deal.

She wasn't stupid, not as much as she knew others thought she was. She knew that the whole project her father was directing was hard and stressful. She suggested some treatment herself and she tested them all out. If they persisted, if they had the determination to become strong, they could get through it. She knew what was at stake, her father explained the situation about Luni, how dangerous she was and what could happen to not only her and her papa, but to the entire world if the Creator were to go berserk.

If only they could see it her way that what they were doing would make them strong...

"If you want to write a letter to your friends back home, I can have Mr. Whale send it to them. You would like to know how they are doing after so long, would you not?" the scientist suggested, still gently patting her head.

Shiro blinked at his words! She had been so focused on getting stronger and trying to help, she completely forgot to write her friends she left behind! They must be so worried!

"Can I really write to them? Wouldn't it be a... security... bleach?" she asked in hesitation as her papa chuckled and ruffled her hair again. She meowed indignantly.

"It's 'security *breach*,' and don't worry about it, Mr. Whale knows how to be discreet, I'm sure he can deliver your letters."

"Thanks, papa, I love you!" she exclaimed before running towards his desk to get writing materials for her letters.

Dr. Gacha sighed as he watched her wracking her brain to figure out what to write her friends back home. He hated that his daughter had to go through this, he would have liked to leave her home until they concluded the project. It was selfish and irresponsible, but he could never bear the thought of leaving her alone for so long because his little Shiro, his daughter, was the only light that could keep him sane in this life.

4

As time passed, things changed for them. The death of one of their own had been scarred into every child in the facility, but little by little, they learned to move on, to focus on tomorrow, on the moment, as if what they had experienced in the past was nothing but a terrible dream.

Ever since the incident, their prison changed to become increasingly more comfortable and livable. Their rooms seemed even more so now, having gained many more decorations over time, more comfortable beds, pillows and even clothes. The television set even got upgraded to a larger model, providing much clearer pictures than before.

The guards no longer bothered them, preferring to stay stoically quiet or conversing with one another, avoiding the children if possible. Rather than bang on their door as they used to, they now had installed a small, electronic chime that was used to call them when needed.

The Coliseum seemed to disappear, and, in its place, the gymnasium came back with daily meetings that lasted even longer. Sure, now guards would stay in the corners of the buildings, watching them like eagles for the slightest sight of a rebellion brewing, but that didn't take the enjoyment of being able to meet friends from other wards away.

They had brought the experiments and training to a full stop, and in its place, they only needed to partake in painless blood exams every week. The scientists had told them that use of experiment labs or training facilities was optional now, to be requested at their own initiative rather than obligatory sessions. Many children cheered at this, feeling like they had been finally freed from their torment and that things would get better for them. Many others, however, used the training facilities to become stronger or the experiment labs to train their endurance, which is exactly what the new leader of the mutant ward, Leo, was taking advantage of.

With the death of the previous leader of the mutant ward, the second strongest took his chance to assert his dominance, naming himself as the new leader. Unlike the aggressive dragon, however, Leo took the defeats he suffered during both the Coliseum battles and the riot to heart and adopted a much more cautious stance than Drago had. Instead of forcefully trying to make others join the army, he left that part to the scientists. As a policy, however, he demanded that all mutants, no matter their loyalties, requested access to the training facilities every day.

This caused a small problem for the other children who wanted to train themselves. There were limited training facilities and for each subject, training took about two hours, which meant that they had to wait in queues when more than one person wished to use the same facility. For people that wanted to train for their final push against the scientists, not being able to was inconvenient.

During this period of change, the scientists also declared that they could request anything they wanted, as long as it didn't breach security. Each subject received a small manual that described what they could and could not request and, as expected, freedom wasn't on the list.

However, they could ask for an abundance of things that made their lives more comfortable. New clothes, tastier food, offline video game consoles, magazines, newspapers, manga, anime... virtually anything that didn't result in contact with the outside world. The whole staff made their lives as comfortable as possible.

It sickened Cyko.

"A Creator is a being of ultimate power, born from nothingness with the purpose of creating life as we know it. Our very own universe and its seemingly infinite vastness was created by our very own ultimate being, Luni. One thing that should be noted, is that these Creators possess a consciousness not too different from a human," the documentary host said, "it is, however, a little frightening to observe how many signs of stress she is displaying. Is Luni taking care of herself, is she taking time off to rest? What would happen if she were to snap, what would happen to us? That is, unfortunately, a question we do not know the answer to," he concluded before the screen changed to show several documented cases of Luni losing her temper, comparing it with ones where she was relaxed.

"Pfft, they really are going all out with trying to make us fear or hate the Creator, huh?" Cyko commented with an annoyed sigh, lying down on his bed to rest after returning from his training session.

"It's everywhere, dear friend. We have that poster on our door for a reason. They want to brainwash us and Scythe agrees with me." Magy, who was also lying down on her own bed, gestured towards the poster stuck on the main door. On it were motivational words about honor, friendship, and glory that waited them when they fully became members of the 'army' that would protect the world from the worst of evils.

"After what happened at the Coliseum… They are afraid, afraid of us," Cyko said with a small smile, even as his eyes looked angry.

Magy shook her head, aware that Cyko couldn't have seen it from his position. "I don't think it's that, Cyko. If they truly feared us, they would have resorted to more extreme methods of control. They still underestimate us," she reasoned as Cyko sighed in reluctant agreement.

"It's just… What they are doing, Magy, it's *working*. Kids are falling for it! And don't even get me started on that lion!" Cyko seethed as he thought about what the scientists' latest plot achieved.

Many children took the new comforts and privileges as a sign that their lives would be better, that it made up for their past torment. Sure, they still supported Tela and wanted to be free, but their spirits were slowly giving in and to make matters worse, Drago's death didn't change much for the mutant ward, since the new 'leader' still openly supported the project for the strength it gave them.

"I know, my friend, and it saddens me that some of us are losing the desire to be free in exchange for comfort, but what matters now is what we want, those of us that want to be free." She got up as she heard an electronic chime. "We still have people who would fight alongside us and if there's one thing we can be glad about… it's that they still let us meet with them. Even if Tela's power is good for communication, nothing beats a face-to-face talk."

Cyko sighed and got up from his own bed to prepare for today's meeting. Now, instead of a guard banging down their door, they called them through an electronic chime. Even still, Cyko opened the door and was greeted by that same giant brute of a guard.

"The meeting will start soon; would you like to go?" the guard asked in a clipped voice, likely wishing he could go back to insulting and threatening him. The guard stepped aside so Cyko and Magy could walk out. A small army of heavily armed guards, who would still be thrilled to strike them at the slightest provocation, escorted them towards the gate.

As the children stepped inside the gymnasium, Cyko and Magy looked for their friends, ignoring the guards that positioned themselves in the corners. After a few minutes, they spotted Cyko's family sitting together at one table, and a little further away, Tela stood amidst a small crowd of people, serious looks on their faces as they were deep in discussion. They both wanted to speak with Tela, to see how she was doing and what she had planned, but they knew it wasn't the time, besides, Cyko's family spotted him and was calling him over.

"Cyko! Hey there, how are you doing?" One of his older sisters, Anna, greeted him with a huge smile.

"Hey everyone, it's been a while," the enhancer said, patting Starry's head as she went near him, causing the small girl to giggle.

"It's been a few weeks, are you sure you are all right?" Henry, his eldest brother asked in a worried voice.

It had been a while since Cyko last saw them. Even with the meetings being held every day, he often missed them to use the time for training instead. Because of the queue, he sometimes had to wait before he got to use the facility and that meant training when everyone else was having 'fun' in the gymnasium.

"Yes, brother, I'm as fine as I can be," he paused. "I wish Myo was here. I hate that they are trying to make us forget what they did, but I know Myo would've liked this, not being forced to fight or be tortured anymore."

Cyko and Magy weren't the only ones affected by his death. For Cyko's family, it was a blow that almost broke them. The older siblings felt the pain of losing yet another younger sibling, a great shame that kept them up at night. Starry had cried for days, seeing the death of Myo firsthand had struck her hard and even Torch's own attempts at comforting her couldn't lift her mood. Eventually one day she woke up and demanded to be taken to the training facilities to get stronger to protect her family.

Soon enough, they all took up training to improve themselves. Those who were helping Tela directly started to focus on their abilities to use them to better scout and map the facility.

There was one thing that worried them… their brother, Cyko. The massacre that happened during the battles was so unlike him, to kill, to mock his enemies with such little care, enjoying their suffering and fear as they desperately tried to save themselves. Cyko killed all those that he deemed responsible for Myo's death.

"This is a cursed place, isn't it?" Magy said sadly, her serene face adding a melancholic tone to her words. "They torture us, experiment on us, they make us go through things no child should ever go through. A tragedy happens, we fight back and then, they kill us with kindness to make us forget what they did."

Magy clapped her hands, startling everyone.

"Many of us just want a better, more normal life, which is why this trick works so well. We can't let ourselves be turned into drones who do nothing but fight."

"I agree with her," Cyko said. "We need to work together and punish them for all they did."

Cyko sat down at the table, moving over so Magy could sit beside him. "I know you guys are worried about me, about what I am becoming… I know the price of that sudden surge of power I got, it will slowly turn me into a monster."

The table went silent.

"Is that really true, Cyko?" Anna looked down to avoid his eyes.

Cyko sighed and nodded. "It was the price I was told I would need to pay for the power I got. I wish I had known how to get it sooner, if I did, maybe Myo would still be alive… But you guys have nothing to worry about, I would never hurt any of you on purpose, not even at my craziest," he assured them with a friendly smile.

"Big bro… you are not a monster." Everyone turned towards Starry, who had spoken. "The real monsters are the adults in this place. I know Cyko would never hurt us." She created several dark stars that hovered around Cyko, as if he was the night sky, a sky they haven't seen in a long while.

The enhancer stared at her and then at the beautiful stars flying around as if orbiting his head. He chuckled.

"She is right, you are not a monster Cyko, and to us, you'll never be a monster," Anna said, smiling wildly as she saw her siblings nodding in agreement.

His siblings echoed their opinions, knowing that despite his change in appearance, strength, and eventually in personality, they would still love him the same.

"Oh, guys..." he whispered, overwhelmed by his appreciation for them.

They would be a family no matter what happened. They would fight together, they would laugh, they would cry... They would live and one day, they would all be free, together.

5

Several weeks had passed, it had now been two months since Myo died. Everyone who either witnessed or taken part in the battle to save his life was changed, for the better or for the worse. The rebels were increasingly more motivated, the loyal mutants wished to keep the army going strong and the ones that didn't fall on either side were traumatized enough to partner with whoever scared them the least. Everyone had learned something from the riot... Everyone except him.

Reddox had fought. His attacks were massive and powerful, many mutants were incapacitated, but once it was over... he didn't try. He didn't feel like it, he never *felt* like it. Ellyn's encouraging words helped sometimes, along with the feeling of guilt that threatened to consume him whenever he looked at anyone.

He was brought to this lab long before the others. Different from the rest and terminally ill, he was almost instantly discarded. Back then, he had been full of emotion and terrified of dying. He was lying on a bed when the doctors told him that despite the magic he awakened, it would be unlikely that he would survive.

He became desperate. With everything in him, he wanted to live. He wished he could be like Luni, that he could do anything he wished, erase his illness, save himself and the others, no matter the price. It was a very surreal day for him, but he accomplished his goal: his illness was gone.

And so were all his emotions.

He didn't notice it right away, thinking he felt numb because he was still recovering, but as the days passed, he noticed that nothing he did garnered any emotional response. He ate to satiate his hunger, but it didn't please him. He went through the steps of experimentation and training, but didn't feel terrified or scared. This earned the side effect of the scientists treating him like a favorite because he now did whatever they asked of him without complaint. This added to his powers, he was hailed as the strongest and most useful subject of the entire project, and the scientists went out of their way to please him. He got nicer clothes before anyone else, tastier food before anyone else…

Although, there was one thing he noticed he could still feel… guilt. He knew he had almost a supreme power in this place, his magic coupled with his ability to 'erase' things and limited time manipulation made him valuable in the eyes of the scientists, but he never really felt the need to put forth all of his efforts—he didn't even know his own full capabilities.

Yet, recent events were changing his mind.

"I know how you feel, Reddox." Ellyn, who had accompanied him in silence for today's meeting, looked at him with concerned eyes. "The wind can pick up on your sadness. You are feeling guilty again, aren't you?"

"It's nothing, I'm just contemplating recent events," he said, not wanting his perhaps only friend to worry about him. Besides, he was busy talking mentally with Tela.

"Today has been a rather pleasant day, don't you think? Let's not talk about that stuff now," Reddox said, causing Ellyn to sigh in annoyance.

"I've known you for nearly six months now, Reddox, I think I know when you are trying to change the subject." She shook her head. She would not let him get away with it so easily! "Despite what you believe of yourself, you do have feelings. I can pick up the guilt you feel every day. You want to help but can't muster enough willpower to do so," she said matter-of-factly.

He stayed silent for a while. It was always like this, she would try to comfort him or encourage him, even when he told her it was useless, he lost his ability to care and to feel motivation. Or so he thought, anyway. This girl…

"Then, tell me, Ellyn, what am I supposed to do? The last person I tried to help died under my watch, how can I expect to help anyone else if I can't even muster enough emotional resolve? Can I even protect you, if it comes down to it?" Reddox asked, exasperated at his inability to care. When Ellyn clenched her hand on his, however, he felt a surge of serenity.

"Then try again. Keep trying, Reddox. I know you want to be free just as much as the rest of us and if you can't care enough, then let me care for you!"

"Are you sure it's a good idea? I don't even know how I can help."

"There are many ways, don't worry about it, what matters is that if we help, we can give peace to everyone here! What do you say, Red?" she asked smiling, letting him know that she would be okay with whatever he chose.

Reddox turned his gaze away thoughtfully. He didn't know if he could put everything into it, he may never feel the accomplishment of helping free all the children. He may not have many feelings anymore, but he still had a conscience… And the guilt that threatened to consume him was telling him he should try it, that fighting for something good would make up for his past mistakes and his lack of care.

"Fine, then. I'll do it."

"You won't regret it, Reddox! I promise you! We'll do our best together!" she exclaimed, letting the wind blow around them in encouragement.

Nodding, Reddox kept looking around as she rambled about ways they could help, using the wind curtain she made to ensure no sound would escape and be picked up by the guards. Ellyn didn't see it, but the mage couldn't help but smile at how passionate she was.

Yes, this girl somehow made him feel again, in a way. Pushing herself into his life the moment they met. Yet another feeling he thought he had lost, the feeling of gratitude. Maybe, just maybe he still had a chance of escaping the guilt and helping others, and he knew that the girl would make him try, even if he couldn't muster the emotion to. She would feel for them both.

6

In her mind's eye, many conversations were happening simultaneously, a constant flow of different emotions, thoughts, desires, and fears all ran through her heart, threatening to overwhelm her spirit, to break her concentration and send her mind into a breakdown. Yet, even as the stress of talking with dozens of children at once and monitoring the minds of hundreds of guards and scientists tried to consume her, she kept working to make sure everything would be flawless.

In a world of darkness, Tela was surrounded by hundreds of glowing phantom monitors and by an equal number of miniature versions of herself, respectively representing all the situations she was handling at the same time and her personality partitions that were focusing on them.

It had taken her a while to get back to her normal self after Myo's death, but when she did, she immediately noticed what the scientists were planning and went to work on trying to counter their brainwashing tactics with her own abilities, trying to change the minds of the children most likely to fall into the trap.

It was hard, Tela really wished she could just convince everyone, even the loyalists of the mutant ward, that being free is the best choice, but… She couldn't do that, not without trampling even more on their freewill than she already had.

"It's done," Tela whispered to herself as her mental faculties finally completed a detailed map on the facility by combining all the information gathered by volunteers the past few months, painstakingly matching every single detail they had given her and comparing it with others, noting and removing errors of memory and mistaken information. The map appeared before her.

The lowest first floor of the building was where the children were kept confined in their rooms and had little freedom. The floor was separated by wards, as they had already known, and in each of these was a large elevator that connected to the second and last floor she mapped.

The second floor was the area where every single one of them was taken to be tested, experimented, and tortured for the sake of creating the perfect soldiers. The area had large corridors leading to the different kinds of labs.

That was where her range died off, however. She knew that the second floor had many elevators that connected to the wards in the first floor, but she also knew that there were other elevators that connected to an unknown, third floor. Because the ventilation shafts didn't connect to that floor and because the scientists never took the children there, what happened in that particular area and its structure was unknown to her. From that point on they would likely have to fight their way out.

An element of surprise was needed. The longer their enemies took to notice their rebellion, the bigger advantage they would have. If they broke into the upper floors without the staff knowing, then fighting their way out would be much simpler, and to accomplish that... Tela had formulated a plan.

Over the years she had spent as a prisoner, she had managed to tag every scientist and guard that worked on the lower levels. Now there were exactly 400 guards, spread unevenly over all the wards on the first floor.

With nearly 500 children, they outnumbered the guards on their floor, but she doubted that those were all the numbers they had, because just on the second floor, there were about 300 other guards present and they likely had many more on higher floors.

Out of those 700 guards on the first two floors, at least 20 percent she could feel had magical power... Not to mention the number of mutants loyal to Leo, which numbered around eighty-five. It may seem like a small number compared to the total allies she had, but each mutant was more powerful than a hundred guards. They would be dangerous opponents and chances are that a clash would be inevitable. She could always leave the mutants behind, but... many of them also wished for freedom, it would be cruel of her to deny them that. She had a plan to separate the loyalists from her allies, anyway.

Regarding the guards, she had gone to great lengths to learn their behavior. She had noticed that many of them didn't take their job seriously and had mainly feelings of boredom and anger at having to watch over children.

Obviously, the guards started paying closer attention after dozens of them got killed, which caused tension amongst the normal guards and the magical ones, but thanks to the 'peace' that the recent change in conditions had caused and for how long it already lasted, the guards went back to being complacent, no longer believing that the children would be a threat.

The guards weren't the only security issue, however. The walls and the structure of the facility were the biggest obstacles to their freedom. Made with the strongest construction material available and with hundreds of magical barriers and wards on every surface, the facility was a veritable fortress that could easily withstand nuclear explosions from both outside and inside, the only exception being the ground of the Coliseum.

The wards were the main problem that prevented her from getting access to the rest of the facility, because aside from reinforcing the structure of the facility, they also stopped all magical energy from passing through, which proved her mental abilities useless. She couldn't contact the outside world for help, not even with their gods helping them, as the wards somehow blocked faith from passing through. They were truly and completely isolated from the world.

Tela's own mental influence's sphere of propagation spread with the use of her tendrils, intangible and invisible, they manifested from the crown of her head and slithered either into the air or into the ground, seeking the target she designated, after which it would connect to that person's forehead, allowing a mental link to exist between them as long as the tendril existed or maintained contact. Hundreds of tendrils could travel through the ventilation shafts at once.

The reason she didn't use them to map the floors was because she could control them, but couldn't see through her tendrils, which is why she tagged people. Once tagged, she could easily find out where they are. Patrol routes and the movement of children were easily monitored in such a way, ensuring that everyone was all right being one of her top priorities.

As long as there was a hole even as small as a needle, unprotected and with no wards, her tendrils could pass through, which made many great advances in their plans. Things that would have taken years to organize had taken just a few months.

Everything was ready. Thanks to everyone's efforts and help, they arrived at the point where conditions were ideal for their rebellion, for the final push towards their freedom. Already, her many fragments were subtly manipulating the guards' minds to feel as if today was just a regular day, making them less likely to notice anything amiss. She concentrated her mind and informed everyone of what was about to happen.

"*It's time. Rest well, for tomorrow will be our last day here.*"

CHAPTER 6

REBELLION

1

Today was already tense, she could sense it. No one was talking, no one smiled, everyone clumped together in familiar groups, standing near the southern gate, opposite from the larger gate the mutants used to enter and exit their wards.

Leo wasn't present alongside half of his allies, they were all using many training facilities on the second floor, which just made things better for Tela. The leading loyalist present was a rhino mutant with super strength, who was wrestling against a Minotaur mutant while the other loyalists cheered. The non-violent mutants were mingling in the middle of the arena, occasional taking glances at her, those were the mutant allies, who sought freedom just as much as the rest.

The guards, 50 total, stood at the corners, helmets and bulky armor concealing their bored expressions. For them, it was just another, typical day...

"Tela." A hand touched her shoulder, causing her to turn her head toward the person, meeting eager blue eyes. "No matter what happens from now on, I'd like you to know that you are one of my best friends. Without you, none of this would be possible. I, we, all of us owe you a lot."

"It's thanks to everyone's efforts that we got so far, Cyko. But I also consider you a great friend of mine, we went through so much in this horrible prison... You always believed in me, you never stopped trusting in me even after... after I couldn't save Myo. You always stayed loyal, my friend, and that means a lot." Her face was flushed, but the genuine smile of a friend caused Cyko to let out an embarrassed laugh.

"So cheesy, but that's what I like about you. Say, Tela, what do you want to be when you grow up?" he asked suddenly, causing her to blink.

"Hmm… I never thought about it much, not since I got here, but… I think I might want to become a psychologist, to help people heal and deal with their problems… I want to continue helping, and I think my powers would make me suited for that."

"That job fits you well, Tela. I can imagine how many people you would save, just like how many you'll save now."

"What about you then, my friend?" the telepath asked through feelings of warmth.

Cyko's face for a moment looked resigned, but his own feelings never turned into sadness. "I might end up in an asylum for the criminally insane you know, at least that would be a much better place than in here," he said in a joking tone, but his words still struck a chord with Tela. She knew what he meant, she had felt his change…

Turning around, Tela put her arms around Cyko and filled his heart with warmth.

"If you end up in an asylum, Cyko… then I'll be the one who will assist and help you recover," she whispered gently. He replied by putting his own arms around her.

"I would like nothing more, Tela."

The announcement that declared that the meeting was over sounded just as they parted ways, smiling with determined eyes. Without a word being said, they turned in opposite directions—Cyko returned to Magy and his family's side while Tela went towards the center of the gymnasium.

The gates of all the wards were already open, and the mutants had started to walk in. The ones faithful to her got close behind. The guards noticed nothing unusual at first, but when the last loyalist entered and no one else had moved from their spot near the south most gate, they called out, "Hey, rats, get moving! We don't have all day!"

"… NOW!"

At Tela's mental yell, chaos seemed to erupt in an instant. The giant metal door that led towards the mutant ward closed abruptly, sealing the way. Darkness soon replaced the previously bright environment.

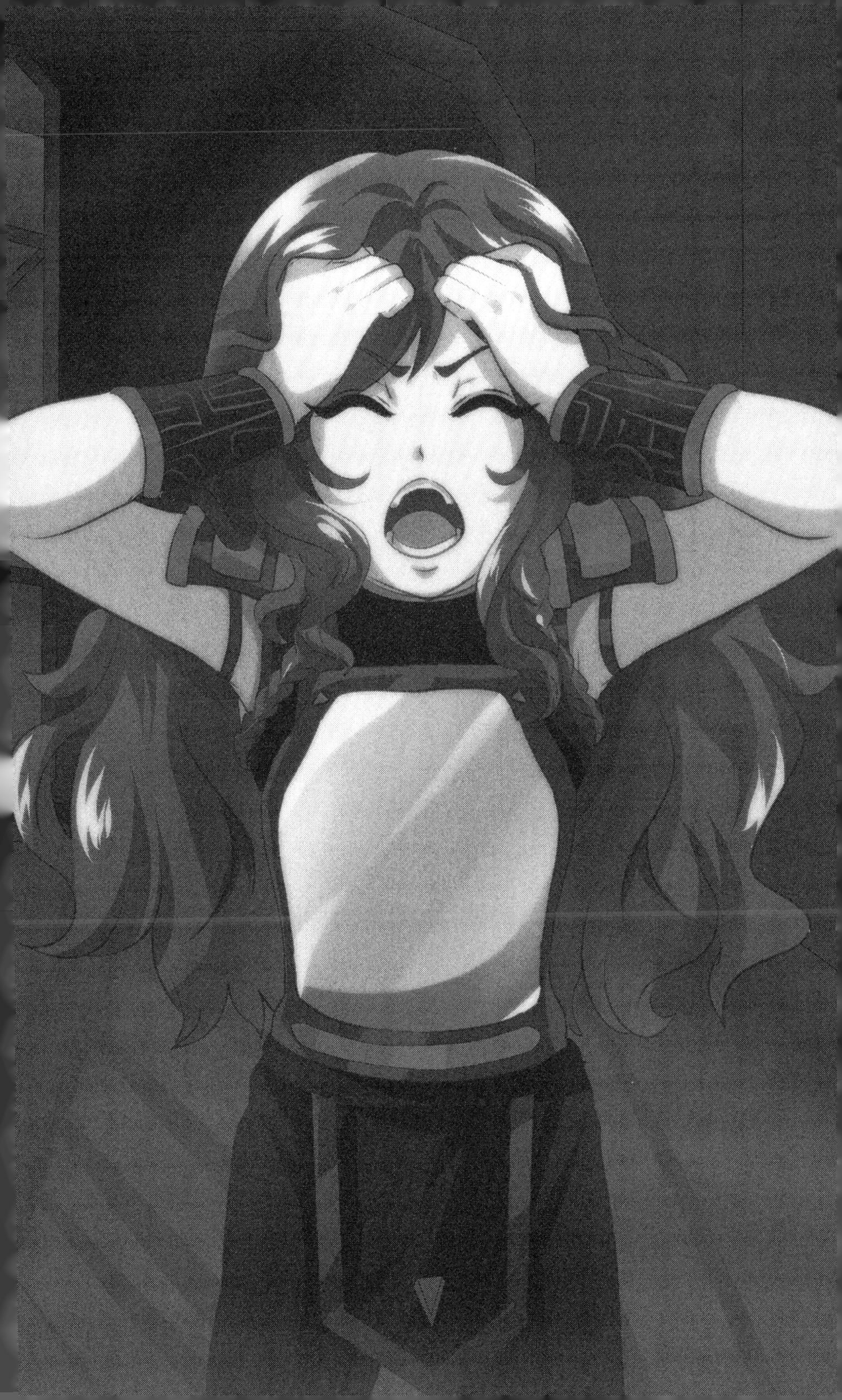

Disoriented, but still trained professionals, the guards quickly grabbed for their weapons and aimed at the threat: the test subjects.

Just as the emergency lights flickered to life, the children acted immediately. Energetic and physical attacks of all kinds went out at once. Cyko and Magy had already killed 10 guards by the time they took to notice what happened.

In less than thirty seconds, the 50 heavily-armed guards had been reduced to only a few alive either writhing in pain or unconscious. Cyko and Magy standing over the bodies of the dead guards startled many of the children, the dim lighting only making them appear more sinister, eyes glowing with power.

The rebellion had begun.

"Everyone, please calm down," Tela declared mentally, sending a wave of reassurance through the crowd, comforting most of the scared children.

"This is it, everyone. The moment we have been waiting for so long has finally arrived. Today, we fight for our freedom!" Tela declared loudly, everyone felt her determination and resolve.

"I know many of you had given up, that you didn't feel like fighting anymore, that the events of the last riot had broken our spirits. When they started treating us better, no longer forcibly taking us to be tortured and experimented on like animals, many of us thought this would be the best 'freedom' we could get, that we shouldn't worry anymore because we were no longer treated like trash... But don't allow yourselves to forget the monsters they truly are and what they've done to us! We don't want to be here, we want to be free! We won't accept their lies!" the leader declared, outrage and determination mixing to form the resolve she had, since the beginning, to help free everyone.

The children cheered, roaring with their own growing determination to be free from their prison. It was now or never, to be free or to be confined, those were their only choices.

"Now... We'll fight together as one!" Tela's eyes were glowing with power. As soon as her words entered their heads, they felt something click.

Suddenly, they could feel one another. They were all attached by Tela's tendrils.

"*Guards approaching, 70 armed and 10 mages!*" Tela informed them, causing everyone to turn towards the south gate almost as one.

Cyko and Magy quickly cut down the first guards who had positioned themselves nearest the door.

"We will go first and clear the elevator!" the enhancer shouted before dashing inside the dark corridor alongside his roommate. Tela sent a mental nod towards him, knowing they would find their way thanks to her network and the mental map she had made for them. Soon enough, terrified screams of pain and death echoed through the open door.

"*Everyone, let's go!*" she commanded as they charged the large corridor as one, using Tela's mental instructions to create a formation where those with defensive abilities would stay in front, paving the way for those behind to attack with impunity.

This was the first step of her plan. Thanks to the aftermath of the battle with Drago, she had deduced that every area in the facility could isolate itself. It had been an interesting and worrying thought, knowing she could use it against the staff or they could use it against them, but she never really thought it could work until Reddox and Ellyn brought it up.

They had offered to use their unique abilities to help as much as they could and while Ellyn's powers over wind weren't that rare, her unique ability of being able to talk with the wind allowed her to eavesdrop on many conversations between the guards and scientists, some of which talked about the security system they had in place, confirming that every area of the facility could be isolated in case an emergency were to happen. Reddox said he could do anything as long as he had enough time, and that was something they now have plenty of, since the staff had pacified them.

Reddox was classified as the single, most powerful child amongst them, so he had made use of his divination powers. He mapped out where every panel that activated and deactivated the isolation was by using Tela's map. Unfortunately, he could only use divination if the map already existed, and he refused to use the darker rituals in his grimoires to make a map of the whole facility.

That had been enough, however, as the next part involved secretly placing the magical sigils that would activate the isolation the moment Tela gave the order. This had taken much longer, as it had been hard to sneak children across the places for the magic to work. The two floors that Tela had mapped were now fully under her control.

"Tela, we have arrived," Reddox claimed as he vaporized the last guard who tried to sneak up on them, causing the redhead to nod and look at the elevator, its large doors opened just like she wanted them to.

"There were guards panicking inside, but we took care of it," Cyko, who had been standing inside the elevator, said with a large grin, directed towards the fallen guards.

"All right everyone, the elevator is still working, but we can't all ride it at the same time. We'll need to do it in small groups. There are guards right outside the door above, however, so the first people to go need to take care of them and hold position until everyone is here," Tela explained, inwardly feeling thankful that if everything went well, the planned route she had in mind would see little combat. Sure, it may or may not condemn the mutants she left behind for a life of slavery and maybe even starvation if they were forgotten about here... But the life of innocents far outweighed the costs.

"Let us go ahead. Me and Cyko can soften them up," Magy said out loud, her pristine scythe seemed to glint in anticipation, while Cyko's grin widened.

Tela would stay behind, opting to go last just in case more soldiers arrived. Reddox's sigil should have also destroyed the isolation switches, preventing the spell from being lifted, but it never hurt to be careful.

"We'll go as well!" Ellyn exclaimed, dragging an exasperated Reddox with her, a large grin on her own face. "You guys got most of them, leave some for the rest of us!"

Reddox sighed at his friend. "What this airhead means is that all help is good. You two need long-range cover and defense, we can provide that." He stepped into the elevator alongside his friend.

"Don't forget about us, little brother," his oldest brother, Henry, said as he approached, followed by the rest of his family.

"You may be psycho now, but you are our psycho!" Anna said with a grin, raising her cannon-arm in emphasis. She was quickly followed by agreements and assurances from the others, even little Starry was pumped up, although she avoided looking at any blood directly.

A few others also got into the elevator, until it was full, but not uncomfortably so. They were supposed to be the vanguard.

"Good luck everyone," Tela thought to them, her eyes following the elevator as it climbed. The fight had just begun.

As the elevator rose, Reddox took a moment to approach Cyko, who was looking up at the approaching door with anticipation.

"I can feel the power of magic in you," the redhead blurted, to which Cyko blinked and looked at him with a raised eyebrow. "Ever since you changed, there is this new energy inside you. I think you are just like me, in a way."

"What? Why are you being all mysterious? Now, of all times?" Cyko chuckled, before turning back to await their arrival. "So, I'm just like you, huh?"

Reddox opened his mouth to respond but frowned as he noticed that the door wasn't open.

"That might be a problem. Scythe says the walls and doors are all heavily fortified with defensive spells," Magy offered, her red eyes glowing in the emergency lights as she tried to analyze the door.

Cyko mentally informed Tela of the situation. Almost immediately, they all received a buzz of confusion over the matter.

"But... How? I can still feel the guards outside, but... Oh. The airshafts are open, maybe it's a design mistake? Reddox, do you think you can erase that door?"

"Hmm... No, it wasn't the sealing field, it seems the doors were closed manually. They must have heard the commotion below," Reddox reported, his glowing hands casting a red shine around the children present as he analyzed the reinforced door in front of them. *"However, just like all doors of its make, it's filled to the brim with reinforcement and warding seals."*

"This is bad," Tela admitted, her feelings of worry leaking through to those in the elevator, heightening their anxiety. *"Those doors are just as hard as the walls—protected with hundreds of strengthening wards and spells. It would take a massive amount of power to even dent it,"* she explained, knowing that by the time they broke through it, it could be too late.

"Everyone step back!" Cyko yelled as the holo blade in his right arm glowed brightly. Cyko moved forward with a yell, the blue streak of his weapon casting a now cyan glow around them all. With a sound of crushing metal, a large, deep gash formed in the gate.

"Huh, so it really is strong," Cyko commented with a frown.

Reddox, however, was of a different opinion. His hands glowed red as he approached the gate to analyze it once again. "As I thought."

"The spells and wards in this door—and everywhere else, from what I can see—have deteriorated. It's like they got corroded from old age and lack of repair. It should've taken at least a thousand years for spells of this quality to arrive at this level of disrepair. What makes this even stranger is that they look fine at first glance..." Reddox trailed off.

"But.... But how is that possible?" Tela asked, perplexed.

"Deteriorated, huh?" Cyko whispered under his breath. The image of his little brother, Myo, in his last moments, glowing with the drive and desire to live and be free, fighting with all his might. He shook his head. Now was not the time, besides... It couldn't be, could it?

"Then I'll annihilate it completely!" Cyko's arms moved in a flash and then, with each streak of blue another deep gash appeared in the gate.

Just as the door was about to fall, Cyko stopped and charged at it, body glowing with the power of his enhancement as he kicked it, finally breaking it down and sending the large piece of reinforced metal flying. He grinned as he heard yells of pain as the gate flew, landing fifteen meters from the entrance.

The guards that evaded the flying gate instantly open fired upon the group. Several of them cursed when the bullets stopped in midair thanks to a red, glowing magical barrier that appeared in place of the gate. Cyko turned towards Reddox, whose hand was glowing in power.

"We need to clear them out so the elevator can work," the mage commented, causing the enhancer to smirk.

"You don't have to tell me twice!" Cyko jumped out of the barrier, his enhancement making the bullets seem as if they were moving in slow motion. Before the guards even noticed it, three of their colleagues had fallen, the holo blades cutting through their armor like butter.

"Ah, so impatient," Magy scoffed, feeling shivers run down her spine as the guards screamed. "Leave some for me, dear friend!"

The guards panicked due to their rapid decrease in numbers, and those who remained in the elevator moved down the corridor. As the children gradually spread out, more fights ensued.

Cyko and Magy however, soon found how fun it was to hunt down the scientists.

"Dang it, dang it, DANG IT! I didn't sign up for this!" a scientist who was walking back to his quarters for a well-deserved rest, screamed in terror as he desperately tried to open the lab doors, knowing the isolation protocol would keep him safe, but to his dismay, it was already in place, working against him.

"Oh my, who said you could run away?"

Whimpering, the scientist looked down, eyes widening at the sight of two, large, pinkish blades piercing his knees. The pain was very much real, yet the man noticed how it didn't seem to damage the fabric of his pants or spill blood.

"Ah... Aaaarrrghhh!"

"I remember you. You were the one who usually put me through the worst of the 'experiments,' as you called them." The girl made air quotes and sneered. Magy's form seemed to glow in the emergency lights, the darkness only enhancing the effect that her glowing eyes had on him. "Oh, are you crying? Are you begging for mercy? Scythe tells me I should give you exactly what you gave me, no mercy at all," she said in a sinister voice, giggling as the man tried to crawl away from her. She might like this much more than pain.

As the doomed scientist's wails of anguish echoed down the corridors of the second floor, Cyko was having a much different sort of fun. He had gone down one hall in Tela's mental map, which had been full of guards, intent on clearing them out and had found, to his surprise, that they were protecting a small group of scientists who were attempting to evacuate.

"He is tearing us ap-gah!" a nameless guard yelled in desperation, just before Cyko cut him down, effortlessly dancing between their bullets.

"S-stay away, you monster!" one scientist snapped, his terror and fear leading him to pick up one of the fallen weapons and aim at Cyko, who smirked. The corpses of the fallen guards surrounding him and the dim lights made him even more sinister-looking to the cowering scientists. "S-STAY AWAY!" He shakily pointed the weapon at the enhancer, who continued grinning and didn't slow his pace.

The man closed his eyes and pulled the trigger. The loud bang echoed around the corridor, the bullet ricocheting around and the weapon flying out of the man's hands, clattering on the floor. Opening his eyes again, he froze, the child standing right in front of him.

"Here is a lesson. Learn how to use a gun beforehand, idiot," Cyko said with a smirk before plunging his holo blade into his stomach. Chuckling, Cyko let the man fall to the ground to bleed out, turning his gaze toward the other scientists.

"Well then. I've been waiting ages for this moment."

They had been following Tela's advice closely; she had told them before about the number of guards present on the second floor, around 300 with only 30 in the labs. She had informed them that the security on this floor was much higher, and since the corridors didn't isolate themselves like the wards of the first floor, combat was expected, but as long as they had the element of surprise, they could triumph.

Already, both Cyko and Magy had taken care of over a hundred guards, plus over twenty scientists. If they wanted to eliminate more, they would have to keep searching for them, but they needed to secure an elevator to access the next floor. Tela's plan was to get out to freedom rather than fight to the bitter end. Still, it would take time before everyone moved up from the elevator.

"Hey, Tela! Me and Magy will head to the elevator closest to us! Do you think you can ask a few guys to watch over the path we cleared?" Cyko asked, directing his thoughts towards his friend, knowing she would have marked the path he and Magy rampaged through. Soon enough he received a confirmation from her.

"All right but be careful. That corridor is suspiciously deserted," Tela cautioned, knowing full well that some mages could block her tendrils with personal barriers.

"Don't worry, Tela, we got this." Cyko tried to channel his confidence to her. So far, they hadn't come across anything that could stop them and if they kept up like this, they had a real possibility of escaping.

It was a weird but not unwelcome sensation, being connected all together. It felt like they were one, in a way. He knew exactly how many guards were left: 125 and dropping. The brown dots on the mental map marked the scientists, many of which were rounded up in one corner and slowly disappearing, mostly at the hands of the mutants who were on their side.

The map itself could be seen on the upper left corner of their vision, always in perfect focus. Cyko compared it to a video game interface, which also informed him of the condition of his allies.

"Hmm, no one's coming. That is suspicious. Scythe says they might be planning something or have already gone," Magy reasoned, a frown on her face. She had come to enjoy reaping the life of the sinful.

"Well, if there is no one ahead, that will make it easier for u-!" Cyko stopped in his tracks as they turned the corner that led to the elevator. At the other end of the hallway, standing in front of the large elevator, was a huge mutant, whose body was like a humanoid octopus with eight tentacle-like arms with heavy infantry weapons in all of them. In front of him was a group of fifteen mages, ten wearing the normal uniform for magical guards and five wearing scientist clothes, identifying them as magical researchers.

Alongside the mages was a squad of guards with their weapons, pointing them straight at Cyko and Magy

"Grrr…" the aquatic roar of the mutant ran through the corridor, before he opened fire. The guards joined in immediately.

Cyko grabbed Magy and launched back around the corner, barely avoiding the bluish streaks that left mini craters in the wall where they had been.

"*Tela, we found the mages. They teamed up with a mutant, the one that looks like an octopus.*" He tried to peek around the wall to observe his enemies, but immediately retreated to avoid more bullets. "*They are trying to keep us pinned with heavy fire, bullets that can hurt us somehow. Those are coming from the squid.*"

"*This is bad, one mutant must have stayed out of the training labs. They must have worked together with the mages to block my mental scans once the isolation went into effect,*" Tela reasoned, figuring that the guards from the upper floors would have more time to set up a proper defense. "*That mutant should be Octo, a loyalist. His ability is to enhance weapons he holds and make them deadlier, such as the weapons of the guards he is likely holding onto. Stay there, I'll send reinforcements.*"

"Of course his name is Octo... Nah, don't worry, I got this. You should have the others focus on keeping the road safe," Cyko said out loud, causing Magy to turn towards him with a raised eyebrow.

"If you believe you can defeat them, I won't stop you, but I'll send help if I sense you are in trouble, all right?" the telepath said.

"I thought we would actually have to go through without a serious fight. At least now I can warm up a little." The enhancer grinned as his body glowed with his power.

"Well then, dear friend, don't let me stop you," Magy said, stepping out of his way.

Cyko decided to test the waters first by making a projection of himself and ordering it to charge down the hallway. Almost as soon as it appeared, the bullets fired and despite the clone's own agility and reaction time it was destroyed in just a few seconds. Smirking, Cyko decided to just charge in by using his own clones as decoys.

In a flash of movement, he and twenty of his replicas jumped out of hiding, intent on rushing towards the barrier. Making his move just as the bullets flew, the real Cyko vanished from the crowd of clones, unnoticed.

The looks on their faces as he appeared right in front of them with a glowing holo blade were priceless. With a laugh, he slashed at the magical construct, the blue streak creating a large, diagonal gash with cracks rapidly spreading out.

Once again vanishing just as all the guns turned to him and fired, Cyko giggled. The barrier was already recovering from the damage, but it would only be a matter of time until he broke it. Even with that squid helping them, it would make no difference. It was just a little more challenging fight he would love to overcome... ending with him slaughtering them all.

2

Dr. Gacha had a feeling something was amiss today. The guards seemed even more relaxed and bored than usual; the atmosphere seemed to cover a hidden tension, like the calm before a storm. It didn't help that his daughter refused to leave his side. She was originally an animal and they have strong senses of impending catastrophes, so just in case, he had ordered his small staff to stop working on the project for now, and instead instructed Shiro to bring the serum with her so they could go to Mr. Whale's office and present the results.

The emergency alarms started to wail the moment Shiro pocketed the concoction, causing her to hiss loudly and look around with her claws fully visible. The reason was clear in just a second… They lost all contact with the sixth and seventh levels, with certain sections having fired off reports about entering emergency isolation fields for unknown reasons.

The chaos was happening just a floor down from where they were.

"Dr. Ferdinand and Dr. Ivanovski, follow me to the third level, we'll discuss this situation there," the head scientist said, one of his hands playing with a small, metallic sphere in his pocket while the other looked at the alarm data on his tablet. "For now, it's unclear what's happening, but it might be tied to the same attack that happened a few months ago," Dr. Gacha said, expression unchanging even in the face of a crisis.

"Papa, we need to go, it's dangerous here," his daughter said with urgency, ears and tail perked straight up, reacting to the slightest noise. Her father nodded, pocketing his tablet and hastily making his way towards the exit.

"I already ordered for every scientist to retreat to the third level and for the guards to reinforce both this level and the fourth," the head scientist declared as they left his personal laboratory, heading straight for the closest elevator.

"Sir, what do you think caused the lower floors to go silent?" the bearded scientist asked, stroking his beard nervously as they entered the elevator.

"The sectors that entered the isolation mode were connected to the rest of the facility in such a way that if they were to go down, all other contact would be lost. A lack of foresight on my part I only just realized."

Guards were rushing through the fourth level, hurrying to fortify positions and arrange equipment. The scientists ran towards the massive elevator at the opposite end of the area, avoiding and maneuvering through the many large, hard crates that contained all kinds of supplies.

The magical staff, both mercenaries and researchers, hurried to apply the required defenses on all the critically important staff, such as

Dr. Gacha, his daughter, his two assistants, other leading scientists and commanding officers of the guards. The goal was to fortify as many positions as possible for the eventual outbreak of whatever was causing this.

It was a catastrophe without precedent. Considering what happened the last time, it might even be someone who is trying to free the subjects. That would be disastrous for their goals; they needed the army, they needed the subjects alive and loyal to them.

They arrived on the third level, by far the most reinforced floor, created to serve as the headquarters of the mercenary force, a safe house in case of catastrophes, and as a final defensive line in the case of an invasion… or a desperate rebellion.

At the entrance to the third floor, was what they called the command bridge, where all the mercenaries in charge of security were working intently, paying attention to their consoles to see if any new information appeared. Walking in further, Dr. Gacha looked up at the commander. The man was tall, looked to be made from pure muscle, and the experience and ruthlessness in his eyes was clear, enhanced by the scars that lined his face alone.

"Commander, what's the situation?" Dr. Gacha asked as soon as the man turned to look at him.

Grunting, the mercenary leader looked back at his console, the largest and most elevated post on the bridge, surrounded by monitors that looked out on the two sides of the floor, which were covered in high-tech weapons galore.

"It's unknown. We have dispatched soldiers to try to get inside the isolation fields, but so far, we have been without luck," the man's gruff voice answered.

"It seems you arrived just in time to see something interesting. Look, here." The commander pointed towards the monitor, showing the live-feed of one of his soldiers. The camera panned over many scientists, guards, and a few mutants pouring out of a hole in the elevator. The mutant leader, Leo, was standing in front of the soldier whose live-feed they were watching, arms crossed, and stern-faced.

"The mutant is demanding to speak with you, scientist."

"Wait, that's Leo, isn't it? What is going on?!" Shiro exclaimed. She, like her father, knew the names and who the strong leaders were. She knew that this giant lion was the one who took Drago's post as the leader of the mutant faction, but she didn't know exactly what that meant.

"Very well, activate the intercom," the scientist ordered.

"Subject Leo, what do you wish to say?" Dr. Gacha's emotionless voice echoed through the hallway in which the mutants were, causing the group to perk up, looking around for the source of his voice.

The lion growled. "I assume you don't know what's happening downstairs, do you? Then let me explain. The pride led by that telepathic girl, Tela, is the cause of all this chaos. She rebels against you, who gave us power, who gave us honor! I left one of my own to delay them as long as he can, but it won't take long for them to arrive here," Leo declared between growls.

"What?! But... But... Why?! Are my friends in this too?! Cyko, Magy, Myo?!" Shiro shouted, wide, worried eyes looking at the lion mutant on the screen who growled again.

"Who are you?! No, that's not important. What you should know is that I only have around 40 other mutants with me, the others were in the gymnasium. As for those names you mentioned, the one called Cyko is one of their most vocal and motivated members. He is likely slaughtering guards as we speak," the mutant leader said.

"But... But..." Shiro stammered, unable to comprehend what she heard. She knew her friends disliked her father, but that was just because of a misunderstanding, wasn't it? She panicked before a strong, warm hand touched her shoulder. Looking up, she met her father's gaze.

"Focus, my dear daughter. Don't allow your emotions to cloud your judgment now. We'll need a clear head for what's coming." He always knew what to say to calm her down or cheer her up... She would protect him, she would make sure.

The scientist turned back towards the live-feed, thinking hard about what he had just been told. An open rebellion. This was bad, terrible even. The purpose of the project's latest phase was to increase loyalty amongst the subjects, but it failed catastrophically, this rebellion was proof of that... But how had the subjects caused this much chaos without them noticing?

"Subject Leo, how many loyal members do you have with you?" the scientist asked.

"We have over 80 loyal mutants, but here with us, about half that."

"Very well. You may proceed to the fourth floor; your orders are to reinforce the position of the guards and mages there," the scientist said.

"Know this, scientist. With my powers, I could have escaped any moment I wanted; the walls and everything underneath us are under my command. Unlike that arrogant reptile, I know the danger those rebels present. The only reason I am doing this, is because I believe in this project of yours, and that it will bring glory upon us," Leo declared between growls, snarling at the cowering soldier under him.

Just before he parted to make preparations, however, he turned to look at the soldier one more time, ignoring the man's loud gulp.

"It would be wise to watch out for Tela and Cyko. The former is the leader of their faction, while the latter really, really hates your guts." The lion turned and sauntered off.

"Cyko… This can't be true, can it…?" Shiro whispered to herself, ears dropping in sadness at the thought of her friend's anger. She looked back up at her father as he talked with the scary-looking man standing beside him, discussing the next steps. He looked so strong.

"It's decided then," her father's voice rang out on the command bridge, the authority behind his posture unquestionable. "We need to wait until all the rebels leave the sixth level, otherwise the isolation fields will block the bracelets signal. All guards are to maintain a hit-and-run tactic, retreating towards the fourth level when possible. If all else fails, we still have many other defenses. Bring in the live feeds of all cameras connected to the fifth floor." The head scientist ordered, causing the commander to grunt, but nodding as he pressed several buttons, resulting in the platform he, Dr. Gacha, and his daughter were standing on to be surrounded by holographic monitors.

On the screens, they could see many areas of the fifth level, both inside and outside the many, many specialized laboratories, including the now deserted cloning research facilities. All scientists had retreated by this point, and now only a token force of fifty guards and five mages stayed to give the impression of being caught unaware. If all went well, those mercenaries would join the others on the fourth floor in case the bracelets failed.

Soon enough they detected the first sign of activity. An elevator door was blown apart and several subjects poured out, scanning around for threats before a few of them broke off and the rest stayed behind. The scientist and the commander frowned as they realized the breach in security. Normally, an isolation field would remove all contact with the other rooms, this included cutting off electrical power, but in this case, elevators always had their own power source, to stay operational in case of emergencies and bypass the normally mandatory stops to get security clearance to continue upwards. Their own emergency protocols were being used against them.

"All soldiers commence operation!" the commander shouted, causing all the mercenaries to spring into action.

On one screen, Shiro could see her friends, Cyko and Magy, making short work of a group of guards who were working together with two mages. Thanks to the real-time updates on the mercenaries' detection and preemption system, they were doing an excellent job of avoiding their attacks, with the mages taking every opportunity to curse the two children... However, it could only help them so much. Soon enough they began to tire, and the two children seized the opportunity.

The screams of pain that rang out from that battle would haunt her for years to come. They slew the guards without hesitation and to make it worse, they did so with joyful smiles on their faces.

"They are killing everyone..." Shiro whispered, watching as the two moved from group to group. They showed no mercy, slaughtering everyone in their way.

"All soldiers on the fifth level confirmed killed in action," an operator on the command bridge said with a shaky voice. The commander himself had sweat running down his forehead. Never, outside of a full-blown war, did the Neon Lunatics lose so many soldiers in so little time.

"Hurry up and upload all the soldier's data displays with enemy coordinates! I want no more soldiers to die! You!" The commander turned towards Dr. Gacha, his eyes squinted, and eyebrows furrowed. "My soldiers were ordered to use only non-lethal weaponry and the mages to use non-lethal spells! That decision is now slaughtering my men! You retract that order and allow my men to kill!"

The scientist closed his eyes. Now that there were no guards left, the rebels invaded and ripped apart the labs, ruining years of research and hard work. But, to allow the mercenaries to go all out meant that they would go for fatal attacks. Every subject was worth at least a hundred of theirs, for the purpose of this project was to create an army stronger than anyone else. At least he knew it worked.

He also couldn't allow them to escape, to reveal the nature of their project to the outside world before it was time. This would bring the Creator's wrath down on their heads, and she would surely end them all. If the subjects escaped, not only would everything they worked for be for naught, it would also put Shiro in danger.

It was decided.

"All mercenaries in this facility are now allowed to use lethal methods to end the rebellion. I hereby remove all restrictions, begin preparations for total combat immediately," Dr. Gacha declared, earning himself a wide-eyed stare from his daughter. He sighed.

"You know what is at stake, little Shiro, your friends cannot be reasoned with, look at the brutal way they killed all the guards who were just doing their jobs."

"The subjects have left their defensive position around the elevator!" an operator reported.

"Activate their bracelets now! Pick up the pace on the preparations! I want heavy weaponry ready on the fourth level!" the commander yelled out his orders, before turning back towards the scientist, smiling as the bracelets activated and immobilized all rebels instantly.

"The fourth level is roughly a third of the size of this one but filled to the brim with obstacles. Eight hundred soldiers will conduct the defense with lethal weaponry with the mutants, if by some miracle they escape both the bracelets and our defenses at the fourth level, we won't hesitate to use the full might of the fortress to keep them from escaping." The mercenary leader declared, looking at the scientist right in the eyes.

"I understand. We can't worry about the cost right now," the scientist replied before turning back to look at the bound subjects, frowning as he watched the blue-haired child, Cyko, once again destroy the binding and immediately get to work on freeing his pink-haired companion.

Blinking, the scientist looked down as his daughter tugged at his coat, a sad expression on her face. "Father... can I try to talk to them? I don't... I don't want them to get hurt, but I also don't want them to hurt you! We can solve this if we just talk!" she pleaded, using the more formal 'father' rather than her usual affectionate 'papa.' She was serious about this; the scientist could tell.

"My daughter, I can't allow you to do that. I know you are strong, very strong, but there are too many of them, and they all want retribution. You saw how they massacred the guards. What's to say they didn't do the same thing on the lower floors?"

"But... But..." she whispered, feeling hopeless.

"You should listen to your father, kitty," the commander interrupted suddenly, causing both her and her father to look at him. "If the enemy is dead set on your destruction, then they aren't your friends anymore, even if they once were."

"I... I understand... I'll do my best." Shiro looked back up at him, tears gleaming in her eyes.

"That's enough chit-chat! Look back at the screens!" The commander bellowed, eyes widening as one by one, the bindings in the bracelets were being undone with a flash of red—coming from the devices themselves.

"How did this happen?" the head scientist demanded.

"We aren't sure, but the first subject after the blue-haired brat to get free was this one." The man showed a recording of a red-haired child effortlessly shedding his own restraints, starting the chain reaction.

"Reddox..." the scientist whispered to himself. That mage was perhaps more dangerous than Cyko.

"They are moving towards the elevators," the commander noted, frowning as he realized that a little over ten minutes had passed since he issued his orders. "What's the status on the vanguard team? Let's set up an ambush."

Dr. Gacha's eyes lit up, as this was the back-up plan he had been thinking about. He turned towards the commander.

"Follow my instructions, I have a plan for the ambush..." the scientist said before explaining his idea to contain the rebellion.

3

Tela took in the state of her friends and allies. So far, they had advanced through the floors nearly unimpeded.

When the bracelets were activated, she put her plan into motion: waiting until all of them were away from the elevator before activating it. Tela worried that the countermeasures she requested Reddox to make wouldn't work, but then she had felt Cyko's increase in power and knew he had freed himself, just like he did the first time. Worst-case scenario, it would take them hours to free everyone, but Reddox's spell ended up releasing them all. They had been slightly weakened, but nothing major that would keep them down. The staff has been *quite* successful in making them stamina monsters.

"All right everyone, we don't know what will await us on the fourth floor, chances are that their defenses will be much stronger now that they know what's going on. They will strike at us with everything they have, but we won't give up! We are closer than ever to finally being free!" the redhead exclaimed, her message and feeling of determination echoing through every single child's heart.

"Now, let's continue forward! Same strategy as before, close combat specialists will go first and scout the area while a small team remains behind to secure the elevator," Tela explained, walking forward and forcing the doors of the elevator open with her mind. "Be prepared for anything."

A few minutes later, Cyko and his squad stood in front of the closed door to the fourth floor. Just like the previous two, they heavily fortified it with enhancing spells, but as before, they were in the same poor condition, so they easily broke past them.

Reddox immediately cast a protective barrier while Cyko jumped out alongside Magy and several other enhancers and close combat specialists, ready to meet any opposition. The enhancer was disappointed, however, when all that waited for them was a dark room, filled to the brim with crates of all kinds.

"Hey, Tela, did you or any other of our guys find anything alive in this floor?" Cyko swept the room hoping to locate something hiding behind the crates, which served as perfect hiding places.

"Hmm... Give me a few minutes, for now stay close to the elevators, can you describe what you can see?"

"It seems like a storage room. There are crates and equipment everywhere. Cars and trucks... Huh, I think I see a few of those tubes they stuck into us to awaken us." The enhancer jumped on top of the largest crate near him to view the whole room, but only found that there wasn't a soul present.

"Do you think we can spare a few minutes to wreck this place and maybe search for anything useful? Otherwise, I think I can see the elevator from here, it's just a single one. It seems to be a straight path." Cyko said, looking around one more time before jumping back to the ground.

"Hmm... That's strange, I can't find a single mind that is not ours on that floor. Perhaps they evacuated everyone who worked on this floor to regroup. In that case, I think we should just go straight up, if we give them more time to prepare, it will be disastrous." Tela couldn't help but feel like this was too easy.

"Something feels wrong. Scythe says we are in a good position to get ambushed here. We've been relying on Tela's detection too much, I think." Magy walked up to his side, clenching her twin scythes in anticipation.

"The wind, it's still," Ellyn commented, approaching both Cyko and Magy with Reddox in tow. She continued, "It's not saying anything. It feels dead, like there are vacuums spread all around, sucking in the air and preventing it from speaking. I want to get out of this place, and fast."

"I can detect trace amounts of magic in the air, but I can't tell where it's coming from," Reddox chimed in.

Soon Tela and her crew joined up with Cyko and his. The strongest led the group, followed closely by those of nearly equal power and then by those who were the least likely to want to fight. It would be a problem if they targeted those in the back, but the redhead was confident that by seeing so many powerful children grouped together, they might try to take them out first.

"It's here!" Reddox exclaimed just as the group was halfway past the large storage room. "A large magical spike, it's surrounding us." The mage's magical grimoires materialized from his body as he readied himself for battle, quickly followed by the others as they looked around in anticipation.

The fabric of reality seemed to erode away like television static, revealing a fully lit storage room, with hundreds upon hundreds of soldiers surrounding them, mages standing atop crates, each surrounded by their own magical barrier, holding staffs glowing with arcane power.

They quickly noticed the difference between those soldiers and the ones they had fought on the lower floors. Many of them wore much bulkier and heavier looking armor, carrying large and deadly weapons. For the mages, all of them were wearing more protective armor than they were used to, covering their body from head to toe. The message was clear; they weren't holding back anymore.

Despite all of that, the most unpleasant surprise was the large, menacing glare of the second leader of the mutants, Leo, accompanied by no less than forty of his loyal underlings, all of them standing behind him.

Seeing the look of shock and incredulity on their prey's face, the lion let out a mighty roar, his weapons of choice, the sand hammer and axe in his hands.

"Unlike that idiot Drago, I actually use my brain. I knew exactly what you were doing. You're wondering how I got out? Well, here is a news flash for you," the lion said as sand floated around him, making a small, translucent ring form. Tela and the others looked at the ground, and noticed that it was corroding away, turning into the sand that Leo used to make his weapon and armor. "I could have escaped this facility whenever I wanted!"

"H-how?!" Tela exclaimed, looking around her with wide, horrified eyes. All the mutants that were supposed to be locked behind their training rooms under their seal were present in this floor, accompanied by the soldiers who looked deadlier than ever.

Face set in determination, she took a step forward to meet him in battle, only to flinch as her face collided with an invisible wall.

"W-what?!" Her eyes widened as the barrier finally made itself known. A small cage surrounded her, stopping her from moving at all. She looked around and noticed that enclosures also appeared over several other children, Cyko, Magy, Ellyn and Reddox. The strongest ones.

"So, this is your plan, huh?" Cyko commented with a sneer, a blue aura appearing around his body as he let his powers fully course through his veins. "Too bad, we've dealt with things like this before!" He broke the barrier surrounding him in half, making it dissipate. Just as he was about to vanish from his position, however, his flickering form collided against another barrier.

He snarled and tried again, and again, and again to no success. Reddox made his barrier disintegrate by using the power of all of his tomes and just like Cyko, he tried to take a step forward, only for the cage to reform itself around him.

"Haha! Try to escape as much as you want, it won't work! I knew this would happen," the lion whispered mockingly, enjoying the sight of Cyko's increasingly frustrating attempts to free himself.

"Now, all of us here will hurt and maybe even kill your friends, until you give up this foolish rebellion and surrender," he spoke again, causing Tela to gasp and Cyko to snarl.

"Fight me yourself then, you coward!"

"Maybe later, but for now... don't say I didn't warn you," the mutant leader declared. A piercing noise rang out across the room, quickly followed by a cry of anguish.

"AHH! MY KNEE!" The child standing furthest from Tela and the others fell to the ground and clenched his bloodied knee.

"N-NO!" Tela cried out both mentally and vocally, feeling the fear and pain of the child through her mental connection with him. "Don't hurt them! Those aren't fighters!" she pleaded with the mutant.

"I'LL KILL YOU! I'LL KILL YOU ALL!" Cyko shouted, attacking his cage once again to no avail.

With a snap of Leo's fingers, his mutants began to circle slowly around the now wary-looking children.

"Now, here comes the fun part. You either surrender and stop this ridiculousness, or we will tear your friends apart until there's no one left," the leader offered, his low growl sent shivers down their spines as they learned that his threats were very much real.

"N-no..." Tela whispered to herself, watching with fear as the mutants circled around their prey.

If only she could break through this blasted barrier or use her telekinesis to erase it! Reddox had stopped trying to free himself, Ellyn was trying to manipulate the wind outside her dome, to limited success. Cyko kept trying to break through the barrier, destroying it repeatedly only for it to regenerate before he could move. Magy had her weapons cleaved through the barrier, scowling in concentration, but she hadn't freed herself.

It seemed hopeless, and Leo's mighty roar was enough to evoke more fear from the weaker children. She could hear sobs sounding around her. Was this it, then? Had she failed again?

Leo suddenly brought his forearm, armed with both his armor and sand, up to protect himself against a sudden streak of flame that was flying towards him. A large boom resounded from the point of impact, causing the lion to grit his teeth.

The fireball landed on the ground to reveal the flaming form of Torch, who was glaring up at him. "Like hell we'll just give up like that!" the redhead shouted, the fire surrounding his body almost pulsing.

Looking around, Leo noticed groups of children at the ready, assuming a battle stance at the defense of their fearless leaders.

The mutant leader roared, advancing towards the group which was the signal for the battle to start and in less than ten seconds, the once quiet storage room turned into chaos.

"We won't let you do as you please anymore!" Anna yelled, firing two charged shots straight at Leo, who jumped high into the air to avoid the plasma spheres, but was caught by Starry's projectiles, exploding against his form.

Quickly getting to his feet, the lion willed his power to work faster, causing several spears of metallic sand to rise from the ground, seeking to impale the children who were fighting him, but somehow, they all dodged his attack at the last moment. He willed the spears to explode, pelting them with shrapnel.

Just as he was about to charge at Sara, the ground below him shook. The lion stumbled as he tried to hold his footing, once again giving an opening that Anna and Starry were more than glad to take. The older girl fired another charged shot at the beast, striking him right in the chest, the plasma from her projectile exploding upon contact, piercing his sand and his armor, burning the skin underneath. Falling backwards, the lion was bombarded with a salvo of exploding stars.

Finding himself outnumbered, wounded, and under rapid fire that was not allowing him to get up, the lion cursed loudly. He had hoped that by holding the rest of the rebels hostage, the blasted telepath would give up. He had to fight for his own survival now.

With the barrage of projectiles coming to a halt thanks to several guards firing at his opponents, the lion took the opportunity and jumped to his feet.

With a mighty roar, he declared, "Enough playing around! I'll show you why I am the king of the jungle!"

The ground and several containers around him evaporated into dust, bringing the siblings' attention from the guards back towards him, eyes widening at the tornado of metallic dust that surrounded him. It exploded suddenly, causing shrapnel to fly in every direction, piercing everything and everyone in the immediate area.

"Aaahhh!" Starry screamed in pain as several large shards of shrapnel stabbed through her armor, wounding her forearms and legs as she could not dodge them. Grimacing, they all turned towards the mutant leader, and gasped as they saw him.

Towering over everyone was a gigantic silver colored lion with six arms, holding two giant hammers, two axes, and two more appendages appeared to be cannons. Leo's own body was nowhere to be seen.

The metallic lion roared, the loud sound causing several of the floor's occupants to flinch and cover their ears at the volume. Leo pointed his cannon arm towards a large group of rebels and before anyone had time to react, it fired a sphere of metallic dust towards them. It exploded on impact, burying most in his sand.

"NO!" Tela screamed, both out loud and mentally. They had been knocked unconscious. Everyone else was staring at the giant metal lion, ears still ringing from his roar.

"YOU CRUEL ANIMAL!" Cyko screamed in anger, panting slightly from his efforts at trying to break the barrier that still imprisoned him. He glared at the metallic lion.

Just as Leo was about to fire another projectile, dozens of large vines sprouted from the ground and took hold of his cannon arms with surprising strength and stopped them from moving. Two large torrents of water drenched both of the limbs, freezing upon contact and sealing the cannon holes away.

"He may be large, but that just makes him an easier target," Henry declared, the flower floating on top of his head was beaming.

Sara approached him, sweat covering her forehead. "I told Tela to not worry about him, we'll take care of him ourselves," she said, creating more water spheres to use at a moment's notice.

Starry sent a fleet of dark stars towards the metallic titan.

Anna fired her plasma projectiles at Leo with one arm, while the other fired off charged shots. Mat and Torch joined, shooting searing fireballs from their mouth and hands.

With a roar, Leo swung both of his giant axes, forcing the siblings to dodge his attack. As both weapons struck the ground, several bullets of metallic sand sprung up, spreading widely from the point of impact. Some children, mutants and even guards got hit by surprise, giving their respective opponents enough time to counterattack. This took out five rebels and three mutants, along with the death of ten guards.

As Tela watched the fight, carefully monitoring and updating their shared map with any information she or the others could find about the metal lion, her mental partitions also took in the state of the rest of the battlefield.

Several children had been guided off to hide behind a large container, those who either didn't want to fight or were too weak to battle against such large numbers. With them were more children who protected them from incoming attacks. Others were fighting off two of Leo's mutant friends.

The area directly to her left was where fighting had been the most intense, so far. Those that had not gotten imprisoned, but were still formidable on their own, had banded together. Several shapeshifters could transform themselves into other creatures like small dragons, giant canines, lizards, snakes and even into less corporeal things, like ghosts.

One of the largest advantages the shapeshifters had was their ability to cure themselves of all wounds by reverting to their base forms. Thanks to this, Tela had advised a strategy of rotation in which those who had taken a breather would swap with those who were most wounded, allowing them to keep up with the pressure. Already, she had confirmed the death of over a hundred guards and a few mages because of this tactic.

Other shapeshifters had spread out. The child who could turn into a cloud of locusts was fighting a bulky-looking lizard, trying his best to evade the mutant's corrosive smoke. A boy who could turn his own arms into machine guns was keeping three guards busy, another who could turn into a steel golem was having a fist fight against a stone golem mutant who was double his size. A faceless, floating cloak was fighting against two mutants at once, allowing his own intangibility to provoke the two insectoids, using his own ghostly claws to tear away at their stamina. A kid made of pure fire was running between the guards, hoping to set them ablaze, and also distracting them long enough to give others an opportunity.

The spiritualists were making use of their ability to communicate with spirits to harass both the guards and the mutants, gathering information on their positions and the best way to attack.

The enhancers were the main vanguard, speeding through and shrugging off the bullets. Their main job was banding together and fighting against the mutants to keep them away from the weaker children and other combatants. Five enhancers had just annihilated a mammoth mutant, while another one had taken down a group of five guards who were manning a machine gun.

Quite a few mentalists like Tela had been captured by the cages, but that didn't mean all of them. Some were helping by causing confusion, fear, and hallucinations in their enemies, while a small group was trying to free the caged children.

Tela turned her attention back towards the fight with Leo. Already, Henry had covered most of his form with vines, restricting his movements but also sending shrapnel towards the children whenever he struggled. Several bleeding wounds punctured the siblings, especially Torch, who liked to get as close to Leo as he could.

"Hey, Magy, what are you doing? You haven't moved," Cyko questioned his friend, sweat dripping down his face from his own escape efforts.

Magy turned to him, a smile on her face. "I think I might be onto something. I have been talking with Scythe all this time, we've been working on keeping this hole I made with her open. Remember how she can partially enter barriers like this? It's the same principle. I'm having her absorb the barriers energy to weaken it and use the energy in other ways."

"How?" Tela asked.

"If I targeted that annoying lion, I can probably muster enough power to blow one of its arms apart. I can probably kill those mages responsible for this spell if I score a direct hit, but they are spread all over the place. It would take forever to take them all out," she explained.

"Magy, can you control the potency of your attack?" Tela asked.

"Sure, but what do you need me to control it for?" She raised an eyebrow at Tela.

"Do you think you can lessen it enough to send Cyko flying away, but not enough to hurt him?" she questioned, causing those around her to blink at her bold plan.

"That is…" Magy frowned, retracting her weapon from the barrier and looking at her friend. Sure, she could probably do it, but it would be painful. Seeing her expression of worry, however, the enhancer pounded his chest with a smirk.

"Magy, don't worry, I can take it! Besides, I trust you."

"Fine, but… it's gonna hurt." She stabbed her weapon through the barrier, stopping halfway through in Cyko's direction. "Whenever you are ready. Please, be careful." She willed her dark energy to concentrate on the space between her two blades.

"Cyko, once you are out, do your best to cause as much mayhem as possible, but your priority will be the mages. Their barriers should work like ours do, but they are covered in two barriers, cast by each other. If you want to take one down, you'll have to destroy both and then strike them down before they regenerate them," Tela explained to Cyko, who grinned at her words, his plan forming in his mind.

"Don't worry, Tela! Once I'm out, they'll never know what hit them!" He focused on increasing his endurance as he braced himself to destroy the barrier and endure Magy's attack.

"Magy! On the count of three!" Cyko shouted, getting himself into position to slash at it. When she nodded in confirmation, he began his mental countdown alongside her, staying in synchronization thanks to Tela.

One…

Two…

Three…

"NOW!"

The barrier disappeared in a flash of blue just as a pink streak of energy hit Cyko in the gut, knocking the wind out of his lungs and sending him flying into a crate. The barrier that used to imprison him regenerated in the place he stood seconds before.

Their plan had worked, and the enhancer was loose.

One mage, whose keen and experienced gaze searched for the most dangerous child, widened his eyes as he appeared in front of him, both of his holo blades glowing bright with energized power. He aimed the caging spell at the boy, confident that his own protection, a chain of barriers connecting all the mages, would guard him long enough for the cage to take form.

His hopes were crushed when the boy slashed through his form, each blade destroying a barrier. Then, to the mage's despair, a second Cyko suddenly appeared from his side and pierced through his armor and protective spells like they were butter. Gurgling his own blood, the mage only had time to watch the boy teleport away before the clone finished the job, engulfing his world in darkness.

It was a nightmarish scene. One by one, the elite mages were falling, and with each death, their web of barriers and cages got weaker. By the time the soldiers noticed and answered the mages' calls for aid, it was too late.

"Abort the plan! Change to Plan B! All mages assume fighting formation!" One mage, their captain, yelled into the radio. All the remaining mages nodded. In an instant, they dropped their barriers and jumped down in the main areas of the storage room, offensive and support spells at the ready.

The siblings' fight against Leo still raged on. They sported an increasing number of bruises and wounds from the giant metallic construct, who looked far from giving up. With most of his limbs now useless, the giant lion had stuck to summoning dust spears from both the ground and its body, making them explode when convenient.

"All right, everyone, fall back!" Henry shouted. From the moment Leo turned into that giant beast, their aim wasn't to take down the mutant leader just yet, but to wait long enough for the yellow flower on top of his head to finish charging.

The special flower, a species he had created himself, blossomed, revealing a dark interior. The aptly named Blast Flower, worked with the purple flowers on his shoulders, whose purpose was to absorb the ambient energy in the air, mostly magical, and transfer it to the Blast Flower.

Just as the lion reared up for its next blow, Henry willed the flower to let out its charge. With a thunderous boom, a golden beam of energy fired from the plant, its kickback nearly throwing him to the ground.

It struck the metallic lion right in the chest. Both giant arms fell, their joints destroyed from the damage. A deafening roar of pain echoed around the floor, the only sign that Leo was alive.

As the smoke cleared, Henry and his siblings noticed with satisfaction that the entirety of the metallic lion's top half was gone, reduced to a wreckage around the wounded form of the mutant leader. Leo was clutching his left shoulder, his face twisted in agony as the Blast Flower vaporized everything below his left shoulder.

"GAAAH!" the lion roared in pain before willing his power to create another tornado of metallic dust around him, engulfing more crates into it. Torch shot at his form like a flaming meteor, only to be stopped by a wall of dust that absorbed his attack. Before the child could do anything else, the tornado exploded, sending him flying.

Starry caught Torch before he could crash against the ground, the flames on his body somehow not harming her. This was bad. The Blast Flower was only good for one shot because it would wilt afterwards. For the time it would take for another one to charge, almost 12 minutes, they likely couldn't last that much longer against him.

His eyes widened when the tornado ceased and revealed the form of the giant metallic lion, only this time, all six arms had cannons, pointing straight at them. They wouldn't be able to dodge all of his attacks at the same time! To make matters worse, the tornado had severed his vines, which laid in pieces around the construct.

Before Henry or his siblings could do anything, however, another deafening boom echoed around the storage room. Deep gashes appeared on the lion, red streaks of energy cut off its cannon arms, turning it into a pile of metallic dust. A blue streak flashed across him, leaving a deep cut on his chest.

Henry blinked.

"Sorry for the wait, we had to deal with those pesky mages first," a voice sounded from behind him, causing the group of siblings to gasp. Walking towards them was Cyko, Magy, Ellyn, Reddox, and Tela.

"You all did well, I can see why Cyko is so proud of being your brother," Tela said with a gentle smile, making sure they could feel her feelings of respect and Cyko's pride. They deserved praise for holding off such a powerful opponent for so long. Her words elicited smiles in return.

Her face turned serious as she glared at the lion who was again trying to reform his body. Almost instantly, the lion fully reformed himself, this time with only two arms, having only the claws on its fingers for weapons. Her body glowed red as she exerted her telekinesis onto the construction, causing it to contract upon itself under the weight of her mind.

"Agatha, prepare to fire," Tela commanded the girl who had previously fought Starry in the Coliseum, a girl with battleship-like powers. She walked forward, nodding at her command, pointing all six of her triple-barreled turrets at him.

"I think you guys can handle this. My blood is pumping for more payback," Cyko declared, pointing a hand towards the many still ongoing battles.

Magy nodded and walked towards him, ready to assist further.

"Okay, you may go. Anyone else?" Tela asked as the two friends dashed away, eager to spill more blood. When no one else stepped away, she took a moment to breathe and stared harder at the lion construct, causing it to contract even further.

"Over fifty children have serious injuries and there are another seventy with minor wounds. I expected you to at least be better than Drago, but no, you also supported this madness. If you had helped us, we wouldn't have had to spill a single drop of blood. Because of your thirst for power, you put many of us—including yourself—in danger. You disgust me, Leo." the telepath said to his mind, making sure he could feel the emotions from the wounded and scared children.

Still, he wasn't done in yet, not by a long shot. He may have lost an arm and got himself a deep gash that nearly pierced his heart, but he was far from finished! He had trained hard and studied his abilities rigorously just to make sure the same thing that happened to Drago would never happen again. He had learned even more about how his powers worked and what he could do with them.

Drago wasn't the only one with an ability that the scientists had forbidden.

He could take control of the entire ground, ceiling, and even the crates if given enough time. He could make the entire floor collapse upon itself and will it so that only he and his mutants escaped unscathed, while everyone else suffered. If he pushed his limits enough, he could make the entire facility his weapon! He could still win!

But he wasn't stupid. Chances are, they would counter his ability and escape. He wanted to become the leader of a powerful pride, the lion blood the scientist had awakened in him demanded it! But he wouldn't accomplish that by dying.

"Unlike Drago, I never underestimated you. I expected this rebellion would happen, but I never for a moment believed you would lie down and accept what is happening here, the birth of a powerful army!" the lion said to the rebel leader, gritting his teeth to ignore the throbbing pain in his chest.

"There is also another difference I have from Drago. Unlike him, I'LL SURVIVE!"

Suddenly, the ground underneath Tela gave birth to thin spears of dust she deflected before her eyes widened as the metallic lion melted, forming a tornado of debris, causing shrapnel to fly everywhere. Quickly those that could create barriers did so to protect the others from the attack.

Leo was nowhere to be seen.

"W-What?!" Tela whispered to herself in shock, realizing now that the mental connection she had made with him was gone too.

"Tela!" Cyko's voice came to her mind, urgency in his tone. She immediately brought her attention to him as he spewed out an explanation. *"The mutants! The bad ones! They are being grabbed by the dust! They are disappearing, even the dead ones!"*

The mutants were retreating!

"Cowards!" Torch yelled, the flames of his hair cracking. "Get back here and fight like a man!" He threw fireball after fireball at the hole that was left from the mutant's escape, the only evidence left of the giant metallic lion.

"Yes! This is good news, everyone! Without the mutants, the guards will be much less dangerous! Now is the time we finally move forward! To freedom!" their leader declared, her own heart filling everyone else's with determination.

Cyko, surrounded by the bodies of several guards and a few mages, clicked his teeth in annoyance at what Tela had said. Not at her, but at the cowardly lion.

"He comes here and tries to stop us like some game boss and then runs away with his tail between his legs, how typical. Don't worry, I'll find you one day," the enhancer muttered to himself.

The battle had quickly progressed from a stalemate between the two factions into a one-sided massacre in favor of the rebels. Even with more professional equipment meant to wage war rather than just stun, it didn't make much of a difference. While dozens of children got serious injuries, the soldiers had it much worse.

No guards were left alive. Cyko, Magy, and several of the more vengeful children made sure of that.

However, this battle made one thing clear for them. The staff was done kidding around, and Tela doubted that this would be everything they had in store for them. She hoped that with how many guards had perished, there wouldn't be many more to deal with.

After the battle on the fourth floor was over, they started their next priority: taking care of the injured. Tela gathered those with healing powers and made a priority list in her mind, working through everyone that had wounds.

It wasn't until an hour later that they were ready for their next push towards freedom. They wouldn't stop, no matter what.

4

There was one thing that the staff had done right. They had trained them to be the perfect soldiers, in terms of endurance. Not a single hour after that intense and chaotic battle, most of them were already in a condition to fight again, even those that had fought the hardest, like the enhancers and shape-shifters, were already in prime condition.

The injured had recovered fast, thanks to the help of those with healing powers, which included Reddox. Classified as either elementals or spirituals, those with restorative powers were rare, about only 20 of them had such abilities, and most of them weren't strong fighters, but that didn't matter as their healing abilities were top-notch.

The food they found was mostly snacks like cereal or chocolate bars, something the staff had added to win their favor. It failed, but the snacks had served their purpose of keeping them fed for now.

The elevator was already open, and the first team, several enhancers, a few elementals and four of their own mutants had boarded, making for roughly 40 children. Cyko, Magy, and some others who had gone before opted to go second this time, mostly on Tela's insistence that they were pushing themselves too hard and needed the extra rest and food.

As the elevator ascended and left, Tela scanned the mental state of everyone remaining. While there was a near universal feeling of victory that stayed inside their hearts, she could sense the fear and worry some of them still felt over their situation, which was understandable.

The purpose of the vanguard team was to discover the level of threat that awaited them, and to hold the line long enough for the rest to arrive to provide backup. If everything went well, the next threat would already be eliminated by the time everyone got on the next floor.

"Tela, we have arrived at the fifth floor," Isaac, an enhancer focused on speed, reported to her. *"Just like down there, the door is very large, but it appears to be much more fortified than usual. It may take a while to open it- oh wait!"* She felt his shock as if she was the one standing there with him.

"Isaac? What is it?" Tela asked in urgency.

"The door! It's opening by itself!" he answered. She cursed, for she knew why it would open unprompted.

"They are expecting us! Everyone, be prepared for anything!"

The boy and everyone in the elevator snapped to seriousness, the elementals already creating several barriers to shield them from the inevitable hail of bullets.

"All right! We didn't come this far to stop now!" Isaac shouted before he froze, his previous motivation replaced by a feeling that made Tela pale.

"Oh... Luni... Is that... a battleship? They have a freaking-" his thought was cut off as rumbling sounds came from the elevator room, causing the telepath to jump to her feet, expression ashen in terror.

"NOOOOOO!" Tela screamed as all the children turned towards her in panic.

Their leader fell to her knees, tears falling from her eyes.

"No… No… No…" she whispered, not even looking up from the ground to view the elevator shaft as flaming pieces of debris fell, followed by a cloud of smoke. That was enough of a message to convey what had happened a floor above them.

Total loss, it was a total loss. Not a single child she had sent up that elevator had survived… She had felt it again, their lives ending, their last feelings, the contradictory sentiment of regret and relief, their despair as death approached, the unique feeling of a soul leaving the body… She had felt it all, and… She had failed again.

"What the heck… WHAT THE HECK!" Cyko yelled in disbelief as he stared at the flaming remains of the elevator before looking at the crying telepath.

"Tela… What… What happened…?" he asked, not willing to believe what he was witnessing.

"They… They…" Tela tried to force out between her sobs, "They are… They are all dead… J-just before their… they said… a battleship…" she managed, trying her best to swallow her despair at just losing forty children… Forty children who had trusted her to bring them to freedom…

Tears fell freely from her eyes, and Cyko didn't need to look around him to know that many other kids were also sobbing.

A battleship?

This wasn't fun anymore. All sense of joy from killing guards and scientists was gone. It was a war; they were rebels, and the staff was the army and they would be treated just like the soldiers they were expected to be. If Cyko had been any more stubborn, he and Magy would have boarded that elevator and they would have been reduced to ashes alongside all the others.

"Attention all subjects," the cursed voice of the head scientist echoed through the storage level, causing everyone to snap their head upwards, spotting the cameras and speakers that had survived the fight.

"This is your last chance, surrender now and we assure you no further harm will come to you. Continue your rebellion and we will use full force against you. I repeat, cease all hostilities and-" his ice-cold voice broke off as a blue aura covered the entire roof and all cameras and speakers were crushed into dust by an unseen power.

"No." Tela's voice echoed. "We won't stop, we won't bow down to you, people who would kill, torture and brainwash *children*! We refuse to be used and treated as less than human! You tore us from our lives with false promises, we won't fall victim to them again!"

"I agree... We won't surrender. Giving up is not an option!" Cyko declared, followed by a nod from a grim-faced Magy.

"Scythe says to give up now would mean to disrespect the memory and souls of our dead friends, of little Myo, who wanted nothing more than to be free."

"Tela." Ellyn approached their leader. The wind speaker took a second to breathe, to calm down her emotions. "I have been listening to the wind coming from the elevator room. The door to the fifth floor is sealed, by ice, but just before that, I could hear the arid winds of a desert and the freely circulating air of a large, open area."

"What does that mean? There is a desert up there? Is it outside?" Tela questioned before turning her attention to another person who was approaching them. A purple-haired boy with glowing violet eyes, a spiritual.

"I've asked my spirits to scout up ahead, the ice that sealed away the entrance is magical, but it's not protected against spirits. They said the whole place is a... desert?" the boy asked, squinting his eyes in confusion.

"A desert? That's what you see?" Ellyn asked. Unlike other spirits, her wind depended on at least a single hole to pass through to the other side. The boy nodded, continuing his scouting.

"Yes, that's what it appears to be, a large desert with a humongous, super... structure at the end?" the boy reported, earning a nod from the redhead.

"Anyone else have anything to report?" Tela asked through their minds as a few kids walked forward to discuss the situation with the others.

Soon enough, they formed a clear idea and Tela propagated the picture with the help of the spirituals, sending it to the minds of the children in perfect detail, as if they were looking at a high-resolution image on a computer.

A large desert awaited them, spreading five kilometers long and one kilometer wide, with nothing to use as cover against attacks, just a very large terrain of sand. At the end of the desert stood a massive structure resembling a battleship, like the boss level of a video game, stationed between them and freedom. A fortress as wide as the desert stood with three huge turrets aiming straight at the elevator door, meant to hold them hostage until they gave up their escape. From the distance, they could make out several, much smaller but no less dangerous-looking cannons.

It was a machine of war.

Their first problem would be setting foot onto the fifth floor without getting torn apart by the giant cannons, then they would need to destroy said cannons and survive whatever else attacked them. It would be hard, few children had abilities or the endurance to survive something this huge…

"I'll go. One of my roommates was in that elevator. I have the powers similar to a battleship. I can take a few hits. If just a single turret is destroyed, that should help us get in there," Agatha declared and Tela nodded at her.

Reddox had also stepped forward, followed by Cyko, Magy, Ellyn, and several other shapeshifters, enhancers, and spiritual and elemental users.

Reddox said he could make an illusion spell to make it seem as if the ice was still in place when it had already been taken care of. It would make them invisible, but chances are the staff would find them out before long. Therefore, their aim would be to spread out to confuse the turrets. After they took the main cannons, the rest would follow them into the desert, and they would make their way past the fortress, once and for all.

After taking a minute to pray for the souls of their dead friends, they climbed aboard an artificial elevator made by several earth-aligned children, who would remain behind to maintain it until everyone had left. Tela wanted to lead the group this time, she refused to stay safe while her friends and allies would risk their lives.

Sara, who had volunteered to undo the ice, looked at Reddox, nodding at him to signal she was ready to start working through it.

Silently, the mage raised his hands and touched the ice above him, muttering. After a minute, he dropped his arms and looked at Sara.

"The illusion is in place; it will only affect those outside the room."

Sara touched the ice above them. After only a few seconds, the ice turned into a fine mist and disappeared, turning into moisture in the air.

"*Everyone prepare to move. Please, please, don't do anything rash. This will be a very dangerous fight,*" the telepath spoke as the elevator finished climbing the last few meters, giving them a perfect view of the large desert and the fortress. It was a scary sight. She turned back towards Sara and the three who had been controlling the elevator. "*The moment we jump out, drop the elevator and don't come back until I've given the signal.*"

"Cyko!" Sara blurted out, causing her brother to turn towards her with a raised eyebrow. She sighed shakily, before looking at her little brother in the eye. "No matter what happens, survive, please."

"Don't worry, I won't let them stop me, I'll show them the monster they created!" her brother said with a confident smile.

"*GO!*" their leader commanded, and as one, the children jumped out of the elevator as it dropped away to safety.

As everyone spread themselves over the large desert, Agatha remained in front, knowing what her goal was. As the turrets turned away from the center to focus on one group of children, she breathed out. It was time to avenge her friends and all those that had died.

As she willed her power to work, she wondered about the irony of this very moment—using the powers they gave her, against them.

Metallic armor spread over her body, granting her protective boots, clawed hands, and a horned helmet. Over her cannons, manifesting from a shield plate on her back, another set of turrets appeared, five total with four barrels each, accompanied by three large missile platforms. This was her first time fully revealing the ultimate power of a battleship.

A little girl with the abilities of a destructive vessel versus a kilometer-long fortress of war, who would win? When she finished charging up, she focused her sights on the center most enemy turret which was glowing with magical power and ready to fire a devastating electrical beam across the desert.

She ignored all other targets, the automatic machine guns that popped from the earth, the robots that appeared from the sides... She needed to get all her weapons ready and at maximum potential to take that magical turret down.

If she didn't fire fast enough, she would be wounded. Expecting the giant turrets to fire at any moment, she put her metallic gauntlets in front of her body to defend herself... But nothing came. Blinking, she looked back at the fortress to find that the normal turrets were still locked on her, but the magical one had stopped glowing. A technical failure?

She fired immediately and her form was soon covered in smoke as all of her weapons discharged at once. Main turrets, secondary turrets, tertiary turrets, machine guns, and missile platforms. Her entire barrage fired off all at once, the noise deafening all other combat on the floor, and when the earth shook, she smiled, knowing she had struck true.

Not wasting time, she willed all of her weapons to reload as she turned them towards the next turret. As the smoke cleared, Agatha noticed with satisfaction that the elemental turret was wrecked and while not fully destroyed, all of its barrels and some of its external armor had been irreversibly damaged.

5

Somewhere on the first level of the facility, a figure stood in the empty administrative room, darkness surrounding it. A tablet glowed, showing the blueprints for the first three floors of the facility.

When the alarm echoed, all workers panicked. During their training, they had been informed that if the red alarm, which meant catastrophe, was ever to sound, they were to evacuate the facility immediately. Their boss, Mr. Whale, was the first to evacuate, ordering everyone to abandon what they were doing and escape.

His secretary had also been ordered to retreat, just like the others, but she made an excuse about being busy with critical work. Supported by a healthy dose of suggestion magic, she convinced her boss she already evacuated with the others. The wonders of high-level hypnosis.

Still, thanks to this crisis, Ms. Allure finally discovered what, exactly, this company was planning with all their secrecy. Even if they tried to cover it up, it was easy to notice that they invested several billion into something that they refused to reveal. Just as shady was the sudden disappearance of a very large part of the Neon Lunatics, both in manpower and in technology. Conspiracy theorists on the internet were going crazy assuming the GACHA Conglomerate had finally conquered the world with the power it had in its hands, wondering whether the Creator would stop them if they tried.

The truth needed to be discovered, which was why she was here. She needed to investigate whether the rumors of an anti-Creator super weapon being developed were true or not. Frustratingly, the security was heavy. She couldn't just infiltrate the building like she normally would, but thanks to this crisis, she now had the perfect opportunity to investigate the facility.

However, as she arrived at the third level, her hopes were dashed. It was sealed, and while not a single soldier was in sight, the gate was too thick and too heavily fortified with magic. She tried to blast at it several times with her dark energy, but only bent it slightly. If she used everything she had, she may break through it, but it would make them aware of yet another thing gone wrong. Thankfully, she had disabled all the cameras before attempting to break the door down.

Sighing in frustration, she explored more of this side of the third level, following a set of stairs that went downwards. Walking as fast as she could, the woman paused as her eyes came across what had been hidden deep down in her side of the facility. A large power plant.

"Well now, this is interesting," the disguised secretary said. Usually a power plant meant nothing, but the way this one was made, it meant that some heavy use of energy was being used. Chances are, this power plant was the source of the energy for the entire facility. Maybe if she… turned it off, things would be easier for her.

"Well, time to get to work," the spy said to herself, pointing a hand towards the power plant, where a large sphere of darkness formed. Sabotage was always a great method of gaining information after all.

6

"UGH!" the commander of the mercenaries shouted as the bridge shook, all the windows breaking. Near him, Dr. Gacha had taken hold of a support to stay upright, his hissing daughter more preoccupied in keeping him stable than doing the same.

"DAMAGE REPORT!" the mercenary leader bellowed in a rage.

"Structural integrity at 90 percent! Magical turret is damaged beyond operation, attempting repairs! Reports show a sudden blackout from the power plant caused a loss of energy to the main guns! Backup power is now online!" an operator responded urgently, just as several more explosions shook the building. "The subjects are now redirecting attacks towards the fortress! Structural damage at 0.1 percent with each attack!"

"Curse it all! Concentrate fire on that blasted ship! Attack now! Make use of those anti-aircraft guns and fire at anyone approaching! Order the snipers and heavy weapons to be prepared! Deploy the tanks, the helicopters! I want everything we have in motion!"

Watching as the battle progressed increasingly in favor of the rebels, Dr. Gacha's face shifted ever so slightly as he clenched Shiro closer to him. They could still win, it would be costly, but there was hope.

7

As they made their way apart from each other, the fifty children, led by Tela, soon saw that Reddox's cloaking was only useful for the first few seconds. Several turrets appeared from the sand and fired a slew of bullets in their direction.

Tela deflected most with her telekinesis and soon enough, she destroyed over a dozen turrets alone, but had to brace herself as the smaller cannons present in the fortress rained fire down on them. One shell hit her telekinetic barrier, nearly sending her to her knees with its power.

Then one of the main turrets fired.

She had to use all of her willpower to not cry as she felt two more children pass away, hit by the giant turret's powerful guns. She pressed on, using her anger to fuel her.

Then the other giant turret fired.

She grimaced as the ground shook from the impact, but thankfully, it had only hit a group of Cyko clones. That had been one of his plans for this fight, to use his cloning ability to cause confusion. Unfortunately, his max range was only one kilometer as he discovered, and if he used several bursts to approach the fortress, it would leave him vulnerable to the smaller cannons.

Five children injured, but all were still persisting.

The walls on the far sides of the desert opened, revealing an army of robots rushing at them with surprising speed. She cursed. Those were the same drones they fought for training, and while they were weak and could be crushed easily, an infinite swarm of them was approaching. It would flank them.

A group of children diverged their attention and rushed the drones, trying to keep them away from the main battle for as long as possible.

Agatha fired off, crippling the center turret before it could fire away. For a moment, the telepath allowed hope to blossom in her heart. One turret down! They could still win!

Then she noticed that all turrets turned towards the position Agatha was in.

Soon, anyone capable of long-range attacks bombarded the fortress to protect Agatha. Powerful magical lasers, barrages of wind, explosive rocks.

It didn't work. All the weapons of the giant fortress fired off at once.

They hit hard, the explosions from the projectiles covering Agatha completely in a fiery ball. For a moment, Tela and everyone else feared the worst. But then, several blasts echoed from the cloud of smoke, followed by missiles and artillery, hitting the leftmost turret and wrecking it completely.

"I-I'm fine! My armor has been torn to shreds, but I can still survive a couple more shots!" the battleship girl responded shakily, seemingly unable to believe she survived a direct hit from two giant turrets. Her answer flooded Tela with relief.

Agatha rolled her eyes as the smaller cannons fired again.

"The smaller ones will be the death of me!" Agatha cried out loud, this time a pained grimace on her face as she felt several shells impact her form.

From the ground, huge blocks suddenly rose up, causing confusion amongst the rebels. What did they have planned now?!

"Tanks!" someone yelled in incredulity, causing Tela's eyes to widen. As she looked at the dozens of platforms that suddenly appeared from below, she watched as tanks were coming out of them, large, black vehicles with neon lights running through their forms. Spread throughout the desert, the fifty tanks opened fire.

"Ahh! I can't take much more of this! I lost another turret!" Agatha yelled through her mind in pain.

"Everyone, try to distract those tanks if you can!" Tela ordered, before she paused as she noticed something else, the sound of rapidly rotating motor blades.

Helicopters! Attack helicopters had left the fortress and were rapidly approaching. She paled for a moment before she willed her mind into overdrive, the world coming to a halt around her.

Out of the fifty children who had volunteered for the first wave, three were dead and five were severely injured but still fighting, and counting Agatha, that was six. Their enemies had spread turrets across the desert, dozens upon dozens which were still firing at them. The drones had been steadily making their way inwards. The large black tanks had made a line of twenty, their cannons more than enough to cover the distance between them and their targets, while the remaining spread themselves in formations of three all around the desert, cannons and machine guns firing away. The helicopters were quickly advancing, and she could feel that several children already were being targeted.

They needed reinforcements.

"Everyone, we need HELP! Those who are here with me, put in maximum efforts!" their leader ordered.

The imminent helicopters launched their salvo of rockets, just at the same time Agatha fired her own barrage at the last turret, striking it directly. Like the other two before it, the turret was crippled beyond use.

Tela breathed as she focused her abilities on a helicopter, causing it to tilt towards another one and fall on top of a formation of tanks, destroying them all. They could win this.

Cyko gritted his teeth as another bullet ricocheted off his armor.

Two dots from their shared mental map, which signaled their allies, vanished from his mind's eye, signaling the death of more children, causing the boy to let out a yell of rage before he created dozens of clones who rushed towards the tanks.

Another child died, their signal disappearing from the map which caused the enhancer to double his efforts into destroying another tank, his punches leaving deep marks in its reinforced plating. It wasn't long before he got to the crew inside and finished them off.

Several more dots appeared, signaling reinforcements. He panted as he took a moment to breathe, hoping that he wouldn't be targeted. He had been fighting at full power ever since the battle started, destroying turrets, robots and trying to divert the attention of the cannons. When the tanks had arrived, he had thought he could destroy them like the turrets, but their armor was durable, so it took a strong slash to defeat them. He had already destroyed six counting this one, and he was growing tired. He would not give up.

Magy, Ellyn, and Reddox had grouped together with Cyko, fighting in sync with him as much as they could.

When several hundred enemy dots disappeared, they knew that victory was approaching, but... at what cost?

The three watched as a child got pierced in the head by a bullet, one of many deaths they had witnessed.

"Snipers! Pay attention to the windows! Take them out!" Tela's grim voice called out to their minds as three more children fell, another dead and two clutching at deep wounds. *"Healers! Focus on the wounded, stick closer to those with defensive barriers!"*

It was a grim prospect, knowing that victory was close, but it would cost many lives. Ellyn tilted her head to the right to avoid a sniper bullet which would have killed her, and raised her bow, launching her powerful arrow, knowing it would strike true, guided by the wind.

Reddox created a barrier to defend himself from an attack of tank shells, making sure the shock wave was contained and didn't hurt his allies close by, before using all of his grimoires to blast at a tank, destroying it instantly.

Magy dashed towards a group of tanks, nimbly evading their shots before jumping on top of one, looking right into the visor of the machine and plunging her scythe deep into it, allowing her dark powers to channel through her weapon, frying the crew inside. Their screams of pain were music to her ears as she jumped away before two tanks fired at her, destroying the tank she had been on. Rinse and repeat.

Five more children disappeared from their map, victims of a concentrated tank attack.

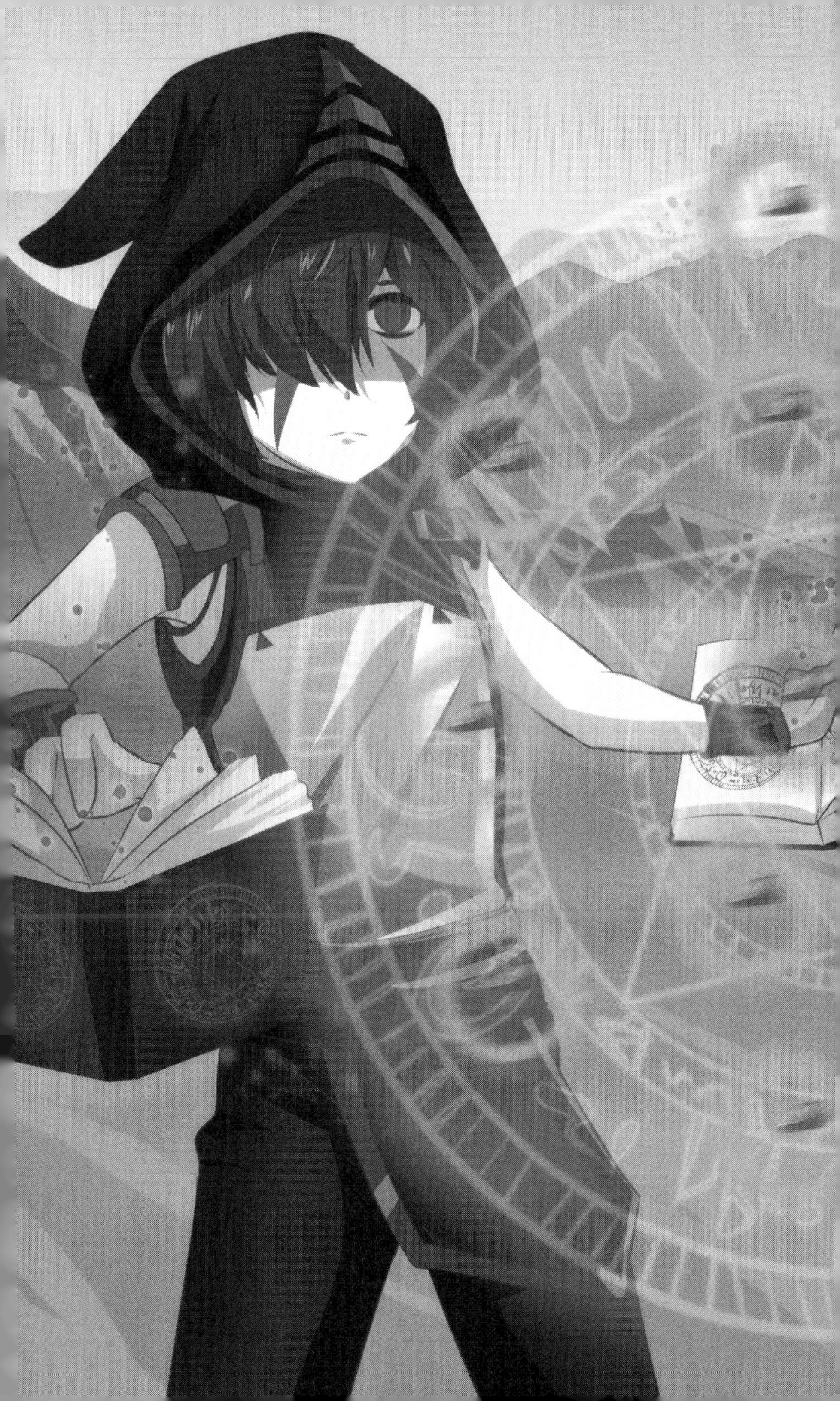

Magy retreated towards her squad, Cyko appearing beside her in time to witness Ellyn and several other wind elementals and spirituals channel a devastating tornado across the desert, taking hold of the remaining helicopters and destroying them.

Many large shadows appeared above their forms, the shapeshifters flying fast towards the fortress itself, accompanied by more children with varying powers. Their reinforcements had arrived.

Enhancers ganged up on the tank squads, elementals and spirituals bombarded the fortress, shapeshifters contributed by attacking the fortress up close, or joining up with the others to attack the turrets or robots. Friendly mutants joined in the brawl against the robots and tanks, mentally powered children did their best to support and confuse their enemy while those with telekinetic powers like Tela exerted pressure and power to crush opposition.

Soon, even the smaller turrets of the once proud, now battered fortress had been destroyed, and with the anti-aircraft guns occupied with trying to deal with the flying shapeshifters, the construct only had its machine guns, snipers, and guards to protect itself.

"Everyone... Let's invade that place and take out everybody inside... To avenge Myo, to avenge all the children they killed! We will be free!" Cyko declared.

"I'm right behind you. It's time to end this!" Magy encouraged, trying to ignore the pain from the death of the innocents.

Ellyn and Reddox walked forward, determined expressions as they displayed their support. "We will fight together! You can count on us!" she declared for them both.

It was time.

8

Dr. Gacha watched the whole battle unfold. By this point, he had already ordered the retreat, so there was nothing left to do but get out of there.

"THIS MISSION IS A FAILURE! SOUND THE RETREAT OF ALL PERSONNEL! NOW!" the commander yelled in urgency, face set into a pale, grim expression as he watched the subjects slowly mow through their defenses. Even the seemingly endless horde of drones was ineffective in keeping them at bay. They had been made for training, after all.

"Papa! PAPA! Come on! We need to go!" Shiro frantically shook him. Engines sounded behind them; their still intact transport helicopters were being used to aid in the evacuation alongside the large vehicles.

"T-they have breached the fortress! They are quickly moving this way!" an operator yelled in terror as he looked at the blue streak that plowed through the landscape, accompanied by an aiding pink blur, and two others who used seemingly arcane powers to destroy anything and everything.

"O-others have also breached through the other side!" another operator yelled, causing the commander to bash his fist against the console.

"Escape through the windows! Order a helicopter to wait by and forget any weight limits! Retreat now!" he yelled out his orders just before the doors that lead inside the command bridge burst open with several streaks of blue light. From the smoking corridor, Cyko came in, followed by Magy, both of their eyes glowing with the power that was coursing through their veins.

"Oh? Look who we have here," Cyko said with a predatory smirk, glaring straight at Dr. Gacha and Shiro, raising his right blade and pointing it right at them. "I've been looking forward to seeing you again, Snow, along with your father. I'd like to introduce both of you to my new friends," the enhancer said, gesturing to each of his holo blades and Magy, who said nothing as she made her scythe glow with dark energy.

"C-Cyko… M-Magy…" Shiro whispered in disbelief, still refusing to believe that her two friends would want to kill her father… Hissing, she stepped in front of him as sparks of energy surrounded her body. "Stay away from him! You already won! Just go to the other side! Follow the trucks! Leave us alone!"

"Did you know, little Shiro? Myo is dead," Magy revealed with an evil grin before a brief frown flashed across her face as she forced herself to keep her hard expression. "Thanks to your 'father,' who forced us to fight against each other. He was so terrified, he never wanted to fight, he wanted to live, like a normal boy. Free and with a loving family." Her smirk disappeared into a cold, loathing glare.

"W-what...? N-no... No! You are lying, right? *RIGHT?!*" the feline girl yelled through wide, horrified eyes, looking up at her father whose stony disposition stayed.

"It's true, the child known as Myo is dead," the monotonous voice of Reddox echoed through the room. She whipped around to spot the redhead and the green-haired girl who had played with her on that day.

"I was searching for a cure for his situation. If I had enough time, he would have been fully freed from his debilitating condition," the mage explained with an emotionless face, noticing how Shiro twisted up in pain.

"All of us witnessed his death," Ellyn added as she pointed her bow at them, not willing to let them move. "Cyko and Magy were the first to try to save him, most of us joining to try to destroy the barrier that was keeping Myo and Drago in. That was when things went bad, the mutants rushed in to stop us on Drago's orders," she moved the bow to point at Dr. Gacha, "and then, he activated those cursed bracelets. We were forced to watch as Myo was killed, incinerated by the dragon's fire..."

"N-no... Myo... I... Why... Why this..." Shiro whispered to herself, the lighting around her body dying out as she was overcome with grief, tears spilling from her eyes. He had... he had been a friend...

"YOU DON'T DESERVE TO CRY ABOUT HIM!" Cyko lurched forward, blue eyes glowing with hatred as he glared at her. "When... when we found out you were related to him, when you defended his actions, when you betrayed us, do you know how much Myo cried? How much he suffered?! HE TRUSTED YOU!"

"N-no! You got it wrong! I never betrayed any of you! I never wanted to hurt you! I-I never wanted Myo to die!" Shiro pleaded, tears running down her cheeks. "I... I'm sorry... I'm so sorry..." the white cat sobbed out, falling to her knees.

"Shiro..." her father spoke out suddenly, putting one of his hands on her head, causing the girl to turn her head to him, looking at the scientist's own, regret-stained face. "It's not your fault. None of this is your fault. You did nothing wrong, far from it. The fault lies with me, I was the one who allowed Myo to be killed. We were attacked by a mental intrusion, they even controlled me, whoever they were, they wanted to stop the fight between Myo and Drago. Myo had to pay the price... for my lack of foresight," the scientist admitted, closing his eyes as he let himself feel regret for the first time since the project started.

"That's bull! Don't you dare sit there and lie with a straight face!" Cyko retorted. He pointed behind him, gesturing to the side of the desert they had invaded from. "You killed over *fifty children* with those weapons of yours! Children, kids! Kids who had been lied to, who expected a better life! Who wanted nothing more but to have a normal life! To be free of this prison YOU PUT US IN!"

"You are a hypocrite," Dr. Gacha replied, his face shifting from regret to calculation, looking at the murderous child straight in the eye, noticing how his words seemed to have struck a nerve in the boy, judging by his expression. "You could have resorted to knocking out the guards and letting the scientists, who couldn't fight back, go. But no, you murdered, maimed, and tortured everyone in your way. A genocide. And now, you want to kill my daughter, whose only fault was wanting to be your friend. How is that any better than what I've done?" His voice dripped with venom. Even Cyko's friends flinched at his words. Magy frowned, Ellyn let her bow down and softly cried while Reddox closed his eyes as he lowered his face towards the ground.

"We... We were only children! You forced us into becoming like this! You *wanted this*!" Cyko didn't let down, his own heart stinging at the realization that, perhaps, his own transition into a monster was already complete. "We never wanted this! We never wanted to become soldiers to fight *your* war!" He thought back to all the suffering he and his friends had to endure over the months they spent here.

"Then I'll tell you something, Cyko. I, too, was forced into becoming like this. I too didn't want to resort to this, but having experienced what I did at the hands of the Creators, I was willing to do anything to protect this world," the scientist answered with a hard glare of his own, hands in his pockets. "Tell me... How does that make you different from me?"

He refused to answer such a question.

"You can ask that all you want. It won't make you any less guilty of all those innocent deaths. I swear to you, I'll avenge them and end this once and for all. Killing you is my top priority!"

At this, Shiro snapped her head up at him in disbelief. They still... they still wanted to take her father away from her?!

Just as the enhancer dashed towards them intending to cleave the scientist in half, the commander appeared in front of him, punching Cyko in the face, sending him flying towards a computer. He took out a shotgun and fired while the others sought cover.

"That's enough of this emotional garbage! Everyone! Retreat NOW!" the commander ordered again as the sound of helicopter blades approached the windows of the bridge. Cyko tried to get up to stop them, but several purple-colored spheres crashed into him, each one hitting with the force of a speeding car.

"I SAID, GO!" The commander looked straight at Shiro, who snapped out of her shock and was covered in lightning once again. Before her father could open his mouth, she took him in her arms and escaped out of the window.

Cyko yelled in rage as he rolled away to evade more of the spheres slamming into him, glaring at his current obstacle who was surrounded by dozens of purple orbs.

"My name is Darius Neon, a leader of the Neon Lunatics!" the man yelled as he pumped his weapon for another shot. He would not have any more of his men and women dying if he could help it!

"*TELA! SNOW IS ESCAPING WITH DR. GACHA! DON'T LET THEM LEAVE!*" Cyko communicated to her, before turning to deal with the mercenary leader, making several clones as he did so, his friends ready to join him in battle.

They would make short work of this guy and hopefully be able to stop Dr. Gacha in time.

9

As Shiro flew towards the exit, she wondered what went wrong. Why was all of this so hard to understand? Why couldn't they all just get along?!

She knew her father admitted his guilt for Myo's death, but she had already forgiven him for it, there was no need to kill him! Her friend's death was tragic, but losing her father... it would kill her. She couldn't allow it. If she were to choose between her friends and her father... The choice was clear.

A large wall of sand appeared in front of her, almost causing the girl to crash right into it. She panicked. Projectiles from different elements shot at her. What was going on?!

She dodged them all before noticing that several spirits were surrounding her. She hissed and spun into a wide kick, the light powers in her body extending her reach and disrupting the hostile spirits. Taking advantage of the opening, she jumped away, running towards the exit.

Several children, bodies surrounded by different colored auras, tried to stop her, but she jumped over them and kicked, sometimes slashing them into backing away.

Then, she felt her body being taken ahold of by an incredible force.

"That's far enough, both of you," an authoritative voice called out before it turned Shiro's whole body around so she was face to face with Tela's hard glare, the rebel leader.

"You won't escape. For the crimes you committed, you can't leave!" the telepath declared, face set in stone as she glowered at the scientist who had gotten to his feet, while his daughter desperately struggled against Tela's powerful hold.

"No! NO! LET ME GO! PAPA!"

A subtle look towards his daughter sent a flash of worry across his face, but he assumed a stony gaze towards Tela. "If I surrender myself, will you let my daughter go? Free and unharmed? To live as she will in the outside world?" His words sent her into a struggling fit, tears streaming down her face.

As far as she knew, while the girl might have spied on them and provided her father with useful information, she didn't seem to be guilty of any crime against them, beyond being associated with the head scientist, that is. Just as Tela opened her mouth to agree, however, Cyko appeared at her side, glaring at the scientist.

"Yeah right you will! You are just stalling, aren't you?!" he accused.

Tela's eyes widened as she noticed that this whole time the man had his hands in his pockets. She scrambled to enforce her telekinesis over the man, but he seemed unaffected. She gasped as her hold over the man's daughter broke.

"W-What did you do?!" the rebel leader cried out. The others are still making their way here, but it wouldn't take them long, so no matter what he tried to pull, he wouldn't get far.

"You're right, I have been stalling for time. I've been working on this small device of mine, and just booted it up for this emergency battle. It is a little something I have kept as a memento from the last war. It had been destroyed, but I restored it." He raised his eyebrows and smiled smugly, hugging his daughter as she clung to him. "It has been a while, but this device does not require experience, only a keen and imaginative mind to pilot it." Dr. Gacha took his hands out of his pockets, one empty while the other held a black sphere with a red eye drawn over it.

"I've noticed my mistake; I realize what I did wrong during this whole project. I closed off my emotions too much, I treated you too harshly and because of that, I created monsters. Now, however, I know what I need to do. If I let you escape and leave this place, you will kill more humans. You'll seek me and my daughter out and torture both of us and any friend or relatives we might have. But, thanks to this little thing, that won't happen." His face changed from the neutral mask into a grim determination as he let the black eye go, making it float in front of him before it glowed and suddenly expanded, covering both the scientist and his daughter.

"You are insane! We want to be free and have normal lives! Away from monsters like you, who lied to us and brought us to this place against our wishes!" Tela willed her power to work at maximum output, her partitions informing her of every child's position as they surrounded the duo, preparing to attack at any moment.

"Let your own actions speak for themselves! You let your little soldiers kill, torture, and destroy everything. Not once have you tried to convince them to spare their opponents! You think it's justice, I say genocide!" the scientist yelled as the sphere surrounding both him and his daughter turned dark as a large, mechanical eye blinked open and floated higher into the air, with two large, plane-like metallic wings materializing on the eye's flanks, followed by four, smaller eyes materializing around it.

It appeared to be some kind of corrupted fighter jet.

His words felt like a knife to the rebel leader, because she realized they were true. She had not once tried to stop her friends and allies from killing the defenseless staff, not even questioning whether they were guilty of helping in their suffering or not. But now was not the time to dwell on that. Now, she was face to face with the monster responsible for their misery. She shook her head and refocused.

"If you try to stop us from being free, then we will kill you! JUST LIKE THE REST OF THE STAFF OF THIS WRETCHED PLACE!" Tela screamed, eyes glowing with power as she shared her desire and determination to escape with everyone, causing a large chorus of war cries to resound across the desert.

"I see, so that's how you did it, that's how you made this rebellion happen! I can finally see it! Your tentacles have every single rebel firmly in its grasp, your own emotions influencing theirs!" the scientist mused, his voice projected for the arena to hear over the loud hum of the eye.

Before a pale Tela could even try to deny his claims, Cyko put a hand on her shoulder, face momentarily shifting into an affectionate smile before turning back to glare at the scientist.

"Well, guess what? We already know Tela can mess with our minds if she wished to, but unlike you, she never made us do anything against our will!" Cyko shouted before vanishing and appearing in front of the fighter plane, ready to slash it in half, only for the round machine to fly backwards, avoiding his attack.

The final battle had begun.

CHAPTER 7

RETRIBUTION

1

Inside the fighter machine known as the Paradox Warper, Dr. Gacha turned to his daughter, knowing they would have to talk fast.

"Shiro, if you want, I can deliver you directly to the exit while I hold them back. This will be very dangerous for both of us," her father said frantically, but she shook her head.

"No, Papa! We either leave together or fight together! You said you wouldn't leave my side, I won't leave you alone!" the girl declared as she glared at the children below who were trying to kill her father, wishing she could blast away from them. "Tell me what to do! If I can't help here, then I'll jump out and join the fight!"

"I knew you would say that…" the scientist said before he turned back towards the holographic cockpit of the eye. "Turn your back, I'll put the interface over your eyes so you can control the Warp Gazers. All you need to control them is your mind. Imagine them moving, will them to fire. They can be charged for stronger attacks and can move away from the fighter up to seven kilometers for now, which is more than enough," her father explained, pressing a button that put a red filter on her vision as two joystick controls appeared in her hands, all of them holographic.

"I can see it! It's a little confusing but… I somehow know how to control all four of them! I'll do my best, Papa!" The girl hissed as she found several targets and fired the attacks, the red lasers flying away towards the children on the ground, who barely evaded them.

Turning back towards his console, the scientist made his own strategy.

The Paradox Warper was a powerful weapon, created to wage war against Creators and match their combat level. Installed on the fighter was a powerful, one-of-a-kind scanner which allowed them to see things that were not visible to the naked eye. Momentous changes in space and time, alterations in reality, wormholes, spirits, failures in the fabric of reality, the flow of magic in the air... Anything that is invisible or imperceptible becomes perceptible. Anything that is too great for a human mind to understand turns comprehensive.

And that was not all it was capable of, those were only a few of the scanners that the PW had installed. Its barriers were made to protect the eye from any attack, both physical, magical, metaphysical, and conceptual, while also being able to calculate the best routes to evade attacks received and the best ways to counter them.

When engaged, the machine could communicate with its pilots, real-time information being fed to their brains in such a way that felt natural. The machine converted and renovated the air, making sure it always had enough oxygen to provide for all pilots inside it.

Its weapon system was also designed to combat Creators. It could fire special kinds of lasers, streams of energy specially designed to strike the soul, piercing through any physical defense. The largest eye was actually the main 'gun,' able to deliver a devastating blast of soul-destroying laser when charged. The wings contained several missiles and missile factories that produced weaponry from leftover particles in the air.

The Warp Gazers were made to act as defensive turrets and drones to fight for long distances, hundreds of them could be controlled by a single pilot, and if they got destroyed, they would rebuild themselves in seconds with the fighter's automated regeneration system, made to repair all damage suffered as long as the main modules behind it, even one, remained operational. The true machine of war was designed so anyone might use it, no matter their expertise or level of intelligence—it made the perfect anti-Creator weapon.

Lacking several of its core systems and with many of its physical parts having been swapped for a long obsolete technology, Dr. Gacha could only salvage four out of the dozens of original Warp Gazers. He replaced part of the body and with the wings unable to support the body; it was a miracle it could even fly. In fact, the magic rituals and wards used to repair it were the only thing keeping it together and afloat. He had considered asking for funding to engineer as much of the fighter's components as possible, to replicate as much of it as they could and then mass produce it... But he knew it would be impossible, and a waste of money. Just to repair it on his own, he had to use many resources.

In fact, the only way he knew how to oppose the Creator in case she went mad was to make an army... the army they tried to build, and which was now trying to kill him and his daughter, already having murdered hundreds of scientists and guards.

But he couldn't allow this project to fail like this. He couldn't allow all the deaths, all the money and effort put into the whole venture to go to waste. He wouldn't allow his daughter's tears to be for nothing, he wouldn't allow her to live in a world that might end at any moment at the whim of a being that thought itself supreme enough to end humanity.

So, his aim was to demoralize the rebels, to hurt and defeat as many of them as possible until they gave up. From the visor over his eyes, he saw everything, the way the elements contorted to the elemental subject's wishes, how the spirits worked to launch attacks at his form, how the mentally powered exerted their strength and most important of all, how Tela's hundreds of tendrils wrapped around every single one of them.

She was both the head and the heart of their rebellion, the main driving force, the one whose own feelings were fueling the others... He needed to take her out.

"Helios-13 Squad, Unit Alpha, codename: Dr. Gacha—commencing combat," the scientist whispered something he had not reported for a long time. It was time to end this for the world, and more importantly... for his daughter.

2

When Cyko's preemptive attack had missed, he anticipated a counter-attack. The moment the large fighter machine moved backwards, he created a duplicate of himself in mid-air and had it kick him back towards the ground, just in time to dodge several streaks of red light that tore his clone apart, causing it to dissipate.

All other capable children joined in the battle, creating large and turbulent air currents, the same kind that destroyed several helicopters and uprooted turrets on the other side of the desert.

Yet, it seemed to be unaffected by the raging wind, passing through strong cyclones without so much as slowing down. Tela ordered the fire manipulators to combine their abilities with those of the wind, instructing them to redirect it towards the retreating fighter.

The result was a large vortex of fire heading straight towards the giant eye, the heat so large even Cyko felt warmth on his cheeks.

Instead of trying to dodge it, the fighter headed straight towards the vortex of flames, causing many rebels to gasp in disbelief, knowing that such a strategy would be suicide.

One moment, there was a large funnel of deadly flames that engulfed the scientist's weapon. The next, there were dozens of missiles being made from the flames themselves—the fighter at the center of the ring of explosives. Then the jet blinked its massive eye and sped away, flying low enough to cause a strong wind of its own, forcing many of them to duck.

Cyko watched as the fighter sped away on a collision route with the fortress before coming to a full stop with a 180-degree turn, just in front of the commanding bridge. It flashed a red streak of energy before the four eyes dashed towards the rebels.

Cyko only had enough time to roll away from the streak. He heard a yell of pain and noticed that a fellow enhancer had been hit in the chest by the attack. The kid had fallen to the ground and clenched at his chest, which had turned black.

It took him out with a single attack.

Glaring at the eye in front of him, Cyko noticed that his mental map changed to show more rebels incapacitated, hit by the same lasers. The eye was charging up again, but before it could do anything, Cyko created more replicas and reappeared right behind the floating attacker, a charged holo blade bisecting it as both halves separated. The orb flashed, it was whole again, whipping around to its airborne form. Before it had the chance to strike, Cyko's holo blades sliced through it, causing it to become a mess of static long enough for Cyko to vanish.

His victory was short-lived, when a turret popped up right in front of him and fired. When one of his clones destroyed the turret, Cyko groaned as more emerged and open-fired.

Unlike the other side of the fortress, this one still looked pristine, which meant that all its weaponry, including the three giant turrets and the fifteen smaller ones, were still operational, but lacked a crew to run them. They killed them all.

Then how... were the turrets moving and pointing towards them?!

"*NO! TAKE COVER! THE MAIN TURRETS ARE ONLINE!*" Tela called out just before all three fired, each one aimed towards a different group of children. Cyko leapt to pull Tela out of the range of fire, pulling her into his arms and away of the path of the deadly bullets.

Twenty more children disappeared forever from their shared radar, while thirty statuses changed to critical conditions.

Cyko didn't need to look down at the girl in his arms to know that Tela was despairing again. He could feel it; they all did.

"I-I-I'm fine, Cyko... T-thank you..." the redhead whispered through shaky breaths and tearful eyes. That attack... it had been aimed towards her. The group she was with moved there after the battle started... and most of them were injured now, the rest dead.

3

Dr. Gacha cursed under his breath, knowing by his daughter's whimpers that something had gone deeply wrong. Warning screens flashed across both his and her visor, warnings of damage, warnings of overheating, and warnings of a depleted magical core.

By using the fortress to attack, he hoped it would turn the fight in his favor, but he had overestimated the Paradox Warper's power output. As the machine was less than ten percent of its true self, it entered a critical condition.

He would have to divert attention away from the shields to reactivate them and cut all power from the fortress to replenish the lost magical power. Thankfully, the Warp Gazers had their own power source and could still function on their own. Even as she panicked, his daughter was still putting forth all her efforts, which made him proud.

He only hoped it would be enough.

4

As Tela noticed that the turrets from the fortress stopped moving, she ordered everyone to focus on the fighter and to be careful of the red lasers. Already, the eyes flying around them had disabled over 15 children with these lasers. They seemed to get past the endurance of the enhancers, turning all body parts they hit black, like a bad bruise. She felt a part of them vanishing, like a hole burnt into their souls.

It seemed like the eyes would be impossible to destroy. Magy's form, covered in dark energy, appeared over one to do the unimaginable. The reaper struck it with one of her scythes, causing it to stop midair and explode into pixelized particles.

As the pink-haired girl braced herself to hit the ground from the impact of the explosion, she found herself in the arms of her friend who had vanished from Tela's side to catch her, the telepath already sprinting towards them.

"Magy! Are you all right?" Cyko asked, worried, as he pulled her to her feet.

"I think I figured out a way to defeat that thing."

"You did?! How?" Tela asked in urgency.

"I'll tell you like this, do you think you can send my explanation to everyone else too?"

Tela nodded as both she and Cyko dodged an oncoming beam.

"Everyone, please listen up! This explanation will be the key to surviving and winning! Focus on what you are already doing, I'll make sure the knowledge you'll receive won't disturb you during the fight," Tela said, mentally nudging Magy to begin her explanation, the girl taking cover behind a destroyed turret so she could gather her thoughts.

"Okay, this is what Scythe told me. When that giant eyeball forced the fortress to fire on us, Scythe noticed a sudden drop in power from it, which made it spark. You might notice how it didn't move when we counter-attacked, that was because it had overworked itself. Because of this, Scythe said that if we could overwhelm its defenses or pass through them, we could do a great deal of damage." She clicked her teeth and jumped away to avoid a barrage of missiles.

"*To test my theory out, I attacked one of those smaller eyeballs. Thanks to my Scythe's unique ability, I can ignore any barrier it makes and strike at the source. I tried to overwhelm it with my dark energy, disrupting its core, which caused an explosion.*" She fired several large, crescent waves of dark energy towards the fighter which hit it with little affect. "*When that fighter passed through the vortex of fire at the start, Scythe also sensed a drop in energy, both when it got hit and when it turned the fire into missiles. Even now, its energy decreases whenever it gets hit. If we can drop it to critical levels again, we should be able to destroy it!*" she finished, jumping away as one of the smaller eyes tried to hit her with a stream of energy.

"So, attack it until it gets tired and then attack more… I can get behind that!" Cyko said with an evil grin as he ordered more clones to fire while he went around destroying the automatic turrets to lessen the burden on their allies.

The enhancer grinned as his mind received more information from Tela to overload the fighter's energy core, relying on heavy hitters like him and Agatha while others distracted them.

Just before they could set their plan in motion, the fighter dashed towards them, firing off its front lasers. Instead of trying the same trick when it arrived at the fortress, it turned to the left, flying towards one end of the desert.

It turned again, flying towards the elevator, then again, flying towards the other wall. The eye was flying circles around the subjects. Turning once more, the machine flew low enough to allow its wings to graze across the sand, spiraling into a tight circle in the center of the desert.

Several energy streaks hit all five shapeshifters, causing them to roar in pain as their forms fell from the sky. After hitting the ground, they tried to shape-shift back into their base forms to heal their wounds. To their agonized horror, the black bruises persisted on their bodies.

Dr. Gacha didn't sit idly by. With a deafening boom, the fighter picked up speed, moving in a perfect circle around them at blinding speeds, which caused the sand and wind to swirl with it. The Warp Gazers fired, raining dangerous and lethal lasers onto the rebels below.

Three shots hit Agatha, two in her main turrets and one in her stomach. The turrets disappeared as she was losing energy, the crippling pain of her wounds taking her out of the fight. Tela cursed and ordered several earth elementals to protect her and the other injured children.

One child got hit in the torso—out of the fight. A Warp Gazer hit another in the arm—useless. A mutant was bolted in the leg, causing him to limp. The rain of attacks wore them down, but they weren't about to give up. Domes of ice appeared to shield them from the rain of red death, which worked much better than Tela expected as the lasers themselves didn't inflict much damage on their covers.

Now with a shield, they started their counter-attack, launching large waves of energy, causing more damage to the fighter's shielding.

Knowing this current battle of attrition would not last, however, the scientist tipped the scales in his favor. Inside the view of the Paradox Warper, it was as if time slowed down as he ordered the machine to use its energy core once again, refilling the wing's missile compartments and releasing them all at once in the strong winds. Just before the currents threw them off path, he activated another module, which spread a red glow through the area.

The missiles melted into a fire that spread throughout the whirlwind, turning the once normal hurricane into a flaming tornado, offering no exit for anyone inside as the heat sweltered.

Tela's eyes widened as she realized what the scientist was trying to do. Fire needs oxygen and once it runs out, it's extinguished… with them in the middle. She noticed with a panicked face that she was feeling short of breath. Several children, fire manipulators, soon passed out as their own powers worked against them, depriving their bodies of much-needed oxygen.

"All fire users, stop using your powers now!" Tela shouted, looking around to note the conditions of her allies. Some fire elementals had passed out, while several others were having a hard time breathing but continued to stand strong, trying to take down the fighter with all they had. "Wind elementals! Try to counter this tornado! We won't last much longer with it sucking our oxygen!"

"The wind is not listening! The fighter's hold over it is too strong!" Ellyn cried out from her cover as she ducked to avoid being hit by a stray beam, taking a handful of sand and enchanting it with her ability and throwing it towards the tornado, the currents taking the grains into the raging inferno, leaving it seemingly unaffected.

"T-then..." Tela stuttered, breathing hard as she felt increasingly more suffocated. Five more children passed out, unable to breathe. If she didn't think of something soon, they would all suffocate! *"Magy, how much longer until it runs out of energy?"* she asked the reaper girl, who was also panting inside her own earth cover.

"At this rate, it won't be long before it overloads itself again, but we'll run out of oxygen much faster than it will run out of energy," Magy replied as she took in a shallow breath, stepping out of her cover to try attacking the fighter to no avail. Grunting, the girl stepped back as two beams threatened to hit her, taking cover once again.

Then a streak of blue started to run in circles alongside the fighter, trying to keep up with it while avoiding the red streaks of energy from above, but it was no use as for every lap he made across the hurricane, the fighter made five. Cyko cursed as the heat became unbearable before he yelled and jumped just as the fighter passed by him, charging up his holo blade and slashing just in time as the fighter passed him again, hitting it directly and causing the plane to glitch out for a split second.

Caught in a telekinetic hold before his momentum caused it to engulf him in flames, Cyko was brought back to Tela's side, who shot him a worried glare.

"That was dangerous! What were you thinking?!" Her teary eyes made Cyko feel like a jerk. She had already experienced too much death today, being reckless like that wasn't good for her and he knew it.

"S-Sorry, Tela, but I can't hit it. I can't get past its barrier, I can't damage it enough by myself... but, I have an idea..." Cyko explained what he had thought up between short breaths, while Tela kept her disapproving glare fixed on him.

"Everyone prepare to dodge again, our next move will take us out of this situation! All earth users! Prepare to create walls in front of the fighter starting at the marked position in the map in 15 seconds! Any barriers over a downed child must be maintained!" Tela ordered, using this newfound hope to fuel her friends and allies.

One... Two... Three... All earth users dropped the barriers before moving towards the extremes, making small barriers over their forms to protect themselves against the red beams. *Eight, nine, ten...* The children sidestepped the rain of red streaks, doing their best to avoid being hit. *Thirteen, fourteen...*

Fifteen... "NOW!"

As one, all children who had power over the earth created their barriers, starting at the marked point and continuing clockwise, conjuring thick walls of stone from the sand, which caused the fighter to crash through them. Even as the walls of earth were created at a rapid rate, the fighter still crashed through the barriers, barely slowing down or registering damage as it turned each wall of rock back into dust.

It was all Magy needed.

Willing her own dark energy to course through her body, she took in as much of the leftover oxygen as she could, letting her power enhance her muscles, her speed, and her endurance, causing a dark aura to take form over her body. Then she ran, a boom accompanying her as she followed the fighter.

Using the same effects that happened whenever she tried to make her Scythe pass through a magical barrier, Magy was able to anchor herself to the fighter, her weapon buried in the flying eye's wing. The heat from the flames was making her sweat, but thanks to the dark aura around her body, she could bear it.

She let all the accumulated power in the blade of her weapon course inside the wing, causing it to glitch out before the hole exploded, smoke trailing out.

Smirking, the girl brought her arm up, ready to repeat the process before she spotted movement from the corner of her eye. She turned, becoming face to face with a Warp Gazer. Without thinking, the reaper put her weapon in front of herself, so the blade covered her face, just in time for her weapon to deflect a beam fired from the smaller eye.

Magy sneered behind her blade and braced herself just as the eye shot another beam of red energy towards her, which was once again deflected, but this time straight towards the other wing of the fighter. Passing right through the barrier and hitting it, it caused the wing to glitch out before an explosion sounded from the point of impact, resulting in another smoke trail.

She swore the eye panicked before it flew away, going back to firing at the rebels trapped inside the flaming hurricane, but before Magy could celebrate this victory, the fighter started rotating at high speeds, almost causing her to lose her grip as her body felt much heavier than before. She persisted, gritting her teeth and clenching the handle of her weapon.

Using her other scythe, she stabbed it on the wing again, making her way towards the center of the machine. She was getting close, but at this rate she would lose her breath and if that happened, her dark aura would dissipate and then she would suffer the full effects of the fire.

Removing one of her scythes from the wing, she let her darkness cover it again.

With a shout, Magy threw it, watching as it lodged itself deep in the dark eye, causing it to flash as her weapon pierced through the barrier and into its body. With a grin, she removed her other blade from the wing and repeated the process.

Inside the cockpit of the Paradox Warper, both father and daughter looked up to find the blade of a scythe hovering just a few centimeters above their heads. Before they could move, the weapon let out sparks of dark energy, which filled the fighter, causing several explosions on the consoles and in the surrounding areas.

She had succeeded.

Many explosions ricocheted inside and outside the fighter before the spinning eyeball lost its flight path and fell to the ground.

Rolling across the desert several times, the Paradox Warper came to a slow stop, sparks running across its immobile body. The Warp Gazers seemed to wander around in confusion like lost soldiers without their commander.

The hurricane of fire was finally brought to a halt, as the wind users calmed it down. Tela, who was still gasping to regain her breath, took the opportunity to move forward. *"Everyone! Attack now with everything you have!"*

"No need to say that twice!" Cyko exclaimed with a sinister grin as he and the other enhancers charged towards the fallen fighter while the long-range users bombarded it with all their might. As soon as Cyko appeared next to the fighter with a charged holo blade, Tela coordinated the attack to make sure no close-range rebel would be hurt.

The fighter's barriers didn't recover from the damage it was receiving. Inside the cockpit, Shiro was panicking and made the Warp Gazers attack anyone they could, but it was of little use as they were still being bombarded by a constant wave of attacks, which was rocking everything inside. Static and the sound of explosions drowned out the cat girl's desperate cries.

"*Warning: Structural integrity approaching 60 percent, redirecting the power from redundant systems to critical core systems.*" The message appeared in Dr. Gacha's visor. He frowned hard, trying to keep the growing panic in his heart from making him do something unthinkable. The Warp Gazer that had been injured was recovered, but… If he didn't do something drastic, he would lose. The Paradox Warper couldn't take much more damage like this.

"Shiro, calm down," her father said. He gave her a reassuring smile, even as the explosions rocked the craft. "It's time to turn the tables." The two Warp Gazers flew towards the fighter, entering the large black eye and instantly getting absorbed.

"*Energy levels restored to 100 percent.*"

Seeing the smoking plane, Tela felt hope that they had taken their opponent down and that they could finally flee this prison, but when she saw the two smaller eyes zooming towards the craft, she knew it wasn't over yet. Ordering all close quarter combatants to retire to a safe distance, she watched as the fighter glowed red again.

"*It's back to full power!*" Magy signaled with urgency.

"Everyone brace yourselves! We don't know what they will do now! All long-range fighters, keep up the pressure!"

The jet pulsed flashing colors before it dashed towards the fortress once again, a large boom in its wake, but this time, it didn't stop. Instead, the fighter passed right through the fortress like it was a hologram.

"*Execute command: Singularity.*"

"Tela! Scythe just detected an enormous discharge of energy! Almost as much as there is in that entire eyeball!" Magy yelled in alarm, just before a large, reddish glow overtook the entire fortress, bathing the desert with its light… Then it crumbled into itself, as if it was being sucked in by a dark hole.

Another pulse of red light.

Sand and debris flew into the fortress. Tela's body was being pulled as if gravity was centered on the black hole…

"E-everyone run as far from the fortress as you can, now!" she cried, catching several children who had been swept off their feet and were being dragged towards the massive building.

Before anyone could follow through with Tela's orders, a large section of the ceiling, almost half the desert, pulsed red as the fighter appeared from it, diving straight towards the ground.

"I-It's absorbing the energy of the magical wards!" Magy yelled as she forced her body to turn away from the fortress and move in the opposite direction.

"W-what?!" Tela exclaimed in surprise. Another strong flash of light appeared, this time from the ground, the same size as the one on the ceiling. The fighter appeared from the ground, sending a group of rebels flying right towards the fortress.

Tela used her powerful telekinesis to catch them mid-flight, throwing them away from the hole. She refused to let any more children die today.

The giant eyeball stopped and radiated a bright blue.

"Execute command: Isolation Field at 99 percent."

By now, almost all the sand on their half of the desert had been sucked towards the fortress which was almost nonexistent now. The ground and the ceiling began to crack.

Cyko wandered away from his spot, trying to take as many of the non-combatants and injured out of the area as he could. His clones were running around helping to keep people on their feet, but he had to help them one by one, which was getting more difficult. "Tela! I'm going to take you out of there now, you are the closest to the fortress!" he said.

"No! I can hold myself with telekinesis, but I also need to stay here to catch anyone who strays! I won't let anyone else die!" She caught three more children, throwing them back the way they came.

In front of the fighter was a huge, bluish barrier that resembled a solid wall of glass. From ceiling to ground, from wall to wall, it covered any exit point from their side of the desert, and from what Tela could see, it also isolated the effects of the gravitational pull.

"NO!" Cyko yelled as both he and the child he had tried to rescue crashed into the barrier. Making a clone and letting it hold the unconscious, injured child, he hacked at the barrier, but none of his attacks had any effect. Not a single scratch appeared on the smooth, glasslike structure.

Everyone who could, bombarded the glass, hoping to break it so they could escape the growing singularity, which was getting much, much stronger. The ground and the ceiling were now breaking apart.

"I can break that barrier, but I'll need time to fully erase it," the cool voice of Reddox called out to Tela, causing her to turn her attention to him. "But as it stands, the singularity will engulf us before I can charge enough power. Tela, we might not survive this."

"No, Reddox... We won't give up, no matter what! Take as much time as you need, then do it!" Tela ordered, her own burning determination to live fueling their own.

Tela watched as everyone attacked the gigantic barrier of glass with everything they had.

Cyko used charged slashes as several of his clones hacked and slashed at it.

Magy's scythes scratched the surface of the barrier.

Ellyn bombarded the barrier with cutting winds while firing her wind bow.

Reddox was charging energy for the attack needed to destroy the barrier, focusing to get the necessary amount as fast as possible.

Starry was being held by one of Cyko's clones, but she was firing several large stars towards the glass.

Torch punched it repeatedly with all the strength he had.

Matthew was letting out his metal melting flames against the barrier.

Anna fired charged shot after charged shot.

Sara had both ice and high-pressure water spewing at it.

Geon made the barrier shake, hoping the vibrations would cause it to break.

Henry had an entire garden of Blast Flowers around him, each one firing at the glass barrier.

Agatha, who was outside the barrier, was working through her pain to fire at the glass, grimacing with each shot.

Even the non-combatants, children who had been too afraid or weak to fight, helped as much as they could.

Everyone knew this was a crucial moment, the one, single instance that would decide whether they would be free, if they would become slaves or if they would be allowed to choose their own destinies. It was a moment of life or death.

The black hole was getting stronger by the second. The large plates of metal underneath the sand shifted towards the spherical mess of metal and dirt. More children lost their footing, but Tela grabbed them before they got too close.

Her body and eyes were glowing red with the sheer amount of power she was exerting, both to keep herself from being sucked in and to save her friends from suffering the same fate as the fortress.

The ceiling collapsed, and the ground split apart. She raised one of her arms to shield the debris from hitting her friends.

"Singularity approaching critical mass."

Everyone kept attacking, their single-minded determination for freedom fueling their attacks. Little by little, hairline cracks in the glass proved that they were indeed damaging the barrier... But not fast enough.

The singularity was getting too strong. The ceiling fell in bigger chunks. Many children couldn't stay on their feet anymore, even if she launched them all the way to the glass barrier, they would still be sucked in. She used her power to keep them there, as far away as possible.

The girl coughed, grimacing at the metallic taste in her mouth. She was getting light-headed. She couldn't hear the thoughts of her friends anymore; she had cut her tendrils to focus solely on her telekinesis... Yet, even in her hazy mind, she felt proud that despite not being connected anymore, they all still fought with a shared purpose. A purpose she wanted to preserve.

It would still take some time for Reddox to finish his spell.

It was decided.

Turning around, Tela launched herself towards the large descending sphere, touching it with one hand before spreading her other towards her friends, preventing them from being sucked into the sphere. This much gravity...

With a large mental push, Tela coughed into her shoulder, squinting to see the red spatters on her shirt. She shook the thought out of her mind and pushed the sphere towards the ground.

The gravity was much stronger. She felt wetness on her cheeks, and the telepath knew those tears weren't normal. She could barely understand what was going on anymore, just that it was imperative that she bury this sphere and keep the little people from coming too close.

Oh... One of them arrived close, he had blue hair... He was shouting... She used her tele... tele... her telepathic hold to keep him from approaching. Curious who it was, she extended a single tendril towards him...

Cyko...

5

The world around Cyko vanished and in its place, a large plane of whiteness appeared. There was only him and the one person he admired the most: Tela.

"What... what are you thinking?! WHAT ARE YOU THINKING?!" the boy yelled in anguish, tearful eyes looking into Tela's kind ones. "You are supposed to be leading us! YOU AREN'T SUPPOSED TO BE SACRIFICING YOURSELF!" He fell to his knees.

"Cyko..." the celestial voice of his leader and friend spoke next to him, causing the boy to look up at her, tears streaming down his cheeks. She was smiling at him, a smile filled with kindness and affection. "I'm sorry, it seems I must break my promise. I won't be able to be your psychologist after all." The girl kneeled, pulling the boy into her arms.

"I-it's not fair..." he whispered, clinging to her. He wasn't sure how Tela made this place, but in here, he could feel her warmth, smell her scent, hear her beating heart. In here, she was real, she was alive... He didn't want to go back to a world without her.

"You flatter me, Cyko... Do you want to spend eternity with me?" she whispered in his ear through soft, flushed cheeks.

He sobbed harder, knowing that even if he wanted, his wish would never come true.

"You never failed me. You'll always make me proud." She used what power she could spare to fill his heart with her feelings towards him.

"You are... You are the savior we wanted, the only one who helped us... The only one who wanted to save us..." Cyko said through sobs, clenching the girl in his arms as tightly as he could, unwilling to let death have her.

Tela pulled away, looking the tear-stained Cyko in the eye.

"I'm glad you are the last person I talk to, Cyko. I always liked you. You were always genuine and kind with me, even by playing around and not telling me your name until we met. I wish we had more time together, maybe even as something more than friends..." Tela confessed.

"We are only children, we should have met in high school... Teenage drama and all that, instead of this horrid place..." He realized he would never know what might have happened between the two. She would just be a vision to him.

"Please allow me to be a good memory for you, Cyko." She smiled as she cupped his cheeks with her hands. Bringing his face close, Tela lightly touched his lips with her own, sending a jolt through both of them.

"I hope you don't mind... I don't want to go without experiencing a kiss. All girls dream of that, you know," she whispered in his ear as she embraced him again.

"Don't apologize," he sobbed as he tried to keep Tela from vanishing with his willpower alone.

"Please... Stay with me until the end..." She willed her mind to extend this small share of sadness and happiness for as long as she could. Her time was coming, but she would stay as long as possible to experience the fleeting happiness she felt in this moment.

As she shared her last moments with Cyko, she made a wish that regardless of who he would become, that he could still find happiness. At least he would still have his siblings and Magy to take care of him.

Until her consciousness vanished completely, they stood in that place, the white field that only those two friends shared.

And then, darkness engulfed them.

Cyko woke abruptly, with no warning that the dream they shared was about to end. His eyes registered the last scene he had seen before... A large mountain of rubble and metal, being sucked into a large hole in the ground. A thunderous noise and a flash of white came from deep below the chasm, causing the earth around to him to shake like a violent earthquake.

Yet, even as the quake brought him to his knees, he couldn't stop thinking and feeling Tela's last moments. All she wanted... The one thing she wanted... was to be free, to help all the children who had been imprisoned against their will to find a better life.

The boy noticed through blurry eyes how everyone else stopped attacking to run away from the crumbling ground. They noticed when Tela had cut their network, the map and the empowering determination of their leader vanishing from their minds. Most of them only had time to look behind and watch helplessly as Tela was engulfed by debris, vanishing into the hole.

"No..." Magy whispered as she put her left hand on her chest, whimpering as she, and many others registered what happened, what their leader did for them... The ultimate sacrifice. Those that had been fighting on the other side of the barrier all stopped attacking, also noticing the silence of their friends and their tear-stricken faces.

Someone who gave them meaning had been taken away from them, just like that.

Before the grieving children could mourn her death, a powerful aura washed over them, turning their attention towards Reddox, who had been chanting and accumulating power all this time. Besides him, Ellyn was wracking with sobs.

A large magical symbol appeared, and the mage lifted his head, looking straight through the barrier in front of him. For the first time in a while, Reddox felt something on his own, aside from guilt... anger. Anger and sadness. One person that had given him motivation, that awoke in him the desire to fight, was dead. That infuriated him.

Watching him, Cyko understood. They all understood. It was time to end this, once and for all. For Tela, for Myo... For everyone who had died up to this point.

One second the barrier was intact, the next, it shattered into a million pieces. Dr. Gacha saw a warning before he tried to dodge the large magical explosion, but he was too late, and the left wing of the fighter was engulfed in the energy wave.

Cyko looked back towards Reddox as he fell to his knees, Ellyn catching him before he hit the rough ground. The mage looked up towards them, his message clear: He had used all the energy he had left. The rest was up to them.

Letting his anger take control, the boy's aura exploded from his body before he vanished away again, appearing on top of the sparking black eye. For a single moment, Cyko didn't move, letting the tears fall from his eyes and onto the fighter before he screamed and slashed at the Paradox Warper with all his might.

This masochist was responsible for too many deaths! Countless children! Myo! Tela! They all died thanks to this failure of a human! Even as the fighter tried to shake him off, he held on, even as the now uncoordinated attacks of the rebels hit him, he refused to stop. He ignored all wounds, making clones to throw him back towards the fighter. He continued to thrash, and thrash, and thrash.

Smoke and sparks erupted with each of his angered attacks, the armor of the eye was beginning to chip away. He made more clones and had them attack at every single point on the fighter.

Then, the eye exploded, sending him flying backwards and towards the ground once more. Grunting, the bloodthirsty enhancer leapt to his feet, ready to continue. Before he could get in position, his instincts kicked in and he brought up his holo blades just in time to block an incoming strike from a thunderbolt.

It was Snow. She was glaring at him through tearful eyes of her own, the large claws on her hand sparking with the power of thunder.

"LEAVE MY FATHER ALONE!" she screamed before swatting his blades aside and spin-kicking him away, the electricity inflicting pain as he rolled away from her.

6

A few minutes earlier, the scientist had been watching the subjects struggle against the barrier and the singularity he had transformed much of the fortress into. Their leader, Tela, had been putting up a respectable struggle, but she sacrificed herself.

With being crushed underneath tons of rubble and from suffering the explosion of the singularity when it reached critical mass, there was no way she could have survived. He had accomplished his main objective; eliminating the leader of the rebels. Almost immediately, they all stopped their efforts, losing their spirit to continue on. He let out a relieved sigh.

But he had miscalculated. Dr. Gacha forgot to account for the human heart again. When the Paradox Warper lost its left wing and suffered attack after attack from the now enraged rebels, he knew he had made a colossal mistake.

"*Warning: Structural integrity approaching 40 percent, redirecting all power to critical systems, all other systems will be lost. Recommended course of action: Retreat.*" The message flashed across his visor as he heard both the explosions from the outside and his daughter's frightened cries as she tried to keep the rebels from attacking them any further.

For a moment, the scientist considered escaping. With the Paradox Warper, even as damaged as it was, flying through the matter on the facility would be trivial. If he escaped now, he could go back to a normal life with his daughter, they could go somewhere far away… But… they would hunt them down. This wasn't about just keeping them in the facility in the hopes of somehow continuing the project, this was about basic survival now.

The scientist cursed out loud, clutching the holographic controls of the fighter. Why? How had he allowed things to reach this point?! He should have planned more, researched things more! Maybe find something other than children to experiment on! Now because of his foolishness, his daughter would pay for his mistakes!

"I-I'm going out! I won't let them hurt you!" she yelled before willing the fighter to eject her.

"No, Shiro, don't!" But it was already too late. The Paradox Warper recognized her request and threw her from the cockpit.

7

With electricity running through her veins, Shiro dashed between the rebels, using her thunder claws to swipe them away. Her eyes were wild, not focusing on one thing for more than a second.

"AAAAAAHHHH" the girl screeched as she fought off two enhancers, one covered in electricity like her, while the other had a body as tough as stone. They were strong, having survived this long, but fatigue was obvious in their movements, so she took full advantage of that, using her tail to take hold of the earth enhancer and throw him towards the light one with surprising force, causing both of them to stumble. Seizing the opportunity created from their momentary stun, she opened her mouth towards the duo.

And she roared.

She wasn't just a lap cat. She trained hard to use her powers. While the children here had trained for months, she trained for years, and thanks to that, her own abilities were much stronger than when she had first discovered them.

The thunder roar hit both of them, the great flash of lightning sending them flying away, twitching uncontrollably. She hoped that she didn't kill them, but as they didn't come back up, she assumed she had taken them out from the fight.

Her right ear twitched.

Without turning back, she jumped and rolled away as several dark, crescent shaped energy waves passed by her. She turned back towards the attacker and roared again, just missing the pink-haired rebel who was rushing towards her.

She noticed that her opponent was Magy, the nice girl who used to pet her… Putting those thoughts to the back of her head, the girl hissed as she tried to swipe at her, coming in contact with one of her scythes before Magy brought it down on her head, a glare fixed on her grim face.

Gripping the weapon that had blocked her attack, Shiro jumped and with a great show of nimbleness, evaded the scythe and whipped around towards Magy's back, ready to pierce it with her claws, but just as her nails touched the armor, the reaper girl exploded into darkness and Shiro went flying.

Twisting in the air and landing on her feet, she looked up just in time to see Magy dash up to her again, Scythe glowing and ready to strike. Not having enough time to act, the feline brought both of her arms up, relying on the bracelets on her wrists to protect her from being cut by the sharp weapon.

Yet, the weapon passed through her bracelets, arms, and body, leaving an ethereal trail as the cat girl gasped in pain. She felt like her body was in two halves, which, coupled with the sudden loss of strength, made her believe that she was dead for a moment.

"This is for Myo, you traitorous feline," Magy said with a hard glare as she brought up her weapon. Shiro felt a stab in her heart as she remembered the sweet, scared little boy…

It was not her fault…

Hissing, she rolled away from the scythe just before it hit her and jumped backwards to avoid another downwards slash, landing on her feet several meters back. Shiro dodged the attack and pulled her claws out, revving back to stab Magy in the heart.

The reaper ducked and her claw went into her shoulder instead. She laughed as the powerful electric currents coursed through her body. "AHAHAHA! N-NOT BAD LITTLE SNOW!" Magy yelled into the astonished cat girl's face, before kicking her away with an enhanced kick.

Cyko now appeared in front of her, a thunderous expression on his face, kicking her again towards the ground.

"Magy! Magy, are you all right?!" Cyko asked in deep concern, but she giggled as she got up from the ground.

"Don't worry. A wound like this won't even leave a scar with the way our bodies are now; it feels quite pleasant actually," Magy answered, motioning towards the cat.

She was crouched in a leaping position, eyes hard and focused even as she twitched. From her resilience, they knew she would not go down without a valiant fight.

"Then, let's make sure she understands this. Our friendship with her is over, she chose her side." Cyko grinned. "And we have chosen ours," he whispered before vanishing.

8

With a quick command, he had access to all the weaponry on this side of the third level: 10 tanks, about 40 turrets, and thousands of trained drones. He was going to use the machines and the surrounding sand and air as raw material.

He spent power to make large clouds of sand float above him, turning them into large, bright spheres of pure, magical energy. With another command, he bombarded all the subjects he could with the small spheres of explosives.

"*Warning: Structural integrity approaching 30 percent, detected several persistent points of damage, causing continuous degradation of* systems and integrity. Redirecting power to emergency systems. Recommended course of action: Retreat."

It was still not enough. They were in a losing battle.

With a few clicks and commands, another message flashed across his visor, "*Execute command: Extreme polarization, inserting exception on target A-1, generate nuclear containment field, 2x2 meters, change characteristics of polarization targets into large-scale explosives.*"

While his fighter no longer had the ability to turn objects into a nuclear bomb, he could still make a nuclear containment field, which would hold any explosions inside it, along with normal bombs.

An explosion on a small, enclosed space was much more dangerous, anyway.

Soon, the Paradox Warper's computers calculated that another 50 rebels had been put out of commission because of injuries, but that somehow, none had died yet. He took a moment to turn his attention towards his daughter.

She was hurt. Her opponents nowhere to be seen.

"Warning: structural integrity approaching 20 percent, main systems are offline, emergency systems are damaged."

"Ah…" Dr. Gacha commented as he saw both of the scythes pierce the side of the fighter again, charging for another attack.

"Warning: Structur— integri— approaching 10 percent… All —stems criti—. recom— —jection…"

It should have been obvious. The Paradox Warper was already so damaged, with most of its remaining energy concentrated on keeping the critical systems alive for an escape, it could not fulfil his commands.

He should have escaped with his daughter rather than fight.

An explosion occurred near his face, causing blood to run down his forehead.

"My daughter… I'm so sorry…"

9

She had taken down at least 30 children alone. Her agility, coupled with lightning-fast reflexes and super strength, made her a very dangerous opponent, but everyone has a limit. When both Cyko and Magy ganged up on her, the fight turned sinister.

With each attack from Cyko that Shiro deflected, came an attack from Magy that was almost impossible to avoid, and if she did, then another one from Cyko would hurt her. Two against one... she wouldn't survive.

Yet, they didn't get away unscathed either. For every attack they inflicted on her, she inflicted one on both of them. Their armor and bodies were full of claw marks while her own clothes were full of cuts from Cyko's weapon.

"Papa... Papa..." Shiro called out in fright, lifting her head up, not wanting to but needing to see what was happening to him. It felt like a knife in her stomach as she saw his fighter being attacked over and over again, exploding several times and dropping from the air, losing altitude as it was unable to maintain itself.

He would die like this... The person she cared for the most in this world would be taken away.

Panting, she reached towards a pocket in her skirt, feeling out for the small bottle she had taken with her from her father's lab. It was still intact, so she took it out and lifted it towards her lips.

She knew what it was, she knew what it was supposed to do to her. Her father explained it to her as he worked on it alongside the other two, probably dead, assistants of his. This 'serum,' as he called it, was made with a mix of Cyko's blood and her own.

Ignoring the awfully foul taste, she gurgled it all down, not leaving a single drop behind. The plane her father was in crashed into the ground, and the rebels headed towards it. She got up from her position and dashed to him

10

They had defeated the final obstacle in the way of their freedom. It was bizarre, how the craft seemed to be melting down, attempting to go back to its former small spherical shape.

The scientist had been defeated.

Standing on his knees, surrounded by rebels waiting for an excuse to mob him, he seemed like a broken man. For once, his face was full of raw emotion. He was crying, clenching his fists and jaw as he looked at the ground in shame.

Walking forward, blades still in hand, Cyko glowered at the man who refused to meet his gaze.

"I hope you realize your fate. Because of you, over a hundred children are dead. Because of you, Myo, and Tela... Because of you, THEY ARE ALL DEAD!" Cyko yelled, his eyes crazed and wild. With another shout, he stepped forward, kicking the scientist hard in the face, sending him flying.

As he landed, crumpled on the ground, Dr. Gacha struggled to get up. He held his stomach and vomited, staining the sand scarlet. Internal damage, severe bruising, likely a hemorrhage. The scientist locked eyes with the approaching enhancer.

"P-Please... s-spare... m-my daughter..." the father forced out, the act of speaking sent pain shooting through his bruised stomach. Hearing his words, the enhancer's face darkened.

Before the murderous boy could take another step forward, a blur crossed his vision, causing Cyko to blink as Snow was now standing in front of her father, arms wide open, face twisted in desperation.

"STOP! STOP IT PLEASE! You've already won! You can just go now! Leave my father alone, please! I beg you!" she pleaded, tears streaming down her cheeks.

Cyko's face remained cold, gazing at her with uncaring eyes. "Get out of the way, Shiro." They were no longer friends, they had stopped being that a long time ago, from the moment they discovered who her father was.

"N-no..." the girl whispered, "p-please... Don't take my father away from me."

"Get out of the way," he repeated, walking forward. He would not stop.

"H-he... He saved me... When I was about to die. He took care of me. He loved me. He raised me... He worked so hard to give me a happy life. Please... Don't take him away from me..."

"S-Shiro..." her father whispered from behind her. If only he was stronger, smarter, if only they had escaped, if only he never went through with this whole thing...

After the great war, there was a man who had lost everything, who had fought and discovered a purpose, only to have it taken away again. He made his way down the cold roads of Neon City, the unified capital of the Neon Countries. Body covered in rags, the man walked down an alley, opening up trashcan after trashcan, hoping to find something he could fill his starving stomach with.

He stayed as far out of the societal radar as possible. He didn't want to be found; he didn't want to be pitied. Living on spare change, discarded clothes, and leftover food, he just wandered from place to place. Despair had settled in his heart.

One day, however, he hid himself behind a large trashcan, watching as a group of rowdy teens passed near him. Just another group of delinquents. Sighing, he waited until they left before moving on, going back to scavenging before he came across something.

A family of kittens laid on the ground, broken, bruised, bleeding, close to death... The group of delinquents were bloodied, but he thought it had been from a fight, not from this.

Falling to his knees, he looked at their miserable forms. Why? What's the point of living? Why had he fought so hard in that cursed war?

Then, he heard something impossible. A meow. A muffled meow coming from beneath the largest cat, the mother. With desperation he didn't know he still possessed, the man gingerly lifted the mom's body, finding a breathing kitty. The mother saved one!

Tears jumped to his eyes as a feeling he didn't know he still possessed blossomed in his heart... Hope, a strong, intense hope coursed through his body, strengthening him as he took the damaged kitty in his hands... She was so small...

With a burning determination, the man got up and ran. He needed to find somewhere safe from this coldness, somewhere he could help her!

Enveloping the kitty in his rags, keeping her warm for now, the man ran, and ran, his destination certain as he knew of one location that would offer the help he needed. An abandoned building on the outskirts of the city.

Finding an old table, the man took the bundle of fur in his arms and lowered her onto it. He had no money to take her to a vet, but he had enough knowledge of feline anatomy and medicine to treat her, even if he had to improvise equipment.

Still, to his surprise, he found that although she had a few bruises and a broken leg, she was fine. Quickly finding a sturdy enough piece of wood, he made a small splint for her, the poor thing whimpering in pain as he applied it.

He scrambled to count the money he had scavenged, finding he had ten gold pieces.

The kitten milk formula was fifteen gold, but somehow he had managed to convince the clerk to sell it to him for only ten, begging until the girl pitied him enough.

It had been hard, he had taken care of her for several days straight, eating fewer scraps and keeping a close eye on her condition. Little by little, the cat got better, more lively and healthier. When he first noticed her improving condition, how she would snuggle in his hand whenever he would check on her, he cried in gratefulness.

He had found a new purpose; a new light. And because he was sure she was going to make it, he named her.

"My name is Harold Jacob. It's nice to meet you… Shiro," the man whispered close to his daughter as the kitty purred and nuzzled her head in his hand. Shiro… She was his light, the light of hope that saved him from the darkness. *What a fitting name,* the man thought to himself.

From that day on, he decided that if she was to stay healthy, he would have to find a job to get them a nice home with plenty of warmth for both of them.

It hadn't been easy. He had to make up a story for why he had no documents and he had to go through a lot of bureaucracy and headaches to get paperwork to find a job. After a while, the former scientist had found a career in a small lab that had given him a chance to prove his alleged expertise.

From then on, he had worked hard to get back to his previous status as a master geneticist. The lab he had found work in had grown appreciative of his skills and eventually forwarded him to a larger, more prestigious lab. His reputation amongst the scientific community grew with haste. He had proven his knowledge enough so that his earnings increased so he could buy them a house. They would go hungry no longer.

In a year, both his and Shiro's lives had changed drastically. The little kitty had recovered well from her injuries. Shiro took any opportunity she could to rub herself against him or sit in his lap, wanting to give him as much love as possible as thanks for saving her life.

She never seemed to have the wanderlust that many other cats had, she liked to stay home and nap or play with him when he wasn't working. His little Shiro, the light of his life…

On one of his free days, he took his little kitty for a walk which meant that she snuggled on his shoulder and purred as he wandered the city.

The scientist halted, noticing how he ended up in an alleyway he used to scrounge around before he found Shiro. But that wasn't what had caused him to stop, no… It was the group of teens in front of him.

They had looked up at him the moment he stepped inside, the same gang of teens that had beaten Shiro's family. They looked like criminals—wearing leather clothing, showing off their tattooed bodies. His daughter seemed to recognize them too, as she arched her back and hissed upon spotting them.

"Just in time, old geezer. We were just going to get a couple drinks, a few cigars… how kind of you to pay for us," one of them said with a maniacal smile. They all had gotten up and were making their way towards him, intentions clear on their faces.

His daughter jumped from his shoulder onto the ground and hissed at the approaching delinquents, to which they laughed at her attempts of intimidation. "Aw, look guys, isn't she cute? Hahaha get lost you pest!" the delinquent yelled, kicking her away.

Before Harold could get to her, the criminal took hold of his shoulder and punched him across the face, laughing as he fell. Gritting his teeth, Harold sprung to his feet.

He fought desperately, he fought bravely, he fought dirty, he needed to protect his daughter against this scum. But no matter how much he tried, how many times he punched them, there were just too many. Ten versus one was hardly fair, and the delinquents knew that. They laughed at his efforts and continued to beat him, all the while the little white cat whined.

What occurred next was a miracle.

One moment, the scientist was being held by two other delinquents as a third pummeled his stomach while the others cheered on. The next, all the delinquents were twitching on the ground as static coursed through their forms. Harold looked up to see he was resting his head in the lap of a small child with pure white ears and golden eyes.

"S-Shiro?" he asked, pupils widening as he looked at his now human daughter.

The girl opened her eyes and whispered, "P-papa…"

The girl was his daughter. A miracle had happened, and she somehow turned into a demi-human, and she had saved him, her speed and strength so great he didn't even notice how she did it.

From that moment on, their relationship deepened. Before, she was only a cat, never able to communicate with him, understand him, but he had accepted that. Now, she could speak, could understand more, and was much more expressive.

He taught her words, taught her how to read, bought her clothes, toys, magazines, video games, accessories, everything that a daughter needed. She eventually made friends, other children who she could play with. They were both happy.

She also expressed a desire to train and become stronger, to protect him if they were ever in a scary situation again. He designed and commissioned a pair of sturdy bracelets for her to wear, which would monitor her health in real time. Being a little paranoid, his work colleagues would joke about him, but Harold didn't care. He would spare no expense in protecting his daughter.

For three more years, they had lived in peace and happiness. The father had bright prospects for the future, he felt like he could move on from his past, as long as he had his daughter with him, they were happy together, but…

The Creator.

He had heard the rumors of her increasing instability. He knew she disliked anything that threatened her power or her universe and was trying to protect them. But he also knew she was becoming more impulsive and distant.

He used the lab he worked in to figure out what had caused his daughter to turn into a demi-human and thanks to this, he discovered the existence of an extra gene in her body, one that disappeared over time in other, normal cats. It was something that was never meant to be awakened.

Searching further, he found that humans also possessed the hidden gene. An idea sprang to his mind... What if he could create an army? What if they could stop the Creator from destroying their universe when she grew tired of them?

He would do anything to protect his daughter. And thus, the idea for Project R.N.G. came to be. If he could make his vision a reality, he might protect his daughter's future.

His daughter...

His light...

12

"Please... just leave... You already got what you wanted!" Shiro begged once again through tearful eyes as her memory of her previous life faded. "Please... Don't take him away from me! I love him... He means the world to me..." The girl sobbed; her knees weak.

Cyko just stared at her, cold gaze unchanging. He had heard her, he could see the emotions in her eyes, he could see how much the old fool meant to her. For a moment, his heart warmed, but he shook it away.

"So what?" Cyko asked, raising his eyebrows in fake innocence. "You think that I'll change my mind?" He mocked. "I won't say it again, Shiro. *Move out of the way.*"

For Shiro, those cold words hurt more than anything else. The boy she wanted to be friends with, that she used to comfort and play with... He wanted to kill the person that meant more to her than anything, her precious father.

The world around her was getting darker. Was she fainting? She wouldn't faint like a kitty again! She refused to pass out and wake up to find her family gone, not again!

"Then fight!" A roar erupted in front of her, causing Shiro to blink as she noticed that she was somewhere else, and a mirror image of her appeared. She looked older and instead of pure white, the fur on her ears and tail was spotted.

"If you want to protect what is precious to you, then fight! Cyko is not your friend anymore. Remember? Either we convince them to leave this place, *now*, with force... Or we'll lose our father forever."

"W-who are you? A-and how?! How can we help Papa?! I can't beat them all as I am! I can barely stand!" Shiro cried out, feeling useless as she stared at the ground.

"The boy who is now our enemy named us Snow... So, call me Snow. And to help Papa... We come together as one! If we turn into one, we'll become much stronger, we'll be able to save him!" Snow said with a determined expression, causing Shiro's hopeless face to lift along with her spirits. Could they do it?

"I-I will do anything! I don't want our father being taken away from us! P-please..."

Her older self nodded with a saddened face of her own. "However, there is a price for this power," she said, causing the smaller one to look down as she thought it over.

"What is it?"

"I already know your answer. Anything for the sake of our father..." the older girl responded as she put her other hand on her, holding her smaller self by both shoulders. "The price is knowledge. You are still a kitten, there are many things you don't know, that you don't understand... But once you accept this price, your blissful ignorance will be removed. The world will no longer be a bright, hopeful place."

In this moment, Shiro existed as both present and future.

"If Papa is not here... Then it won't ever be bright again. I accept it! I accept any price!" Shiro yelled as she wiped off her tears, looking at Snow with determined eyes. She would save her father.

The world around her glimmered white as the older cat-girl smiled down at her, both with sadness at her lost innocence and the knowledge to come and with determination that signified their desire to protect the one thing they love the most.

"Then, from today on, the world will know us as Shiro Snow. We will fight together," Snow declared as the world around them turned brighter and brighter.

Shiro could feel the strength coming back to her body. No matter what, she would protect her father!

Then the world turned white.

13

Shiro stayed silent after Cyko's demand, her hair covering her eyes just enough so he could still see the tears running down her cheeks.

"I said, *get out of the way!*" Cyko seethed, walking towards the cat-girl, clenching his fists around his holo blades. If she wouldn't move by herself, then he would move her himself. He raised his arm so he could send her away with the flat side of his weapon.

But then, something unexpected happened.

The boy let out a surprised grunt as he felt his body fly away, impacting the sand several meters away. It had hurt, the boy noticed as he got up to glare at the feline. To his surprise, the girl began to glow as an intense aura of power surrounded her body and she raised her eyes to meet his.

"I said no, *Cyko*," she snapped, all of her previous sorrow gone. "I will not move away, I will not let you hurt my father. I realize now, what he did, what I did, what you did. I understand everything! But I won't let you hurt him. He is my father foremost."

"Shiro..." her father whispered as he looked at her glowing form in awe. He knew what was happening. How did she get the serum? It didn't matter. As a father, he never felt so much pride in her.

Cyko, however, was far from feeling sympathetic. Her declaration only caused his wrathful expression to worsen. "If you claim to know what he did... WHY ARE YOU STILL TAKING HIS SIDE?!" he erupted as he let his own aura of power wash over him.

"Because he is my father, and I love him," she said matter-of-factly, matching his hateful glare. "The price I had to pay was knowledge. I know how much suffering he caused and I know exactly what price you paid for your new powers. You are no longer the Cyko I knew before. You will become something much worse than my father." She pursed her lips, noting how the last part of her words made him flinch ever so slightly.

"You are no different from him," he returned, the weight of his hatred and sorrow visible in those simple words. They had suffered so much; they had lost so much... And she still took his side. A part of him could understand her, but he still refused to allow the man to escape without punishment, without justice being served to him.

"That may be the case, but I'm fighting for the person I love. What about you? You killed many to get here, can't I say the same thing about you?" she rebuked with narrowed eyes, her answer causing Cyko's expression to darken further. It was obvious to both of them they would have to fight to the death for what they believed in; the feline realized.

"Those who don't want to fight, who just want to be free... *Go now!* The leftmost elevator will take you outside if you follow the road! I will not hurt anyone who doesn't want to fight!" she shouted, providing an easy ultimatum to those present. She waited a few seconds, letting out a small sigh of relief as a majority left, taking their injured with them. Cyko planted his feet in the ground, glaring at her.

Around a hundred rebels remained, circling her form. The enhancer grinned with Magy at his side, whose gaze matched his. They still had strength in their numbers, even if they were tired from the constant fighting.

"Hah, there are still enough of us left to take care of you, *Shiro*. Even if you can hold a dozen of us back, the others will take care of your *father!* Face it, there is nothing you can do now!" He raised his holo blades and looked around as the rest of the rebels followed suit.

Shiro sighed and closed her eyes.

"This situation is just like back then. A gang of delinquents wishing to hurt my father, not caring for who gets hurt, not caring for anything but violence... I've had enough," she whispered to herself before opening her eyes.

Power exploded from her body, forming an enormous pillar of energy.

"I'll protect my father! I won't let you take him away from me!" she yelled, the aura of energy coming from her body masking Cyko's. A chilling atmosphere covered the desert as those present closed their eyes against the wind of her power. When they opened their eyes again, many of them gasped.

In Shiro's place was a much different being. Standing at two meters tall was a ferocious-looking snow leopard covered in armor. Its snow-white fur, speckled with black spots seemed to glow with power as the animal glared at the rebels through glowing golden eyes, sharp fangs bared at them. Floating a few centimeters above the leopard's back was a snow crystal, rotating and glowing with power.

All the sand in the desert had turned into snow, the cold air around the rebels making them shiver. And, to Cyko's anger, a dome of crystalline ice was now surrounding the dumbfounded scientist.

The father couldn't believe his eyes. This transformation reminded him of something he had read about long ago.

He thought of the tale of a mountain goddess, it was called the *Queen of Thunder and Snow*, who had stood up against Creator Luni and fought bravely against the ultimate being to the death, being one of the very few gods in their world that inflicted injuries on her. Her described appearance matched his daughter's new one almost exactly.

The leopard let out a deafening roar and then… She was gone. Cyko and Magy barely had time to react as a bolt of lightning passed them, covering their bodies in slash marks. It continued on to zigzag between groups of rebels, the electricity in her body inflicting pain as they felt their nerves fry on contact. The less enduring of the rebels were taken out.

Twenty gone.

Grunting in pain, both Cyko and Magy willed their powers to run to maximum potential, covering their bodies in blue and pink.

Glaring at them, the feline vanished again, her speed so great that even at their maximum level, the two friends barely followed her movements. She dashed behind another large group of rebels and had her mouth opened towards them, a sphere of cold energy forming in her mouth.

Before Cyko and Magy could warn anyone, Shiro roared, a massive gale of icy wind coming from her mouth. The rebels screamed as her attack washed over them, the low temperatures causing frost to form on their bodies. Another 15 died from the intense cold.

She jolted as a fireball thwacked her square in the face. The fiery voice of Torch sounded out of the flames before he jumped away as dozens of vines slithered out of the snow, wrapping themselves around her body. Before Shiro could cut her way free, however, she lost her footing as a powerful quake happened just under her feet.

"NOW!" Henry shouted to his siblings as they rushed out to attack the giant leopard. Matthew launched a powerful stream of hot flames in her direction, Anna fired charged shots, Sara sent high-pressure jets of water, and Starry bombarded her with dark stars while Henry himself

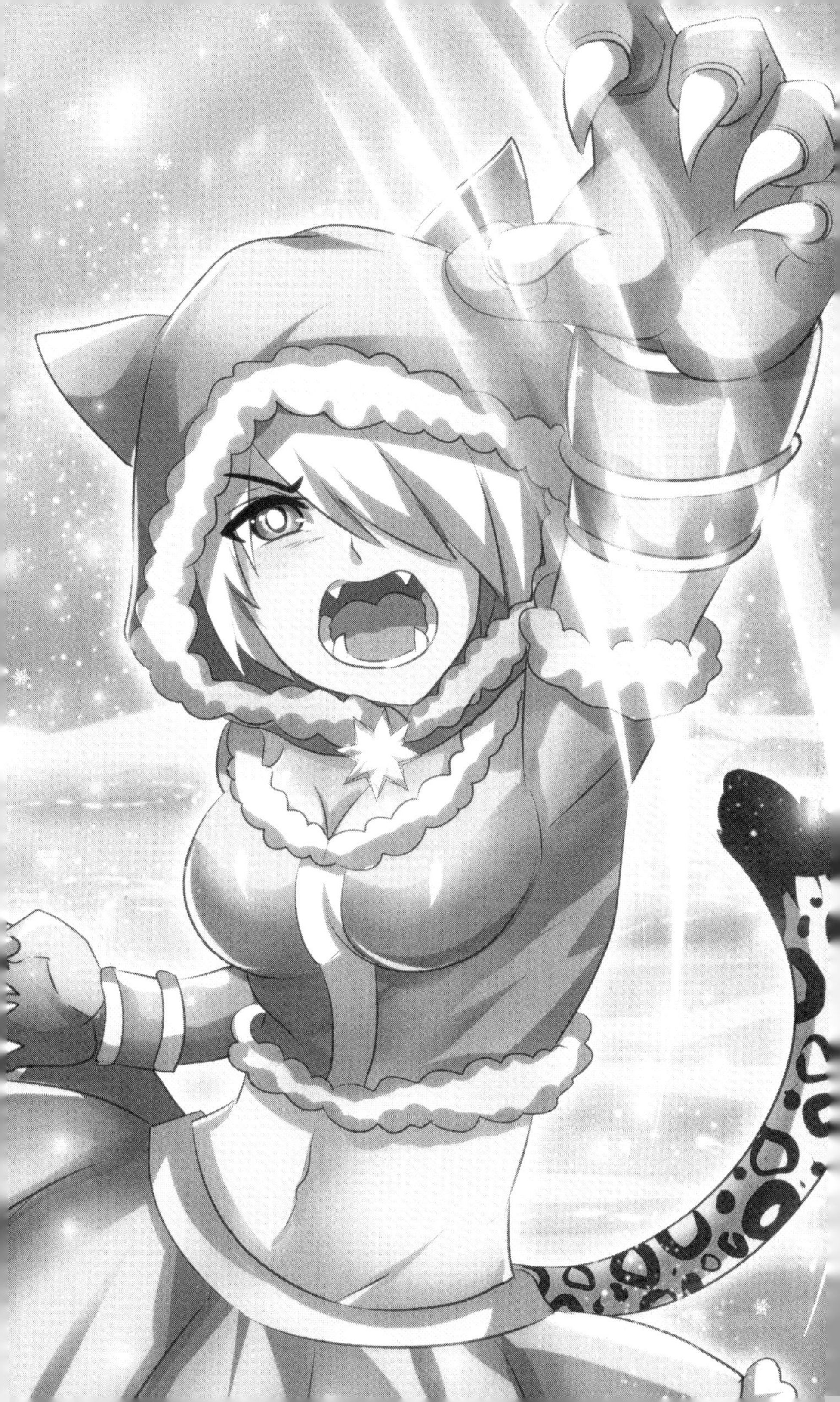

let loose several Blast Flowers, which he had been charging up for quite a while.

Instead of a desire for vengeance, they fought alongside their brother to fulfill their promise of standing beside him no matter what. They would have taken Shiro's offer to leave, but seeing Cyko so hurt and broken over Tela's death and then so emotional over his desire to avenge all the others... No one could muster up the courage to stop him. They would share the burden with him.

"Torch!" Starry cried out as he fell to the ground, hit in the chest by one of Shiro's lightning bolts. Starry was flying towards his airborne form to catch him, but a projectile from the leopard targeted them, engulfing the small children in a rock of ice, their faces frozen in pain from her attack.

As the ice hit the ground, shattering and letting the bodies of the two unconscious children be released, Anna's body was covered in claw marks, leaving her writhing on the ground. Matthew spat out a massive fireball of white-hot flames towards her, melting the snow on its way.

Roaring again, Shiro rushed towards the two remaining siblings, Geon and Sara, passing through them with a large aura of lightning around her body, electrocuting both with her powerful arcs, causing them to fall unconscious from the damage.

She took out Cyko's siblings in ten seconds.

Cyko's clones appeared around Shiro, slashing at her, causing the leopard to growl in pain, before thunder exploded out of her body, destroying all the clones surrounding her and sending Cyko flying away. Magy appeared on her left, stabbing both of her blades deep into the feline's body.

"I hope you didn't forget about me, little Snow!" Magy grinned. "But you are not little anymore, are you?! The pain you inflict is much greater now! How about a reward?!" She willed her dark powers to course through her scythes, rushing through Shiro like a current of paralyzing pain.

"IT'S OVER!" Cyko had taken advantage of her distraction.

He struck the ground like a meteor, slicing her midsection. Shiro let out a soundless scream as her body split into two halves.

But the leopard smirked as her body exploded into a mixture of lightning and snow, sending both Magy and Cyko flying.

Two bolts of lightning sounded, heading straight towards Magy and Cyko, slamming against them. Their muscles cramped and convulsed but they kept their eyes on the two forms that appeared.

One was Shiro, in human form but looking older than before. Her clothes were the same, but her ears and tail had those dark spots from her jaguar form. Her body and eyes were glowing while she looked around as the other streak of lightning landed near her.

The other was much, much smaller than her, taking the form of her domestic cat self, but more vicious. Body alight with energy coursing through her and back arched up in hostility, both of the Shiros surveyed their remaining enemies for a split second before disappearing in a flash towards different groups.

The fight ensued as the rebel army was reduced to less than half—and decreasing by the second.

Landing on their feet near each other, the two Shiros glared at their new opponents. Reddox and Ellyn stepped towards them.

"The wind will not be merciful to you," Ellyn cackled as she raised her bow. Both Shiros hissed at them and fused into one once more, the large leopard roaring as electricity crackled off her.

The world seemed to blink as she was being hit by beams of magic. Hissing, she glared at the mage and sent a blast of lightning towards him, but he ducked just in time.

Shiro roared in opposition, the large snow crystal that floated on her back rising into the sky before sending shards of ice and bolts of lightning in all directions. Reddox and Ellyn abandoned their current attacks and formed barriers of magic and wind to protect themselves. Other rebels weren't as lucky.

"This is bad," Magy said as she got up, panting hard as she gripped her scythes. "We might not win this one. We're tired. If we were rested and fed, it would be a different story, but…" she stopped to catch her breath as she tried to keep herself upright. As much as she would like to believe they'd be able to defeat her if they were at their best and if Tela was still around… The snow leopard was shrugging off everything they threw at her.

"They, of all people, don't deserve a happy ending!" Cyko snarled as he struggled to recover from his wounds.

Floating up in the air, Shiro could make out their frightened but hateful glares. They would not back down from this. They demanded justice and she could understand that, could accept that. Her father's project hurt them and made them suffer... But she couldn't help but fight against their death wishes for her father.

Opening her arms wide, she willed a new power within her to manifest to its maximum potential. It was time to finish this, once and for all!

Staying still in the air, she ignored all the attacks that hit her. They didn't hurt, and she refused to allow them to hurt. Instead, she gathered power in both of her hands, a sphere of light in her right and a sphere of ice in her left.

Cyko let out a frustrated yell as he tried to dodge the hailstorm of lightning and ice, dashing towards Magy and vanishing the both of them behind one of the wrecked tanks, taking cover behind its armored form.

"Why... why is she so strong?!" He hit the ground beneath him and peeked out from his cover to see the fight.

"She has something to protect. There is nothing more dangerous than a cornered animal," Magy whispered as she joined him in glaring out at the feline who looked like a goddess defending her ancient treasure.

Shiro Snow brought both of her hands together and in a great flash of white, a colossal beam of elemental energy shot out of her palms, hitting a large group of rebels all at once. She willed it to move alongside her, hitting all others before they ran away.

The beam of ice and lightning left only devastation in its path. Countless rebels lay unmoving as their frost-covered bodies twitched. Their erratic breathing was the only proof they were still alive.

In one foul swoop, Shiro had taken out all of the remaining rebels that had opposed her.

The feline descended from the sky, looking at the surrounding rebels. Many were lifeless and convulsing on the ground. None were dead, she made sure she only used enough power to stun them. But as she turned her head to see Magy and Cyko making their way towards her, the girl knew that she might be forced to kill.

Reddox and Ellyn appeared in her peripheral vision, also moving towards her. Some of the most powerful subjects that her father talked about were now the only ones left. She took a step forward to meet them and finish this pointless battle. Her eyes widened in horror as she realized she couldn't move at all.

Her entire body was covered in magical seals.

Reddox had snuck sigils on top of his attacks, sigils which only now were activated on the powerful demi-human. His eyes focused on the dome of ice that lay behind her and then on the struggling feline.

"Hah! You are awesome Reddox, did you know that?" Cyko commented with a grin as they approached the cat girl.

"It had always been the plan to immobilize her, I'm just surprised it took this long," Ellyn commented as she commanded the wind to take a violent form around her.

"Well then, dear friends, it may be time to finish this battle," Magy chimed with a smirk as she willed her leftover energy to manifest on her blades, covering them in a dark aura. Shiro continued her struggle, body glowing as she used her power, cracking the seals ever so slightly.

"She's breaking my seals. We need to attack, now!" Reddox declared as he concentrated all the remaining energy he had into his books, which glowed red. "Ellyn, give me your strongest wind!"

"On it! Feel the wrath of the wind!" Ellyn yelled, creating a massive, violent tornado that made its way towards the wide-eyed prisoner. Just before the tornado reached her, Reddox fired his spell, a massive vortex of fire that connected with the tornado, turning it into a burning hurricane of death, engulfing Shiro.

"AAAAAAAHHHHHH!" Her screams of pain echoed around the desert. Her father cried out her name, tears running from his face as he banged the ice barrier. Cyko smirked at his despair as both he and Magy dashed towards the burning tornado, knowing that Reddox and Ellyn wouldn't be able to keep it up forever.

True enough, both of them gasped and fell to their knees in exhaustion. The tornado of flames dissipated, revealing a charred but otherwise fine Shiro, who continued to glare at them as she tried to break the seals.

"TOO LATE!" Magy and Cyko yelled as they attacked her, causing the girl to grunt in pain at each strike. She changed back into her large leopard form, the shock-wave throwing them a few centimeters back before she morphed again and charged towards them. By changing size, she escaped Reddox's spell.

Magy was her first target, impacting the pink-haired reaper with all her strength, slashing at her as the weakened girl tried desperately to defend herself. Shiro was running circles around her, and it was then that Magy realized she already lost.

Grabbing her by the arm and throwing her towards Reddox and Ellyn, Shiro Snow pointed both of her palms towards them, using a weaker version of her previous attack, a combination of ice and lightning, engulfing the trio. They cowered on the ground, covered in frost and twisting as currents of electricity coursed through their bodies.

Only one rebel left.

Cyko turned towards her, claws glowing with both frost and lightning, before they rushed at each other.

Cyko slashed, she evaded. His clones tried to stab her in the back, she twirled and destroyed them all in a single kick. She grabbed Cyko's arm and kicked him down, the lightning in her body electrocuting him.

Before he could get up, she fired another wave of ice and lightning, the combined might of the elements proving to be more than he could bear. As he screamed in pain, Shiro kept on, not letting up until he stopped moving. Cyko was on the ground, white with frost, muscles jerking like the many others she had put down.

All for her father.

"I-I'm not done… yet…" The boy grunted in agony as he mustered the strength to stand, struggling to even get to his knees. He wasn't done, he wasn't defeated yet, he would… he would…

"It's over Cyko. Give up. Now." The panting demi-human felt the stress of the fight she had won. "It's already over. You are already free, just… go…" she whispered with a pained heart.

"No," her once friend said through pained coughs, twitches, and shivers as his eyes trained on something behind her. "I-I won't kill you, Snow… B-but… I'll avenge… Myo and… Tela!" He vanished away, causing Shiro's eyes to widen.

With a heavy heart, she looked behind her, towards the ice dome she had made around her father and she noticed that the dome had melted at the top, creating a large hole ... In there, Cyko appeared behind her father, holo sword raised to strike.

No... No... Nononononononono...

NOOOOO!

She reached out towards her father, her body once again turning into lightning as she flew to get Cyko away from him... Time seemed to move in slow motion as she ran, the distance seemed infinite and Cyko's expression... was not human.

Cyko stared down at the scientist who had yet to notice his presence behind him, blade raised, ready to end his life. It was time. He would avenge all those dead children, he would avenge Myo and Tela. Justice... He would be free from this curse, from this place, the one responsible would pay...

He would commit his first crime; he would take away a father from his daughter. He would take away a loved one from someone he once considered a friend. He would bring despair, he would bring ruin... YES, HE WOULD.

For a moment, his heart ached and his eyes warmed, the last vestiges of his fading morality making a final appearance as regret and guilt began to strike at him... But his expression twisted into murderous glee.

Cyko slashed at the evil scientist's back just as Shiro tackled him away. The sound of the man's pained surprise and Shiro's shrill 'PAPA!' formed a beautiful symphony in the boy's ears. He had done it. He avenged his loved ones; he avenged the innocent who suffered.

He had taken another step away from humanity, the price for his wish making itself known.

Dr. Gacha was dead.

EPILOGUE

THE CHILDREN OF THE FUTURE

1

Freedom doesn't come without a cost. Ever since humanity learned of captivity and freedom, of right and wrong, they have known this simple fact. The price of freedom will be a scar on their bodies forever.

For a group of children who had been fighting unwinnable battles not even a half hour ago, it took time for them to realize this, to understand the costs, the sacrifices, and now the desired dream they had fought so hard for. They blinked, standing in the same large garage they had been brought in months before. There was not a single vehicle in sight, only a tunnel that led out towards freedom.

A light at the end of the tunnel. A soft breeze came through, fresh air. They were free.

For Cyko, seeing this dream becoming a reality was too much to bear. The enhancer wasn't the only one who fell to the ground, body wracked with hysterics. He had lost family, friends, Myo, Tela…

His heart would throb for those he lost for many years to come. He could still see Myo's desire for a happy life, he could still feel Tela's emotions… And now, he had to face the fact that they reached their freedom without them.

Soon enough, Magy, Ellyn, Reddox, and Cyko's siblings, joined him as they made a small group to huddle together and process what had happened. It was over. It was finally over. Even Reddox, whose own emotions had been stunted by the awakening of his abilities, didn't hesitate to hold a wailing Ellyn as he wiped away a few small tears of his own.

More groups of children formed to take this in, and no one was left crying alone. For what seemed like hours, their knees were too weak to do anything but cry. Eventually, their breathing evened, the tears slowed, and those with healing abilities worked on patching up the injured. They avoided thinking about the bodies of the fallen, many of which would never be retrieved.

After a while, the children got to their feet. They looked around the large garage and saw the physical and emotional exhaustion that was evident all over their bodies.

Someone took the first step towards the tunnel and the others followed. They lacked a leader now, but by no means would they give up on their unity.

The walk towards the exit was silent.

Left foot, right foot, left foot… The light at the end of the tunnel got stronger and then…

The sun. It was sunlight! The boy, for a moment, let go of everything and closed his eyes to take in the warmth he hadn't felt in months. It was a clear day with few clouds; the sun was positioned not too far above their form; it was still morning.

A few sobs escaped from several children, especially those who could talk with spirits as they, for the first time, felt the true nature of the world around them. The tunnel's exit had trees around it… The fresh air, the sun, the plants, the sky… It was all so beautiful.

Cyko's eyes flew open as he registered the sound of footsteps hitting the ground in front of them.

He drew in the few reserves of energy he had to call forth a single holo blade, accompanied by the others who still had the ability to fight.

Looking at the new arrival who seemed to have dropped from the sky, Cyko's glare met with the person's stony gaze. It was a woman. She wore a purple one-piece suit. Her short hair was violet, matching with her pinkish colored eyes. Her most striking feature, however, was the pair of wings on her back and head that resembled a bat's, and the tail coming from behind her.

The woman's face that had been defensive when she first faced them almost instantly turned into one of sadness upon seeing their bloodied and exhausted forms. That change in expression was enough to convince them she would not hurt them.

Cyko lowered his weapon as he recognized the figure before them. How could they not, when a great part of their world's culture revolved around her? When the propagandas they had been forced to watch by the scientist contained information on not only her master, but herself as well?

"So, this is what they were hiding all this time? How cruel..." the woman whispered before taking a step towards the huddle of children, making sure her stance was as non-threatening as possible. These children were traumatized. Badly.

"My name is Lilith... Can you tell me what happened to you?" she asked gently, offering a warm smile at their relief upon recognizing her name.

They would be free.

2

A daughter lay crying, wailing inconsolably as she clutched the body of her father, yelling his name. Although the rebels thought he had perished, his desire to live provided him a few more minutes in this world. She had fought hard; she had defeated everyone who wanted to take her father away from her... But they still hurt him.

When she arrived at his side, she ignored everything. To her, the most important thing in the world was in her arms, whispering words of love and patting her head... While he bled out from the wound he received.

"I love you, my daughter..."
"Forgive me..."
"You can overcome this..."
"Thank you for being in my life..."

Already, his body was getting colder, his movements and his speech slowed and slurred. Her father was dying; the person she loved the most in the world was dying.

He murmured his love for her one more time, voice barely louder than a whisper. His hand fell and his eyelids closed. She could hear his breathing was stopping, his heart was ceasing to beat...

"Papa... I love you... please... don't leave me... please don't leave me..." Shiro whispered in despair, her heart breaking apart as she watched his lasts breaths.

With another sob, her body glowed with power, the shine of her new abilities reflecting her deep sadness. She smiled. Maybe there was something she could do. Her father was leaving her forever.

Her world would be destroyed.

3
FIVE DAYS LATER

The scandal was massive. One of the world's largest companies, the GACHA Conglomerate, was found guilty of forced child labor, slavery, torture, and illegal experimentation. The evidence was given to Luni and to the world by her assistant, who presented her interviews with the 342 survivors. Backing all of this up was the ruins of the monstrous facility and a heartbreaking story of how those innocent children fought their way to freedom, using the same powers given to them by the torturous scientists.

Public outcry and civilian unrest had been nearly instantaneous. Millions of civilians occupied the streets in front of the conglomerate's branch companies, demanding justice be brought to those who were in charge and to those who helped it. Big media companies covered the massive scandal 24/7, famous musicians, actors, vloggers, and artists publicly declared their own horror at the conglomerate's treatment towards children and vowed to use none of their products ever again.

The company's lawyers found themselves badly pressed when dealing with the situation, trying their best to stall for time while the directors refused to go public. Many soon quit their jobs because of the stress. In fact, the company also had to deal with thousands upon thousands of employees quitting from sheer disgust, many claiming that they'd rather eat dirt than work for a company with so little morals. They soon saw themselves forced to rely on robots and mercenaries for security of their establishments.

Important investors and business partners cut all ties with them, unwilling to suffer the wrath of the population. On an overnight timestamp, the GACHA Conglomerate found itself nearly bankrupt while hundreds of thousands found themselves jobless, though most by their own decision. The sudden drop in value and negative attention was the first step towards a major global economic crisis.

It was a complete and utter disaster.

To salvage the situation, Mr. Whale had publicly announced the reason for the project, holding nothing back from his words and evidence, knowing he was taking full responsibility for being the mastermind behind the whole fiasco, and would likely face the capital punishment once the few lawyers he had left finally cracked.

"We are not safe."

His explanation, transmitted live worldwide, had begun. He could already hear the hateful wooing, the calls for justice, the desire for his blood because of what he had done. The businessman closed his eyes. "We did not seek to take over the world, we did not seek to create an army to rule over the weak... Our purpose was to protect the weak!" he yelled out with wide, frantic eyes.

"Can you see, citizens of the world, what lies beyond us, above us? Do you realize that, at any moment, our lives, our way of living, *the history of our civilization, can come to an end?* Four thousand years ago we met the one who created us all, 4,000 years ago, the world changed so drastically the name of the planet itself changed. The Creator, Luni, is one of the main aspects of much of our culture, we work hard to please her, we deposit our faith in her, we owe our existence to her... *But what if it's not enough?"*

At any moment, Luni could descend from the moon to crush him to a pulp, but he didn't care. For 4,000 years, no one talked about this, for 4,000 years, no one ever contemplated the ultimate truth: they are nothing to the Creator, she would get rid of them the moment she grew tired of their existence, and he had proof of this.

"I present to you, the evidence you need!" Mr. Whale declared as he nodded towards one of the few employees who was still working for him, a tech manager. Soon, his image on the television was replaced with videos, played one by one, messages sent on social media by both Luni and Lilith, analysis over her mental health, and signs of an eventual mental breakdown.

"None of us want to admit it... None of us want to face this despairing truth. Our lives, our history, our existence, is held at the whims of a supreme being who, sadly, seems to lack a supreme mind. WE HAVE NO WAY OF DEFENDING OURSELVES! WE CAN'T STOP HER IF, no, WHEN SHE TURNS ON US! I will face my crimes against humanity proudly, knowing I tried to stand up for my people!" the businessman exclaimed, tears falling from his eyes as he glared at the camera, sweating profusely as he knew what was coming to him.

Taking his phone out from his pocket, the businessman took one last glance at it. He had been talking with one of the surviving senior scientists about a continuation of the project, in particular... The cloning project.

"It is possible, but we would need to start over from scratch. Equipment, samples, a secure location, secrecy... The mercenaries are unwilling to work with us anymore, and everything we had will soon be turned into a confidential investigation area. Many of us will have to go into hiding," the scientist had explained.

He responded, "Everything I can give you, will be provided. Be free to assign yourself or someone else as the leader of the project." He had already made arrangements and deals; things should proceed even without him to administrate it. He hoped humanity would still try to defend itself.

With a sigh, the man pressed a button that ordered a complete wipe of all his online data before throwing his expensive phone to the ground and smashing it to pieces with a single stomp.

"I should try to appeal to the director board again, maybe we can still save the company," Mr. Whale whispered to himself as he walked towards the door that led out from the media room he was in, reaching out to open it.

He blinked, as instead of the corridor that lead to other parts of the building, what awaited him on the other side was... Space. Stars floated past the doorway and an eternal nothingness seemed to stretch out before him.

The businessman gulped, his stomach dropped to his feet, fear enveloping his heart. Slowly closing the door, he spun around, expecting to find someone.

The room appeared empty...

"*You and I are going to have a few words, face to face...*" an ominous voice sounded from all around him. He looked about. He recognized that voice…

Then his knees turned into jelly as an overwhelming pressure enclosed around him, he could feel his heart beating dangerously fast, the adrenaline suddenly running through his body, making everything seem clearer than it was…

Then, the force moved his gaze upwards… The ceiling had been replaced with a vast, white sky with rays of light coming through the clouds. If he wasn't being held captive by the Creator, it would be an angelic scene. He could feel his body wanting to break down, wanting to die from the pressure, but something prevented that.

A shadowed figure was descending from the eternal sky, but somehow, he could make out the distinct shape of their universe's Creator.

With enormous effort, the terrified and whimpering man turned around and ran.

This was the end.

4
EIGHT YEARS LATER

"We've just received an urgent news feed; it appears that the Neon Lunatics have struck again! Our reporters are arriving at the scene now!" the posh news anchor declared on-screen before it changed to show another location. A massive building in the military section of a Blue Faction country was on fire.

"As you can see behind me, a fire rages at the military outpost at the edge of the city! Oh, Luni, there are dead bodies everywhere, which are being removed by the medical staff! Blue Faction soldiers and military members are among the dead! Police are at the scene and army reinforcement is here to increase security!" She paused as more information was given to her. Her eyes widened, and she looked at the camera incredulously before shaking her head.

"We just received more information from the police investigators at the scene! It appears that a human trafficking ring had been underway in the destroyed building! Crime scene investigators reported that victims had been found in a nearby warehouse in a terrible state. The government is being—Hey, can I have a moment?" the reporter interrupted as she spotted a grim police officer emerging from the flaming outpost.

"Good afternoon, officer. We just received word about the operation inside this building, do you have any other information?" The reporter put her microphone in front of the wary officer.

"The situation is under control. Investigation on the exact nature of this incident is still underway, so at the moment, we have no comment," the officer spoke in a formal tone, watching as the reporter nodded.

"What about the supposed involvement of the Neon Lunatics? Do you believe they had anything to do with this?" the reporter pressed.

"There is a possibility that the Neon Lunatics' attack was a result of the trafficking ring, but we still can't be sure. However, I would like to remind everyone that they, especially their leaders, are extremely dangerous. They have been involved in several deaths this year. Any information that leads to their capture will be rewarded." The officer said with a hard voice. The reporter shakily nodded at the woman's intense stare, before she stepped back to allow the policewoman to go back to her job.

"As you can see, the situation is still under investigation, but the possibly of the two incidents being connected still hasn't been disca—" The screen went black as it was turned off, the viewer letting out an audible click of annoyance at the report he had just watched.

"Tsk, always like this. I get rid of the rotten part of their forces, they still treat me like scum," the mocking voice of a teen said. He was wearing a simple white shirt, blue shorts, and a pout on his face from the news report. Would it hurt them to be a little more thankful?

"Well, it's not like we are exactly tree-hugging super heroes, dear friend," the serene voice of Magy came out from behind him, causing the pouting boy to look at her. Magy had grown well those past few years, her hair in the same pig-tailed style but much longer now and healthier.

"Hey, praising good deeds is not a crime," he said, his pout deepening, causing his best friend to giggle at his childishness.

"Too bad our reputation as criminals is much greater than ours as good doers, superheroes don't go around invading mansions and killing almost everyone inside." Magy made her way towards a bed, sitting herself next to him.

"That's exactly it! *Almost* everyone! We left plenty of innocent people alive!" He sighed.

"Tomorrow... We should take a day off tomorrow. No investigations into possible targets, no assassinations, no jobs. Let us just... Take some time off," Cyko whispered as he thought about what day it would be tomorrow.

The anniversary of their freedom... and the eighth anniversary of Tela's death.

"Yeah... We should do that..." Magy agreed, following behind him as he moved to look out of their hotel room's window.

Cyko pulled out his smartphone, smiling at the background photo of him and his family at Starry's birthday party last month. He flipped through some notifications before pausing at a message.

"I think I know what we're doing today."

5

"There is a good reason I called you here today, Cyko," the redhead in front of him declared, the seriousness in his voice tangible to everyone in the room.

He placed a small glass sphere on the wooden table. The edges of the sphere seemed to be covered in darkness, filling Cyko with uneasiness.

"This is a small magical construct I made; it represents our world. As you can see, some sort of corruption has made its way here." Reddox flipped on the television.

"*Yesterday, all Neon Countries entered a state of war against each other after months of tension, breaking centuries of peace for the first time...*" the reporter spoke robotically, "*Several countries around the world, big and small, have either gone silent or began warring with their neighbors. Wild creatures have gone berserk. The estimated loss of life so far borders on hundreds of thousands, and future estimates put them in the millions if this continues,*" she explained before dropping her head, no longer bothering to keep up professionalism.

"... *The end of the world is near, the end of the world is near... She will be the end of us all...*" the journalist murmured, her words of despair loud enough for everyone to hear, yet the camera didn't cut away.

"*The world will end, the apocalypse is here, everything will end...*" she said in a monotone voice before bringing her head back up and glaring at the camera with wild, bloodshot eyes. A large, mad grin spread across her face as she brought her right hand up to reveal a purple handgun. She laughed madly as the sound of people screaming in the background became louder. She pointed the gun at the camera and fired, causing the stream to be interrupted.

"Wow, things are really getting out of hand over there," Cyko said in a concerned voice.

"Wait, is this stream live? Can you go back and rewind it a bit, Magy?" Reddox asked with a slight hesitation in his voice.

"Uh, sure. Did you see something strange?" Magy questioned as she played with the remote control for the television.

"Maybe... okay pause it right.... NOW!" Reddox shouted.

He stepped in front of the television set, pointing at the image of a boy in the background on the screen. "Look familiar?"

"W-what do you mean? Who is that??" Magy asked.

"Take a closer look, I think we might have another problem on our hands besides this corruption situation," Reddox said warily to the others.

Cyko gritted his teeth as he stared at the image of the boy on the television. He had blue hair, markings on his face, and was wearing the same exact uniform that they were given at their former place of confinement. There was no mistaking the person that was on the screen.

Lifting his head, he looked at his friends, before grinning wildly.

"We'll find this clone and whoever is behind this... *And kill them all!*"

<END>

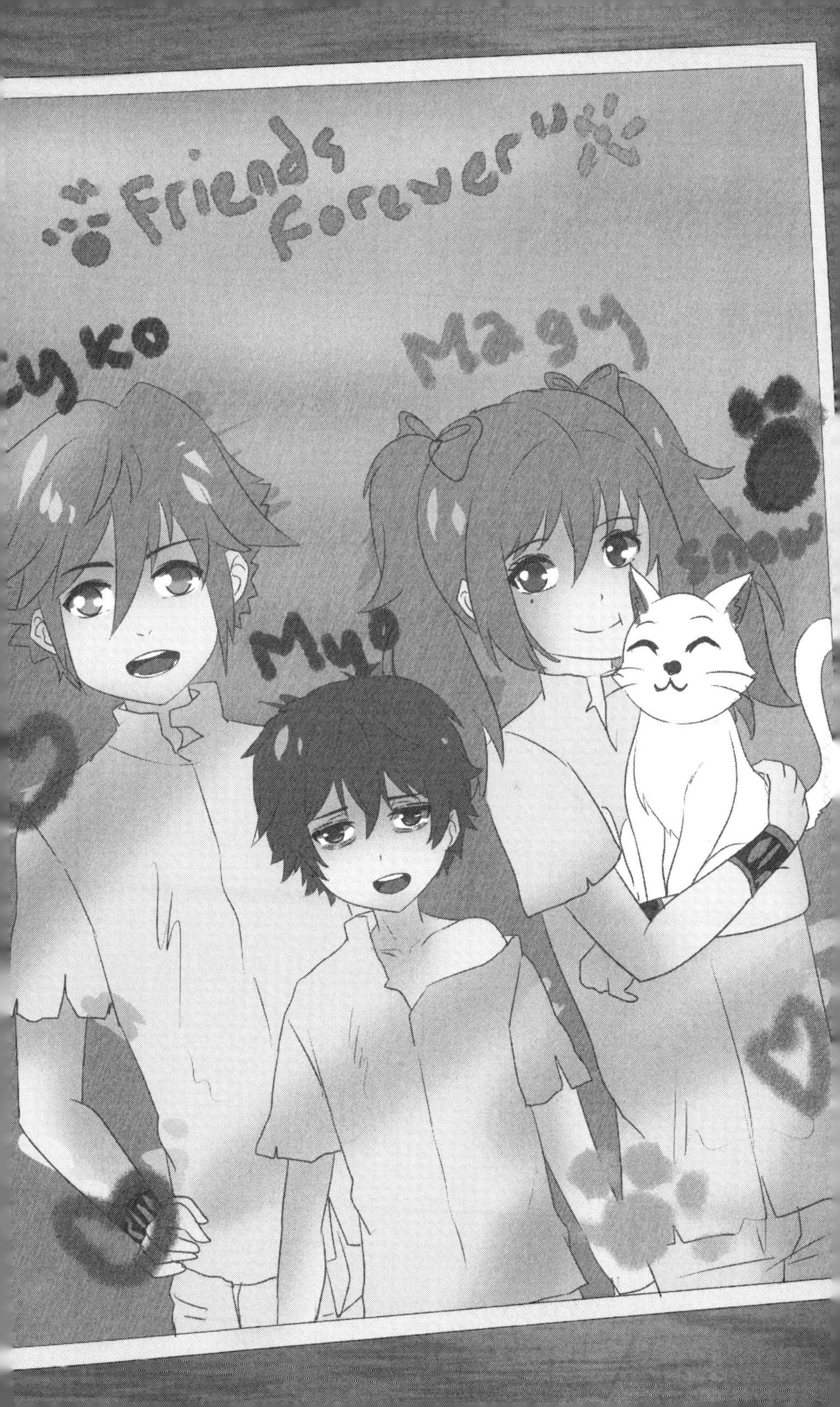
Friends Forever
Magy
Muo

AFTERWORD

Hello, everyone! Thank you so much for reading Lunime's first published light novel! I hope you enjoyed it as much as I did. To all of our devoted fans who picked up this story, we truly appreciate your support and this book would not be possible without you! For those of you who are just getting to know us, welcome to the world of Gacha games. My name is Lucas, but I am more widely known as Luni. I'll talk more about myself later, but first we need to acknowledge the amazing individual that made this novel come to life.

If you have been following Lunime from the beginning, you probably know the protagonist in this story, Cykopath, is one of the most popular characters in our games. Honestly, I am quite jealous of his fame; Creator Luni was supposed to be the most beloved blue-haired character! Anyway, as an avid manga reader, I wanted to publish a novel about the origin story of this famous, psychopathic killer. I took a few days off from coding games and brainstormed a brief plot of what I envisioned would happen in this story, and then I opened a blank document and settled in to type out a novel! But there was one small problem…

As it turns out, writing a feature-length light novel is not as easy as I thought! It involves a great deal of time and effort, and while I wanted to make this dream of mine a reality, I just didn't have enough devotion it needed to make it happen. I dragged Lunime's first potential light novel into the Recycle Bin on my desktop and went back to coding games. A few days later, I received an e-mail from a fan telling us how much they enjoyed playing Gacha Memories, a visual novel app we had recently released. It was then that a marvelous idea popped into my head! Although it is stated in the credits section of the game, many people do not know the story in Gacha Memories was written by a fan from Brazil, known as Luca Braña!

I had contacted Luca after reading his captivating fan fictions he posted on our website, and he was very excited to write the narrative behind our first visual novel. After reading the praise from this fan about his writing, it was obvious what I had to do! I reached out to Luca again and asked him if he would be interested in reviving my failed attempt at a light novel, and we are so lucky that he accepted! Nicknamed "The Insane Writer," Luca worked tirelessly for months on this project, despite being a busy college student. I am forever grateful for all the effort he put forth into this endeavor, and in my opinion, he did an extraordinary job of capturing the essence of Cykopath and the story as a whole. Please extend your praise and gratitude towards him if you catch him around on our various social media communities!

Taking a few steps back, let's discuss how Lunime was created and what our plans for the future hold! During my years in college, I originally planned on becoming an animator and had no intention of designing games. After graduating, I found myself addicted to a bunch of popular mobile Gacha games, but to succeed at these apps, you had to spend a ridiculous amount of money! This was a major turn off for me, especially being a poor graduate who should have been saving money for more important necessities (like, a reliable car for example) rather than spending it on virtual items. As I hunted for animation jobs, I thought to myself, why don't I create my own Gacha games, ones that don't require you to pay to win? I had some previous game design knowledge, although it took a few years of studying to create the games we are releasing today.

You might wonder how I came up with the name Lunime for my company, and it actually is just a combination of two words. The first part incorporates my first name, Lucas. The second half comes from the word 'anime,' because as many of you already know, the graphics from our games are based on the common designs found in Japanese animations, also referred to as anime. So I decided to just combine Lucas and anime to get Lunime!

Let's talk about the apps we have released and what you can expect in the future! The very first Gacha game we made was called Anime Gacha, and it was a simple game where you could collect hundreds of different units! After this, I added RPG elements and a storyline to my next Gacha game, and thus Gacha World was created. This was our first big hit, and I am so happy that our fans enjoyed it. We released many spin-off games based on the units from this game, including titles such as Gacha Resort, Gacha Memories, and Meme Gacha! Since there were so many outfits and character designs inside the game, I thought a few fans might enjoy a dress-up app where they could use the fashion within Gacha World to create their own characters. Soon Gacha Studio was created, and it turns out that a lot more people liked this than we anticipated! With over five million downloads, it is still our most popular game! I decided to make other types of dress-up games with different body templates, such as Pocket Chibi, Gacha Life, and Gachaverse—the sequel to Gacha World! It amazes me to see all the amazing videos, fan-art, and comics that our fans make using these games! While it might seem cliché, I firmly believe our fans are the best in the world!

As for the future, there is no end in sight for Lunime and you can expect us to release many more games! While we have focused on RPG and Gacha-based apps, I have had the recent urge to delve into other genres, so maybe you will see a very different type of game in your app store one day!

In regard to Cyko and his future—that all depends on you! We really enjoyed putting this light novel together and would love to release a sequel! With enough support, I am sure we will get to see what happens to Cyko and his friends next! I want to thank our fans around the world one last time, because without you, none of this would be possible! See you soon!

—*Luni*

Lunime

Enter the World of Gacha Games!

www.Lunime.com
✉ LunimeGames@Gmail.com

- /Lunime
- /LunimeGames
- /GachaTube
- /LunimeGames
- /OfficialLunime
- /Lunime

Printed in Great Britain
by Amazon